THE LEGENDARY DUKE

PUT UP YOUR DUKES BOOK TWO

MARGARET LOCKE

LOCKED ON Love PUBLISHING

THE LEGENDARY DUKE
Copyright © Anne Tjaden, 2018
Locked On Love, publisher, Harrisonburg, VA

ISBN
Paperback: 978-1-946553-05-8
Kindle ebook: 978-1-946553-06-5
EPUB ebook: 978-1-946553-07-2

Cover designs by Lankshear Design
www.lanksheardesign.com

Edited by Tessa Shapcott
www.tessashapcott.com

Formatting by Emily June Street for Luminous Creatures Press

Manufactured in the United States of America

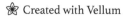 Created with Vellum

PROLOGUE

CAMLON, HOME OF THE DUKE OF ARTHINGTON - NEW YEAR'S EVE 1788

*B*ertram Laxton, Earl of Grennet, eyed the man he was about to kill: Loughton Knight, Duke of Cortleon.

His wife's seducer. Bertie couldn't bring himself to say "lover," though Albina had been quite the willing participant in the fervent coupling he'd just witnessed before Cortleon sent her off. How dare the bastard dally with *his* wife in this field minutes from Camlon? Any of Arthington's other house party guests could have stumbled upon them. Had she no shame?

He swallowed. Did everyone know she was cuckolding him with the loathsome duke? Had they laughed behind his back, even as he'd glowed with pride over his little Bee's current condition? But whose child did she carry, his or Cortleon's?

He clutched his pistol. The honorable thing would be to call Cortleon out, not shoot him without warning. But when had the duke ever been honorable? His lecherous exploits were infamous. Why his wife stayed by his side was beyond comprehension.

Bertie flexed his fingers on the weapon. His source of retribution. Of revenge. Unbidden tears sprang to his eyes. He blinked them away. *Damn it all*. No sign of weakness. Not now, not with his honor at stake. Not with *everything* at stake.

He stepped from the trees. "Cortleon!"

His voice was sure and strong, though his hand shook as he raised his arm toward the figure some thirty feet away. The object of his malice whirled, a smile on his face. Until he saw Bertie. And the gun.

Cortleon held up his hands, palms out, his mouth whisking into that grin that led women to swoon and men to fawn over him. Blasted cur. Charming and debonair, he drew courtiers wherever he went, like an emperor of old. He had it all: rank, looks, wealth. And women. Women everywhere, from the time the blackguard had turned fourteen.

Though they'd been at Eton and Oxford together, Bertie had never had whatever it took to become one of the duke's inner court. Oh, Cortleon had always been hospitable, especially after he'd married Albina's friend Anna, but a deep friendship never developed between the men. Perhaps now he knew why.

"How long?" he called out.

"How long what?" The smug smile never left Cortleon's face, though he stilled at the wavering of Bertie's hand.

"How long have you been swiving my wife?"

The duke's amiable look faltered, wariness entering his eyes.

About damn time.

Cortleon smoothed his hands down the front of his velvet overcoat, a bold scarlet embroidered with birds and gold stars. Stars, of all things, as if forever proclaiming his lofty status. He opened then closed his mouth, evidently at a loss for words. That was a first; the rogue was known for his glib tongue—a tongue that moments ago had been licking Bee's breasts.

"I am sorry, Grennet," he said at length. "Truly. I love her. I always have. I wanted to wed her. But Anna and I had been promised since we were but children." He sidled his fingers to the edge of his coat.

Bertie's brow furrowed. *What was he about?*

"She loves me, too. She wanted to marry *me*, never you. You were her duty, as Anna was mine."

The words shot arrows through his heart even as his nostrils flared. Why was the duke provoking him when he had a pistol trained on the man?

"How long?" he bit out. *How long had his wife and this jackal been fucking?* He took a step closer, dry grass cracking under his foot. Dead. Like the duke soon would be.

"Eight years."

Eight *years?* He took another step. "You seduced her when she wasn't even out in society?"

Cortleon's lip curled. "*She* pursued me at her parents' house party, not the other way around."

His Bee had been intimate with this lecherous rakehell at her own initiative? Sweat pearled on Bertie's forehead. A goshawk called in the distance, the only sound besides the rustling of a light winter wind. His arm steadied as his eye narrowed down the length of the gun.

Cortleon's eyes widened. "Gr—" he began, as a deafening crack rang out. Birds scattered from the nearby forest.

Bertie blinked. Had his aim been true? One look told the grisly story. The duke lay on the ground, face up. Or where his face had been. *Holy Mary, mother of God.* Bile rose. What had he done? Still gripping his weapon, he walked toward the felled man, fighting the urge to vomit.

A high-pitched scream sounded from the trees bordering the clearing. A small boy darted forward, legs and arms pumping, his face purple and cheeks wet. "You killed my papa! You killed him!"

Wynhawke. Cortleon's son. Why was he here? Had he overheard everything? Did he know who Bertie was? *What to do?* He raised the pistol once more, aiming directly at the boy. The chamber was empty, as it held only a single bullet, but maybe Wynhawke wouldn't know that. Bertie's mind spun, his gaze darting from Cortleon's son to the mess of a man a few feet away.

"Stop!" he yelled, his voice echoing around the silent clearing.

The boy did, though whether from the command or from seeing his father's disfigured face, he didn't know. He closed the distance between them, grabbing onto Wynhawke's collar. Leaning down, he pressed his nose near the child, whose eyes leaked tears despite the rage they reflected—a murderous rage matching his own.

Wynhawke was but five. Bertie flexed his fingers. He could settle his hands around the lad's neck and choke the life from him. If the boy revealed what he'd seen, it'd destroy not only Bertie but also his entire family. He might as well hold the pistol to his own skull should that happen. If caught now, he'd hang for sure—unless his peers shot him first. But was his soul so lost that he'd stoop to murdering a child?

He raised himself to his full height, releasing the child. Wynhawke sucked in a breath, his face whitening. Bertie stood a head above most other men and had a chest of such width that his friends teased he was a giant. "You must never say what happened here. Do you understand?"

Mutiny etched itself across Wynhawke's features. Despite his visible fear, he pushed out his chin. "You killed my father! You'll pay for this!"

"Do you know who I am?"

"I know you're a murderer!"

Bertie exhaled. "I don't want to hurt you. Your father deserved it. You, on the other hand ..." He *didn't* want to kill the boy. *One ought not to visit the sins of the father upon his sons.* He scowled, contorting his face into the most monstrous expression he could muster as he bent down, piercing Cortleon's son with his eyes. "Say *nothing*. Should you do so, I'll find you and chop off your head. And that of your mother."

Wynhawke gulped but didn't move a muscle.

"Your father was a bad man. You and your mother needn't pay for his crimes."

The boy's gaze darted toward Cortleon's body. He steeled his shoulders, his little brown eyes tightening.

Bertie's heart—what there was left of it—sank. Wynhawke wasn't going to let it be. That he could kill the father but spare the son had been a far-fetched notion. He grimaced. He was already damned; what would one more heinous act matter? He must spare his wife and unborn child.

As he stepped forward, a roaring pop sounded. Pain exploded in his neck. His eyes widened at the gun in Wynhawke's hands—*where had it come from* —and then he fell, his hands clutching at his cravat, warm blood oozing between his fingers.

Bee, he thought, as consciousness left him. *Forgive me.*

GAVIN SCREAMED. A duke's son was permitted to scream if he'd killed a man, was he not? If he'd seen his papa murdered? He dropped the pistol he'd pulled from his father's coat pocket and leapt to his feet.

"Papa," he wailed, his eyes on the bright red coat he'd long admired for its pattern of stars and hawks.

"In honor of you, my son," Papa had said the first time Gavin saw it. "For you are the Marquess of Wynhawke."

"The birds look so real they seem like they will fly away at any moment."

Papa had laughed, that rich, booming laugh Gavin loved, and allowed him to feel the soft fabric to his heart's content. But now blood darkened the velvet. The birds looked as if they were crying. Gavin stared at them, for he couldn't peek any higher. His papa's face was gone. How could a face be *gone*? A strange, metallic, meaty smell stung his nose. What was it?

Was it Papa?

His stomach emptied itself until there was nothing left. He grabbed his father's hand, fixing his eyes on the large ring, the one with the golden lion's head on top of a red stone. The Cortleon crest. Papa had told him he'd wear the ring when he was Duke.

"I shall be a duke, too? Like you, Papa?"

"Yes. After I'm gone, you'll be the next Duke of Cortleon."

"Gone? But where would you go? I don't wish you to leave me!"

"Nor I, you, my child. But it is the way of the world. That's why you must live with all you have, my boy."

A groan sounded, and he jerked around. The giant green man stirred. How could that be? He'd shot him! A low moan came again, and the man's eyes opened, now rimmed in red. He must be a monster. How else could he come back from the dead? Those red eyes moved to him. *The monster is going to kill me!*

Gavin shrieked, jumping up. Then he ran.

〜

BERTIE LAY ON THE GROUND, agony burning his throat like a hot iron. But he was alive. By some miracle, he was still alive. At least for now. He had to leave this field before anyone found him.

With agonizing movements, he removed his coat then held it to his neck. Rising painfully, he stumbled away. Somehow, he'd have to make it back to Camlon. Howsden would help him. Howsden would never betray him. That was the advantage of employing a valet besotted with him. Bertie never acknowledged the man's desire, of course, but he didn't mind taking advantage of it when needed. Such as now.

Yes, Howsden would help disguise this wound—provided Bertie made it to his chamber undiscovered. What if Wynhawke had already revealed what he'd seen? *Whom* he'd seen? If the boy didn't know him by name, he certainly would know him by appearance. Bertie did not blend easily into a crowd.

But the lad had shaken with terror. Bertie's threat just might keep him safe. If Wynhawke held his tongue, he'd have to act as if nothing were wrong, as if his own body didn't presently bear witness to the morning's violence.

The neck wound may prove superficial, but if Cortleon's son told of what he'd seen, the consequences wouldn't be.

"MERCIFUL HEAVENS, Wynhawke! Whatever is the matter?"

The Duchess of Arthington's startled voice flowed over him as he raced across Camlon's front grounds. He ignored the question, launching himself into his mother's embrace and flinging his arms around her neck, her familiar vanilla scent enveloping him as he clung to her for all he was worth. Nurse would cluck at him. Such behavior was unseemly for a boy his age, but he didn't care.

"He's dead, Mama!"

"Who's dead, my child?" Her tone was sharp, though the hand smoothing his hair remained soft and steady.

"Papa! Papa's dead!"

Without warning, she gave way beneath him, and they both fell.

"Anna!" Mama's friend cried out. She crouched beside his mother, who lay unmoving on the ground.

Just like Papa.

A servant ran off, calling for the duke.

"What do you mean, Wynhawke?" the duchess asked again, a calm in her voice—the kind adults used when they wanted to convince him nothing was wrong.

But everything was wrong and always would be.

"He's in the field. He's dead! He's in the big field."

The Duke of Arthington ran across the lawn. The duke never ran. He was always everything "proper and fitting to his highest of stations, as you ought to be, Pendrake, you rap*scallion*," Gavin's friend James had repeated just that morning, imitating his father's rigid posture and using such a funny voice that Gavin had fallen onto the nursery floor in laughter.

No one was laughing now.

"What is this, Wynhawke?" the duke demanded.

Gavin swallowed but stood up tall, as Papa would want him to. "My father is dead, Your Grace."

"You saw this?"

"Y-yes." He hiccupped, dashing a hand against his wet cheeks.

"There's blood on the boy." The duke frowned, immediately calling for horses. "Take him into the house, madam."

Mama's friend reached for his hand. "We shall go in," she whispered, gently squeezing his fingers. "But with your mother."

A maid knelt by his mother's side and waved a bottle

beneath her nose. The smell was funny. It tickled Gavin's nostrils, making him want to sneeze. His mother's eyelids fluttered open. She sat up abruptly, looking to the duchess. "Irene? It isn't true, is it? Is he—my husband—dead?"

"Shh ... do not speak so now. Arthington has ridden out with several men. We will have answers soon."

A footman helped Mama to her feet. Gavin pulled free from the duchess's hand and ran to her. Though her skin was pale, she gave him a smile. "Come, my son. Let us go inside."

A short time later, noises from the rear of the house indicated the men had returned. The duke strode into the front drawing room where Gavin sat with his mother, four lords following after him. One of the men looked like he was about to be ill. The duke shook his head, his mouth a tight line.

Mama wept, clutching Gavin to her.

"What happened?"

He didn't know to whom the voice belonged, but it didn't matter. He kept his eyes on the red carpet. Red like his papa's bloody coat.

"He was shot in the face. A cowardly act."

"Shot?" Mama whipped up her head. "*By whom*?"

"We don't know, though his own pistol lay near his side. It'd been discharged. We found blood a short distance away."

"A duel?" said his mother's friend, the duke's wife, who sat to their other side, her arm laced through Mama's at the elbow.

"Perhaps. Though if so, not one conducted in an honorable fashion. No seconds, no doctor? Absurd."

A short man with a sizable stomach approached Gavin. "Wynhawke," he barked. "Did you witness the event? Did you see another man?"

Gavin gulped but said nothing.

"There was blood on your clothing." The duke's thick brows wrinkled together. Did he think Gavin had shot his own papa?

He swallowed. "I ... I hugged him."

His mama's body trembled, and she made sad sounds at his words.

They weren't true. He hadn't hugged Papa. He'd only held his hand. But if he told from whom the blood had come, the monster would kill him and Mama. He didn't know the giant's name, anyway, so what could he tell? Of a green man? The man—the *monster*—had worn green from head to toe: green coat, green waistcoat, green breeches. Even his hose and shoes were green, though his periwig was white, like Papa's. Did it cover green hair? A green man with red eyes, like those of a demon. Maybe he *was* a demon!

He'd spoken to Papa as if they knew each other, though. Surely Papa hadn't known any demons?

"Gather the guests," the duke snapped. "Servants, too. Have them assemble in the ballroom. We must make them aware of what's happened, though everyone's likely heard by now. We must see if someone knows anything."

"At once, Your Grace," said a footman, who then sent servants scurrying.

"Wynhawke needn't come, need he?" his mama said. "He's been through so much. Too much. No boy should see his ... should see ..." She broke off with a sob.

The duke's voice gentled. "I'm sorry, Madam. Truly. But we must determine if your son recognizes or reacts to anyone."

Gavin's heart seized. He did not want to go into the ballroom. He wanted to go to the stables and hide among the horses with James. He did not want to risk seeing the green monster again. But he obeyed when his mother, her own throat bobbing, beckoned him.

A great number of people had already crowded into the room and more trickled in from the doors on either end. If only he were a real hawk and could fly away! He didn't see the green man. Perhaps he'd died. Though if he had, wouldn't the duke have found him?

Maybe the bad man had run off and would never return. Oh, how he hoped so!

But at that moment, a round-bellied lady waddled in, followed by the monster he'd prayed never to see again. There was no mistaking him. He wasn't in green now, however, but a dark brown coat with a checked waistcoat.

He looked to the man's neck. There was no blood. Maybe the giant's high-collared coat and neckcloth hid it. Or had he been healed by magic?

The air would not move from Gavin's lungs. The monster that had shot his father stood at the back of the room and nobody knew. Nobody but him. His stomach turned, and he feared he might be sick right here, though nothing remained to come up.

The duke entered the ballroom, his mouth turned downward. "The Duke of Cortleon has been fatally shot."

People gasped and cried. One lady swooned.

"There is a murderer among us!" squealed a plump older woman wearing a silly bonnet. Several other ladies shrieked.

"Let us not make assumptions." The duke's tone was at once both chiding yet calming. "Perchance a ruffian attacked the duke at random."

"A ruffian?" called someone else. "Was Cortleon robbed?"

The duke held up a hand. "I'll say no more at present. You shall each present yourself to me, however, so that I may ascertain privately if anyone has useful information."

The green monster, now in brown, acted as surprised by this news as everyone else, until he saw Gavin. He lifted his hand and pointed up. Gavin gulped at what hung directly above the giant. An axe. A huge, double-headed axe. Lots of old swords surrounded it, but the axe was the only thing he could see.

The green giant might use that axe to chop off his head if he said anything. Gavin pressed his lips together. No words would cross them. He turned away so nobody might see him looking at the monster. He wouldn't let anyone or anything hurt Mama. He would protect her, just as Papa would want him to. Always.

CHAPTER 1

ROME, ITALY - AUGUST 1812

*T*welve years. Twelve years Gavin had waited to commence this quest. Longer, really: twenty-four, counting from the day his father had died.

He'd been only five. He couldn't remember much, though two images never left: a man in a red coat on the ground, and a green monster, giant, brutal, who'd come at him to kill him, as well.

He had few memories other than Rome and their small dwelling on the outskirts of the city, though he recalled playing in a castle. He'd asked his mother about it once, years ago.

"Did we live in a castle, Mama?"

"A castle? Heavens, no." She laughed at the notion, but her eyes grew misty, distant. "Merely a house. Larger than this cottage, I admit. But we're happier here, are we not?"

He didn't know how to answer. He *was* happy with his mama, the two of them, together. He wished for playmates, though. His mother preferred to keep to herself—and to keep him busy with his many tutors.

"I suppose. But why must I learn Latin and Greek and

history and such? What will I ever *do* with them?" He far preferred being outside, running and jumping and exploring.

"You'll need to know such things someday. It will be expected of you." She hugged him tightly. "So much will be expected of you. But for now, you are mine."

"Of course, I'm yours, Mama!" He rested his head against her familiar chest, taking comfort in the notes of vanilla that always surrounded her. "I'll never leave you!"

And he hadn't. Not even when, a few months after his seventeenth birthday, she'd taken severely ill and called him to her bedside. "Gavin, there is much you need to know." Her breath was labored.

"Shh, Mother. You must rest. We'll talk later," he said, as he wiped her forehead with a damp cloth.

"No." Her arm shot out, her fingers clamping onto his forearm. "You must know now. I fear my time grows short and I've kept who you are from you for far too long."

"Who I am?"

She swallowed. "The doctors told me that when a young child suffers a terrible event, his mind sometimes chooses to bury it. When you seemed to forget our life in England, I let it be. It was better if you didn't remember." Her lips pulled into a line. "If only I'd been able to forget as well."

He stilled the cloth. She'd never spoken in this way. Whenever he'd had the nightmares and woken screaming of a wild man in green, blood everywhere, she'd soothed him but pushed discussions away. "You are all right. You are safe."

Her brown eyes rose to meet his now, anguish swimming in their depths. "You are Gavin Knight, that is true. But you are so much more. Your father was the Duke of Cortleon, a powerful man. Now you are Duke."

He pulled away, tensing. What was she talking about? He, a *duke*? Impossible. He was no more than a commoner.

His mother coughed, a weak, feeble sound. "I'm dying, Gavin."

No. She couldn't die. "Don't say such things!"

"I do not want to leave you, but the doctors agree I'm unlikely to recover. So, you must know the truth. I owe you that, though I'd prefer never to visit those memories or the past again." She lay back, seeming to drift into sleep. But a moment later, her voice came again. "You are the Duke of Cortleon, Marquess of Wynhawke, Earl Walwen. Scion of one of the richest and most powerful noble families in England. Son of a man who, despite his many faults, loved you dearly." A sigh followed her last statement.

Images rushed at him. A tall man with brown eyes, lighter than his mother's, like his own. A cheeky grin and laughter. His mother in a never-ending gown of lilac. A field, a loud crack, and a coat peppered with blood.

"You couldn't—or wouldn't—tell more of that awful day, my son. No clues were found, no man arrested. So, we fled. I couldn't risk losing you, for you mean more to me than life itself. I couldn't risk the chance that whoever had done this horrible thing might come back for you." She paused, drawing in several shallow breaths.

"I made the right decision. I know I did. For on the ship to Italy, you screamed in your sleep of a green monster that had promised to chop off your head should you ever reveal him. When fully awake, you claimed to remember nothing. But your nightmares told the truth. You hadn't just found your father; you'd witnessed his death." Her eyes welled up. "I hoped with time the nightmares would cease, that no trace of the tragedy would haunt you. That you and I could start anew."

She reached for his hand, her cool fingers small within his own. "When you pressed me about the dreams, perhaps

I should have told you the entire truth. But I feared for our lives, Gavin. So I brought you to Rome. I acknowledged no trace of our former status. I worried the murderer—this green man, you insisted—would come for us. For you."

The green man. Gavin still occasionally dreamt of him. Sometimes he was a magical creature of immense height and width, entirely green save for red eyes. At others, more a man—clad in green, but a man, nonetheless. The images blurred into each other. Which was the truth? He didn't know, but he'd abhorred the color for as long as he could remember.

"Surely if I were a duke, Mama, I'd know it," he protested, thinking of the lords who pranced through Rome, powerful men well aware of their position and sure of their dominance. English, French, German, Italian. Whatever their nationality, they were the same: men proud of their status and wealth who dressed and acted accordingly.

"I am glad you didn't." Her mouth tightened as she set a hand to her chest, drawing in a ragged breath. "Bring me my box."

Her dressing room box? Why would she want that now?

He sent their single manservant for it, not wanting to leave her. When he returned, she motioned for the box to be set at her side then waved the servant away. Pulling her ever-present necklace with its silver crescent and golden ring over her head, she handed it to Gavin.

"The crescent opens it."

He raised a brow but inserted the crescent's tips into two small holes on either side of the large red stone on the lid, then turned it. A click sounded, and the top sprang up. Inside lay a number of papers and a ring—a thick, heavy ring featuring a lion's head, its mane shaped like a star, set into a red stone very much like the stone on the top of the chest. The one his mother had insisted was paste.

He looked up.

"Yes, it's real ruby. Your father's signet ring. The Cortleon family crest. It's yours now." She gestured to the necklace still in the chest's lock. "That, too. My wedding ring and a silver emblem Loughton found in Egypt."

"Egypt? My father went to Egypt?"

"Yes." She smiled, her face softening. "He always was one for adventure. When he had to return from abroad to take up the ducal title, he sought it at home." Her smile twisted. "Whether with horses, fighting ... or women."

"Women?"

She coughed again, then nodded. "It hurts to tell you this, Gavin, but your father was a well-known rake, even after we married. My greatest source of pain is that my love was never enough for him. And that I always forgave him, though each time I learned of a new affair, another piece of my heart broke."

His father had forsaken his vows and been unfaithful? No wonder his mother spoke so often of honor and fidelity. She'd been denied them. Moments ago, he'd been proud to have had a sire of such noble standing. But to know the man had dishonored Mama in such a way? He balled his fists, wanting to take the ruby ring and throw it across the room.

"Is that why ...?" He wasn't even sure what he was asking.

"Is that why he was murdered? I've always believed so. His pistol lay to his side, more blood a short distance away. The Duke of Arthington believed it to be a duel. It wouldn't have been the first in which your father fought for such reasons. He usually deloped, and the other man accepted his apology. Only once did a husband fire at him, but he missed."

Gavin ducked his head, not wanting to face her, shame for his father's actions coursing through him. He studied the ring instead, noting the intricacies of the design, the defiance in the lion's gaze. He slid it onto his finger. The image of a different hand, a different ring, bombarded him. An emerald ring on a threatening hand.

The green man had had such a ring.

"Mother," he said steadily. "Do all men have such rings?"

"Certainly not. Signet rings are symbols of the peerage."

The monster had been a peer, then. A mere mortal.

"Tell me more of Father's death."

"I know little more. He was shot in a field near Camlon, the Duke of Arthington's country home, at their annual Christmas house party. Arthington queried everyone on the estate, but no one, from peer to servant, witnessed anything, nor was anyone injured."

"Was there anyone present who might have borne Father ill will?" He hated to upset her by asking, yet he needed to know.

"No. We were all good friends. I did ask you that evening if you had anything else to tell, if only to me. You insisted you knew nothing." She took a breath. "Irene wrote once to say that despite Arthington's best efforts, he'd found no further clues."

"Irene?"

"Arthington's wife and my dear friend. I miss her still. But I asked her not to write again. I couldn't risk anyone learning of our location."

What would his life have been like had he grown up in England, the son of a duke? A son who might have had friends? Had his mother truly needed to take such drastic action?

Though his scanty memories affirmed the green man *had* threatened his life. No wonder; if a peer, the murderer risked losing everything were he discovered—his life, but also his family's honor.

His hands shook. The monster had stolen not only his father's life but Gavin's, as well. He loved his mother, but life here could be lonely with no siblings and few people with whom Mama wished to associate. He ground his teeth to keep from roaring. He'd kill him. He'd find this fiend, and he would kill him. If only the emerald ring's details were clearer in his mind; doubtless, many peers had rings of green, that detested color.

"You needn't go back, Gavin. You've everything you need here. I have money in my accounts. You'll lack for nothing. The estates are under good stewardship; I do hear news from time to time." She paused to catch her breath. "But should you choose to return, these papers prove who you are, as does the ring, of course. Promise me, though, you'll stay until my end."

He whipped up his head. "Of course, Mama. I promise. I'd never leave you."

"And promise me ... promise me you'll not repeat the sins of your father. When you marry, Gavin, be faithful. Please."

He swallowed. The dark-haired maid from the neighboring farm had taught him much in their furtive escapades. He shouldn't have trifled with her, though. He'd never have married her. Certainly not now, when his future lay in England. No, he would not be his father. He'd not dishonor women in such a way. "I promise, Mama. Rest now."

Her eyes closed. "If I do not wake, know this, Gavin: I love you with my whole heart. Everything I've done, be it right or wrong, I've done out of love for you. Let love be your guide, my son. Not hate. Not revenge. Love."

∾

ANNA KNIGHT DID NOT DIE that night. "A miracle," her doctors said. "She must be touched by God."

She lingered twelve more years, in fact, though the effects of the illness never left. She remained weak. And Gavin stayed, as promised. He took up new hobbies, however: boxing, fencing, riding, and shooting. He sought out the finest instructors, rewarding them handsomely with the coin to which he now had access. But he revealed nothing about himself, not even his name. "I pay you enough to make anonymity part of the contract."

"*Si, signore.*" Soon they'd begun calling him *il falco*—the hawk. Amusing, given his marquessate title, Wynhawke, of which they, of course, were unaware.

"Because of your aquiline nose," Sulpicio, his fencing master, explained. "But also, your intensity. You fight like a hawk. The most talented man I've ever trained, as good with your fists as with sword or pistol. Your legend will ever grow."

"Not if you don't tell anyone." Gavin winked, but his voice held steel.

"Of course, of course, *falco*. But to hide such prowess is a shame. Your mother would be proud."

"My mother is the last person who needs to know." She wouldn't approve, for he trained in pursuit of a singular goal, his holy quest: to find the man who'd destroyed his family and denied him what should have been his. The monster, if still living, must pay.

The blood thirst that had driven Gavin at age seventeen had given way to more rational thought. Simply slaughtering the man, as he'd first longed to do, would make him no better than the murderer. No, he'd avenge his father, his mother, and himself by means of an honorable duel, the kind denied Loughton Knight. And he would triumph, by means of pistol, sword, or even bare hands.

"I don't seek revenge, Mama," he whispered to himself

many a night, clutching her crescent necklace he wore around his neck. His touchstone, symbol of everything he'd had and lost. "I seek retribution."

The green man had robbed him of his father; he'd not rob him of his future. No, Gavin would find him and exact justice. He'd take all that had been taken from him. As soon as he determined whom the monster was.

CHAPTER 2

WAINSBURY HALL, ENGLAND

"*Y*our Grace, will you be taking breakfast this morning?"

Gavin stood at the window in his study, staring out at Wainsbury's grounds. Land as far as the eye could see, all belonging to the Cortleon estate. To him. *Incredible*. He'd been here two months, and yet still it seemed alien. Not like home. With Mama.

His chest constricted. Her passing hadn't been unexpected; she'd declined rapidly in the last year. And yet, when it came, when she left this world, his arms around her, a howling grief had descended, pinning him so tightly he could hardly breathe. His mother was all he'd had. Now she was gone. Some might say he'd been too attached. Let them. He swallowed against the pain.

"Your Grace?"

He turned, the original question just now registering. His housekeeper, Mrs. Stewart, stood at the door, her expression polite and patient, as always.

She'd thrown her arms around him when he'd first arrived. "I never thought to see you again, Your Grace. How overjoyed Monmouth and I have been since receiving word of your return." But after that quick display, she'd stepped back, starch returning to her posture. "Do forgive me. That was most improper. I was momentarily overcome."

"There is nothing to forgive."

He rather wished at times she'd embrace him again so that he could close his eyes and pretend she was his mother.

"My apologies, Mrs. Stewart. I was distracted," he said. "No to breakfast. Gringolet and I need a good ride. But if you could please alert Malory I'd like a bath upon my return?"

"Of course, Your Grace."

With that, the housekeeper made her exit, and he was alone. Again. He pulled at his well-tailored coat. This loneliness was both familiar and foreign. As was England. At least in Rome, he could slip in among the crowds to bestow a flower upon a pretty signorina or spar with Sulpicio. At least in Rome, familiar faces had greeted him on his occasional roundabouts through town.

No one at Wainsbury was familiar. Mrs. Stewart and Monmouth had served here since he was a child, but he didn't remember them. Malory, Gavin's valet, had taken his position a few days after Gavin arrived. He liked the man already, however. Malory took his duties seriously but had bantered with him while acquainting him with the finer points of a ducal wardrobe. Gavin preferred the more casual clothing he'd worn in Rome, but one couldn't deny the richness or warmth of the new silks and woolens he wore.

Slapping his riding gloves against his thigh, he left the study and made his way to the stables. He'd meet with White, Wainsbury's steward, that afternoon, but for now, nothing appealed as much as galloping across the fields atop Gringolet, the most magnificent horse he'd ever seen.

"A gift from the Duke of Arthington," Malory had read from the note accompanying the horse. "He's most pleased to hear you are alive and returned to England and looks forward to renewing your friendship." The valet's mouth tipped up. "But adds, 'Perhaps we'd better avoid the lake.'"

The lake. He and a blond-haired boy with a crooked-toothed smile had gone hunting in one once, hadn't they? Not for fish or frogs. For a sword. They'd been friends, James and he. He remembered the name but knew nothing of the man that blond boy had become. If James was now Duke, he, too, must have lost his father.

"He includes an invitation to their Christmas house party and says his mother is beside herself with joy to see you again."

The Duchess of Arthington. James's mother. Mama's closest friend. Would he remember her face? The idea of a connection, any kind of connection, appealed. But *Christmas.* He'd never liked the feast after learning his father had perished at a Christmas party. A party at Camlon, the Arthington estate, in fact.

His gut had heaved, almost as if he'd been punched or were about to lose his stomach's contents, but he'd accepted the invitation at once. His father died at Camlon. To Camlon he must return, then. Perhaps the duchess might remember a man with a green signet ring.

He rubbed the lion's head ring as a groom saddled Gringolet. He did not wish to make his social debut at a Christmas gathering. He didn't wish to make his debut at all. He'd hidden at Wainsbury since his arrival—his *return*, the servants insisted—his mourning a painful reality and a convenient excuse not to venture into society.

Pulling on his gloves, he mounted the horse, glad for the fresh but chilly November air. He missed the scent of the oregano and rosemary his mother had grown in her garden, though. He missed his mother.

Squeezing Gringolet with his thighs, he directed the horse toward the fields behind Wainsbury. Other invitations had come, letters expressing astonishment and delight at his reappearance. Unfamiliar names pressing acquaintanceship. Strangers wanting information on where he'd been and what he'd been doing. Most weren't so bald as that, instead housing their questions within their own recollections of foreign travel and the like.

Once Gringolet reached the open expanse of grasses, he urged the horse into a canter, his body flowing easily with the horse's movements. He'd answered none of those other invitations. He'd done little else since stepping onto the estate, as a matter of fact, than ride Gringolet and survey Wainsbury and its lands. Thank God for White, who, as Mama had promised, had the estate so well in hand, Gavin needn't even be here. Between White and Malory's ceaseless instruction and his mother's tutoring her last few years, he was as well versed as he might ever be in the particulars of English society.

He pulled up the horse, staring out over the hills and valleys beyond the eastern edge of the estate. To carry out his quest, he must take up his position and make himself known to the *ton*, in hopes that someone could provide information ... or that the monster might seek to finish what he'd started so long ago, before Gavin had shot him.

Gringolet pulled at the reins, and Gavin gave him his head, exhilaration surging as the horse sprinted across the vast stretches of land.

Yes, to Camlon he'd go.

For the dragons of his past called.

CHAPTER 3

EN ROUTE TO CAMLON – LATE DECEMBER 1812

*L*ady Elinor Greene fidgeted on the carriage seat, longing to pull her skirts free from under her derriere. A sharp fold of fabric had been tormenting her for the last half hour. Not only would her mother disapprove of such an indelicate maneuver, however, but the narrow vehicle allowed no room to lean, much less stand.

She crossed her arms, shooting daggers at her fellow traveling companions. Her mother, back rigid as ever, her father, dozing with loud snores in the corner, her sister Lucy-Anne on the other side of their mother, eyes dreamy, fingering a curl as she soaked in the passing scenery.

Nelle's two other sisters, Tabitha and Prudence, surrounded her, bickering over whether Mozart or Beethoven was the better composer. This followed on the heels of their previous argument over whether dogs or cats made the more ideal pet. She'd suggested rabbits, thinking fondly of Caera, her white, floppy-eared bunny left behind at Inglewood. She'd gladly have stayed behind, as well, though she *was* desperate for alternative company to her incessantly squabbling sisters.

"I do believe you could fight over air!" she huffed now, irritated by their snappish talk. Both sisters stopped and stared. When they weren't at each other's throats, they united against anyone who dared challenge them.

"You're one to talk, Nelle!" exclaimed Pru. "You've been nothing but disagreeable since we set out. For heaven's sake, we're going to a house party! Oh, may many a handsome lord be there."

Their mother tut-tutted. "Prudence, you are not out. You've no business socializing with any young man and will only be in company when I allow it."

Now it was Pru's turn to fold her arms over her chest. "I *would* be out, were it not for our reduced circumstances! If I shan't have a proper Season, why can't I at least dance with a gentleman at a private gathering?"

Lady Rutley sputtered. Tabby leaned around Nelle with a sly grin. "Even if you could work up the nerve to talk to a gentleman," she said to Prudence, "*I* shall be so busy commanding their attention that they'll have no time to notice you. Or your freckles."

The sound of their mother's fan smacking Tabby's knuckles roused Lucy-Anne from her daydreaming. "Don't be unkind, Tabitha," she said, stroking her fingers against the curtain lining the coach window. "Pru's freckles are endearing."

Tabby rubbed her hand, scowling at her mother.

"How much longer to Camlon?" Nelle asked, sounding like a petulant child herself. But truly, how much time could one stand trapped in such close quarters with one's family? Carriage rides were a necessary evil. Horses, too. The motion of either often tied her stomach in knots, and the odors horses produced made such excursions a lesson in olfactory survival.

Smells had always powerfully affected her. She relished the aroma of hyacinths, warm bread from the oven, or a newborn's head. Horse manure and her father's hair pomade, on the other hand ...

Staying in London meant any number of scents to embrace, or more often avoid—such as the stench of the streets and the distinct fragrance of want. That sad odor permeated the Home for the Salvation and Advancement of Abandoned and Illegitimate Infants and Small Children, founded thirty-odd years ago by her Great-Aunt Theodosia. Nelle spent as much time there as she could—when the Greene family was in Town, at least.

Oh, she loved the theater as much as anyone and savored disappearing into someone else's story for an evening. Nor was she averse to dinners and balls. But her heart lay with those unwanted children, born into an unkind world and dropped at others' doorsteps in hopes someone would care for them. Such an action was better, at least, than exposing the infants and leaving them to die.

Once, when Nelle was thirteen or so, she'd cried out as she'd clutched a tiny bundle of wriggling, screaming newborn. "How could a human be so cruel as to discard a living part of themselves in such a way, Aunt?"

"A lack of love does not usually lie behind abandonment, Nellie, but rather the lack of means, of help, and of options. The Foundling Hospital cannot and will not take in every needy child. Neither can we, but I do my part. That's one advantage to having married for money over affection; now with Neville gone, I may use his resources for what I actually care about."

"Did you never want children of your own?" Nelle had asked, pressing a kiss to the newborn's brow.

Her aunt's eyes had clouded. "Yes. I did. But I could not. Sometimes God gives us what we want through different means, dear child. We just have to be open to seeing it."

How she missed her aunt, who'd passed on six years ago. Their age difference hadn't mattered; they'd been like sisters, two souls who'd thought and felt in the same way. Two souls who'd resorted to a cool, practical approach to the world, lest the sorrow and suffering they witnessed overwhelm them. They showered love upon the children in their care but kept their own emotions to themselves.

Nelle rested her head against the squabs. No one had bothered to answer her question about time, each returning to their earlier pursuits: Lucy-Anne daydreaming, Mother scowling, her younger sisters arguing. Their father snored through it all.

A stone cottage similar in size to Inglewood appeared on the horizon. Her heart leapt. What a joy returning to Inglewood at the close of last Season had been. She relished the cleaner air and simpler living, for the sake of her nose as much as anything else. No doubt the rest of her family had wished to be at Rutley Manor, the larger estate her father had had to let the year before.

"With three of you out yet still unwed, we must economize," he'd said after announcing the sudden change in residence. His wife's sour mouth and blazing eyes showed full well what she thought of this measure.

Nelle had avoided that heated gaze, knowing Mother put much, if not all, of the blame squarely on her shoulders.

"I rather like it here, too, Nelle," Pru had confessed just last week. "More privacy without so many servants about."

More privacy and more freedom; Nelle could roam the modest grounds or even walk into the nearby village without a chaperone. She'd spent many a happy hour in the gardens, tending to Caera and any other creature that wandered her way.

She missed the children at the Home, however. She wrote frequent letters to Mrs. Piper, its matron, seeking news and making what arrangements she could for food and clothing. While they always hoped a family would claim a child, either its birth parents, which happened on rare occasion, or other husbands and wives willing to open their homes to the less fortunate, the majority of the babies —the ones who survived, at least—remained until the age of three or four. At that point, though it broke her heart, they transferred to orphanages for older children. The Home simply hadn't room to keep them longer.

Mother often fussed about Nelle's work. "Charitable endeavors are laudable, my dear. No one disputes that. But must you be so *directly* involved?"

She meant, must Nelle spend so many hours at the Home herself? Many ladies contributed money rather than time. She'd little of the former but much of the latter. Too much of the latter, in her parents' eyes.

"You must marry, Nellie," her father insisted. "You ought to have a husband and your own children. You do not wish to end up like Cousin Joan, do you?"

Cousin Joan, a distant relative, lived with them at Inglewood, spending most of her time tucked away in her meager, cramped room on the upper level. What Joan did in there all day Nelle didn't know, but the woman never seemed unhappy. She'd a far sunnier disposition than Nelle's mother, in fact.

Nelle could think of worse ways to end up—such as trapped in a loveless marriage. Aunt Theo had despised her husband. Nelle's parents tolerated each other but never spent any length of time together unless forced to do so— such as during a carriage ride like this. Even now, her mother had somehow managed to put an inch of space between her and her husband.

Lucy Abbott had married John Greene, Earl of Rutley, out of her desire for a title and the means she'd assumed accompanied it. She'd made no bones about that when discussing her daughters' own marriages—marriages she prayed were in the immediate future. "Your father and his family gave every appearance of great wealth. The truth proved different and thanks to Lord Rutley's mismanagement, we're struggling to launch and keep our four girls in society well enough to secure good matches."

Her mother's remonstrations were growing ever louder, especially since Nelle had just completed her seventh Season, though with much less fanfare—and expense—than that for Lucy-Anne and Tabby.

"If you'll make no effort to find a husband, you do not need new gowns," Mother had said. In fact, Nelle hadn't had new dresses in two years. Their mother had turned her efforts to Lucy-Anne, who, despite several suitors, had herself failed to make a match.

"No one wants to look at me when they can look at you," Lucy-Anne had pouted at one soiree. "Why could the daughter who actually *wishes* to marry not have been given your beauty?"

What to say to that? Lucy-Anne's features were quite pleasing, but Nelle had always garnered excessive attention. Men complimented her clear skin, her golden tresses, her blue eyes ... One more reference to gemstones and she'd scream. As if she'd anything to do with how she looked. She'd no more control over that than over the family into which she'd been born, same as those poor foundlings. Was it so bad to want to be admired for who she was or what she valued rather than for her appearance?

This morning, her mother had pressed marrying yet again. "Honestly, I don't understand, Elinor. Your comeliness is beyond compare. Why haven't you landed a husband?"

"Perhaps because I don't wish to have one?"

Even her father, who rarely got between his wife and his daughters in a row, let out an oath. "How do you propose to live, then, dearest Nelle? As a spinster in our home?"

"I thought I'd save that honor for Lucy-Anne. I'm sure she'd take me in," she responded tartly. She and Lucy-Anne might be opposite in temperament, but they were the best of friends.

"Where do you think she'll be if you don't marry?"

"How do you mean?"

"I mean your sisters cannot marry before you do. It's not seemly. And then what will become of them?"

Nelle's mouth dropped. "You're saying you'll not let my younger sisters wed until I do? You'd give such an ultimatum?"

The earl sighed. "I don't wish to, my dearest Nelle. Truly. But your mother speaks the truth; to put it indelicately, we are living well beyond our means. We must find ways to increase our funds."

"The best way to do so is for you to marry into money. A title is of less importance at this point than wealth." Her mother's cheeks spotted red. Never had they had such an indelicate discussion about money. It wasn't done; such frank talk was to be left to merchants and tradesmen. "You're the beauty of the family, Elinor, the only one with allure enough to land a rich husband despite your small dowry. You shall be our salvation."

Sacrificial lamb, rather. She'd had no chance to rebut her mother's notions, however, as their solitary footman had announced the carriage was ready, and her parents had hastily departed the room.

Her mother cleared her throat, rousing Nelle from memories of that undesired conversation. Everyone looked to Lady Rutley at her not-so-silent command for attention.

"We're fortunate to have received an invitation to the Arthington house party. No doubt men of good breeding, men of *means*, shall be in attendance. Including the Duke of Arthington himself." She eyed her eldest daughter. "This is your last chance, Elinor. Even the loveliest blossom eventually withers away. We expect you to make a match."

"By the end of a *house party*?" Nelle's stomach churned, though whether from the carriage's jostling or her mother's sudden announcement, she knew not. "That's the space of a fortnight!"

"You'll certainly know all of the eligible gentlemen there, by name if not acquaintance. Seven Seasons have given you plenty of time to make connections."

"I'm sure you can find someone to love, Nelle," Lucy-Anne interjected, pulling herself away from the window. "Perhaps an older gentleman. He might not mind your advanced age and might grant you more freedom."

Advanced age? At twenty-five, she was only five years older than Lucy-Anne. Why did a woman cross from nymph to ape leader if she remained unmarried much past the age of twenty-one? For heaven's sake, men and women first reached their majority at that age! Must females immediately go from child to wife?

"A sound idea, Lucy-Anne," their mother said, nodding. "If you find a man significantly your senior, you'll likely have many years to live independently."

Mother hadn't yet managed to marry her off but already talked of her being a *widow*? How heartless could one be? Apparently quite when it came to the business of marriage.

Had Mother never wanted a match built on more than pedigree and pounds per annum, never once felt pangs of love or desire? Not that Nelle could attest much to that; while Lucy-Anne fell in love every other week, she was more reserved in her affections. Few men had commanded her attention and fewer still had sparked attraction. She enjoyed thought-provoking conversations, but such were few and far between—either because lords found certain topics unsuitable for women—anything much beyond dresses, balls, and society gossip, apparently—or because the men themselves were dullards. Plus, most men of rank brought with them a fine dose of conceit. Superficial self-regard held no appeal for her.

She closed her eyes to avoid her mother's perusal. Her stomach lurched as the carriage swayed and rocked, pulling her to and fro, much like the unseen ropes of familial and societal obligations binding her. Was it so selfish to want her life on her terms? In this society, yes. For what woman lived such a life? Not any she knew.

Lucy-Anne was right. If she must marry, an older man of means was an ideal choice. Well-off widows controlled their own money and time. They made their own choices.

Nelle cringed. She didn't like to think herself as ruthless and unfeeling as her mother. But perhaps an older man *would* allow her the freedom to continue her work. And if he were a widower with progeny of his own, maybe he wouldn't desire more children, or even wish to share the marital bed.

Hours. She'd mere hours before they arrived at Camlon. Hours in which to accept the fate she'd long denied. She must marry. Though she struggled on occasion with her family, she loved them, even her oft-prickly mother. And if she could save them, didn't she owe that much to her parents and sisters?

But what did she owe to herself?

CHAPTER 4

*G*avin puffed out his cheeks upon his first sight of Camlon. Wainsbury was no small estate, but it paled in comparison to the lavish construction of brick and stone before him. The house looked like a bloody castle, what with its castellated roof and spires. A memory hit of walking across the rooftop, pretending to be on patrol for invading armies.

He'd been here before.

Of course he'd been here before. His mother had told him so. Might Camlon arouse other recollections of his earlier life? Of his father?

Exhaling, he fingered a waistcoat button as the coach made its way up the long drive, a myriad of emotions cascading through him. Anticipation. Grief. Nervousness. Were dukes allowed to be nervous? Had he grown up in full awareness of his elevated status, he might have commanded that degree of security peers seemed to possess.

He straightened. He was no less than they were. He *was* a peer, their equal—in fact, he outranked most everyone. He merely hadn't known it. Wasn't having grown up as he had better? He'd been free to be who he was and to explore what he'd wished, rather than bound by upper society's strict dictums.

He had no reason for doubt. He'd never lacked for confidence and he'd not start now. He knew who he was, and he knew his purpose: justice. Justice for everything the man in green had cost the Cortleon family.

But first he must pass his initial introduction into society. No matter his high rank, he was at a disadvantage. He didn't know these people, people who'd associated with each other since their earliest days. Malory and White had instructed him as best they could in proper social etiquette, as had his mother. She'd also shared anecdotes and details about numerous noble families, using the periods in which she was relatively well to educate him in the ways of the aristocracy. Anna Knight's knowledge and connections were years out of date, however, and of course neither White nor Malory had any true experience circulating amongst the *ton*.

It was up to him.

Show no fear. Sulpicio's first rule. His second, *Command the stage*.

"The man who acts the champion becomes one. Set your mind so that you never lose, so that you are never at risk of losing, and you will make it so."

"That didn't work for my father," Gavin had muttered mulishly the first time Sulpicio said thus.

"Perhaps he was caught unawares. You'll learn to ensure that never happens."

And so, he had. Hours upon hours of physical and mental training had given him an acuity few men had.

"No English peer could match you," his pistol master, Vero, had sneered. He held a low opinion of the English lords in Rome. "Dandies, each with purses—and lives—easily snatched."

As his coach halted before Camlon's imposing edifice, Gavin steeled himself for whatever was to come. He might not know anyone, might not have grown up in England, but he'd step forth with confidence and show everyone he was no less a man than any of them. A smirk played at his lips. *Likely more.* He peeked through the curtained window. Several gentlemen and ladies loitered about. They drew close to the carriage, one young woman pointing before a matron struck down her hand.

Undoubtedly, the coat of arms emblazoned upon the carriage had caused a stir. Gavin had insisted the large lion's head and bright red five-pointed star be refurbished and painted anew so that there was no question as to the occupant of this coach. The Duke of Cortleon had arrived.

A footman opened the door, and Gavin stepped out, flashing an insouciant smile. A pretty, pert brunette's mouth dropped and he sent her a wink. The English *ton* might be new to him but flirting with beautiful women was not.

"The Duke of Cortleon," the footman announced.

A hush fell as a handsome, well-built man of similar age to Gavin stepped forward, hand extended. "Cortleon. Such a pleasure to welcome you! How I've looked forward to seeing you again." He smiled, revealing a snaggletooth. "I'm Arthington."

Ah, the ducal host. His former friend. Gavin took the hand as he searched the man's face, hoping to recognize the boy he'd once been. Though the blond hair remained, gone was any hint of childhood, as evidenced by his firm grip and the solid form filling out his well-tailored coat and breeches. His muscled calves indicated the Duke of Arthington was no stranger to exercise.

An older woman, her blonde hair woven through with gray, stepped forward, as well. "Cortleon," she said, warmth infusing the single word.

"The Duchess of Arthington. My mother."

The dowager duchess tipped her head. "I long to embrace you," she said, her voice lowered so that only he and her son could hear, "but I understand you may not remember me. I remember you, though, dear boy. How striking you've become, though that should surprise no one, as your father's looks were legendary and Anna quite beautiful, herself."

At the mention of his mother, her eyes took on a veil of sadness. "I was so grieved to hear of her passing. Anna was and remains the dearest friend I ever had. How I wished to see her again, but she'd not hear of me coming to Rome. She feared so for your safety."

He nodded, his chest aching. Discussions of his parents were to be expected, he supposed. Though six months had passed, a period Malory assured him was sufficient enough to allow him to enter society, mentions of his mother still stirred those ferocious pangs of loss. Hopefully, others would not speak as directly, but he laid no blame at the duchess's feet. She'd known his mother and had cared for him.

"No doubt it's been a long journey," Arthington said, as he beckoned a servant. "Luc will show you to your chamber. We convene for dinner at six. Should you wish to join us beforehand, the gentlemen will engage in sport on the south lawn in an hour."

A slender footman in lavish livery stepped forward at the duke's word. He nodded at two other footmen to gather Gavin's trunk, then waited for him to step through the front entrance. Gavin turned in the doorway to address his host. "Thank you, Arthington."

"Please. Arth. It's what my friends call me."

Gavin's throat caught. For the duke to speak as if they were familiar friends was unexpected yet moving. *I'd like a true friend.*

He followed the footmen through an expansive hall, wide stairs running up its left side. Holly and evergreen boughs circled the banister and columns supporting the upper landing. The scent of pine filled the air. *Ah, yes, Christmas.* The reason for which they gathered.

Luc led him up the staircase and down a broad corridor, pausing to open the third chamber door. "Your Grace," he said, extending his hand.

Gavin entered. The room was quite large, a sizable poster bed dominating its center. The walls were papered in a rich cream and dark blue, and a walnut dressing table stood to one side. Two long windows afforded a generous amount of sunlight. He neared them, glancing out at a garden through which several ladies strolled. A flat expanse of lawn extended from its side. At its center, a number of gents observed a fencing match. He snickered. The man in the burgundy surcoat would lose, given his weak command of his rapier.

The footmen deposited his trunk then left. What should he do now? After hours cooped up in his coach, he had no desire to rest. He supposed he ought to join the men. He took a minute to wash his face and hands at the washbasin, then exited the lush chamber—and nearly bumped into a group of young women. "My pardons," he said, as he took them in.

Two, both with an appealing shade of reddish-blonde hair, tittered, and a third, her hair a darker brown, stared at him, wide-eyed. None of them responded, until the fourth, standing at their rear, muttered something under her breath. She'd been fussing with her reticule but raised her head now and looked directly at him.

"It is we who should beg pardon, my lord." Her lips pinched. Why? In disapproval? Impatience? For her companions or for him?

Despite her obvious irritation, the woman was beyond

compare. Striking brows a few shades darker than the sunlit honey tresses framing her face arched over long-lashed eyes of a rich, clear blue, not as light as aquamarine but not as dark as sapphire. Precious gems were an apt comparison, however, given their sparkle. A pert nose swept down to lips a shade pinker than a ripe raspberry. And like a raspberry, he wanted to eat them.

"We beg your pardon, *Your Grace*," one of the reddish-blonde ladies said, emphasizing the last two words.

The beautiful woman with the berry lips reddened. "Then I must beg your pardon again, Your Grace."

"There is nothing to pardon, Lady ...?" He paused, waiting for her to give her name.

"Elinor," supplied the one who'd spoken before. "I'm Lady Tabitha. That's Lady Prudence, and that's Lady Lucy-Anne," she said, gesturing toward the other strawberry blonde, then the brunette. "We're the Greene sisters."

Lady Elinor. The syllables melted on the tongue. But why did her surname have to be *Greene*? Even the mention of the color sent a shiver of revulsion through him. He did not wish to think of the green man. Not with this heavenly vision before him. Her sisters were attractive, but they didn't hold a candle to her.

"A pleasure to make your acquaintance, Your Grace," the vision said, her tone crisp. "But I fear our mother shall send in the troops should we not appear soon for the requisite garden stroll." She dropped a curtsy and stepped forward, nearly pushing into the darker-haired girl in front of her.

"Oh, yes, indeed," said the girl—Lady Lucy, was it? — before moving off, though she turned her head for a final glimpse as they made their way to the stairs.

Lady Elinor, however, gave him no further acknowledgment, her figure tall and proud as she shepherded her sisters in front of her.

Suddenly, this party seemed not such a dreadful thing, after all. Two weeks. Two weeks he'd be in the company of that jewel-eyed beauty.

And two weeks he had to find out as much, if anything, as he could about the events of twenty-four years ago.

~

NELLE'S STOMACH knotted as she descended the stairs. To have made such a mistake as addressing a duke as "*my lord*?" But how was she to have known? She'd never seen him before, and she'd thought by now she'd met every man of rank in England.

She'd never met one like *him*, though. Those brown eyes—so light as to be almost amber. That long nose, regal in its bearing, and cheeks that creased most handsomely when he smiled. Both his nose and mouth were slightly crooked, yet somehow that didn't detract from his attractiveness. His jaw held an unexpected hint of stubble. Stubble! What gentleman didn't ensure he was clean-shaven at all times, according to the current fashion?

And that hair. A rich sable brown, it dipped just past where his neck met his shoulders, brushing across the top of his coat, far longer than any man under forty wore his hair. She longed to touch it. To touch *him*.

"Who *was* that?" she asked bluntly, desperate to know both whom she'd insulted and how he'd escaped her previous notice.

Tabby rolled her eyes. "Weren't you with us on the lawn when he was announced?"

She had been, but then again, she'd lost track of the number of arriving coaches and various peers tripping out of them. She'd occupied herself rather by counting the windows on Camlon's front aspect. Surreptitiously, of course, lest one think her unconscionably rude. Once she'd finished the windows, she'd tallied the spires and castellations circling the roof and balconies.

Such ostentatious wealth. How many children could the cost of one of those windows feed? How many dresses and breeches could the Dowager Duchess of Arthington's diamond necklace purchase? Nelle might be an earl's daughter, but such excess had never sat well.

Then again, this house was centuries old and probably the necklace, as well, an heirloom passed down from generation to generation, along with wealth and land. If one had sons, that was. As it stood, Cousin Alfred would inherit the Rutley earldom, given her parents had produced only daughters—a fact her father openly lamented.

"Not that I don't love you, my dears," he always added. "But the cost of daughters ... and then to lose the Rutley estates ..."

"When that happens, it shall be because you are dead," her mother had admonished him once. "*We* must then deal with the loss of lands and income, not you."

Nelle shook off that unpleasant memory.

"He is the Duke of Cortleon," Lucy-Anne said, twirling one of her curls. "Is he not of handsome countenance?"

Her sister's dreamy eyes signaled infatuation. *Oh, bother.* The girl lived with her head in the clouds, convinced her grand love was just around the next corner.

Nelle didn't answer Lucy-Anne's question, instead murmuring, "The Duke of Cortleon." *Cortleon?* The name wasn't familiar, though not entirely unfamiliar, either. She must have heard it in passing conversation.

"Oh, for heaven's sake, Nelle," Tabby groused. "Where've you been? His return made all the papers since he's been away from England some twenty-five years. We've talked about him over breakfast several times. London society has waited with bated breath for when he'd make his appearance. He's been in mourning for his mother, God rest her soul."

She snickered at Tabitha's suddenly pious tone. Her sister was anything but pious. Rather shrewd and calculating, if you asked Nelle, and therefore the Greene sister most likely to make the best match. Did Tabby have her eye on this duke? That'd be a high aim for the third daughter of an earl.

"Where was he?" *Drat*. She should have kept silent. Her sisters were sure to mark this unusual interest in a man.

"Rome," Pru said.

"Why Rome? And why for so long?"

"Good heavens, you goose!" Tabby exclaimed. "Surely you remember the story? His father passed away at Camlon —during their Christmas house party, as a matter of fact. Shot in a duel when the current duke was quite young. His mother spirited him away, fearing for his life! No one knew his whereabouts or if he even still lived. Until his return, of course. He is a *mystery*."

"For all that is sacred, Tabby, you say that as if it were a desirable thing, like something out of one of your dreadful Gothic novels."

A duke had died here, and now his son had returned after nearly his entire life away to the very place his father had been killed? How horrible.

"Lady Gertrude said His Grace found his father in the field," whispered Pru as they walked to the gardens.

Nelle swallowed. She did not want to think of such a monstrous thing. Seeing the bodies of children who'd died from exposure or disease was devastating. But to discover her own papa in such a state? Her heart went out to the brown-eyed duke.

She straightened as they reached the other ladies gathered at the garden gate. He was a *duke*, a man born to wealth and privilege, at the pinnacle of power, with a freedom she'd never know. Why would she think him someone for whom she should feel sorry?

Why was she thinking about him at all? Why had their brief, awkward interaction stirred her so much in the span of a few minutes? Whatever the reason, she didn't care for it. No, she was here to find a husband. A young, handsome duke was not on the cards. She might be renowned for her looks, but also for two other things: her advancing age and her frostiness.

"The Ice Princess," a lord had called her that very morning, assuming she couldn't hear. Or perhaps that she could.

"Frigid," another responded.

Both men's eyes had flashed to her, but she'd refused to dignify them with any sort of reaction except a polite dip of the head, as one might give a stranger when out for a stroll. No one need know the sting those comments dealt. She was not made of ice. She was not cold. But how was she to turn around and play the empty-headed flirt in the evenings when she spent her days caring for unwanted and unloved children?

So many of her age and social standing seemed of little substance. Theater and dinners and balls, the latest bit of gossip, riding in Hyde Park, shopping for new finery; those were uppermost on so many fops' and debutantes' minds. Did they never want something *more*? She enjoyed the escape those activities provided, as well, but she always returned to her work, for she'd found her calling.

According to society—and her mother—a young woman's primary purpose was to land a husband and bear him children. At what point were women allowed to turn their minds to more weighty matters? After their children were grown? Never?

The peers who sat in parliament made decisions affecting the well-being of people at all levels of society. At some point, then, lords who in their youth cared for nothing beyond hunting, shooting, and riding must embrace a more serious outlook.

Yes, older men had more substance. An older gentleman would make a better husband than a young, frivolous lord—or a man with velvety eyes and an entirely too charming grin. A man in the prime of his life, as his figure showed. And much to her chagrin, she'd noticed. Oh, how she'd noticed.

She turned to the ladies, insisting that despite the chilly air, she, too, wished to spend the afternoon walking through the gardens. *And probably every afternoon for two long weeks.* Or two weeks entirely too short, given her parents' ultimatum. Indeed, endless walks along paths winter had deadened to dismal browns and grays were exactly what she needed.

Anything to take her mind off the enigmatic Duke of Cortleon.

CHAPTER 5

*G*avin strode across the lawn, angling for the one man mildly familiar: Arthington.

The duke held court at the center of a throng of young bucks. A lanky, black-haired man to his side cracked a grin at something Arthington said. The blond duke beckoned with a welcoming hand as Gavin neared. "Cortleon. Come, let me make introductions."

Gavin nodded as he reached the small enclave.

Arthington gestured to the black-haired man. "The Marquess of Emerlin."

Blue eyes shone out of an oddly charming face, nearly elfish when he grinned, large dimples decorating his cheeks.

The duke nodded next to a gentleman of brown hair and square jaw. "The Earl of Stoneleigh." In quick succession, he introduced several others. "Viscounts Keswick, Borswell, and Bedeville, and the Marquess of Pallemeade." All were of similar age.

Holding his arms wide, Arthington flashed a toothy grin and gave the barest of head tips to the left. "We welcome you to Camlon and the bounty it holds."

Gavin turned. A congregation of young ladies meandered through a maze of low shrubberies, empty flowerbeds, and leafless trees, Lady Elinor among them.

"It's like the Holy Grail of beauty," he said, and the men broke out in laughter.

"Fitting," added Arthington, after their chuckles died down. "My family claims Arthur as a distant ancestor, insisting Camlon took its name from Camelot and Avalon, homes of the fabled king."

"That must be why you're always on the hunt for old swords, my friend. Hoping to find Excalibur?" Emerlin's words came out with a hint of Irish lilt.

Arthington gave him a friendly shove. The two were obviously close.

"I suggest you resist the temptations of this castle of maidens, however," Stoneleigh interjected. "Unless, of course, you wish to find yourself leg-shackled before this party is over."

"My mother would certainly enjoy that." Arthington wrinkled his mouth. "I've a feeling that was her intention behind this year's particular group of guests. Mother sought out families with eligible daughters of a certain age, hoping, no doubt, I might find one to my liking."

Gavin cocked an eyebrow. "If all the young ladies in England look like that, I'd think it an enjoyable pursuit." He glanced toward Lady Elinor, who turned away. Had she been watching him? More likely the group of men in general. There was no reason to believe she'd singled him out.

Arthington gave a harrumph. "First, they only have eyes for Em." He brushed off his friend's protest. "You know it's true. And second, I've no desire as of yet to give up my freedom."

"To give up the women fawning over you," Borswell

said. "Married, unmarried, demimonde ... A duke may have whomever he pleases."

Arthington snorted. "I doubt you're suffering in that department, Borswell. A title is a title, and viscounts as well as dukes command their share of attention. Especially ones with all of their teeth and no need of laces, like you." He patted his own middle. "In fact, if I'm not careful, I may soon have to let out my breeches. Cook's meals are entirely too appetizing."

"You could be bald as a baby and have two clubbed feet and the ladies would still want you, Arth." Bedeville pointed ruefully toward his own thinning hair.

Arthington eyed Gavin. "How about you, sir? What's your preference when it comes to the fairer sex?"

Gavin hesitated. Was it common for men barely acquainted to speak so frankly? Or was his childhood friend bestowing a sign of acceptance, a welcome into this circle of friends?

"I myself like a blonde," the duke continued, without giving him a chance to respond.

Emerlin gave a comical roll of his eyes. "Yes, everyone knows you like blondes."

Gavin looked again toward Lady Elinor. She'd fallen behind the other women after stopping to investigate something. A flower? Nothing bloomed this time of year. The foliage at her feet rustled, and a rabbit dashed out, much to the lady's amusement. Her delighted laugh echoed across the lawn.

"Ah," said Arthington. "Lady Elinor has caught your eye."

Several of the men snickered, as if sharing a secret joke. Gavin raised a brow.

"Quite the beauty. But uninterested in men."

The other brow joined the first.

"Not in *that* manner!" the duke exclaimed. "I've seen

her dance, even flirt, but she's refused a reputed eleven marriage proposals, including one from Keswick here."

The man in question shrugged, as if to dismiss the whole affair.

Eleven? "Why?"

Emerlin's cheeks creased. "Who are we to understand the ways of women?"

"Says the man who attracts them in droves?" Bedeville's tone was half-teasing, half-lamenting.

"Exactly," Emerlin rejoined. "There's no accounting for taste."

"Don't say we didn't warn you, Cortleon," Arthington said. "She's charming, intelligent, a diamond of the first water. The *ton*'s darling during her first two Seasons. High-ranking suitors lined up in droves. Everyone speculated she'd make a brilliant match. And yet—"

"The closer a man gets," Keswick interrupted, his shoulders slumping, "the colder she becomes. She was a sparkling wit the night we danced the cotillion and the few additional times we encountered each other at dinners or the theater. Yet, when I asked permission to call upon her parents, she turned to ice."

Pallemeade gave him a good-natured poke in the ribs. "Perhaps you should try again. She might say yes, this time. She's not growing any younger. Moreover, I've heard the Rutley family fortunes are suffering."

Keswick snorted. "I may not achieve the kind of marriage Claremont now has, but I do wish to wed someone at least a little interested in my person over my purse. Plus, can you imagine taking such an ice princess to bed?"

Gavin's breath caught at the idea of that mass of blonde hair loosened, falling to her shoulders, maybe even lower. Of her bounteous breasts freed from the stays binding them. Of her eyes dewy with pleasure. *What the devil?* He shifted his stance to disguise the tightening of his breeches. He couldn't claim he never fantasized about being with a woman. Indeed, since his vow to his mother, fantasies and his hand were all he had. Still, to lose such control in public over a woman with whom he'd exchanged no more than a handful of words? If he didn't know better, he'd add sorceress to her name.

Arthington clapped him on the back. "I wish you luck, Cortleon."

Gavin opened his mouth, but no response came.

"She's quite passionate about the Home," Emerlin said, admiration in his tone.

"Home?" Arthington wrinkled his brow.

"The foundling home her aunt established. Surely you know of it. Not far from the Foundling Hospital itself?"

Bedeville sniffed. "Why open a separate home, then, when such a hospital exists?"

"Perhaps because vast numbers of infants need care?" Stoneleigh's voice was quiet but firm.

Bedeville's cheeks reddened. He said nothing more.

The same as in Rome. Perhaps the same everywhere. Rome's poor had always tugged at Gavin's heart, especially the women, young and old alike. Their struggle to survive, many forced to sell their bodies, struck at his very core. He'd given them what he could, but it'd never been as much as he wished.

It could be now. As duke, he held wealth beyond his wildest imaginings. For all Loughton Knight's faults, he'd done well by his estates. The Cortleon coffers had grown considerably in Gavin's absence since his mother had requested only the minimum to get by. How a former duchess could be happy living as they had, he didn't understand, but he was grateful. And proud. Material goods had never mattered much to Mama; she'd concerned herself more with spiritual growth and with raising him to be honorable, courteous, and loyal.

"Like a chivalrous knight of old," she'd said many a time, only half teasing. "London society would do well to return to such ways."

Gavin presumed people more pleased to live in an era in which the violence and illness endemic to the Middle Ages weren't so prevalent, but he'd held his tongue.

"Don't many members of the *ton* support charitable measures because it's currently 'in fashion'?" he said to Emerlin, his emphasis on the last two words betraying his disgust. He may now number among them, but he'd grown up in a manner far removed from these men and women.

"Yes," Emerlin conceded. "Yet, I believe it means more for Lady Elinor. I've seen her cuddling children in its yard a number of times."

Arthington spun to his friend. "I didn't realize you followed her movements so closely, dear friend. Is she about to receive her twelfth proposal?"

Emerlin held up his hands. "Not I. A cousin lets a house directly across the street. When I visit, I have occasion to notice things."

"Yes, ever the observer," Arthington commented wryly.

Gavin cast another glance toward the gardens, but the women had moved on, Lady Elinor with them. That was likely for the best; he'd already paid her too much notice. He was here to discover what he could about his father's murder, not to chase after this alleged Ice Princess. Though Emerlin's revelations proved her heart must be warm, at least where children were concerned.

She'd certainly set him on fire.

CHAPTER 6

*B*ertie pulled at his beard as the carriage approached Camlon's gates. He'd agonized over whether or not to attend this year's party. The younger Cortleon had returned to England and might be at Camlon this very moment. The Duchess of Arthington and Anna Knight had been best of friends; surely, she'd have issued an invitation to the newly returned duke? Or would Cortleon have remained at Wainsbury out of mourning for his mother?

He picked at a piece of dust on his breeches. He'd had to come. He had no other choice. What excuse could he have given his son when they'd attended every year since Hugh was an infant? He'd done so to keep suspicion away. After all, what murderer would return to the scene of his crime time and again?

As the years had passed with no sign of Wynhawke, Bertie had relaxed his guard. At present, however, every muscle had tensed and a cold sweat coated his hands. He must be mindful not to press them against the fabric covering his thighs, lest the moisture leave a telltale mark.

He shouldn't have come. He should have sent Hugh on

his own. Why risk discovery? If Wynhawke—no, Cortleon now—recognized him, Bertie faced prosecution at best or the immediate end of a pistol at worst. Either way, the ensuing scandal would taint the Grennet reputation.

This was madness. And yet ... he had to know if Cortleon would recognize him, would see him for whom he was. Had to know if he'd finally be freed from his past, if he was at last safe from discovery and from the grievous crimes of his youth.

He had a pistol of his own in his pocket, of course, and a dagger in his boot. They'd do little good if Cortleon called him out publicly, however. No, he had to pray that age, his beard, and the ephemeral nature of childhood memories would work in his favor.

"You're tugging on it again."

"What?"

"That beard. Why ever did you grow such a thing? It can't be comfortable, and it certainly isn't *á la mode*."

"I needed a way to hide." Bertie hadn't meant to say that, but his son merely laughed.

"No man your size ever goes unnoticed. You look like a red-maned lion. You really ought to have trimmed your hair."

A lion. Symbol of the Cortleon line. *Lion against Lion*. How fitting.

"And from whom would you be hiding, anyway?"

Bertie cracked a grin. "Why, Lady Brownhouse, of course."

"Lady Brownhouse has shown interest in you?"

"That a lady might pay attention to an old goat like me surprises you?"

"I ... uh ... no. It's rather, you never pay attention to ladies."

"Hence the desire to hide."

His son straightened, looking once more out the

carriage window. "There's the house! Isn't it wonderful to be at Camlon again, Father?"

Ah, Hugh. His pride and joy, his only child. What a man he'd grown into. Brawny, like himself, to be sure, but also reasoned, sensible, charming ... and innocent. Everything Bertie wasn't. *Thanks be to God he's not like me.* Hugh was a bright light, the future of the Grennet earldom. Cortleon would not rob Bertie or his son of that future—not like the man's father had done. No, he'd be on guard from the start.

"Indeed, my son." He pulled again at his beard. "I apologize for our delayed departure. I know you wanted to be here for Christmas Day itself."

Hugh made a dismissive gesture. "'Tis understandable, Father; one cannot help when one takes ill."

That had been a lie, too; he'd been fit as a fiddle. But he'd needed more time to consider his course of action, to decide whether to show or not.

Now his time was up. He must meet the past face to face.

～

THE TABLE OUGHT to have sagged under the weight of the multitudinous items laid out for the New Year's Eve feast. A fantastical castle constructed of sugar dominated the center, surrounded by fowl and meats, puddings, mince pies, and vast spreads of every delicacy one could ever desire.

Nelle's mouth watered at the oranges piled high in a central basket. How she loved the fruit's scintillating, sweet citrus smell. Given its high cost, however, she hadn't enjoyed one in some time.

"An unnecessary expense," her mother had decreed.

Would anyone notice if she took two?

Her attention flew from the fruit, however, when a

gentleman took the seat to her left. Her heart sped up in spite of itself and she ducked her head, lest the color no doubt mottling her heated cheeks betrayed her.

The Duke of Cortleon.

She'd been entirely too aware of him since their accidental, awkward introduction a few days past, though they'd yet to exchange another word. Surprising, given the house party, though of considerable size, was not so large people didn't regularly encounter each other—unless he'd intentionally steered clear of her. *Had he?*

She frowned. She wasn't used to gentlemen avoiding her. Outside former suitors, at least; they opted to keep their distance. One such suitor, Keswick, was here. Had he warned the duke away? Not that that should bother her. No, despite her unsettling reaction to him, the Duke of Cortleon, was *not* on whom she should be concentrating. He was entirely too young, too ... virile. If she *must* marry, better to someone who didn't affect her so. For she couldn't deny he affected her. Far too often she'd admired the way his coat spread across his shoulders and how his long hair feathered around his cravat.

That Tabby continuously gushed about him didn't help. "He's so mysterious. Don't you think so, Pru?" she'd exclaimed as they'd descended the stairs for dinner. "The tales about him are legendary."

"Legendary? In what sense?" Nelle had interjected, unable to help herself.

"That he ... that he ... well, so little is known about him."

"Ah. So, you've heard no tales."

Tabby scowled. "Lord Keswick insists he's the best fencer, rider, and card player he's ever seen."

"Lord Keswick's opinion doesn't mean much."

Pru leapt to Tabby's defense. "Isn't it legend enough that everyone thought him dead and he's not?"

"Exactly. Mama said the former duke was legendary, as well, but for different reasons." Tabby lowered her voice to a whisper. "He was a complete rogue—charming and captivating, but a shameless philanderer. Young or old, married or not—Mama said it didn't matter."

"*Mama* said?" Nelle couldn't imagine their mother ever speaking so frankly.

"To Lady Brownhouse. I happened to overhear."

More likely she'd set out to eavesdrop.

"And has the current duke the same reputation?" It ate at Nelle that it mattered.

"No one knows. I imagine so; he commands attention wherever he goes, does he not? Half the ladies here are no doubt in love with him!" Her sister's sigh suggested she was among those besotted.

Nelle had raised her eyes heavenward. The duke taking an interest in any of the Greene girls was highly unlikely. At least not for any honorable purpose. She'd have to be on alert. God forbid he seduced one of her sisters.

Or her. The man exuded sensuality. His brown eyes positively smoldered the few times their gazes had met, though he'd not sought a nearer acquaintance. He must look that way at every woman, which would explain why so many fell at his feet.

He hadn't shown any one lady preference, however. He'd danced, but never more than once with the same woman, and he'd chitchatted with nearly every female there, despite age or status. Of course, who knew what he did behind closed doors? Many an illicit liaison took place at parties such as this.

No, he'd never singled anyone out. Except for her. In terms of *lack* of attention, that was; he'd never asked her to dance nor engaged her in conversation. Why not?

My reputation precedes me. The Ice Princess. Though the

moniker bothered her, it served to keep most men at a distance.

Was it Nelle's fault so many had chased after her those first few Seasons? She'd never given any sincere indications of interest, wanting only to be pleasant, courteous, and polite, and yet a number of lords had professed their undying love, sometimes within hours of meeting her. As she'd declined one after another, they'd declared her cold and unfeeling.

Ridiculous. None of the gentlemen knew her. None of them made the effort to look beyond her face. They praised her beauty, but what had that to do with the real her? How she looked was not who she was.

Then again, what had she expected? Men and women married more often for practical purposes such as gaining titles or wealth than for love. And when betrothals were arranged after short acquaintance—a few dances, a ride in the park, perhaps a dinner or two—how could either party know the other well enough to establish if they were in complete accord, a true match that could last a lifetime? Her parents certainly were not. She didn't want to live like that, one half isolated from the other.

She tucked her hands in her lap, cognizant of the man sipping wine to her side. She was forthcoming about her desire to retain what independence she had. No one knew the impossible romantic notion she'd kept close to her heart, that she could love—and be loved—like some fairy tale princess of old. She neither wanted nor needed a knight to free her from her self-imposed tower, however. Her friends, her animals, her sisters, and her cherished orphaned children kept her quite content. Why marry when life was perfect as it was?

How naïve to have thought it could stay that way. She was aging, thus losing her value to society. A bloom fading. It wouldn't bother her but for the sake of her sisters. And despite her struggles with her mother, she loved her parents. She must do right by them, by the family. She must land a husband in order to save them.

Just not the living, breathing Adonis next to her.

~

GAVIN HAD STAYED AWAY from Lady Elinor as much to mute his curiosity as whet her own, disturbed by the strange reactions she stirred in him. Surely light flirtation at the dinner table was safe, however. By all accounts, she'd no interest in either marriage or taking a lover, so teasing conversation, perhaps even a dance or two, held no danger. The house party ended in a week; what harm could come from a little fun in the midst of his search, especially since it'd not yet yielded fruit?

"Good evening," he murmured, setting down his cup. The wine was heady, full-bodied, and succulent, like the woman next to him.

She started.

"My apologies. I didn't mean to frighten you."

Blue eyes met his, her expression serious. "Thank you, Your Grace, but you did not. I was simply adjusting my chair."

Where was the smile she bestowed so freely on the other gentlemen? He gave her the most dazzling grin he could muster.

She hit her hand on the table, then muttered as her fork clanged against her plate.

Ignoring her discomposure, he pressed on. "How are you enjoying the party?"

"It's fine."

A footman dipped between them to pour more wine.

Gavin tried again. "Did you and your family travel far to be here?"

She sipped her own wine before answering. "Not so far as you, Your Grace. Inglewood Cottage is near Kingclere." His face must have betrayed his lack of knowledge, as she added, "A little less than twenty-five miles from here."

"Ah." He really must improve his English geography. "May I ask what your connections are to Arthington and his mother?"

She narrowed her eyes. "Think you we're not of sufficient status to be here?"

"I meant no offense. Perhaps you're unaware, but I've not been back in this country for long. I'm afraid your knowledge of English families and friendships is vastly superior to mine."

Her shoulders dropped. "I beg your apologies, Your Grace. That was woefully rude of me."

He could accept her apology as gracefully as she gave it, but if he did, she might take her heavenly eyes off of his. He remained quiet.

"The dowager duchess and my mother are childhood acquaintances," she said after a moment.

"Ah. Similar. My mother is a friend of the dowager, as well. Or was, rather." His throat caught, and he swallowed, forcing down the thick knot of grief. Damned if it didn't hit him at the most unexpected times. He gestured toward a platter. "Would you care for duck?"

"Please."

He served a generous portion before taking some for himself. She sent him a grateful smile, but then a copper-haired older gentleman to her other side offered her mince pie, drawing her attention away. They continued in conversation, though the hubbub of other speech in the room rendered their words inaudible.

Gavin glanced around the table. Elegantly clad men and women partook of the bounteous feast, drinking liberally from glasses footmen quickly refilled. At the far end,

Arthington held court, amusing those near him. Catching his eye, the duke winked, raising his cup toward Lady Elinor.

Aha. So that explained this particular seating arrangement. On previous evenings, they'd been at opposite ends of the table, seated according to precedence. He'd wondered about the change. At least he wasn't next to the portly woman in the deep emerald gown, her turban and feathers dyed to match. He avoided looking her way as best he could, lest he lose his appetite for dinner. How absurd, this visceral response to that deuced color, green. The unfortunate surname of the Venus to his side.

His eyes closed at a sudden vision of a brown-haired man shouting something before falling, his face melting as he went. *Father.* What had he shouted? Gavin pinched his brows together, replaying the moment. "Gr—"

He sucked in a breath. Green? Had his father yelled green? Or *Greene*? He jerked his attention to Lady Elinor's father, seated a few places down. Could he ...? *No.* Lord Rutley was short, nowhere near the giant figure of his nightmares. Though didn't all adults seem huge to a child? He looked again. The earl's round, affable face matched his round form. Even with the addition of age, this couldn't be the man. Plus, his mother had never mentioned the Earl of Rutley or his family in her catalog of *le bon ton*. Had Rutley been at Camlon twenty-four years ago, she'd have said so.

Gavin relaxed, his fingers easing their grip on the knife he hadn't realized he was clutching. He took a bite of the duck, using the respite to study the others at the table. Borswell and Pallemeade hovered about one of Lady Elinor's sisters, each doing his best to charm her. Lady Tabitha? Which one had the freckles, again? Emerlin edged away from a buxom brunette who'd practically climbed into his lap. Lady Elinor still spoke with the man to her other side.

How could he recapture her attention? Without giving himself a chance to reconsider, Gavin let his right leg loll enough so that his thigh met Lady Elinor's under the table. When she snapped around with a bewildered gasp, he hid his chuckle beneath his fingers. "I beg pardon, my lady. No offense intended."

She turned away, leaning forward to fetch an orange from a center basket, allowing him a clear view of the man to her side. Sulpicio's third rule: *Observe your opponent. Note their strengths and weaknesses.*

Strong features dominated a rugged face. His coat strained over his broad shoulders, and he sat a good half a head higher than everyone else. The lines on his skin and strands of gray in his red hair and beard suggested a man around fifty years or so of age. How unusual to see such a beard when clean-shaven faces were fashionable; no other gentleman present sported facial hair.

The fellow dipped his head in polite acknowledgment. Despite the man's placid expression, Gavin skin pricked. Why? Who was he?

Lady Elinor sat back, blocking much of the stranger from view again. She sipped from her cup, and when she licked her lip, any thought of the other man evaporated. How he longed to press a kiss to the corner of her mouth, where a glistening drop of wine remained. She looked to him, her cheeks coloring.

Damn. He'd been openly staring.

"Are you enjoying the dinner, Your Grace?" Her voice squeaked on the last word.

"I'd enjoy it more if I could hold as much of your attention as the gentleman to your other side." There. Let him be direct. He enjoyed discomfiting her. No doubt she usually set men at dis-ease and not the other way around.

"I beg pardon." Her tightened mouth suggested no real

sincerity in the words. "Lord Grennet was asking about the children in my care."

Grennet. Gavin's jaw clenched. Another name beginning with *Gr*—though there were many such names: Grenville, Gray, Griffin, to mention just a few. Was he to jump at every one? This Grennet *was* massive, though. Gavin could hardly accuse him of a crime on account of his size with no other evidence, however. And who was to say his father had yelled a *name*, even if this unexpected memory was accurate?

He'd ask Arthington about Grennet later. For now, he wanted to keep those Sevres blue eyes on him and to watch those raspberry-hued lips as she spoke and ate and drank. He wanted to set Lady Elinor Greene as much out of kilter as she did him so that her cheeks infused with that delectable scarlet color.

He angled toward her. "I'd also like to hear about them. I'd like to hear anything you wish to tell me."

That was too much. But damn, what a pleasure to flirt, to lose himself in the moment rather than think of his mother, his father, or his true purpose for returning to England—which wasn't to sit at a table laden with more food than he and Mama would have seen in weeks and make verbal love to a lady. He ought to be careful, lest she misconstrue his regard as being more serious in nature.

Then again, this was the Ice Princess. If anyone was in danger of hoping for too much, it was he.

CHAPTER 7

*N*elle rubbed her fingers over the stem of her wine glass. The Duke of Cortleon was entirely allure and seduction, and he was close. So close. When his leg nudged hers, she'd sworn the heat of his flesh flowed into her, though that was impossible given the numerous fabric layers separating them. Had he done it on purpose to gain her attention? She couldn't be sure.

She should apologize to Lord Grennet for twisting away in such a rude manner. She'd encountered the earl a time or two in London, despite his rare presence at social events. He was always pleasant and tonight had expressed admiration for her charity work.

"I once wanted more children, though a father could not be any prouder than I of my son," he'd said, gesturing to Lord Ashvere, who sat next to Lucy-Anne.

Her sister's face glowed with adoration as she listened to the young lord. *Oh, heavens.* No doubt Nelle would hear of nothing but him for the few days.

Neither Lord Grennet nor his son concerned her at the moment, however. *Why* was the duke paying her such attention this evening when he'd hitherto ignored her? He had his pick of the crème de la crème of the female *ton* right here. So why her? Why now? Had he sincere interest in her activities, or had he simply deemed her a mild diversion for the evening? After all, the spinster Ice Princess posed no threat to his marital status, whereas the other women's increasingly desperate attempts to attract his regard were hard to miss.

She pressed her lips together. This figurative dance was so tiresome, with its complicated steps to determine the interest and intentions of one's partner. Could not two people move to the music of flirtation out of sheer enjoyment, rather than fret about what might be expected or assumed after?

Truth was, she loved to dance. Actual dancing, that was. She loved the movement, the feeling of freedom, the music tickling her skin. She savored the thrill such exertion brought forth, the festive feeling it induced. Yes, she loved to dance—but the idea of partnering with the Duke of Cortleon held far more appeal than it should.

Everything about the man did.

BERTIE STABBED AT THE VENISON, bringing the meat to his mouth and chewing without tasting. Cortleon's parentage was indisputable; he was the spitting image of his father. The blasted resemblance clearly went more than skin deep, as the Lothario had drawn Lady Elinor Greene's attention and worked at present to charm her with that familiar crooked grin.

His temples throbbed. *Calm yourself. This is of no matter.* Indeed, he should be thanking his stars Cortleon had shown no signs of recognition. When Bertie spied the unmistakable duke so near, frenzied energy had consumed him—half fear, half anticipation. His moment of reckoning was at hand.

And then ... gone? He'd used every ounce of control to remain expressionless upon the duke's frank appraisal. Cortleon had shown curiosity, but nothing more.

Was that it, then? Were his secrets safe? If so, this irritation—no, this *rage*—at the duke's attention to Lady Elinor made no sense. Bertie had only struck up a conversation with her in order to keep an eye on Cortleon—and to avoid Lady Brownhouse to his right. The *widow* Brownhouse, as she oft repeated, her beady gray eyes devouring him. She'd made it apparent she'd be most willing to share his bed.

"I do fancy myself a large fellow," she'd cracked, the double entendre quite clear.

He'd no interest. She was everything he abhorred in women of rank and supposed refinement: loud, brazen, overly plump ... and lascivious. He may pay good coin for quick tumbles with whores, but aristocratic women ought to hold themselves to a higher standard; lustful appetites did not become them.

His lips curled back at the thought of his wife. The harlot. If she had entertained other men beyond Cortleon, it'd not surprise him. She'd been a renowned beauty, too, like his dinner companion. In fact, Lady Elinor bore a startling resemblance to his feckless first wife, with her artfully arranged blonde hair and fine eyes a shade or two lighter than Bee's.

Bee. The bitch who'd dealt him a near-fatal sting.

Unlike Albina, Lady Elinor showed no aptitude towards wantonness. Her reputation preceded her. Not once had any impropriety attached itself to her name, despite the many rakes who'd attempted to seduce her. His last time in Brooks', several bucks had boasted of seeking a kiss—or more. She'd rebuffed them all.

"A cold fish," one scoffed.

"Firmly on the shelf," another said.

"Nobody shall ever thaw her ice," sneered a third, to a scattering of laughter.

"A waste of a beautiful woman, if you ask me," the first replied.

Lady Elinor had never given *him* the cold shoulder. In fact, she'd been quite amiable. Her back was to him now, though, as the duke monopolized her. The captivating Cortleon and the blonde beauty, intent only on each other. They could easily be the elder duke and Albina. Would *this* Cortleon corrupt an innocent lady, as his father had Bee?

Bertie's legs shook, as wrath thought long buried burst through him. He clenched his fists, his jaw aching from the force with which he ground his teeth. *No.* He would *not* cave to his fury, would not let his actions destroy everything he'd worked so hard to regain. Unless this damned duke deduced the truth, he'd leave him alone. History need not repeat itself. He would not jeopardize Hugh's future.

A chair scraping drew attention to the head of the table as Arthington stood. "Gentlemen, let the ladies leave us whilst we enjoy a glass of port. Those interested may then join us in the red drawing room for charades and such." He gestured to Emerlin. "Perhaps Emerlin here will entertain us with his magic tricks."

The dark-haired man laughingly shook his head as the women filed out, shrugging, palms up as if to say he'd no idea what the duke meant.

Oh, to be that carefree again. To go back. Bertie closed his eyes as unwanted memories washed over him.

"Did you do this?" Bee's face was ashen.

He walked toward her. "Albin—"

"No!" She clutched her abdomen, scurrying back several steps.

He flinched. How could she think he'd ever hurt her? He loved her. Except now he also hated her.

"You must have seen—"

"Seen what?" He feigned surprise as best he could. Let her think his face bloodless out of confusion rather than rage.

Her mouth opened, her eyes darting to the side. "Never mind. I feared—" She broke off, squeezing her lips together.

Like the vise squeezing his heart—and the agony searing his shoulder. He couldn't show her. Couldn't let on. No one could know.

"I want to leave. We must leave."

"Bee—"

"Now! I must go now."

"What would we tell the duke and duchess?" His fingernails inside his shaking fists dug trenches into his palms. If she truly thought him ignorant of her affair, she wasn't covering her tracks well.

She clasped a hand against her pale forehead. "Tell them ... tell them this has been too much for me. I need to return to Swythdon for the sake of the babe's health."

He nodded, and his wife's shoulders relaxed, even as her tears flowed anew. "It's horrible. The poor man. Lou—" She turned toward the window.

Behind her, Bertie seethed, his chest rising and falling. He should kill her, too. Perfidious bitch. How could she betray him like this? When he loved her and only her? His fingers itched, but he forced a slow breath, then another. He must consider the child. Was it even his? He refused to think about that. He had to get his wife, get himself, far away from Camlon and the chance of discovery. Wynhawke had said nothing, though he'd had ample opportunity in that gathered crowd. Bertie's threat seemed to be holding. Should he seek the boy now to end any chance?

NO. He was not a monster. A momentary fit of madness had overtaken him, but he'd carry it no further. Unless given reason to.

AND HE HADN'T, not even when Albina wept for weeks after Hugh's birth. The midwife had tried to assure him this wasn't unusual in a new mother and that the doldrums would pass. He knew better. His wife lamented that the boy's red hair and green eyes were not the deep brown of her lover's. She'd sobbed as much in the nursery when she'd thought she was alone. The child was the Grennet heir: Hugh Laxton, Viscount Ashvere. And he was Bertie's.

That miracle was all that had sustained him in the dark few months that followed. Bee took more and more laudanum, claiming she needed it for her nerves. One evening, when he'd gone to bid her goodnight, he'd found her ghostly white and listless, a note caught in her flaccid fingers.

Grennet, it had begun. No sign of the love he'd thought they'd shared.

> *I can't go on any longer. You deserve the truth. I had an affair with Cortleon. I love him. I've always loved him. Now he's gone. I thought you killed him. I truly did. But your continued regard for me since our return from Camlon convinced me otherwise. Still, I've no joy any longer. I haven't my Loughton, nor, as I'd hoped, his son. I'm sorry I could not love you in the way you wished to be loved. You deserved better. Hugh deserves better. Give him the life he should have, not the one he'd have with a mother like me.*
>
> *Goodbye, Bertram.*

He'd stared at her body, his own flushing hot and cold as fury and grief warred within him. How dare she betray him one last time by deserting him? By deserting their son? This, after he'd tried to forgive her, after he'd prayed that with Cortleon gone, she'd return to him. He wanted to choke her, to stab the life out of the traitorous whore. He would have done so had she not denied him the pleasure.

Then she'd stirred, the lightest breath escaping her. *She wasn't dead.*

His hands snaked out to wrap around that alabaster neck. *Wait. No.* He mustn't leave marks, not after she'd granted him the perfect alibi. He reached instead for her goose-down pillow. As he moved over her, her eyes flew open and she raised an arm against him. She was no match for his giant form and brute strength, however, especially with the laudanum leaching away her resistance.

The housekeeper had assumed it was an accident. "She were taking more and more, milord," she'd wailed when Albina's body was discovered the next morning. "But I'm sure she did not mean ta die, ta leave the wee bairn witho' his mother. Oh, the poor wee laddie!"

A loud cheer roused Bertie briefly from his recollections. Arthington raised his cup in a toast, but to what, he couldn't say. He rubbed his shoulder, its ever-present ache a constant reminder of what he'd suffered—and who'd shot him.

He'd bitten onto the thick bed covering to keep from crying out as Howsden stitched up his torn flesh. Next had come several layers of bandages and a heavy dose of laudanum—thank goodness his wife had taken it for headaches even then, so a draught was on hand—and then, excruciatingly, a fresh set of clothing.

"His Grace asks the guests to gather in the ballroom," his valet murmured. "The Duke of Cortleon has been found dead."

Bertie had given the tiniest of nods, then chewed his cheek against the pain—and fear. How he'd got through that afternoon and evening, he didn't know. Luck was with him; Wynhawke kept his silence. Perhaps it was God's grace for his sufferings.

In the time between their arrival home at Swythdon and Hugh's birth, Albina noticed nothing. Then again, they hadn't shared a chamber in months.

"Because of the babe," Bee insisted. "We shouldn't be intimate. We don't want to risk it."

He'd taken her at her word, of course. He hadn't known how he'd explain the wreck of his upper shoulder, but it proved a pointless concern, as they'd never shared a bed again.

And poor Howsden. The devoted servant had succumbed to a fever a year later. Bertie still missed him, though it was one more piece of the puzzle gone before anyone could find it.

Arthington's voice intruded again. "Shall we rejoin the ladies?"

As the men rose, Bertie flexed his shoulder, his eyes fixing on Cortleon's back.

Only one piece remained.

CHAPTER 8

*T*he next days passed swiftly, the men absorbed with fox hunting and sport, the women with whatever they did while the men were away. Gavin found himself looking forward to the evening meals as much for the welcomed sustenance after hours of intense physical activity as for the opportunity to see Lady Elinor. He hadn't been seated next to her again, though.

"Mother is enjoying defying convention by mixing up the company," Arthington explained, "though I've no doubt it's to assure I'm seated next to a different eligible lady each night."

"We're enjoying it, too, as it allows us the same," Keswick had quipped.

Lord Grennet had been her dinner companion tonight, and the spark of jealousy that ignited left Gavin in a sour mood. What was it about her? She was an otherworldly sprite, a nymph, a siren who'd cast her spell on him. None of the other women captivated him like she did—to their noticeable chagrin. Several had moved on to Emerlin or Grennet's son Ashvere, though like Gavin, he only had eyes for a Greene daughter. Luckily, it was Lady Lucy-Anne and not her older sister.

Gavin dressed now for the evening's entertainment, the crowning event of the entire house party: A Twelfth Night ball. Dinner had held avid discussions of the festivities to come and the roles everyone might play. The dowager duchess had assigned character types that afternoon but directed they be kept secret. Positively exuberant over the entire affair, she'd had several trunks rife with old clothing, masks, accessories, and the like brought into the red drawing room and then invited each guest to privately select their desired items, which the servants delivered to the appropriate chambers.

He was to play a medieval knight. Appropriate, given his surname. A suit of armor no doubt belonging to some Arthington ancestor had been among the costume offerings, but after lifting one arm, he'd decided against it. How could a person move in such a suit, much less dance? And he wanted to dance with Lady Elinor tonight.

Thank heavens Sulpicio had insisted upon lessons alongside Gavin's other training. "The complex dances of courtship and war are of the same essence—sometimes one and the same. Skill in both is essential to a gentleman's success."

Would he have trouble identifying her? Doubtful. Masks and costumes couldn't hide height, after all, or figures—albeit the many pillows among the accouterments suggested he couldn't claim the latter with certainty. But surely the guests would surmise each other's true selves with ease. He'd said as much to Emerlin at dinner. "What's the point of a masquerade? After several days of acquaintance, our speech and mannerisms will immediately betray us."

"Not all are as observant as you. And a masquerade is most often a pretense."

"A pretense? Of what?"

"Of anonymity. When masked, people feel they can behave in ways ordinarily considered too risqué were their real identities known."

"So, this is an excuse to engage in open debauchery?"

The marquess's rich laugh echoed throughout the room. "For some, I'm sure. Though most probably keep to a stolen kiss or two. Regardless, what happens under the guise of a masquerade is not usually acknowledged once the event has concluded."

"Strange habits, you English."

"We English? I'm half Irish. You're more English than I."

Gavin shook his head. "It doesn't seem it."

"We're both foreigners of a sort, I suppose."

"I gathered from Arth that although your family is in Ireland, you've spent a good part of your life here."

"I have. But my heritage and my destiny mark me, much as your decades of absence mark you."

"Destiny?"

The blue-eyed man pulled at an ear. "My father wishes me to return to Armagh. To an Irish life—and an Irish wife."

"But you don't?"

Emerlin looked away. "I'm not sure. I miss my family. And it might be easier to be Irish in Ireland," he conceded. "The land of my birth feels no more my home now, however, than I imagine this one does you."

Gavin had nodded. He felt a strong kinship with Emerlin. He liked Arthington, too, though there was no doubt the duke had been raised for his role from the day he was born; the man exuded nobility, his bearing downright regal. Thank goodness he had a wicked sense of humor and a fondness for informality.

Gavin traced his fingers along the finely wrought chainmail tunic—a hauberk—draped upon the bed. It spoke of an earlier period but allowed greater freedom of move-ment. An iron helmet wrought to cover the eyes and nose lay next to it. At least the bottom half of his face would be bare. Were the eye slits large enough for him to see? Crashing into others for the sake of a disguise held no appeal.

Malory aided him into the hauberk, which Gavin wore over his own shirt to protect his chest from the metal loops. A long, solid, armless tabard of brilliant red cloth followed, which the valet secured with a belt that boasted an ornate scabbard.

"Do I get a sword, too?"

"I'm sure we could procure one, but if you wish to get close to any ladies, you might not want your blade bucking between you." The valet's face crinkled. "Though perhaps that's exactly what they *would* want."

Gavin let out a bellow. "Now, Malory," he said when his laughter had abated, "as a noble knight of old, I'm to save rather than take a woman's virtue."

"I doubt knights were as chivalrous as the tales and legends lead us to believe. Now, if you don't mind, could you kneel?"

"Kneel? You needn't take things so far as to dub me."

"No, but I'm shorter than you, Your Grace, and if you'd like to wear this helmet, I need you to stoop."

He snickered but complied.

"I suppose it best to forgo the metal shin plates and foot coverings," Malory said, sighing ruefully after fitting on the headdress.

"These black pantaloons and leather shoes must suffice, I fear, lest I wound a fair maid with said footwear."

His valet retrieved one last item from the bed. "The Cortleon coat of arms."

He craned to see the object in Malory's hands: a large red shield bearing a giant golden lion's head. His family's crest ... but why would it be here? "My father must have worn this at a previous Twelfth Night celebration."

A curious feeling struck. His father had once been in this very place, doing exactly as he did now. Gavin gave a forced chuckle as he rubbed his thumb over his signet ring bearing the same lion's head. "It's a shame he didn't have it the morning he was shot."

"Even mail such as this could not stop a bullet, Your Grace."

"A good point." He shook off the emotions threatening to cloud his thoughts. He'd no time for grief or regret. Or rage. He must keep a cool head.

Was the killer here? Unlikely. Less than a handful of party guests were of the right age, and of those, the dowager was adamant none could have committed that crime. "Only Lords Macomston, Rotland, and Grennet were in attendance that year," she'd said when he'd asked privately that morning, "but all were friends of your father's—and none showed any sign of guilt, much less injury."

Gavin had thought Grennet had watched him during the most recent foxhunt but dismissed the notion when their vixen quarry had proven to be behind him. Though their paths had somehow otherwise not directly crossed, nothing in the earl's behavior marked him as anything less than a proper gentleman, much less a suspect in such a heinous act. Still ... Grennet had been at that party. The earl was a giant. And Gavin *had* had that moment of unease upon their first meeting. *Was it possible ... ?*

Not according to Anna Knight. At his pressing, his mother had named every party guest she could recall but then gave reasons each could not have shot Loughton—including Grennet.

He hadn't made the connection when he'd first met the earl, as Mama had called him by his Christian name, Bertie, rather than his title.

"We were close friends. Albina and I more so than Bertie and Loughton, I suppose, but we were often in each other's company. She took Loughton's death extremely hard. Bertie was beside himself, lamenting your father's loss but also fearing for Albina's health, as she was expecting."

Arthington's mother had sung praises of the fellow, as well, insisting he was an upstanding member of the *ton*, well regarded for his close attentiveness to his son after his wife had died. "Many a peer leaves the care of their children to their servants, but not Lord Grennet," she'd said, admiration in her voice. "He doted on that boy and has brought him up to be a shining example of a proper English gentleman."

"Will you take the shield, Your Grace?" Malory asked, pulling Gavin from his thoughts.

He shot his valet a smirk. "Think you I need such defense?"

"The ladies might. Every fair maid shall swoon at your feet, Your Grace. They always do."

He waved his valet off, the metallic rings encasing his arm producing a quiet but noticeable sound. *Hopefully, I won't have to sneak up on anyone tonight – friend or foe.*

"I'm off to slay a dragon." He tipped his head to Malory before exiting the chamber.

"Don't forget to rescue the princess," the valet called.

Lady Elinor's blue eyes flashed before him. Perhaps he needed rescuing from her.

Or by her.

～

NELLE FUSSED with the narrow folds of fabric on her shoulder. "Are you sure this is not too much?"

"Too little, you mean?" Tabby gave her a mischievous grin.

"Yes, exactly." She turned to her mother, who was adjusting a large mask with ostrich feathers springing up from its top. "Mother—"

Before she could get out another word, Lady Rutley snapped open her fan. "You are Athena, Goddess of Wisdom. A toga is entirely fitting."

"Yes, but to have my entire arms and shoulders on such display?" She tugged at the white cloth again.

"Many a ball gown reveals nearly as much. Besides, it might aid you in landing a husband."

"I think you look wonderful, Nelle." Lucy-Anne gave her an encouraging smile. "At least you aren't a nun. I have to wear that awful wimple! No man will look at me twice."

"Haven't you already secured a certain young lord's admiration?" Tabby teased.

Lady Rutley's feathers bobbed comically as she whirled. "What's this? Have you formed an attachment?"

"No, Mother." Lucy-Anne's rebuttal was instant, if not exactly convincing. "Nothing formal, at least."

"Who—Do you mean Lord Ashvere? You've secured the attention of the Earl of Grennet's heir?"

"Why are you so surprised, Mama? We are earl's daughters, after all," Tabby said, giving a shrug. "Such a match is hardly a coup."

Lady Rutley huffed. "I meant he's rather young. And Lord Grennet, while eminently respectable, is not ..."

"A duke or a marquess? Really, Mother, we must be reasonable. I don't think any of us has a chance of that." Pru's voice was matter-of-fact. As was Prudence most of the time, though she rarely challenged their parents.

"Do not set your sights too low." It'd not have surprised Nelle had their mother continued with, *you see what happened when I did for your father.* "It will all be in vain, however, if Elinor does not secure a betrothal forthwith."

"Oh, for heaven's sake." Nelle thrust back her shoulders in defiance.

"We need you to marry soon, but also *well*. With your beauty, though aging—"

"You speak as if the flesh is dripping from my face!" The biting words rebounded through the room. She'd not apologize, however. She would *not*.

Her mother changed tack. "Don't you want Lucy-Anne to be happy?"

Nelle thinned her lips but remained silent.

"She might be if she marries Lord Ashvere. But as the son of a hale, healthy, still-living earl, he'll probably not come into his inheritance for some time. And who's to say Lord Grennet would see fit to help our family if it's his son who marries?"

"Who's to say any husband *I* might land would? You've made increasingly clear that I'm losing what charms I have by the hour."

"Now, Elinor." Her mother approached, setting a hand over Nelle's bare shoulder, raising goose bumps where her cool fingers touched. "That's not what I meant. But the more matches we secure for you girls, and quickly, the more likely our family fortunes are to recover."

"If for no other reason than three of your dependents would be off your hands. Right, Mother?" Tabby's razor-sharp tone belied the angel wings on her back. "Why not throw in Pru, though she's not formally out? Perhaps we should plan a quadruple ceremony right here at Camlon?"

Lady Rutley's cheeks darkened with red splotches. "That's enough." She fidgeted with her mask, its ostrich feathers waving in an absurd fashion. "Let us go below and join the ball. I'll brook no further rebellion tonight."

~

THE MOMENT LADY ELINOR ENTERED, everyone's attention turned. And no wonder. With that creamy skin on display, her hair intricately styled and decorated, and the loose folds of her toga dress flowing gracefully over—but not disguising—her curvaceous figure beneath, she was a sight to behold.

Gavin knew her in an instant, despite the ivory mask covering the upper half of her face, for it didn't hide that golden hair, those berry lips, or the elegant curve of her neck. Her sisters swept in behind her, followed by their mother, but he couldn't have said what they wore, as he only had eyes for the goddess before him.

A chuckle emerged from the monk next to him. "Is it a sin to have eyes for a holy sister?"

Ashvere, by the voice. Gavin looked to a lady clad in a nun's habit, complete with a wimple. Scarcely any of her was visible, given the black mask over her eyes, but a single lock of brown hair escaping from the white cloth and the small mole near her lip marked her as Lady Lucy-Anne. "Perhaps you are Abelard and Heloise."

Ashvere grimaced. "If so, I'd hope for a happier ending than that poor couple."

"Then you should invite your nun to dance."

The young lord drew up straight. "Indeed. Thank you, Sir Knight, for your gallantry in championing love." He strode off before Gavin could respond.

Love. Did the younger man already fancy himself in love? Hadn't Ashvere made Lady Lucy-Anne's acquaintance at this very party? That wasn't possibly enough time to develop deep feelings. Desire Gavin could accept; the fair goddess across the ballroom certainly aroused that. But love was something else entirely. He could indulge in neither, but that didn't mean he couldn't dance. Lady

Elinor had taken position across from a Quaker, however, so he asked a woman bedecked in the brightest of yellow, a round mask in the shape of the sun covering her face. Lady Agnes Merriweather, if he wasn't mistaken.

"With pleasure, Sir Knight." She giggled while dropping a curtsy.

Lady Agnes was the first of many with whom he partnered that evening, but Lady Elinor captured his complete attention. Every time he neared her, another lady intervened, requesting the privilege of a dance. Such forwardness was entirely acceptable at a masquerade, according to Arth. Was dancing several times with the same woman also not looked upon with the same significance it might otherwise be? Hopefully so, as the sun had asked him to dance for a third time.

At last, the end of a country reel set him directly next to the divine vision he sought: Lady Elinor. He wanted to nibble those milky shoulders, the delicate hollow of her collarbone, that chocolate mole on her cheek, hidden now by her mask. He bowed with great flourish before rising again. "Good evening, Goddess. May I beg a dance?"

CHAPTER 9

*N*elle's stomach quivered. The knight's headdress hid his eyes and part of his nose, but his lower face, with that distinctive jaw, remained bare, and his unmistakable long hair hugged his neck. The Duke of Cortleon, without a doubt, only more spectacular than ever. What a magnificent knight he made. The chain armor enhanced his Corinthian form and the scarlet tunic set off his darker skin. Was it naturally dark? Or was that a consequence of the Italian sun? And how strange to see a man without his cravat. If only she could stroke the uncovered flesh at his throat. Was it soft? Rough?

Then again, more was allowed on Twelfth Night, was it not? *Not to a young lady.* But perhaps to Athena? How would he react if she touched his bare skin? If she pressed for a kiss? Heat crept up her cheeks. It wasn't as if she hadn't kissed a lord or two. She had if only in hopes it'd beget an attraction otherwise missing. It hadn't. Kissing Cortleon might prove different. Never had a man induced such strong *feeling* in her. All parts of her.

The corners of his lips tipped up as he awaited her

response, merriment, and something else, sparking in his eyes. "Well, Goddess?"

"No," she blurted. She couldn't dance with him, couldn't step closer to him without possibly making the biggest fool of herself by leaping into his arms.

He flinched, his courtly grace gone, as was his smile. "No?"

"No, I'm sorry, but I am ... in need of the retiring room." Her whole face burned. If only the floor would open and swallow her whole. What lady mentioned private needs in front of a gentleman? Especially when untrue?

"I see."

Had his shoulders gone rigid?

"Perhaps at a later time this evening," he said evenly, though his mouth pulled into a line.

If only she could see his eyes. She nearly reversed her refusal but bit her lip to keep from speaking. That'd mortify her even further, and how would she explain?

He bent once more before her. "I remain in your service, Goddess."

Before she could respond, he left the room. She pressed her fingers to her mouth, sure every eye was on her. She'd declined a duke. Publicly.

Then again, people weren't supposed to know he was the Duke of Cortleon or she the infamous Elinor Greene. So much for being Athena, the Goddess of Wisdom. She'd shown no such attribute this evening. Her mother would be livid. Had she seen?

Lucy-Anne whirled by in the arms of a monk. How fitting. Several curls of reddish hair had escaped the man's artificial tonsure and mask. Ah, Ashvere.

"Might I have the pleasure?"

Nelle jerked around. Before her stood a Fool as found in royal courts of old, complete with contrasting red and green coat, his hose opposite, and a ridiculous three-pointed hat upon his head. Given his height and size, it must be Lord Grennet. How had the costume even fitted him? She looked down. It strained across his thighs and rode up at the wrists. It also revealed that despite the earl's age, he remained in prime physical condition, no extra flesh upon him.

For the third time in as many minutes, her cheeks tingled. She'd openly examined him. How to disguise the awkwardness? "I admire your willingness to play the Fool."

Good heavens! What kind of thing was that to say?

He hesitated. "I do hope you see me as such for one evening only, my lady. No man likes to be thought a fool."

"Of course." She extended her hand, pushing away the embarrassment of their initial exchange. "Just as no lady wishes to be thought a goddess."

"Oh?" He took her fingers.

"We're flesh and blood, same as you, and wish to be treated as intelligent, capable humans rather than objects for the opposite sex to admire." *Where had that come from?* She'd never spoken so boldly. Every word was true, however. How tiresome to always be valued for her looks rather than her spirit. Her soul. She was more than a pair of fine eyes. Was it so bad to want people to see that?

The music swirled around them. She concentrated on the steps in an effort to regain her composure, though she cast an occasional glance toward the door through which the duke had exited. He did not return.

The earl's hand tightened on hers. "Are you seeking someone else?"

Shame on her, looking for one gentleman while dancing with another. "My apologies, my lord. I thought I saw my mother."

"Would you rather be with her? I suppose no one likes to be seen with a fool." His voice held a note of teasing— and something else. Sharpness?

Not that she'd blame him.

"Tell me, Lady—?"

"Athena," she supplied, though he must know her.

"Ah, Athena. Renowned for her wisdom and, tonight, her beauty. Are you enjoying the ball?"

A reference to her looks. How irritating. "Actually, I'd prefer to be at home. I miss the quiet."

"A forthright answer. So refreshing in a lady."

A motion from a few feet away caught her eye. Her mother's ostrich feathers bobbed as she gave her daughter a decisive nod of approval.

Nelle looked back to the earl. He'd been polite and pleasant the few times they'd conversed. His features remained handsome, even with the lines marking his face and the unusual beard. He was of a decent rank and wealthy enough that her mother would consider him an advantageous match. *Could she?*

That strange, unsettled sensation hit her again as her thoughts drifted to Cortleon. *Blast the man!* Why did he stir such a reaction? Every time he'd danced with another woman, the queerest feelings ate at her. Jealousy. She'd been jealous, wishing she were his partner instead of those ninnies. She hadn't liked it. No, much better to engage with someone such as Lord Grennet, who fostered feelings of friendliness but no more. He'd been widowed many a year, though. If he'd had interest in marrying again, wouldn't he have done so already?

She tilted her head, considering. If she were to set her cap for anyone, he was ideal. And if he dissuaded her atten-tions? Well, then, she could tell Mother she'd tried. Nelle fixed a broad smile on her face, giving him her full regard. Yes. The earl made for a far better matrimonial candidate than the duke.

She started, nearly tripping over Lord Grennet's feet. When and why on earth had she begun to consider the

Duke of Cortleon an option? He wasn't. She was no medieval princess, nor he her champion. She was not trapped in a tower, guarded by a ferocious dragon. No, if anything, he *was* the dragon.

So why did she long for his return?

~

BERTIE STUDIED the woman before him. Lady Elinor's resemblance to his wife was unsettling. The blonde hair, the fair skin, the blue eyes. Many an English lady had those, to be sure, but something in the cut of her jaw and the shape of her brow reminded him very much of his long-dead wife. Bee had not been quite so beautiful, though. He clenched his jaw. This young woman dragged forth memories and emotions he didn't want to revisit— including desire.

Agitation gnawed. For as with Albina, this lady had arrested not only his attention but also Cortleon's. And as with Bee, Lady Elinor returned the duke's interest, as evidenced by their earlier exchange. Despite her refusal, her eyes had lingered on the duke, her cheeks flushing pink as her body leaned toward his. And when her gaze drifted time and again to the door through which he'd exited, it'd erased any doubt.

A different, dangerous desire sparked. A desire for revenge, at long last. If Cortleon wanted Lady Elinor but Bertie wed her, would that not be fitting? He could steal her from *this* Cortleon as the previous duke had stolen Bee. A final strike at both Bertie's unfaithful wife and her lover and at the brat who'd hurt him all those years ago.

You wouldn't have to marry her. You could bed her and be done. Take her innocence first as Loughton Knight did Albina's.

No. He'd not stoop to a Cortleon's level. Seducing and discarding Lady Elinor would be the height of dishonor.

85

He'd never do that to a lady of good breeding. Wedding her, however, would serve two purposes: he'd keep her from Cortleon and he would salvage her family's battered finances. *See? I am better than he.*

What if she were to follow in Bee's footsteps and land in Cortleon's bed, however? Blood thundered through his temples at the thought. No. She wouldn't. Not with her frigid reputation. And yet, she'd melted in the damned duke's presence tonight.

Bertie tensed, pulling her more forcefully through a turn than intended. This duke's father and Albina had robbed him. They'd taken his honor. His faith. His *love.* They'd destroyed everything he'd thought he had. Avenging the wrongs they'd done him, the shame they'd brought on him, had not only been justified, it'd been the only way to defend and protect the Grennet name. But Wynhawke—*Cortleon*—had nearly cost him his life before disappearing. Now the worm had returned, no worse for wear. It wasn't fair.

This idea was pure madness. He'd thus far escaped recognition. Why tempt fate?

Because now was his chance for the justice so long denied him. Cortleon would not have her.

But who was to say the duke's interest would outlast this gathering? Bertie's brow knitted. No matter. Whomever Cortleon decided to court—for surely now that he'd come into society, he'd take a wife so as to continue the cursed Cortleon line—Bertie would do his best to save her from the man's clutches.

He tightened his grip on Lady Elinor's fingers, eliciting a gasp and a wince. "My apologies, dear lady. Sometimes I do not know my own strength."

She gave a pained smile. "I don't doubt it, my lord. You are not a dainty fellow."

He actually laughed. "'Tis true. None have ever described me as such."

The music stopped. He gave a bow then released her hand. "Thank you for the dance, my lady."

She curtsied before making her way to a woman clad as a nun. Lady Lucy-Anne, her sister. His son approached the two women. After exchanging a few words, Hugh took Lady Lucy-Anne's hand, leading her into a dance. Wasn't this the third time they'd partnered? Hugh had sought her out on other evenings, as well. Hopefully, he didn't have serious designs on the lady. He was only twenty-four—far too young to consider a permanent attachment. Given his youth, his tendre for Lady Lucy-Anne would likely sputter out, however, and thus Bertie need not worry.

Then again, a connection between the two might give him an advantage. If Lady Lucy-Anne wished to wed, wouldn't her parents want their eldest married first? The Earl of Rutley was down on funds. Lord and Lady Rutley must not only want but also *need* their daughters to marry men of means. Bertie was such a man. The Grennet earldom boasted wealth greater than a number of marquessates and even a dukedom or two. He could erase whatever debts Rutley held without seriously denting his own coffers.

He tugged at the neck of his coat, sweat pooling beneath its heavy weight and under the brow of his Fool's cap. Ire flared. Why had the dowager assigned him this degrading role? He'd not been able to beg off, however, when every other guest had embraced his or her character. At least he hadn't been assigned the part of the glutton. That poor fellow had stuffed his waistcoat so full of pillows he could hardly move.

Still, didn't Bertie deserve better? Why should Cortleon play the gallant knight and he the lowly Fool? On the other hand, he, not the duke, had gained a dance with the goddess. Where the knight had failed, the Fool had succeeded. He'd continue to play it if it aided him in his goal.

~

GAVIN ATTEMPTED to lose himself in cards, but his concentration wouldn't hold. He'd lost a fair sum to Arthington.

"Not that I'm complaining," the blond duke said. "But I find fleecing people more fun when they're actually trying to prevent me from doing so."

Gavin set his cards down with a rueful grimace. "I suppose I should return to the ballroom."

"Especially if your liege lord commands it." Arth's cheek quirked up as he adjusted the crown on his head. "If my mother insists I be King Arthur, I might as well play the part to the fullest."

"Ah, but who is your Guinevere?" Emerlin asked.

"A blonde with large ... *fortunes,* of course."

Everyone around the table chuckled.

"But come." Arthington rose. "It's nearly midnight. Let us rejoin the ladies." He flipped his fur-lined cape over his shoulder. "This blasted thing is choking me. However do kings do it?"

"At least you needn't wear this scratchy white hair and beard." Emerlin pulled at his whiskers.

"You could have got a worse role than Merlin, my friend," Arth said, clapping his friend on the back. "You could be wearing Grennet's Fool costume."

"I know your mother has joked you and I are incarnations of those medieval legends, but this is ridiculous."

"You're merely annoyed because the beard and mask obscure your fine countenance and you haven't the normal number of ladies dancing attendance upon you," Stoneleigh commented.

When Arth snorted and Emerlin shot him a look, Stoneleigh held up his hands. "Don't blame me. I'm only playing my role of the drunkard to the full. And does not a drunkard always tell the truth?"

The group chortled as they made their way from the card room, Stoneleigh stumbling as if deep in his cups. *Was he?* Gavin hadn't seen him partake the entire party.

When they reentered the ballroom, Grennet, who stood less than a foot away, shot them a surly look. Had he somehow overheard Earth's crack about his costume? Or perhaps the older man simply begrudged the younger peers' reappearance, as women flocked at once to Emerlin's side. So much for the long, white beard as a deterrent.

Arthington took a butterfly in hand—Lady Tabitha—and Emerlin accepted an invitation from a woman clad as a horse. Poor thing, especially since her natural nose only emphasized the comparison. Gavin sought out Lady Elinor. She stood to the side, her fingers toying with her toga. Why had no one asked her to dance? How could they leave such a goddess to herself? Unless she'd refused all requests. Should he try again?

A hulking figure passed him, striding purposefully towards her. Grennet. The Fool held out his hand, and she took it. She'd accept Grennet but not him?

Gavin pulled the mail shirt away from his neck. He was hot, likely as much from the port he'd drunk as the many bodies and candles warming the room. His slightly muddled head might explain why he'd read something personal into Grennet's actions.

He shrugged. If he couldn't partner with Lady Elinor, he'd dance with the tavern wench before him. And perhaps, just perhaps, he'd try once more for the Holy Grail: a waltz with the Ice Princess. No, not princess. Goddess. His Ice *Goddess*.

How he wanted to make her melt.

CHAPTER 10

*N*elle spun in Lord Grennet's arms, her stomach lurching at the sharp turn. She shouldn't have had the punch. Her head was swimming and not because of the energetic country reel.

Across the room, her father's jowls jiggled enthusiastically as he spoke with a gentleman attired in beggar's rags. Father's cheeks were blotchy and his nose red. He held a glass of punch in each hand. She wasn't the only one feeling the beverage's effects. How much alcohol did it contain? Perhaps she should have expected a strong brew, given the nature of the evening.

She'd taken a turn on the dance floor with Lord Ashvere, obliged several other gentlemen, and partnered once with Lord Stoneleigh before he'd slipped out the same door as Cortleon. Thereafter she'd pleaded the need for libation and had stood to the side, observing the dancers while sipping two more—or was it three?—cups of the tasty punch. Drinking had given her something to do, to mask her constant looking for the knightly duke—ducal knight? —and to keep her hands from toying with her toga.

"It's a pleasure to dance with you again, my lady," Lord

Grennet said, his olive eyes intense on hers through his jester's mask.

"Th-thank you," she stammered, concentrating on the steps lest she should lose her footing.

"We've only a few days left at Camlon," he continued, "but I do hope we might spend more time together."

She hesitated. What to say? She should encourage the earl's interest, but now, with the duke returned the room ... "Do you know me, sir?" She injected her voice with a light, teasing tone. "We are, after all, masked."

He paused as the music stopped. "I'm no Fool, Lady Elinor. I am sure every one of us knows who hides behind each costume tonight."

"You think we're hiding?"

"Are we not all hiding some truths in one way or another?"

He stepped away after that peculiar comment, leaving her staring at his retreating back. What had he meant? And why had his words made her uneasy?

Goose pimples peppered her skin, but not on account of Lord Grennet. No, she'd turned to seek out Lucy-Anne only to find the duke across the room, his regard wholly on her.

"Whatever's the matter, sister? You are the color of a pomegranate."

Nelle flinched. Tabby's voice had startled her. Her sister lowered her voice. "Did the jester do something untoward?"

"No, no. I'm merely ... out of breath."

"No doubt. I've never seen you take so many turns around the floor." Tabby linked an arm through hers, pulling her to the side of the room, farther away from Cortleon. "I've danced twice with the boar," she said, waving an arm toward a man in a pig's mask, "and he really does live up to the title of *boor*." She laughed at her own witticism. "Shall we have some punch?"

Nelle held up a hand. "No, thank you. And you ought to be careful, Tabby; it's stronger than it seems."

"More reason to have a second cup, don't you think?" Her sister's eyes twinkled. "Especially since Lord Emer—I mean, the wizard—has returned. I believe I'll ask him to dance."

If you can cut through the crowd around him.

"Ladies and gentlemen." All conversation ceased as Cleopatra—that is, the dowager—stepped to the middle of the room. "Midnight is nearly upon us, at which point comes the unmasking! Thank you for your gracious participation. I invite you now to select your final partner for the year. Choose wisely, for you may end up under the mistletoe before we reveal our true selves."

She pointed to the boughs hanging from several of the chandeliers. How had Nelle not noticed them before? Much tittering began, and one matron near but not quite under a bough pulled her husband beneath it and pecked him on the cheek, much to the guests' amusement.

"More!" someone yelled.

"Will you do me the honor now?" The low, rich voice was so close to her ear that its owner's breath caressed her bare neck.

The Duke of Cortleon. She shivered and turned. "Sir Knight." Was her voice unsteady? Or just her head?

He didn't smile, as expected. Those hazelnut-brown eyes never left her face. He held out his hand. Nelle took it, shocked by the feeling of his bare fingers. They curled around hers as he pulled her forward, closer.

Her foot caught on the hem of her toga, and she tripped, falling against him. "Oh!"

His hands were sure upon her naked arms, steadying her. The warmth of his fingers soaked into her skin, and her breath grew shaky. He set her upright then took a step back. "Are you all right?"

She touched a shaky hand to her hair. "My apologies, Your Grace. For a supposed goddess, I've proven quite clumsy."

"On the contrary. You've given me what I sought all evening."

This time her breath caught completely.

"A knight is always in need of a damsel to rescue. You allowed me to carry out my quest."

She giggled. A high, nervous giggle. Why did this man fluster her so?

"You are certainly a goddess, Lady Elinor." He took up her hand again, leading her smoothly into the dance as the music began.

"You're not supposed to know who I truly am." Where had that hint of coquettishness in her voice come from?

"Nor you I, but as you just addressed me as 'Your Grace,' I surmised you've identified me."

As if there were any disguising this man.

"Tell me, my lady. What do you wish for most in this new year?"

He was making small talk now? She nibbled her lip. "My parents wish me to marry."

Oh, heavens, why had she said *that*? Blast that punch! Nothing made most eligible men scurry away faster than the mention of matrimony, and now that she was in his arms she wished to remain. At least for the duration of the dance.

To his credit, his step did not falter. "But what do *you* wish?"

Their eyes locked. His reflected true interest in her answer.

"I ..."

Stop acting the calf-eyed debutante, you goose! You're twenty-five, not some girl barely out, for Heaven's sake, and this is not the first time you've danced or conversed with a man, even a duke!

Though none of them stirred her the way this duke did.

"I'd like to find permanent homes for abandoned children. I'd like to improve the amenities in my Aunt's foundling home and work to better the conditions there." She stuck out her chin. "And I want to be independent. I don't need a husband."

He laughed, a full-bodied chuckle. "My mother sometimes spoke similarly." His grin faltered. He swallowed, his bare throat bobbing in a strangely attractive manner. "My apologies. Occasionally my grief still takes over. This is the first New Year I've faced without her."

"You have my sympathies, Your Grace." She winced. That was too much a platitude, a meaningless statement people offered in the face of loss.

His smile didn't quite reach his eyes. "I should apologize, Lady Elinor, for injecting this pleasant moment with sad feelings." He clasped her hand firmly, but not in the earl's bruising manner. "In fact, this is the most pleasurable part of my evening. You have my admiration for your care for children. I can tell your devotion is sincere, not just a part you play."

She bristled. "Of course, it is!"

His hand at her waist pulled her closer, enough so that the space between them was slightly improper. "I meant no insult. While a number of Rome's rich helped the poor, most gave money, not time. Those who directly interacted with needy children often did so with clear distaste."

"How awful!"

"Agreed."

Silence fell, though they moved together.

"Is it strange to be back in England?" she asked after a moment. It was a bold, overly nosy question. But then again, his own had been rather personal. She tried to cover it by adding, "What do you wish for this year?"

"It *is* strange. I concede I feel more Italian than English." The wistfulness in his voice pulled at her but before she could respond, he went on. "As to the other? To complete my true quest, beyond rescuing a goddess from her offending garment."

He didn't continue. What did he mean? What quest? And had he intended that last to sound so ... seductive?

"'Tis nearly midnight!" someone shouted. "Ten—nine—"

Others joined in, the ballroom coming to a standstill as the musicians ceased playing. "Eight—seven—six—"

People shuffled about.

"Three—two—one!"

Great cheers rose as couples kissed. Nelle flushed, not used to such open displays.

"May I?" He leaned in, leaving the barest of spaces between them, but waited, his eyes on hers.

"Is—is—it not for married or at least betrothed couples?" Even as she said the words, she arched toward him.

"Ah, but we are ..." his arm raised, and her eyes followed it, "... under the mistletoe."

Had he intentionally maneuvered her there? Did she care? She didn't. Fueled by the punch and an unfamiliar longing, she nodded. When would she have the opportunity to kiss such a man again without consequence? At a Twelfth Night ball, under the mistletoe, at least she could claim it was not untow—

His lips closed over hers, warm, piquant, tasting of something at once unknown and familiar. She'd thought it'd be only a light peck, but he didn't release her. Instead, he pulled her so close her breasts brushed his chest and opened his mouth, tracing the seam of her lips with his tongue.

What? *Did people do that?*

She parted her own lips in return, shivers racing through her as their tongues touched and then danced away. How peculiarly wicked. The feeling of his mouth against hers, the tingles it raised throughout her body— she'd never experienced anything like it.

The room spun, but whether from the kiss or the drink, she didn't know. If only this could go on and on, forever and ever ...

"*Elinor!*"

CHAPTER 11

*T*he sharp cry broke through Gavin's fantasies of taking this goddess to his chamber and into his bed. Her flavor was like nothing he'd ever tasted. Honey and manna. And that little noise she'd made when their tongues had touched? Reluctantly, he broke off, turning to whomever had dared interrupt them.

Lady Rutley. *Merda.*

"Mama." Lady Elinor's voice shook as she backed away from him. "I'm s-sorry."

"There's no need to apologize." He kept his voice calm, despite the desire twisting through him. They'd done nothing wrong, only shared a midnight kiss under the mistletoe, at a masquerade, no less. If anyone should apologize, he should, for wanting more. He pointed to the green boughs above. "We followed tradition, Lady Rutley. As did other guests."

The countess sized him up. "I care not what others do; I care only about my daughter's reputation. Who are you, sir? Have you noble intentions?"

She'd spoken loudly, drawing further attention. Lady Elinor shrank in front of him, a quiet groan escaping.

Bloody hell. How dare she embarrass her daughter like this? And to ask such a pointed question in front of everyone? Ludicrous! They'd kissed *once*, not been caught in a truly compromising situation. No. He'd no intentions toward Lady Elinor. He'd not be forced into a union, especially not now, with his quest unfinished. He pulled off his helmet and mask, then donned his most charming grin, though a muscle in his cheek spasmed.

Lady Rutley gasped dramatically. "Your Grace!"

His eyes narrowed at the woman's artifice. His knightly helm hadn't hidden his longer hair, a style no other gentleman wore. She had to have known his real identity. Did she honestly believe she could trap him into marrying her daughter? He forced insouciance into his voice. "No intentions, noble or otherwise. My only goal was to secure a kiss from a goddess as a good omen for the New Year."

Murmurs and chuckles emerged around him. Lady Elinor's face crumpled, her lower lip trembling. *Damn.* He hadn't meant to imply ... What *had* he meant? Why *had* he kissed her? She was beautiful, of course, but he'd resisted many a beautiful woman before.

Momentary doubt struck. Could one kiss truly be so bad? Dishonoring a woman went against his innermost code, but surely no one outside of Lady Rutley could fault them, especially as the dowager herself had given her blessing to such mistletoe kisses?

Lord Rutley approached, nodding to him before setting a hand on his wife's arm. "I daresay I don't blame His Grace. Who among us hasn't taken advantage of mistletoe at least once?" He dropped his voice. "I seem to recall *you* kissing a gentleman on a long-ago Twelfth Night. And he wasn't me."

Lady Rutley looked as if she wished to say something disagreeable, but stopped herself, giving Gavin a swift nod as she pulled her daughter away. "It is time to retire, my dear."

Lady Elinor made no response. Nor did she look back, as her mother ushered her through a side door.

Bloody hell indeed.

∽

BERTIE'S HEART hammered as sweat dripped from under his cap. He yanked off the offending item, clutching it in his hands lest he strike at something. Or someone. How dare Cortleon? How dare the bastard kiss her so publicly? So *avidly*?

Red swam before his eyelids. History was repeating. Cortleon was no better than his father. Worse, for all Bertie knew. How many affairs was this miscreant carrying on? Had he seduced other innocents? Or other married women, cuckolding their husbands as he'd been cuckolded? Dishonorable cur.

She'd returned the kiss. Was she less pure than her reputation suggested? Or had the Casanovan duke, the seductive nature of the masked ball, and the powerful punch led her astray? Bertie himself had imbibed too much. He knew better, knew the lengths to which alcohol could push him. He'd indulged out of relief that nothing in the last week had jarred Cortleon's memory.

He closed his eyes, counting to ten, then twenty. Counting was one of the few things that reduced the rage. Counting and waiting. Difficult under duress, and yet something he'd trained into himself over the years. Anger still came that he couldn't help. But he could choose how he responded. Better a cold, calculated strategy than an impulsive move. He'd learned that with Cortleon. The other Cortleon. Not only would challenging Loughton Knight's son here and now deny Bertie the satisfaction of taking the object of the duke's desire, but he could lose his own life.

He massaged his scarred shoulder, a reminder of the price he'd paid for his rash actions. He'd killed the man who'd wronged him, but he'd also lost his wife and his honor. One he could never regain; the honor he'd spent his life attempting to recover. He'd not throw it away again. Not here. Not openly. But he'd find some way, somehow, to make *this* Cortleon pay.

Exhaling, Bertie approached the duke. Though he itched to strike him, he willed a benign smile onto his face and dispassion into his voice. "I don't suppose you'd care for a round or two of cards, now that our real selves have been unmasked?"

If he couldn't best the man with women, he'd at least best him at cards—and perhaps glean useful information at the same time.

"I say, that's a devilishly good idea," Arthington broke in from Cortleon's side, clapping both the duke and Bertie on the back. "I'm not quite ready to call it an evening, but I've had enough of evading daughters and their match-making mothers. Including mine."

Cortleon chuckled. Bertie did not.

"Come, Emerlin. Stoneleigh. Let me recoup my losses from earlier in the evening."

"Or add to my gains, you mean," tossed in Emerlin, as he neared them.

They adjourned to the card room, seating themselves at a round table.

"Mind if I join you, my lords?"

Hugh. *Damnation*. He loved his son but did not welcome him at present.

"Certainly, Ashvere." Their ducal host nodded to a seat next to Stoneleigh, as Emerlin began to deal.

The first rounds passed quickly, Bertie taking most of the pot.

"I'm clearly no match for all of you," Cortleon said, as the guineas in front of him dwindled.

"Ah, but some of us would prefer your winnings from earlier in the evening." Arthington fixed the fellow duke with a mirthful stare.

Cortleon winked. "Whatever do you mean?"

Bertie nearly pounded the table. How dare the ass make light of his boorish behavior?

"I'm surprised Lady Elinor permitted it," Stoneleigh said, pushing his lower lip out as he mused. "We must learn your secrets, Sir Knight. If you can thaw the Ice Princess, I dare say you can have any woman you wish."

Cortleon snorted. "How lucky for you, then, that this Knight serves all ladies and not just one."

Several more rounds passed, the conversation circling to the hunt earlier in the day.

"'Tis a shame you didn't accompany us, Cortleon. Do you, like Emerlin here," Arthington shoved the Irish lord good-naturedly in the arm, "have a soft spot for animals and cannot bear to hunt? Or do you simply prefer female targets?"

Bertie pretended to study his cards, though his fingers shook. For conversation among gentlemen to turn to ladies wasn't unusual, but speaking about Lady Elinor so cheekily was beyond the pale.

Arthington tipped his head toward him. "Grennet secured quite the buck."

"As he's now securing all of my guineas." Cortleon chuckled as he motioned to the pile in front of Bertie. "I must determine how to win them back from you, sir, lest my reputation at the tables should be forever tarnished."

Bertie attempted a smile, leaning back in his chair. "I might rather have caught what you did, Your Grace."

The last two words came out with a harder edge than intended. Cortleon furrowed his brow. The other men chortled.

"You want Lady Elinor, Father?" Hugh's tone bespoke his bemusement.

Bertie leveled a pointed stare at his son. The pup should know better than to speak so coarsely.

"Not that any of us blame you, Grennet," Arthington said. "Who among us wouldn't want to kiss the incomparable Lady Elinor Greene?"

The table fell into an awkward silence.

Bertie took a sip from the glass at his side. With great effort, he winked at Cortleon. "Perhaps I meant a kiss from His Grace himself. Given how the ladies fawned over Sir Knight this evening, I do assume that's what each wanted." He fingered the holly branch hanging from the arm of his chair. "Considering your ... *friendly* nature, sir, and Lady Elinor's frosty reputation, I think I'd have secured one more easily than the other, don't you?"

$\sim$

"FATHER!"

Gavin held a hand toward Ashvere before leaping up. He'd had enough. Grennet had made snide comments and innuendos more than once since they'd sat down to play. Now the earl openly baited him, impugning both Lady Elinor's and his honor? He leaned over the table, pressing his fisted knuckles onto the playing board's surface. "Had I a glove, as the knights of old, I would throw it down in challenge, Fool."

Emerlin set a hand against his forearm. "Come now. We've all jested about the evening. Let us attribute it to an abundance of spirits and not enough sleep, given the many late nights."

Grennet rose as well, his eyes fierce under his bushy brows. The man might top him by several inches, but Gavin would be damned if he'd stand down.

Ashvere clasped his sire's arm. "Father, please."

The earl looked to his son, then Gavin, his face rigid. After several tense, silent moments, he gestured toward the marquess. "Emerlin is correct. This Fool is deep in his cups. I beg your deepest pardon, Your Grace, for any unintentional insult."

Gavin's chest heaved with agitated breath. How he'd love to meet the man at dawn. This Grennet had aggravated him from the start.

His mother's face floated before him. *Gavin, my son. You must not let your temper rule you. Your father's great passions got him killed. You must do better. You must* be *better.*

He swallowed, glancing at the other men. Arthington wore an angry scowl. Emerlin and Stoneleigh's eyes expressed concern. Ashvere's pallid face radiated fear. At length, Gavin gave Grennet a crisp nod. "I grant it."

He could not bring trouble onto these men; men he already considered friends. Dueling was illegal and although Arth clearly would stand by him if he pursued this course, he couldn't risk repercussions that might taint these gentlemen. Or himself. Plus, though he doubted Grennet could best him, *should* the earl kill him, he'd never know the truth about his father.

"Thank you, Your Grace." Ashvere rose. "I think it's time we bid a good night." He pulled at his father's arm.

The older man hesitated briefly before following his son. He left his winnings on the table.

"Whew," said Arth, breaking the tension.

Gavin sighed. "I should not have invited conflict under your roof. If you wish me to leave—"

The blonde duke pointed at Gavin's chair. "Don't be silly. Sit. Worse has been said and done at our house parties." He winced, wrinkling his nose. "Now I must apologize. I didn't mean to reference—"

"—My father's death?"

Everyone stilled. It was Gavin's turn to dispel the discomfort. "I'm happy to be here. How else might I find clues as to who shot him?"

"You think you can solve this mystery after all these years?" Emerlin said.

"I certainly intend to try. Whoever killed my father not only robbed him of his life but also stole from me the life I should have had. I must know who he was. And when I find out, there will be no backing down." He shot Arthington a meaningful glance.

The duke tapped a finger against his lips. "I'll help in any way I can, but my father found no additional clues or information, and no guest raised suspicion. Camlon is remote, but not so much that someone couldn't sneak onto our land through the surrounding forests. According to my parents, we'd had problems with poachers that year."

"Do you recall anything of that day?" Gavin was grateful for the frank discussion; though he'd been at Camlon more than a full week as if by unspoken agreement neither he nor Arthington had broached the subject. Perhaps Arth had wanted to spare him further pain. For his own part, he'd needed to first take the measure of his host.

Arthington shook his head. "No. I was practicing with my riding master at the time. I do recall the ballroom full of people and your face, so very white. But that's all."

"And you don't remember anything, Cortleon?" Emerlin's voice was gentle.

Gavin swallowed. "Not directly. Only the nightmares that followed. A faceless man. A green monster. Red eyes. A loud noise—a gunshot, I presume. According to my mother, I insisted in my dreams that I'd shot the monster."

"Further proof no one at the party was involved, I suppose, since none of the guests were wounded."

Stoneleigh broke in. "Could someone have been injured but feigned health?"

Arth drummed his fingers on the table. "I suppose it's feasible. It's too late to know now. Many of the guests then present have since died, my father included."

Gavin leaned forward. "But Grennet is of the right age, isn't he? Our mothers listed him among the guests."

Arthington nodded slowly. "Yes. Though I've never known him to be anything except the highest example of honor."

"My mother insisted the same. As does yours." Gavin pulled a hand through his hair.

Stoneleigh cleared his throat. "He wasn't the highest example tonight."

Everyone turned to him.

At Arth's sputtering, the earl added, "Let me be clear; I make no accusations. Only an observation."

Emerlin shook his head. "You're right. His age and presence might raise suspicion, but given his character—outside of this evening—I find it highly improbable he had anything to do with your father's murder. Plus, *were* he culpable, why would he come back to Camlon year after year? Especially now, when you've returned? That'd be beyond brazen."

The marquess had a point.

"I must concur with Emerlin," Arthington said. "Grennet doesn't circulate much in society, preferring to stay at Swythdon. Understandable, given its distance from London. It makes for quite the journey. But by all accounts, including my own personal experience, he's a man of principle. One devoted to his son."

"What of Ashvere's mother?" Gavin asked. "I've heard nothing of her."

Arth frowned. "Mother said she died from a lingering ailment a few months after Ashvere's birth. Grennet shut himself up in Swythdon for some time in mourning."

Grennet's wife died only months after my father? Gavin swallowed. Could there be a connection between the two? Could Grennet have had a hand in both their deaths?

He pressed his fists to his forehead, closing his eyes. That wild theory flew in the face of everything everyone said about the earl—including Gavin's own mother. And despite Grennet's antipathy toward him, the earl was indeed exemplary in his manners with everyone else.

Was he so desperate for answers he'd twist an innocent man into a murderer? "My apologies, gentlemen. For my temper and for bringing up the past. It's time I retire."

"No need for apology, Cortleon," Arth said as Gavin made to rise. "Each of us, to a man, understands your need for resolution. And we're all friends here."

The men circling the table nodded. Gavin's chest swelled. Friends. He had friends. What a wondrous feeling. Still, when everyone had vouched for Grennet's character, why did the earl unnerve him? Was it just that the older man held an interest in Lady Elinor, then?

So did he. But she was not an option. Tomorrow, he'd seek her out to make amends for his boorish behavior. That he had hurt her pained him, even as memories of her soft lips and the tangy sweetness of her mouth taunted him.

Lady. Goddess. Siren.

He best be careful, lest his honor crash on her shores.

CHAPTER 12

"*G*et up, you goose! I've never known you to lie so long abed."

After a screeching noise, rays of dagger-sharp sun flooded the room, digging their way into Nelle's pounding head. She held up a hand as if to ward off both the light and Lucy-Anne, who towered over her at the side of the bed.

"Lucthy," she mumbled. Her mouth felt stuffed with cotton and her own voice made her wince, as it increased the hammering inside her skull.

Lucy-Anne flounced onto the bed, unaware or uncaring of her sister's wretched state.

Why, oh why, did I imbibe so much punch? Images from the previous evening assailed Nelle. Dancing couples. Cortleon in armor. Their midnight kiss. Her skin went hot at the memory, and her cheeks had almost certainly turned that scarlet Lucy-Anne so loved to tease her about.

Her sister was paying her no attention, however, as she played absent-mindedly with a loose curl. "Isn't he the most handsome man you've ever seen, Nelle?"

Sherry-brown eyes in a dramatic face, a regal nose, that jaw. Yes. Yes, he was.

"Such green eyes, like grass in the springtime."

Green? Oh. The realization came slowly, tripping its way into her head alongside a further company of drums. Her sister wasn't referring to Cortleon. Of course not.

"And we danced, not once, but thrice! Surely that means something, even at a masquerade. Do you think so, Nelle?" Lucy-Anne looked down at her. "Good heavens. Whatever's the matter?"

Nelle groaned. "Too much punch is the matter." Too much punch and one entirely unforgettable kiss.

Would he say anything of it today? Unlikely. He'd made it quite clear their kiss had meant nothing to him whatsoever. How mortifying. She'd not only kissed a man in front of a crowded ballroom but wanted to do so again despite his dismissal. Absurd. Men wishing to steal a kiss were nothing new. She'd granted a few, refused most. But none of them had been in a crush of mixed company.

She lay an arm across her eyes, shutting out the sun. Shutting out everything.

"A kiss at midnight!" Lucy-Anne exclaimed with a squeal.

Nelle wanted to kick her sister. Couldn't Lucy-Anne see she needed quiet? Quiet and whatever kind of cure a gentleman took after he'd dipped deep.

Wait ... kiss? She groaned. Was Lucy-Anne truly bringing that up now? *Of course.* Why wouldn't she? Nelle's flagrant display, her open embrace of the duke, combined with her mother's emphatic reaction, ensured their kiss would keep tongues wagging for days.

Tongues. *The duke has a delicious tongue.* Spicy, yet sweet. Like the aroma of his skin. She yanked the pillow from behind her head and covered her face with it, wanting to block out the memory of his tongue teasing at her lips.

Teasing and tasting until she'd opened her mouth and joined in the game.

Lucy-Anne dragged the pillow away. "Did you not hear me? He kissed me!"

"Kissed *you*?" Had he kissed other women after she'd left? She threw off the pillow and sat up, ignoring the shrieking in her temples. "*Who* kissed you?"

The cloud suddenly cleared. Lucy-Anne was talking about Lord Ashvere.

"Ashvere." The syllables came out a caress, while Lucy-Anne's fingers stroked over the coverlet. "Isn't he the finest of gentlemen?"

Nelle had thought Cortleon such. Until those final moments. "He has paid you a great deal of attention this past week."

Lucy-Anne nodded vigorously. "He has, hasn't he? Oh, why must this dratted party end tomorrow? How will I see him again?"

"We remove to London for the Season in two months. He'll likely be there, as well. If his intentions are serious, he'll seek you out."

"Two months is an *eternity*!" Lucy-Anne leapt up and paced the room.

Nelle threw off the coverlet and swung her legs out from the bed. "You've made it some twenty years without Ashvere. I hardly think a few months more will do you in."

Lucy-Anne crossed her arms at the chest. "They will when you are in *love*. Have you never been in love, sister?"

Nelle pressed on her temples in an attempt to abate the pain. "You think yourself in love?"

"I don't think so. I *know* so."

"Lucy-Anne, dearest. Be practical. You scarcely know him. A fortnight is not enough time to fall in love."

"Love knows no timetable."

She peeked through her fingers. Lucy-Anne's chin

tipped up defiantly. This clearly required a different tack. Trying to talk her sister out of her feelings was like Sisyphus pushing that rock; Nelle had never succeeded before and wouldn't at present, either. "Has he expressed his feelings? Are there promises between you?"

Lucy-Anne's mouth twisted. "Well, not in so many words. But I know he feels something for me. Surely he'd not seek me out and wouldn't have kissed me if that weren't true."

Nelle snorted. "Just because a man kisses you does not mean he has serious intentions."

The bitterness in her tone must have cut through Lucy-Anne's lovesick euphoria, as she halted her steps to scrutinize her older sister. "Why would you say that?"

Before Nelle could answer, a rap sounded at the door, and their mother sailed through. She halted, taking them both in. "I see yestereve's events have left their mark this morning, Elinor."

Nelle didn't respond, even as Lucy-Anne exclaimed, "Events? What events?"

Lady Rutley raised a brow. "You must have been the only one not to see your sister in the arms of that rogue, the Duke of Cortleon. *Kissing* him. In the middle of the ballroom!"

Nelle groaned. If God were going to smite her for her wanton behavior, now would be an apt time.

Her sister squealed. "You kissed the *duke*? Oh, how could I have missed this?"

Nelle gave her a meaningful glance. "Perhaps you were otherwise occupied."

Lucy-Anne cast their mother a guilty look. *Ah.* Her sister had not told Mother. Only Nelle was to be taken to task for a kiss, apparently.

"This is not something to make light of, Elinor."

Nelle threw up her arms. "Of *course,* it is. One kiss at a

Twelfth Night ball is hardly the scandal you are making it out to be."

Her mother tutted. "It might be one thing if the duke had intentions of courting you. He made it clear he does not, yet you kissed him anyway."

"Mother!" Annoyance flared. "A kiss does not a formal declaration or an engagement make!"

Lucy-Anne shifted at her words, but Nelle ignored her. "Nor is it enough to now castigate me as a lady of the evening."

Their mother sucked in a breath. "You shouldn't speak of such things."

"I'm twenty-five, Mother. I'm not completely unversed in the ways of the world. Think you I haven't received at least one or two proposals to become someone's mistress?"

Her mother's face blanched. "*Who*? Who would dishonor you in such a way?"

Nelle pinched her nose. Goading her mother hadn't been wise, especially since the woman's voice had reached volumes heretofore unknown. "That's unimportant; I didn't accept. I may not wish to marry, but I value myself more than that."

"Thank goodness for that. But you must avoid the Duke of Cortleon. I fear him a Don Juan, just like his father."

"You knew his father?"

"Only of him, my dear. And that's enough." Her mother fixed her with a pointed stare. "I hope you've not ruined your chances with Lord Grennet."

Nelle snickered. "Alas, I must disappoint you once again, as I've not managed to secure *any* match in the precious space of two weeks." She gave Lucy-Anne a meaningful glance. "I daresay one could not even fall in love in such a short span."

Her mother exhaled heavily. "I suppose expecting a full betrothal was unreasonable. But hear me: you've one final

Season, Elinor. You must marry. We are depending on you."

Nelle swallowed. Never had she felt so trapped, like Rapunzel in her tower. But which key to pursue? Cortleon, whose kiss had set her aflame? Or the acceptable but rather uninspiring Lord Grennet? A maniacal giggle threatened to escape. As if she could force either to offer for her! She'd commanded any number of proposals as a fresh debutante, had, in fact, turned down a dozen. But now, in her twenty-fifth year?

Was there a third key?

Lucy-Anne clasped the bedpost, leaning in. "Oh, surely you can find *someone*. Love is the grandest thing, is it not? What I wouldn't give to marry the man I love."

Nelle squirmed under her sister's calf-eyed stare.

"Pshaw," their mother said. "Love need not figure into things. It's certainly not the best basis for a marriage. Love and passion fade." She pointed a finger. "But marry you must, Elinor."

The weight of the world settled on Nelle's shoulders.

Oh, you goose. You are not Atlas. Many people faced far more dire predicaments—including the Home's orphans. *Concentrate on them. And your sisters.* A wealthy husband might help not only her family but the foundlings and orphans, as well. Yes. She must make the choice that most benefitted others. It was the sensible thing to do. What she herself desired didn't matter.

Did it?

~

A SHORT TIME LATER, Nelle halted on her way to the break-fast room. Would Cortleon be there? What would she do if he were? She ought to comport herself as if nothing had happened. After all, it'd meant nothing to him beyond a meaningless mistletoe kiss; he'd said as much. For her, however, it was a different story. She couldn't stop thinking about him, had in fact dreamt of them dancing, kissing—and then entangled on a bed, the kissing continuing, and more …

She frowned. The "more" she'd heard described in hidden whispers and titters among women. Though she understood logically what happened, in reality, she couldn't fathom it. To be naked, to be so intimate with another human being. A man. And to lie together, to have parts blend into each other. It'd never appealed to her in the least. Until last night. Now the scandalous idea of Cortleon without his shirt, perhaps even without breeches, held a tantalizing, disturbing allure.

She smoothed her skirts, forcing her back straight. She'd hide from no one. If he were here, so be it. The room, however, proved empty of men, save the doddery Lord Cobshire, although several ladies lingered over pots of chocolate.

Nelle selected a small number of items from the sideboard and took a seat next to Pru and Tabby, both of whom were eating toast with strawberry marmalade. The sisters' tastes in food were amusingly similar.

"So," Tabby said, a knowing gleam in her eye, "how was *your* evening, dearest sister?"

Nelle shoved a forkful of eggs into her mouth. Indelicate, perhaps, but it kept her from having to respond, at least momentarily. After a sip of tea to wash down the food, she said, "Fine. And yours?"

Her sister's mouth dropped. Nelle might have laughed if she weren't so irritated.

"Surely you've more to tell?" Tabby pressed.

"Whatever do you mean? I danced any number of dances, the same as you." Two could play at this game.

Tabitha glanced around to ensure others weren't listening then leaned in. "You kissed the Duke of Cortleon!"

"That is hardly news. In fact, I was present for the event."

"And?"

"And what? We were under the mistletoe. It was to be expected."

Her sister sat up, annoyance marring her features. "But what was it *like*?"

"You should kiss him yourself if you truly want to know."

Tabby's eyes widened, whether at Nelle's acerbic tone or the suggestion itself, she didn't know. Nor did she care.

Pru put a hand on Tabby's arm. "Let her be. If she doesn't wish to speak of it, we must respect that."

Nelle shot Pru a grateful grin.

"Maybe *you* must," Tabby retorted, "with your goody-two-shoes sense of honor. I, on the other hand, want full details."

"Well, you shan't get them."

Tabby set an elbow on the table, pouting as she rested her chin in her palm. "If only this party could last another week or so. Inglewood will be so dull after this affair. I shall perish of boredom until London."

"Then I suppose that'll spare me further questioning." Nelle dabbed at her mouth with her napkin, as much to hide her smirk as anything.

"If only we could go hunting, as the men have done," Tabby grumbled. "I'd like something exciting like that to do, rather than spend another afternoon strolling in the gardens or associating in the drawing room."

"Scarcely a minute ago you wished this party wouldn't end." Pru gave her sister an innocent stare.

Tabby returned it with a glower, as Nelle choked back a laugh. *Hunting.* So that's where the men were. Had

Cortleon accompanied them? If so, her goal of avoiding him for this final day would be easier.

Why did that disappoint her?

Lucy-Anne swept in, decked in her finest day dress, her hair over-styled for morning. After surveying the room, her shoulders sank. She crossed to their table. "Has Lord Ashvere already broken his fast?"

Tabby shrugged. "Likely so, if he accompanied the others on today's hunt."

All grace gone, Lucy-Anne slumped onto a chair.

"So, two of my sisters have found themselves beaus, I take it?" Tabby swirled her chocolate with a dainty spoon.

Nelle looked daggers at her.

"Oh, yes. Isn't Ashvere divine?" Lucy-Anne exclaimed. "Oh, if only there were another ball this evening. How I long to dance with him again!"

Tabby rolled her eyes. "Mother must be pleased she might marry off two daughters instead of one, then. And one to a duke."

Nelle nearly spat out her tea. "Tabby! I'm in no way interested in, much less affianced to, the Duke of Cortleon!"

A hush fell. Few guests were present, but those who were gave her curious stares. She wanted to drop her head into her hands. Why was it every connection with the duke left her mortified? Ire bubbled up, her skin pricking. If he hadn't pursued her yesterday evening, she'd not be the current seven days' wonder. She swallowed. Could news of this pass beyond the house party? Heavens. Surely one kiss was not *that* remarkable?

With a grunt, she pushed away from the table. Respite was what she needed. Respite and solitude, to soothe her still-aching head as much as to avoid further discussions of the vexing duke. With any luck, she'd not see him before departing tomorrow morning. Then again, Fortuna must

have deserted her. Why else would she face a parental ultimatum of matrimony?

And why else would Cortleon have such constant hold
over her thoughts?

∼

THE REST of the day passed swiftly, thank goodness. Nelle
had sunk into a novel, grateful to escape company and
conversation. But now, as she dressed for dinner, nervousness hit. In half an hour, the full house party would assemble. Would anyone comment on the previous night? Surely
not. It'd been a Twelfth Night masquerade! And for what
purpose was a masquerade other than to provide an opportunity to be someone you weren't for a short time? Everything reverted to the way it had been—fire to ice, a knight
to a knave—once the masks came off at midnight. The
visible masks, at least.

She tucked a strand of hair behind her ear, studying
herself in the mirror. The lady's maid had woven a delicate
green lace ribbon through the blonde mass. "It sets off your
gown wonderfully, don't you think, milady?" she'd said
when she'd finished.

It did. Green was Nelle's favorite color. It flattered her
paleness, bringing a pink to her skin that other colors
muted. She preferred vivid shades of emerald and now that
she was no longer a young debutante destined only for dull
pastel muslins, her mother had acquiesced to her making
over this one bold dress that had belonged to Aunt Theo.

"Accessories go a long way to combat decline," Lady
Rutley had said, touching her own fruit-festooned turban.
"I suppose a bright color might attract notice and remind
suitors of your plumage still to be plucked."

Nelle touched the green ribbon once more, grateful her
mother hadn't insisted on a feathered hat to complete the

avian picture. Should she add color to her cheeks and lips? Normally she didn't, but perhaps it'd assure others at dinner that she was fine and not the least bit dismayed, ashamed, or in any way affected by the previous evening's events. Taking such care with her appearance had nothing to do with the duke. Nothing at all. For if she must now play the trussed goose to be served up to the highest bidder, ought she not baste herself accordingly?

A bell rang, and she drew in a breath. Dinner. She was late. Mother would be furious. She grabbed her wrap and hastened out the door, all but running to the dining room. She clasped her hand against her midsection as she entered, unsure if the exertion or the trepidation and anticipation warring against each other in her stomach caused her rapid breath. As nervous as she was to face the general company, much less Cortleon himself, frissons of excitement tickled her skin at the idea of seeing him.

A footman guided her to her seat. Her throat caught at spying Cortleon at the opposite end. At least he was not on the same side of the table as she, which meant she could observe him covertly. Most of the party guests turned their heads to acknowledge her entrance. He did not. He talked with Lady Agnes, the sunny, young blonde woman next to him.

Nelle sucked in her cheeks. Had he not noticed her arrival? Or was he giving her the cut?

"Good evening, Lady Elinor."

She looked to her right. Lord Grennet. Though his smile was amiable, his olive eyes held a touch of something else. Judgment? Displeasure? "Good evening, Lord Grennet. Please excuse my tardiness."

"Nonsense." He bent nearer. "A man never minds waiting upon a lady."

She must have misjudged his initial reaction, as his manner now bordered on flirtatious. Or was she imagining that, as well? Had she lost all ability to discern whether a man was interested or not?

"Did you enjoy your day?"

An innocuous enough question, thank heavens. "Yes. It was a fine day for reading."

"One for hunting, as well."

"Did you catch anything?" Hunting didn't interest her in the least, but she ought to engage him if she wished him for a—she swallowed the lump in her throat—husband.

"A wild boar surprised us. Nearly took my horse down."

"Heavens! Is the horse all right?"

"Yes. As am I." He gave a rather forced chuckle. "I'm still an agile horseman. I outmaneuvered the beast quickly."

"I'm glad to hear it," she said with sincerity, though inwardly she admonished herself. *I ought to have asked after him first, not the horse!*

"Cortleon nearly caught a vixen, but she escaped. Until I got her."

Nelle resisted the urge to look toward the duke. "Is that so? Poor fox." She drank from her cup, the wine tasty on her tongue. She determined to consume very little given the escapades of the previous evening, however. "I'm sorry to say, Lord Grennet, but many men chasing one helpless creature never seemed quite fair."

"It's what gentlemen do, is it not? Chase vixens and outfox each other?"

She shifted. Nothing in his manner was entirely off-putting, and yet something about his words sent a chill through her. *Goose.* Doubtless, she was making something out of nothing, the same as she'd done with last night's kiss. "Ah, perhaps." She chuckled with false levity. "But did gentlemen never once consider vixens might not wish to be caught?"

"Some would say the vixens are who do the chasing,

waiting for the right moment to ensnare an unwitting chap."

This time her laughter was genuine. "We're no longer talking about animals, are we, Lord Grennet?"

"The hunt for one bears an uncanny resemblance to the hunt for the other, wouldn't you agree?"

"Perhaps."

She took advantage of the footman serving the next course to glance down the table. Cortleon had been looking this way, she was sure of it, but he now sent Lady Agnes that roguish smile. Forcing her attention back to her plate, Nelle took tiny bites of whatever fowl Lord Grennet had served to her. She barely tasted it, her nerves on edge between the earl's attention, the duke's lack thereof, and the severe glances her own mother cast her way. At least she needn't worry about dividing her attention between the gentlemen on either side of her. Lord Cobshire sat to her left, and the man was deaf in his right ear. As the dinner progressed, Lord Grennet and she talked of mundane things—of riding, the weather, the food.

She'd just taken a bite of a lemon custard when he said, "My son has developed a tendre for your sister."

He tipped his head toward the pair, seated side by side near Nelle's mother.

She hesitated. Was he indicating approval or disapproval? Nothing in his manner made his thoughts or feelings clear.

Before she could decide upon her response, he spoke again. "Will your family be in London for the Season, Lady Elinor?"

"Our mother would not let us miss it."

"We shall see each other again, then."

How did he mean that? Did he speak on account of Ashvere and Lucy-Anne or of her personally?

"It'd be a pleasure, Lord Grennet." What else could she say?

Arthington rose from the head of the table. "Gentlemen, let the ladies leave us to our port this one last time. Lady Tabitha has agreed to play the harp and pianoforte this evening. Those who wish may reconvene in the conservatory in an hour."

As Nelle stood, the earl rose, also.

"We've a long journey and need to make our start with the sunrise, so I will say my farewells now, Lady Elinor." He dipped in a formal bow. "I hope you and I may continue our personal association in London."

His meaning was unmistakable. But why had he waited to say something until the eve of his departure? So that if she refused him, he could retreat with his pride intact?

What arrogance on her part to assume her rejection would injure him! She'd held such power over men in her first few Seasons. But not now, as that devil Cortleon had proven. Not once had he acknowledged her this evening, despite her conviction he'd looked her way several times. She now felt the injured party—an unfamiliar and unpleasant realization.

"Indeed, Lord Grennet." She summoned a smile. No more throwing unwanted attention at Cortleon. Lord Grennet held the very advantages she sought in a marital partner. An unwanted partner. How she hated thinking of marriage in such terms, as a list of advantages and disadvantages, of blessings and curses. Emotion mattered not, merely the best match. The best catch. Lord Grennet's analogy was apt; everyone wanted the prize buck, the most ferocious boar, the wiliest fox. Nelle, however, loathed playing the predator.

Nearly as much as she hated being the prey.

CHAPTER 13

*G*avin downed the glass of port and beckoned for
another.

"Whoa, Cortleon. Are you still upset about
ceding the vixen to Grennet?" Arthington's cheek
popped up.

"I cede nothing to that man."

"I do hope you've put the previous evening behind you,
my friend." Arth ran a finger around the rim of his own
cup. "Though he was out of order, Grennet is an old family
friend, and I'd hate to think you bear him any ill will."

"Of course not." The earl irritated him but had made
his apology for the previous evening. No, Grennet was not
the source of his surly state of mind. Lady Elinor was.
Nelle, as he'd heard Lady Lucy-Anne call her. He'd been
painfully aware of her all evening but had studiously
avoided any interaction. For one, the deep green of her
gown had roused that stomach-churning reaction he
detested. It made him feel weak, vulnerable—like a child
again.

For the other, he didn't want to remind anyone of the
previous evening's kiss—not that people were likely to

forget. He was not the kind to dally with a woman. He certainly did not wish to marry. Not yet, anyway, with his quest unfulfilled. And yet, his attention drifted to her time and again, and to Grennet, with whom she'd spent the entire dinner talking. Could the earl have serious intentions? He was nearly thirty years her senior and long a widower. If he'd wished to remarry, wouldn't he have done so? Then again, Nelle was a singular woman. She'd captured the regard of most men at the party, despite her icy reputation.

She'd certainly caught his own.

He took a sip of his port, making every effort to slow himself down. It was early yet in the evening, and he didn't want to make a fool of himself. No, leave playing the Fool to Grennet. Gavin felt the idiot now, however, given how much he'd envied Grennet's seat next to Nelle. *He'd* wanted to serve her the meat, to engage her in conversation, to watch those lips move so prettily as she spoke. He was undoubtedly under her spell.

Several times she'd looked his way, though he'd averted his eyes lest she catch him watching her. Was she thinking of the previous evening? With joy? Regret?

He'd accompanied Arthington and Stoneleigh on the day's hunt, despite his head pounding like the marble workers' hammers in Rome. He'd gone to avoid her and memories of that heavenly kiss. Had he feared she'd make no acknowledgment of their connection the previous evening? Or that once again her parents would make too much of it?

He knew he was among the most eligible men in England. As were Arthington, Emerlin, and Stoneleigh— not to mention many of the other peers present. With such a group of high-ranking bachelors, no wonder the female house party guests repeatedly cast eyes—and in the case of one particular widow, more—at the men.

"My mother's doing," Arth had said with a groan that first evening after dinner. "She wishes me married by next year's end. I wish to disrupt her wishes. There are still too many ladies to enjoy before I settle for just one. And who'd want to give up the company of such fine gents as you?"

Emerlin raised a brow. "Who's to say you have to?"

Arth threw a bread roll at the marquess. "You're suggesting I be unfaithful? I may be many things, but I am not that."

"No, you clot pole. I meant Claremont is completely besotted with his new wife, yet he made time to see us when he was last in London." The marquess took a bite of the roll he'd caught in one hand, smirking as he chewed.

Stoneleigh gave a nod. "'Tis true. Though one might hope a newlywed would prefer the company of his wife to that of a group of men."

"Given the fact he and his new duchess are not here because she's increasing, I daresay he does," Keswick had quipped, evoking knowing chuckles from the other men.

"Gentlemen, our hour is up." Arth's voice brought Gavin back to the present. "Let us repair to the conservatory. May the young women about to entertain us do so on key. And may their mothers realize their matchmaking hopes must now be postponed since our Christmas gathering has made it to its end without any promises exchanged."

Gavin drained his cup and followed the men out of the room.

No promises, but one hell of a kiss.

THE MINUTE CORTLEON entered the room, Nelle drank him in. *Drat and blast!* She didn't want to give the duke any more of her time or attention. His intentional avoidance of her at dinner spoke volumes. He did not wish to extend their acquaintance. Neither did she.

Except memories of those lips, far softer than expected, tormented her, as did the heady, masculine smell of his skin and the shadow of stubble on his chin. The man must shave every day, perhaps twice, to keep his beard at bay. The curl of his brown hair around his neck warm her nearly as much as the heat in his amber brown eyes had when he'd leaned down to kiss her. Or when she'd stretched up to kiss him, rather, as that's what had truly happened.

He and his friends took seats on the far side of the room, opposite to where she sat with her family. The music room wasn't particularly large, but a number of chairs separated them. As other guests filled those seats, they blocked her view of the duke. All for the better. She straightened in her own chair, flapping her fan with vigor, though the room wasn't overly warm.

Tomorrow they'd leave, and the frustrating duke would no longer vex her. Once out of his presence, she'd have no trouble turning her attention to securing a more ideal husband. Lord Grennet, if he proved amenable.

Her brow knitted. What if Lucy-Anne's tendre for Ashvere faded, as had happened with her other "true loves?" How uncomfortable might it be if Nelle married the earl, but Lucy-Anne and his son broke with each other?

Oh, why when she'd finally found someone she'd consider marrying must a potential obstacle arise? *That is putting the cart before the horse, Nelle.* Yes, it was too soon to think in such a way. She'd take measure once they returned to London. If Lucy-Anne no longer cared for Ashvere or, heaven forbid, he for her, then Nelle would rebuff any attentions, should they be forthcoming, from Ashvere's father.

His father. Would society frown upon Nelle marrying

the *father* of her sister's husband? She flapped her fan even more furiously. At least Lucy-Anne would know that upon Lord Grennet's demise, Nelle, as his widow, would make no unfair demands of the new earl or her sister. The fan stopped. She was imagining the death of a man she hadn't even married yet. She was the vilest of creatures.

The beginning strains of the harp pulled her from the horrible thought. Tabby's face puckered in concentration as she strummed a most extraordinary melody, its simplicity haunting, and Nelle couldn't help but get caught up in the music, her attention solely on the sounds. At some point, her eyelids drifted shut. When the music stopped, they fluttered opened again, blurry for a moment against the intense colors of the room.

Several houseguests called for an encore, and so Tabby began again. After two more songs, another young lady came forth to play the pianoforte. She was accomplished enough, but nowhere near as remarkable as Tabitha.

The evening flew by, making it a shock when the dowager stood and thanked them for their company over the holiday.

"We look forward to seeing everyone again in London, come the Season," she said, then crossed the room to speak with a friend, indicating the guests were welcome to retire.

Numerous young lords crowded around Tabby, who preened at their sudden attention. Lucy-Anne and Ashvere whispered fervently near the back. Where had Cortleon gone? Nelle didn't see him. *It's for the best.*

She'd already made to put him completely out of her mind, pleasantly surprised the music had allowed that to happen. In less than twenty-four hours, she'd be well away from Camlon, and Cortleon would be en route to Wainsbury. Or perhaps London. Where didn't matter. It'd not be Inglewood.

As she worked her way to the exit, the duke stepped out from behind a side column.

Her breath halted.

He bowed. "Good evening, Lady Elinor. Your sister is quite talented."

"Thank you, Your Grace."

"I—" He paused. "I'd like to wish you well in the coming Season."

Of course. Whatever her future plans may hold, once again he'd made it quite apparent he'd no wish to be part of them. Something stabbed at her heart, tiny knife pricks of pain. Rejection. She sucked in a breath. *No.* She'd not grant him power over her.

"Thank you, Your Grace," she repeated, this time with an edge. When she made to turn, he put a hand on her arm. She looked down. He removed it almost as quickly as he'd placed it there, but then moved his fingers up to stroke her cheek.

She jerked back, bewildered by the unexpected action.

"Playing your knight was pure pleasure, Goddess." His eyes smoldered, sending unexpected tingles tripping through her. But in the next instant, his lips thinned. He dipped his head then strode from the room.

She held her hand to her cheek as if to trap the warmth of his touch. What had just happened?

CHAPTER 14

EN ROUTE FROM CAMLON - JANUARY 1813

*B*ertie groaned as the carriage rocked to and fro. Two nights of heavy drinking had resulted in a throbbing head and sloshing stomach, rendering the poor traveling conditions even less bearable.

Cortleon was to blame. Between Bertie's initial fear of discovery and then that damnably disgusting kiss, the duke had propelled him toward the brandy. Baiting the man had been the height of folly. At least Bertie had had the good sense to stand down at Hugh's urging, though it'd tortured him to apologize.

The cool light of day had brought him to his senses. He'd lost so much to Cortleon; he was not going to lose the rest to the blackguard's son. Though he'd escaped recognition at Camlon, if he were to ward off future suspicion he needed to keep to the upright, respectable, and non-threatening manner he'd assumed for the sake of his son.

Hugh sat across from him, his expression wretched. Bertie suspected his son's misery stemmed not from an upset stomach but rather his parting from Lady Lucy-Anne. As he hadn't confessed his feelings, however, Bertie asked no questions. Instead, he let his mind drift to Lady Elinor. He'd enjoyed their dinner conversations. He'd begun them in a concerted effort to draw her away from Cortleon, but the young woman had enchanted him. She had a good head on her shoulders and was devoted to her family. Loyalty was a trait he admired.

Her physical resemblance to Bee both drew and unsettled him. Unlike his wife, however, by all accounts, bodily passions did not drive Lady Elinor Greene. No scandal had attached itself to her name. She was a woman of honor, one who'd make a fine wife. And if her lack of passion meant she preferred to avoid marital relations, he could accept that. After they'd consummated the marriage, of course. He always had recourse to other options for sexual congress, and it'd be far better than taking another woman to wife whose fidelity was in doubt.

He made a low noise in his throat. *Was* Lady Elinor as virtuous as she seemed? She'd kissed Cortleon, after all— and Bertie had thought Bee faithful until he'd caught her in that field. His hands gripped the coach cushions, fingers biting into the fabric. *No.* Cortleon had drawn Lady Elinor in like a spider an innocent fly. Like his father had Albina. Had the rakehell not seduced her at such a tender age, things would have been different. Bertie's love would have been enough.

He might not love Lady Elinor Greene but marrying her would keep her from the current duke's clutches. He slammed back against the squabs, longing to strike something. By all that was holy, he'd be damned if a Cortleon ruined another lady.

Especially his future wife.

～

THE RAIN PELTING the carriage's windows aptly mirrored

Nelle's mood. At least this time she had a side seat, but next to her mother, whose stiff posture set her on edge.

Pru and Tabby half-chatted, half-argued about the various happenings at the house party—who'd flirted with whom and other such nonsense. Why they needed to revisit it all was beyond her. She only wished to forget.

Except she didn't, not really, and that's what bothered her most. If any man, her attention ought to be on Lord Grennet, but it wasn't. Cortleon haunted her thoughts. She'd never before experienced such an obsession. How disconcerting not to be able to rid her mind of him. Of watching discreetly from the gardens as he'd disarmed every challenger in fencing, struck the target every time he'd shot, and outplayed every opponent in lawn bowling. Of his insouciant charm, tossing that absurdly longish hair over his shoulder as he flashed that winsome grin. Did he know what such a grin did to women?

Of course, he did. The man was well aware of his appeal, his allure, his ... prowess.

Had he had amorous congress with any of the women at the house party? She bit her lip. She oughtn't think of such things. If he had, what concern was it of hers? Yet, she couldn't help it. She hadn't seen him kiss anyone else, but then again, what did any lady know of what occurred behind closed doors? Tabby insisted she'd witnessed Lord Effingham and Lady Blareweather exiting the orangery late one evening, only to return to their respective spouses with virtuous smiles on their faces.

Why had the duke ignored her after the masquerade but then cornered her at the musicale? And *had* he looked at her at dinner? Her instincts said yes, but whenever she'd turned his way, he'd been conversing with those around him. But that touch of her cheek, that look in his eye ... what did they mean?

She drummed her fingers on her thigh in frustration.

She didn't understand him. She wasn't used to being ignored. Not at first, at least. Despite her mother's implication that Nelle had one foot in the grave, gentlemen still pursued her. She'd thoroughly rebuked Lord Galwright at Camlon, in fact, after he'd made an unseemly proposal.

Yes, men continued to profess their admiration and devotion, comparing her eyes to the heavens and her lips to the most delicate of roses, christening her Aphrodite or Venus. What would these same men think of her conviction that every child deserved a good home and education or her belief that social status and sex did not automatically render anyone better than others?

Her stomach rumbled with hunger; she'd hardly eaten anything that morning, too consumed by the anticipation —half worry, half hope—of encountering Cortleon, but then she'd overheard Arthington tell his mother Emerlin and the duke had already departed.

"I quite enjoyed Gavin," Arthington said. "He wasn't entirely as expected or remembered, though I suppose that should come as no surprise; he was away for so long."

Gavin. Cortleon's Christian name was Gavin.

"The poor boy, to have suffered such a thing in his youth. Yet I saw no sign of it. One would expect such trauma to scar him, but he was entirely charming and full of humor."

"Not all scars show, Mother."

"As we both well know."

Yes. Not all scars showed, including those one's own family inflicted, intentionally or not. How often her sisters lamented they hadn't her looks, yet how she envied Lucy-Anne's open, loving nature, Pru's nimble mind, and Tabitha's musical abilities. Each earned her sisters praise for something other than their appearance. At nearly every dinner or soiree they attended, in fact, people asked Tabby to perform. Nelle only had to sit and look pretty.

Then again, did Tabitha feel as much the trained monkey as Nelle the Christmas goose dressed to be put on display and then consumed by all who saw her? How often she'd wished to disappear from the *ton* to live a quieter life —that of a schoolteacher, perhaps, or the matron of an orphanage.

Horrid tales of cruelty and deprivation at the hands of teachers abounded, however. Each broke her heart, both for the children entrusted to their care but also for the masters and mistresses themselves. What fostered such harshness? A dearth of advantages, most likely. She'd never had to worry about material things. Although her family had had to economize of late, they still held the advantage of rank and far more wealth than those of the lower classes. Certainly, more than the children for whom she helped care.

What would happen to her family if she didn't marry? What would happen to *her*? Would her parents truly cast her out? If they did, could she make her own way? Dreaming of taking over a foundling house and orphanage was one thing, actually doing so another. Maybe she wasn't up to the task, for all her wishing. She shifted in her seat, her shoulders falling.

Oh, to be a man and have more control over her person and her purse! To not have to rely on others for a place to live or for money to spend! Her father had lost most of the Rutley wealth through a series of bad investments. Upon Father's death, the Rutley earldom and estates would by law pass to the nearest male, Cousin Alfred, for whom none of them much cared, nor he for them. Money and marriage, then, were her mother and sister's only sure source of future security—which was why her parents demanded she marry a man of means.

The Duke of Cortleon certainly fit into that category.

She nibbled at a fingernail, turning toward the window

lest her mother notice. She didn't need another scolding. No, she was scolding herself enough. *Why were her thoughts of Gavin so all-consuming?* They'd shared but a handful of conversations. A few dances. A number of looks. And one wondrous kiss.

That kiss and her incessant preoccupation were why she needed to keep her distance. In body, that wouldn't be difficult, at least until the Season started. But the blasted man had taken up residence in her mind's every nook and cranny—exactly what she didn't want. Her attention needed to remain on the ways in which she aided others. Selfish desires served no one.

The carriage hit a rut, tilting to the side. Nelle pressed a hand to her abdomen as her sisters gasped. Everyone soon fell to their earlier pursuits, however—and Nelle to her thoughts.

For as long as she could remember, she'd wanted to be valued for what she gave more than for her looks or any alleged accomplishments. She wanted to help others, especially those poor, parentless infants she'd first seen as a young girl of nine when her aunt had taken her to visit the Home. Why should those babies have to suffer? Wasn't there enough for them to receive food, love, and a home? The contrast between the aristocracy's vast excesses and the living conditions of London's poor shocked her. Her mother had lectured the sisters on their duty to help the less fortunate while making it clear that they were above those they helped. Mother saw their position in the *ton* as well deserved and understood. They'd been born into status and wealth and rightly so.

Nelle had never felt comfortable with that notion of innate superiority. Why did others easily accept realities she never could? Wouldn't it be simpler to think only of the next ball, dinner, or opera? Of marrying and raising children, as expected? Yes. But it wouldn't fire her heart the way aiding those children did. Marrying someone rich would, however, save her family.

Sherry eyes taunted her. Gavin had wealth. Immense wealth, according to gossip. And he certainly set her on fire. But she did not want to burn. Better to keep the fire at bay and don that layer of ice everyone ascribed to her. Fire should fuel her service, not her selfishness.

Lord Grennet was the wiser choice. For one, he seemed to hold a steady regard for her, not one that ran hot and cold, as with Gav—the *duke*. For another, he fitted her qualifications for a suitable husband: older and thus presumably less passionate, supportive of her charity work, and hopefully willing to be financially generous to her family and her causes.

Though what certainty did she have of any of those?

"You must be missing Lord Ashvere," Tabby said, jarring Nelle from her reflections.

Her younger sibling turned toward Lucy-Anne, done with needling Pru for the time being.

Lucy-Anne's gaze flitted to their mother. "I am," she admitted, a dreamy sigh escaping.

Lady Rutley let out a sigh, as well—a soft, gentle sigh, completely unlike those full of irritation to which Nelle was accustomed. "He does seem an admirable gentleman."

Lucy-Anne sat up straight. "Oh, he is, Mama. The best of men! I can't wait to see him again."

"Do you have an understanding with this Ashvere?" Father's voice was sharper than Nelle had ever heard it.

"N-no, Papa," Lucy-Anne stuttered. "We'd never arrange such a thing without your permission. But we *are* fond of each other."

He exhaled. "Then we shall invite him and his father for dinner one evening."

"Truly? Oh, that'd be heavenly."

"Yes, and Nelle could spend time with the earl," their mother said. "He showed you interest, did he not?"

Nothing escaped Mother's eye.

Nelle swallowed. She wished to deny it to stave off any discussion of her imminent future. But she must shake off that selfish desire and do what was necessary for the family. She set her hands on her thighs. "Yes, I believe he did."

Lady Rutley sent a rare, beaming smile toward her eldest daughter.

"Marvelous. Two daughters married off by the end of the Season. Is that not wonderful, John?"

He grunted. "Indeed. Now to marry off the other two."

When all four daughters gaped at him, he held up a hand. "Said with love, dearest daughters. Said with love."

With love.

Father did love them, of that Nelle was certain. Her mother, too, in her own way. But the couple's disregard for each other was a deciding factor in why she'd never wished to marry.

But she would, to save the ones she loved.

CHAPTER 15

LONDON - SPRING 1813

*H*ugh bounded down the stairs into the front hall of their Berkeley Square townhouse. "It's good to be back in Town."

Bertie smiled at his son's exuberance. Hugh had chafed at being holed up at Swythdon these last weeks. Normally, Bertie preferred his quiet ancestral home to the never-ending chaos of London, but this time, to his surprise, he'd looked forward to their return, as well. "Is it *London* you're so delighted to see or Lady Lucy-Anne Greene?"

Hugh's cheeks beat their way to a fiery red. Like father, like son. Bertie's own passions had also once blazed hotly. For Albina. He swallowed. May his son make a better choice of spouse than he had. Bertie had spent the time since Camlon making discreet inquiries about Lord Rutley. Though the earl had run into financial difficulties, he and his family were upstanding members of the *ton* with no scandal attached to any of their names. Rutley and his countess held no great love for each other, but neither had been connected with a lover. That pleased him.

"I do hope to see her again, I confess," Hugh said, as he fiddled with his finely knotted cravat.

"Then you're in luck, as I've heard Lord Rutley and his family will be in attendance this evening. We shall make sure to stop by their box."

"That'll be the only reason I look forward to this performance, then. I can't say I enjoy the opera, Father."

"Ah, but the drama off stage can be more informative than that which is on."

A scant half an hour later, they'd settled into their box. Men and women milled about on the floor below, conversations echoing throughout the large theater. Silk dresses shone and jewels glittered under warm candles. People came to the theater as much to be seen as to see.

Bertie had greeted many an acquaintance, given a handshake here, a nod there, but he'd yet to spot Lord Rutley and his family—or Cortleon, though Arthington and Emerlin had taken seats in a box across the theater.

"Father, I see them." Hugh leaned forward, peering somewhere in the distance.

Bertie followed his son's gaze, the bright blonde of Lady Elinor's hair gleaming in the candlelight as she sat in a box opposite and one level higher than his own. Her sisters surrounded her, with Lord and Lady Rutley behind their daughters. Lady Elinor studied a paper in her hands, seemingly disinterested in the goings on around her, while Lady Lucy-Anne used a pair of opera glasses to scan the crowd. When she swung in their direction, one hand flew to her lips.

His son touched his fingers to his head in acknowledgment, an expansive grin lighting his face as the lady smiled.

"I take it the opera pleases you now, my son?"

"Only some of its attendees."

As the performance began, Bertie sneaked covert glances at Lady Elinor. She'd edged forward in her chair, her hands resting on the front of the box. He couldn't make out her exact expression from this distance, but the singing clearly riveted her. Her two younger sisters chatted while Lady Lucy-Anne shifted her glasses between the singers and the Grennet box, but Lady Elinor remained unmoving, perhaps even unaware of the people around her.

For a woman supposedly made of ice, opera melted the eldest Greene sister. Bee had loved the opera, as well. Bertie, like his son, had never seen its appeal, preferring a much more comprehensible play to wailing arias. But Albina had been a performance in and of herself at the opera; she'd exclaimed over the sopranos, wept at the tenor solos, swooned with the lovers, and wailed with those wronged ... His nostrils flared as he tugged at his beard. Had his duplicitous wife been thinking in those moments of how she'd wronged her own husband?

Shaking his head as if to rid it of unwanted memories, he turned his attention to the stage. Soon, though, as if by its own volition, his gaze drifted back to Lady Elinor. She made none of the same histrionic displays, yet it was almost as if he were watching his wife. The distance and low light blurred Lady Elinor's face enough that it was easy to impose Bee's features onto hers ... or Lady Elinor's onto Albina's. He closed his eyes, the jarring effect unnerving him.

At the intermission, Hugh immediately rose. "I should like to make my greetings to Lord Rutley and his family."

Bertie stood, as well. "If you don't mind, I'll accompany you."

His son's face fell and he almost reconsidered. But if things were to go to plan and Lady Elinor became his wife and Hugh married Lady Lucy-Anne, well then, shouldn't Hugh get used to his continued company? If Cortleon still held a tendre for the eldest Greene daughter, of course.

Bertie hoped he did. Marrying Lady Elinor, with her

marked resemblance to Bee, might allow him to replace the pain and shame of his deceitful wife. And rescuing her from Cortleon's clutches, as well as from spinsterhood and potential penury, might just erase his sins.

"Of course, Father."

Ever the dutiful son.

The sheer number of bodies crowding the theater's corridors created a stifling atmosphere. Maneuvering with any speed was difficult, but at length, he and Hugh made it to the other side of the theater, where they found Lord Rutley and his entire family in the hall outside their box, the younger two daughters sharing nuts out of a paper cone.

"Lord Rutley," Bertie called, raising a hand in greeting.

"Ah, Lord Grennet. Good to see you've made it to Town."

The two men shook hands, and then he and Hugh greeted each of the women in turn. His son saved Lady Lucy-Anne for last, moving to her side to speak in quiet conversation. Bertie tipped his hat to Lady Elinor.

"My lady, it is a great pleasure to see you. I so enjoyed our time together at Camlon." *Damnation.* Why had he mentioned Arthington's estate? He did not wish to bring Cortleon to mind. Then again, avoiding the topic of the house party would be difficult since that's where he and the lady had spent time together.

"Lord Grennet, it is good to see you again, as well." Her lips tipped into a gentle smile. "What do you think of the opera?"

"I think I am not nearly as entranced as you."

Her smile twisted into a puzzled frown.

Fool. He'd made it plain he'd been watching her. But wasn't that what people did at the opera? Observe the audience as much as the stage performance?

"Lord Rutley!" came a familiar voice from behind, and

everyone turned as the Duke of Arthington approached, Cortleon next to him.

Cortleon. Bertie's mouth twisted. Devil take it! When had he arrived? How had Bertie not noticed? He'd have expected quite the stir at such a high-ranking yet relatively unknown peer's appearance. Discussion of the maggot filled the papers. One rag had even termed the man *the Legendary Duke of C-*.

Hugh had read from it that morning, the words etching themselves in Bertie's brain:

"The Duke of C- remains a figure of legend to most of society given his mysterious formative years, about which he says very little, according to one Lady T., and given his highly selective acceptance of invitations since his return to Town. Now His Grace has developed a new following among the Fancy for his exemplary prowess at Gentleman Jackson's, Angelo's, and Manton's Shooting Gallery. Ladies are quite aflutter about this Corinthian Nonpareil. Will his longer locks become the vogue among the fashionable set?"

"Your Grace," Lord Rutley responded to Arthington, pulling Bertie to the present.

"A pleasure to see you," the duke said before addressing the Greene ladies with that snaggle-toothed smile. "And you all, as well." He tipped his hat. "Grennet, Ashvere."

"How is your mother?" asked Lady Rutley.

At her question, Arthington's face lost some of its joy. "She's decided to remain at Camlon for the Season, as her health has been ailing. Pleurisy."

"Oh, I am so sorry to hear that." The words were Lady Elinor's, but the rest of the women nodded and murmured in agreement.

"Thank you, Lady Elinor." Arthington nodded to Hugh. "Ashvere. I hope you join us some evening at White's. I do believe there's a bit of coin I need to win back from you. You, too, Lord Grennet."

Bertie gave a crisp nod but gritted his teeth. Must the duke reference gambling, given their last table encounter? No matter Bertie's dislike of Cortleon, his behavior at that masquerade had been inexcusable. As had Cortleon's. But *he* was a man of honor, an honor he'd fought to regain and protect, and he shouldn't have been so reckless. So rash.

"What do you think of the opera, Lady Elinor?" Cortleon's tone was courteous, his words the same as the lady's to Bertie, but the sweep of his eyes over her form revealed he was not so nonchalant as he appeared.

"It's marvelous, isn't it?"

Cortleon gave a shrug. "I'm not used to opera being sung in English."

Her face fell, but she lifted her chin. "You must have seen many operas in Italy, I suppose."

"No." His answer was short and succinct. He said nothing else, but his eyes remained on her.

Bertie wanted to kick him—or almost kiss the idiot when Lady Elinor pinched her mouth and returned her attention to him.

"I believe the intermission nearly over, but I wanted to thank you for stopping to talk with us, Lord Grennet. Your and Lord Ashvere's presence has been most welcome."

He gave her a genuine smile. In singling him out, she'd both acknowledged interest and slighted Cortleon, had she not? Out of the corner of his eye, he caught Cortleon's frown, but then a woman laid a hand on the duke's arm. Cortleon looked to its source, that irritating grin reappearing as a buxom brunette spoke with him in hushed tones.

"Excuse me, Mother. We should return." Lady Elinor slid by the men without another glance, disappearing into the theater. The rest of her family made their good-byes to the men, Lady Lucy-Anne sending Hugh one last look of longing before following after her sisters.

The brunette sidled away from Cortleon, and then the two dukes excused themselves, moving to rescue Emerlin from the gaggle of ladies surrounding him. Bertie gave both men a polite nod, feeling generous in his victory over Cortleon. The duke still very much wanted Lady Elinor Greene—the lust in his eyes proved that—but the lady had made her preference for Bertie known.

Hugh whistled happily to himself as they returned to their box, but Bertie's thoughts remained on Lady Elinor—and Cortleon. For although she'd acted indifferently to the duke, something in her voice on her last words caught at him.

A discernible tone of hurt.

∽

NELLE FIXED her attention on the stage as she awaited the second act, but the joy of the performance had dimmed after Gav—no, the *duke's*—coolness toward her ... a coolness that had altered upon the appearance of Lady Tutledge. *Tartledge*, rather.

It shouldn't bother her. He'd made his disinterest clear two months ago. Two months in which his cognac-colored eyes haunted her far too often, in which she'd catch herself stroking her lips at the memory of their kiss, wondering, as always, why he'd behaved as he had. And how he might act should they meet again.

She had her answer. She was of no consequence. He'd spoken to her as if she were no more to him than a potted plant. The intensity in his eyes, though ... But it was always there. She'd marked it upon their initial acquaintance. He must give every lady the same sultry stare—which would explain why his reputation continued to grow.

Just that very afternoon, while strolling along Bond Street with Lucy-Anne, she'd overheard Lady Betsy Plympton comment on the duke's form and the exceptional cut of his clothes. "So ... fitted," the vapid girl cooed, her fan working overtime.

The ladies surrounding her tutted, another one adding her two-penny's worth regarding his well-formed backside.

"I'd rather look at his front," Lady Betsy replied. "That face. Those *eyes*. There's something ... exceptional ... about him. Legendary, even."

"My husband says he's the most skilled fencer he's ever seen and that he nearly knocked poor Lord Emerlin senseless at Mr. Jackson's earlier this week!"

The lady in question—Lady Bebbers, wasn't it?—whispered the last as if it were some great secret. Nelle rolled her eyes. No conversation about his character, merely sentiment and sighs over his physical appearance.

Though what did she herself know of his true nature? She'd enjoyed their exchanges, but he'd revealed little of himself in speech, and his actions had shown him to be more rake than gentleman.

Lucy-Anne had pulled on her arm. "Why have you stopped? We must meet Mother."

Why *had* she stopped? She'd been no better than a silly schoolgirl making calf eyes at the mere mention of his name.

Nelle leaned forward as the operatic actors reappeared. She'd *not* give the Duke of Cortleon any more thought.

Lucy-Anne bent toward her. "He was even more handsome than at Christmas, wasn't he, Nelle?" she whispered.

Yes. Yes, he was.

"He seemed most happy to see me." Her sister pressed her hand to her heart. "Oh, may the time fly until the Malford ball. How I hunger to be in his arms again."

"Lucy-Anne!"

She'd spoken more loudly than intended, and their mother shushed them. Nelle stiffened at the reprimand. Lucy-Anne's frankness had surprised her, though it shouldn't have. If she'd never met Ga—the *duke*, she'd have dismissed Lucy-Anne's effusiveness as absurd. Now for the first time, she understood. Her pulse leapt at the merest memory of their midnight dance. At least he wasn't visible from this box. What misery that'd be after his curt behavior, especially if he sat with Lady Tar—Tutledge.

Lucy-Anne held the opera glasses to her eyes, training them not on the stage, but somewhere to the side.

"May I look?"

Her sister's mouth rounded at the unexpected request, but she handed them over. Nelle briefly studied the stout soprano but then turned them in the same direction Lucy-Anne had. *Ah.* Ashvere. No great surprise. She shifted her view to Lord Grennet.

He was staring directly at her.

She dropped the glasses. Lucy-Anne made a noise and grabbed for them, but Nelle hardly noticed. The glasses had given her a close view of the earl's face. Stoic. Unsmiling, though he hadn't appeared *angry*, merely intent on her.

It unsettled her, though it shouldn't. Men's gazes had followed her for years. Though each of the Greene sisters was comely, the *ton* agreed Nelle's beauty blazed brightest. Her flame was close to burning out, however; this was her final Season.

The soprano's voice soared with emotion, clutching her hands to her chest as she sang out her agony.

Nelle had never understood the opera better.

⁓

GAVIN TUGGED at his signet ring, working it over his knuckle and down again. His mind was not on the interminable wailing emanating from the stage. It was on Lady Elinor.

Nelle.

Damn. Time away had not dimmed his desire. She was a distraction he couldn't afford, and yet the moment he'd seen her, every muscle in his body had leapt to attention. He'd wanted to trace his fingers over those pearlescent cheeks, to take her into his arms and plunder her mouth, to pull her into a private box for a more intimate interlude.

Shame gripped him. That was not how a gentleman treated a lady—at least not how *he* treated a lady. He flirted, yes. Engaged in banter. Danced. He'd even exchange a kiss, provided each party understood it'd go no further.

It wasn't that he didn't want more or that he never struggled with lust. Hell and damnation, he certainly did. He was a male in his prime, after all, and temptation lay everywhere. His oath to his mother and his vow not to be the rake his father had been kept him from indulging, however. He thrust his unslaked desire into sport, into exercise, and into training, so that when he found his quarry, he'd be prepared.

He was not ignorant of his father's sins. He didn't venerate the man. But honor demanded retribution for Loughton Knight's ignoble death. The murderer must pay. Gavin's desire for justice burned brighter than anything. Anything but his desire for Nelle, that was. And that frightened him.

In all honesty, he didn't want to be in London. After years of living in Rome, he'd grown fond of the extreme quiet and solitude at Wainsbury. But "holing up in a musty old house," as Mrs. Stewart was wont to say, would not move him forward in his search, so he'd acquiesced to Arthington's request to join him in London.

Arth had invited Gavin to stay with Emerlin and him in his St. James's townhouse. "We'll carouse with Em in the finest clubs and seek the best in sport. It's a shame Tom Cribb has retired from boxing—I bet you could have taught him a thing or two!" he'd scrawled in his bold hand, signing off as simply "Arth."

Since Gavin's arrival, they'd passed many an hour fencing and milling at Gentleman Jackson's, much to his delight, especially when he imaged his opponent as his long-sought but faceless enemy. In the late afternoons, they rode in Hyde Park, a welcome respite from Mayfair's noisy sprawl, even when the park crawled with crowds. Just yesterday, a carriage had nearly knocked Gringolet sideways in the crush of mounts and vehicles.

Gavin preferred their occasional morning rides, as the park and Rotten Row were far emptier then, but Arthington enjoyed their evening rounds more.

"Not so many fine ladies in the wee hours," he'd said.

"Not so many Arths, either," Emerlin retorted. "You're nearly always abed until mid-afternoon."

"And you often rise at dawn, do you?"

Em had shrugged. "You don't know everything about me, my friend."

How Gavin wished he'd grown up with friends like these. He could have had these very friends, in fact, as Arth and he had played together as children. Had Gavin stayed in England, he *would* have had this. He wouldn't have been so lonely. He'd loved the Italian villa in which he and his mother had lived and the rugged landscape surrounding it, but some part of him had always sensed they didn't truly belong there. Italy was incredibly beautiful, but it was not his homeland.

Now he was in London, a city familiar in its chaos and cacophony, not dissimilar from Rome, but also foreign. And he was at a loss as to how to go about his hunt. Not only would discussing items of such a personal nature with strangers be the height of impropriety, but if he revealed his hand, the man in green would hold the advantage. If the monster yet lived and moved in polite circles, that was. Still, Gavin must always be on his guard—for who knew from where an enemy could strike?

"No one will ever challenge you, my friend," Emerlin had said, cradling his jaw after Gavin had given him a particularly rough strike the previous week.

"Not in milling, nor swordplay, nor in pistols, I dare say. Your reputation has reached legendary status, Cort," Arth added, his mouth twitching into that toothy grin. "Much to my dismay; you need to leave some of the ladies for the rest of us. They all swoon and sigh as you walk by."

"I thought all that swooning and sighing was for Emerlin," Gavin parried, giving the marquess a light punch on the arm.

Emerlin held up a hand. "Please, no more."

"Come now, Em." Arth gave him a tap on the other arm. "No more what? Punches? Or women?"

"Both."

Arth chortled. "I daresay Lady Rebecca will be greatly saddened to hear that."

"Lady Rebecca?" Gavin had met many young ladies in Town, but no Lady Rebecca.

Emerlin's ears flamed an amusing shade of red. "Lady Rebecca Mattersley. Sister to an old friend. And *sister* to me."

Not if those ears had any say about it. Why hadn't Em pursued this lady? With the way women gawked and tittered in his presence, it was as if the Irish lord possessed some kind of magic.

That wizard with women stood now, clapping his approval at the prima donna and other company on stage, as did everyone else. Thank heavens. This torture was at an end. Perhaps a true gentleman appreciated opera, but

Gavin was willing to exert ducal privilege in this case. With any luck, he'd never attend one again.

Arthington scooped up his hat and overcoat. "Come, let us to White's."

Gavin nearly cried off, longing for nothing more than peace and quiet. But not only was White's Club an ideal place for learning gossip and secrets, it'd also provide respite from the Cyprians pressing close on all three men as they made their way from the theater.

And perhaps respite from this obsession with Nelle.

HOURS LATER, Gavin careened out of the carriage and up the stairs at the rear of Arthington's townhouse. He might have asked for help from Arth and Em, but they were in a similar condition. One hundred percent foxed. Were his mother here, she'd wave her finger and chastise him for excess.

"At least it's not excess with women. A woman. That woman," he muttered as he stumbled through the back entrance. Thoughts of Nelle had tormented him at every turn, and every time memories of those succulent lips taunted him, he'd taken a drink.

There'd been many drinks.

Light eked its way across the horizon. He should go to bed. He didn't feel like sleeping, though. What if he were to dream of her? His goddess?

"Good God, she is not mine!"

"Beg y'pardon?" Emerlin raised one, then both brows.

"Nothing, nothing."

"Gentlemen, what say we toast the evening one more time before retiring for the night?" Arth staggered toward the front parlor, Em shuffling after.

Night? It was morning. He most definitely should go to

bed. Instead, he trailed after his friends, slinging himself into an armchair as Arth retrieved a decanter of something —brandy? port?—and three tumblers. His blond friend must be less inebriated than he if he could carry those glasses without dropping them.

Pouring a generous amount of liquor into each glass, Arth handed one to Em and then him before raising his own in the air. "To a successful London Season!"

Em halted the glass at his lips. "And what would that mean? Will your mother finally get her wish?"

Arth shrugged. "If not this one, perhaps in the next."

"Wh—what d'you mean?" Gavin's words were slurred, and he had to work hard to make the two Arthingtons swimming in front of him merge into one.

"Why, marriage, of course. What is it Mother quoted to me from her most recent novel? 'It is a truth universally acknowledged, that a single man in possession of a good fortune, must be in want of a wife,'" Arth responded, holding his hand to his heart in melodramatic fashion.

Em snickered. "You could rival Keane."

"A wife ... and an heir." Arth threw himself into the nearest chair, all signs of levity draining away.

"You don't wish to wed?" Gavin did. Someday. When he found resolution.

Arthington rasped his lips, resulting in a most childish, unrefined noise. "I'll have to. But ..."

"He's waiting for his one true love," Emerlin broke in.

Arth mocked throwing his now-empty cup at his friend. "What are *you* waiting for, Em? Your great love is right under your nose."

Gavin's head swung back and forth as he tried to follow the conversation.

"You know why I cannot." Em grimaced.

Arth crowed. "Because she's too young?"

"Because I must accede to my father's wishes." The marquess had never looked so troubled.

"And you, Cort?" Arth said.

"And I what?"

"Will you get yourself leg-shackled this Season?"

Emerlin smirked. "You're this year's top prize, Cortleon. A handsome, *unmarried* duke, legendary in his prowess and with a mysterious past? No debutante—or her mother— could resist you."

Gavin snorted, taking another drink from his nearly empty glass. "The question is, can I resist her?"

Both men leaned forward. "Her?" they said in unison.

"It's Lady Elinor, isn't it?" Arth added. "I knew it!"

Damn. A slip of the tongue. "It is no one. Not until I fulfill my quest."

"Quest?" Arthington's nose wrinkled, pulling his lip up with it. "Are you perhaps taking your knightly role too far? The masquerade was months ago."

Gavin set his tumbler on a side table. "Perhaps duty is a better word. However you term it, I returned to England for one reason and one reason only: to find the man who assassinated my father."

Arth blew out a long breath. "More than twenty years have passed, Cort. My father searched. The whole of the country searched. The murder of a duke is not taken lightly. They found nothing. You think you can after such a length of time, with nothing to go on?"

"I must. I promised my mother. I made a vow to myself. And upon my honor, I'll see this through."

"But what if you can't?" Em said. "Will you spend your whole life hunting ghosts?"

Ghosts. Yes, his father's ghost haunted him every day. As did the dying figure of his mother, her skin stretched thin over her bones, agony writ in every part of her face. Gavin's throat caught, his heart lurching. His father's death had robbed them of their intended life; she'd done everything she could to save his. "As men of honor, would you not do the same?"

Arthington mused. "I don't know. No love was lost between my father and me."

"Might it not be best to live your own life now, friend?" Emerlin's voice was soft. "Enjoy yourself. Marry. Start your own family. Begin anew. Always chasing after your past will destroy your future."

"What else have I to live for?" Bitterness reinforced every word. "I did not grow up as you did, secure in my place in society. With the assuredness you both possess. With friends."

"You have that now," Arth said.

Gavin snorted. "What have I got?"

"Me," Em answered earnestly. "Arth. Stoneleigh. Keswick and so on. *We're* your friends."

Gavin sucked in a breath, his eyes growing moist. *Good God, he was soused.* He hadn't cried since his mother died. He wasn't going to do so now.

Arthington launched himself from his chair. He raised his arm high as if clutching a sword, tottering on his feet. "We shall be your fellow knights, aiding you in your adventure. If we can. Have you learned anything new?"

"No. I'd hoped your party might shake my memories loose or at least jar *something*. But I have nothing more than what you told me. Given my father's libertine reputation, however, my mother suspected a cuckolded husband." He snarled, pounding his hand on the arm of his chair. "I wish I could *remember*. I was in the field. *I saw the man who shot him*. But the only thing I ever spoke of was a green monster, and Mama said I didn't single out any of the guests."

"Perhaps you were too frightened," Emerlin said. "A child that young? Faced with accusing a murderer?"

"Perhaps." Gavin traced his fingers over his thigh.

"I stand with Arth; we'll help all we can. But ..." Em hesitated. "Consider letting go and moving on. You are not at fault for your father's sins. Nothing can change the past. But you *can* choose your future."

Arth's head swung toward Emerlin. "There are times, Em, when you display a sort of wisdom."

"Surprising, isn't it?"

Gavin stood. Despite the extra drink, he was far steadier on his feet than when he'd first entered the room. The serious turn in the conversation had erased most of the alcohol's effects. "The thing is, the murderer knows exactly who he is, even if I don't. So, you see, the danger is always there. I saw him—and I shot him. Two very good reasons for him to seek me out, don't you think?" He sighed. "My mother slept with one eye open, always shrinking at shadows. I don't want to do the same for the rest of my life." He pulled at his cravat, loosening its folds. "Now you understand why marrying is out of the question. I'll not subject a wife to potential harm. She could be used against me. Or worse, murdered."

"I do think you are overstating things. Believing someone from two decades ago would murder your future wife?" One side of Arth's mouth quirked up. "You can seek out other sorts of female companionship, if nothing else, I suppose. A mistress, maybe."

"No."

"No? Are you saying you've no interest in females? Do you prefer—"

"No, no. I'm definitely one for the female sex. But I vowed to my mother—and myself—I'd never be my father. I will not take any woman to bed who is not my wife. Honor in all things is my highest code."

"I see now why you exert yourself so at sport. You must be in great need of ways to work off that ... energy," Em quipped, before finishing his alcohol.

Arth roared with laughter.

Even Gavin chuckled. "Indeed. Though I don't mind a bit of flirting. Or a kiss at midnight. I'm not dead, after all."

"No. Merely a monk." Arth's eyebrow cocked up. "Like Claremont. Until he fell in love with his wife. You'll have to meet him, Cort. You'd like him."

"And that after swearing he'd never marry again, much less have more children." Emerlin crossed to Cortleon, slinging an arm around his shoulders. "So, you see, one cannot know what the future holds. It's entirely possible one year from now you could be cradling a babe of your own."

Gavin held up his hands. "Gentlemen, when the talk turns to infants, it is time for me to retire."

He strode from the room as steadily as he could, ascending the stairs with gratitude in his heart for these two men who'd become dear friends in a short amount of time. And with images of brown-haired, blue-eyed cherubs, cherubs with beauty marks in the exact same place as their mother's, taunting him the entire way.

CHAPTER 16

$\mathcal{N}$elle claimed a megrim for the next few days, then her monthlies the week after that. In truth, she wanted no part of the social whirl. The morning calls, the afternoon promenades, the evening dinners, and the late-night balls exhausted her. But staying in her room curtailed her visits to the foundling home, too, so she'd forced herself from bed this morning, determined to shake off her gloomy spirits and go about a normal day. A normal day feeling trapped, that was.

Lord Grennet had called with Ashvere the day before. Her mother had pleaded with her to come down, but she'd refused. She shouldn't have, of course, but she'd been out of sorts since the opera, angry at Gavin's dismissive treatment and her own desultory reaction. So what if she hadn't enthralled him? Was she so vain, so spoiled by the years of attention, that she couldn't imagine someone *not* being bedazzled by her?

The idea didn't sit well.

She fastened her redingote before collecting her gloves. She'd much rather walk the distance between here and the

Home—the exercise would do her good—but Mother would never allow it, even in the company of a footman.

"One cannot be too cautious, Elinor. Lady Marthorpe says footpads have been committing atrocities in broad daylight."

Who knew where Lady Marthorpe heard such rumors, but Nelle daren't fight back or Mother might prevent her from going altogether, and she needed to spend time with the children. In the country, she had her small menagerie to care for: cats and rabbits and pups and the occasional squirrel or hedgehog. London's strays were far less friendly than the creatures roaming about Inglewood. Who could blame them? Town made her less amicable, as well, though she honestly enjoyed balls and the theater. This Season, however, everything held an air of finality, which was nonsensical, really. Marriage was not the same as death.

Nelle climbed into the hackney ahead of Polly, the maid her parents insisted accompany her. Normally, she enjoyed chatting with Polly, but today she remained silent, absent-mindedly watching out the window as the cab rumbled through the streets.

She sat straight up at the sight of Gavin riding a gorgeous gray horse. *What was he doing?*

He tipped his hat at several passing coaches and nodded at a group of ladies crossing the street.

Sit back! It wouldn't do to be caught gaping. And yet, she couldn't look away. Just as they were to pass each other, he looked up, his eyes meeting hers. But he didn't touch his hat. He didn't smile. He didn't do anything. And then he was gone.

She threw herself against the squabs. Infernal man. Then again, she'd stared like a child pressing her face against the glass in order to see a spectacle. Tonight, if Lord Grennet were at the Waltham dinner, she'd do her best to encourage him. She wouldn't think about the duke. She wouldn't.

Thankfully, once at the Home, the children chased away any thought of Gavin. Little Nancy had been ill last week, and Nelle was grateful to see her recovered. The number of infants and children who perished in London each year devastated her. She'd witnessed the loss of far too many.

If people knew the harsh realities abandoned children and orphans endured, they'd understand why she'd had to wall part of herself away, lest the sorrow and tragedy lead her into madness. The poor's struggle for basic necessities contrasted with the aristocracy's elaborate dinners, luxurious carriages, and fancy tailcoats and gowns was deplorable. Yet Nelle partook of the latter. She was caught between two worlds.

"It's good you have a heart for the less fortunate, Elinor, but you cannot rescue them all," her mother had said many times. "We are born to our stations in life and each must play his part."

Yes, far too often she felt she was playing a part, living a life not really hers, like the actors and actresses who donned masks every night on the stage—if not literally, then in the characters they assumed. She'd far prefer to spend her days with babies and animals, but she was an earl's daughter and with that came certain expectations.

Her causes were the only thing that had sparked that fire, a true passion, in her—until Gavin. How aggravating. She'd been the belle of the ball, infamous for her refusal of repeated proposals. Why was it only now, as a near spinster, that she'd become infatuated with a man? Only now that desire distracted her at the oddest moments?

What *was* it about the Duke of Cortleon? He was of fine countenance, but to be fair, not nearly as handsome as some. Yet he drew people to him. He drew *her* to him. Was it his seemingly carefree nature? The energy and vitality with which he pulsed? He'd thrown himself into every house party activity with verve and vigor, whether riding, fencing, or playing battledore and shuttlecock. He differed from the majority of peers. Less restrained. More ... free. He was full of life, a fire to her ice. Was that what drew her?

He did everything with a physical intensity she envied; women weren't to exert themselves in such ways. He moved as if he reveled in his own body, his own strength. It'd drawn her eye—and that of nearly every other woman, of course. And the way in which he danced—not like those concerned with maintaining proper posture, or, worse, counting the steps, but more innately. Naturally. He'd swept her into his joyful passion and she'd reveled in it.

She longed for that feeling again. And feared it.

A week later, Lucy-Anne burst into Nelle's room, her hands fluttering in her familiar manner. "Oh, Nelle! I cannot wait! Oh, to see him again."

Nelle glanced in the mirror, her sister reflected next to the maid styling her hair. Lucy-Anne glowed. The deep rose at the waist, hem, and sleeves of her ivory muslin gown complemented her brown hair, which had a ribbon of the same rose encircling it. The color—or the excitement bubbling from her—brought a beautiful pink hue to her skin.

"Didn't he call this morning?"

"Yes, but that was *hours* ago."

"Oh, heavens, Lucy-Anne! You are such a love-stricken goose."

"Love-stricken," her sister murmured, her eyes rounding. "Love-stricken. Yes, yes, I am! I love him. I love Hugh!"

She clapped a hand over her mouth before adding, "I mean Ashvere."

He'd given Lucy-Anne leave to address him by his Christian name? This had taken a serious turn. No doubt her mother would rejoice, but she dreaded the lecture sure to come if she didn't increase her own efforts to land a husband.

"And how went your conversation with Lord Grennet?"

Unabashed interest—and hope—lit Lucy-Anne's face. Nelle had sat with the earl while Lucy-Anne and Ashvere took turns around the drawing room. "He's pleasant."

"Handsome, too, is he not? And he's not so *very* old ..."

She laughed at her sister's barely disguised line of questioning. "Should I summon the minister to tonight's ball or wait until tomorrow to wed him?"

Lucy-Anne clapped her hands thrice, then stilled. "You are teasing?"

"Truly, Lucy-Anne? You think my nuptials imminent when he and I are of such limited acquaintance?"

"But you *are* getting to know him. Surely you'd consider him?"

"You wouldn't find it strange for your sister to become your mother-in-law?" Nelle countered, dodging the question.

"Not at all! Think of how close that would allow us to remain, perhaps even under the same roof!"

"There, milady," the maid said, pinning one final piece of hair atop Nelle's head.

"Lovely as always, Polly. Thank you."

Polly nodded. "Do you wish a necklace or earrings, milady?"

Normally she refused, feeling no need to adorn herself like a fancy dessert for display. Tonight, however, she said yes. Because of Gavin, though she didn't want to admit it. *Who was the goose now?*

She fussed with her bodice, tugging it higher. Her new

gown was far too low-cut for her taste, but her mother insisted it was the height of fashion and might aid her in securing further interest. As if breasts were all that ought to matter in a marital decision.

"A difficult expense to spare, but we must have you looking ..." Her mother had trailed off.

Nelle had been sorely tempted to add, *like a piece of meat offered up to the nearest tomcat?*

At least the gown was green, a deep mint with a sheer overlay of cream silk embroidered with delicate lace flowers.

Polly returned with a selection of her mother's jewels; likely Mother had pressured the maid to get Nelle to acquiesce to them. "The pearls, milady?"

"No. The emeralds."

"A spot of Pear's for your cheeks? The Alkanet?"

"Yes, why not?"

"I knew it!" Lucy-Anne exclaimed.

"Knew what?"

"That you *do* like Lord Grennet. Your attention to appearance proves it."

"Or I'm simply trying to keep up with you, Lucy-Anne. Though you far outshine me tonight."

It wasn't the earl's notice she sought. It was Gavin's. Nelle didn't even know if he'd be in attendance. Ashvere and his father would, however. She must do her best to enchant the earl; far better to set her cap for him than to chase the elusive duke. Lord Grennet didn't fire her blood, but that was for the best. This wild attraction for Gavin was distracting, unsettling, and interfering with her stability. It was inconvenient, uncomfortable, and unrealistic. And it would only lead to heartache.

She closed her eyes as Polly dabbed the tinted powder onto her cheeks. Gavin did not have the makings of an ideal husband. He was too intense. Too passionate. His energy would consume her whole. And he flirted widely, perhaps more. She may not have many demands of a husband, but fidelity was one of them.

"Done, milady."

She opened her lids. The jewels drew attention to her clear, creamy skin, and the coral rouge enhanced the color of her eyes. Tonight, she appreciated her beauty. For she wished to hook Lord Grennet ... while perhaps baiting the Duke of Cortleon. "Thank you, Polly."

The maid dipped a curtsy and left. Nelle rose and laced her arm through Lucy-Anne's.

"Shall we, dear sister?"

CHAPTER 17

"*T*he Earl and Countess of Rutley; the ladies Elinor, Lucy-Anne, Tabitha, and Prudence Greene."

Before the announcement had even finished, Gavin spun to the ballroom's entrance. Nelle. She was here.

Several other gentlemen turned, as well. "Beautiful as ever," whispered one near him. "But as cold as a statue."

"A pity. I like to think I could melt any heart, but not one as hard as marble."

He wanted to punch the overconfident young blade who dared utter such nonsense. Nelle was no statue. He'd held her in his arms. He'd tasted those lips, lips a thousand times softer than the finest leather. He'd seen the fire that intoxicating kiss kindled in her. And the way she'd stared at him through that carriage window, her exquisite eyes never leaving his? No, she was no ice princess. She was a goddess.

And he wanted to touch divinity tonight.

She glided through the room, emeralds glittering at her ears and delicate neck, her dress flowing over her sumptuous figure like cream over strawberries. How he wanted to take a bite. If only she weren't clad in that dreaded green. And yet ... this minty confection looked good enough to eat.

For the first time, his instinctual tensing at the color evaporated. Even the bright green jewels at her throat didn't disturb him. Rather, he'd like to drop kisses onto the ivory flesh they covered.

Ashvere approached to greet Lady Lucy-Anne, blocking Nelle from view. Grennet joined them a second later. Gavin ambled closer and to the side, wanting to see Nelle's face. White teeth gleamed between those sumptuous lips as she laughed at something one of them had said. She looked to the earl, her beatific smile remaining as she touched her fingers to one of her earrings. As Grennet spoke, she stroked her throat as she tilted her head to the side.

She was flirting. With *Grennet*, a man twice her age.

The earl held out his hand, and she placed her gloved fingers into his, allowing him to lead her to the dance floor. A minuet began, and Nelle executed each step gracefully, her form elegant, a bright smile on her face. Something gnawed at Gavin. Something quite unpleasant. He wanted to cock the earl. Wanted to pull her attention away from that oaf and hoard it to himself. Wanted to keep all other men from her. Especially Grennet. He simply did not care for the man.

"I was going to invite you to cards, but I see your attention is happily engaged elsewhere."

He turned at Emerlin's voice, and Em flashed that dimpled grin. Several ladies cooed.

"They drop like flies whenever you near," Gavin teased.

"Oh, they aren't sighing for me, I'm sure. Your legend only grows. Many are whispering of your prowess as a lover."

"*What*?" He hadn't so much as kissed a woman since the masquerade. "But I—No," he stammered. "You know I'd never dishonor a lady in such a way. Why would—"

"Why claim you'd bedded the Duke of Cortleon? Notorious flirt? Man of the Town, a Corinthian buck outperforming every other lord in fencing, boxing, riding, and more? Given your mastery in those areas, is it not natural to assume those skills extend into the bedchamber?"

Gavin's cheeks grew hot. "I didn't realize ..."

"Of course not. But I have because it's drawn attention from me. And for that I'm grateful." Em gave a humorous little bow. "I shall leave you to it."

"You won't dance?"

The Irish lord's face stilled. "There's no one with whom I care to partner at present."

Ah. This Lady Rebecca must not be in attendance. "You'll leave these young ladies disappointed."

"Oh, no." Em's blue eyes sparkled with mischief. "I'll leave them all to you. The Legendary Duke."

Gavin sighed as Emerlin slipped through the crush. He was about to follow when the music stopped. Nelle dipped a curtsy to Grennet just as Lady Tabitha neared and said something to her. The earl gave a polite bow before walking off toward a quartet of older gentlemen. The two sisters spoke for a moment, and then Lady Tabitha scampered away. To where, Gavin didn't know—nor did he care. His only interest was the goddess before him.

He quickly crossed the few feet separating them, lest she depart before he could speak with her. When Nelle spied him, her eyes rounded and one hand went to her bosom, that sumptuous expanse of flesh rising from the gown irritatingly concealing the rest of her. Not that he'd want her exposed to the other men in the room. *Not that you should want her exposed to you.* But he did. Oh, yes, he did. Still, thought and action were not the same. Surely one dance was not a danger. He bowed before her. "Lady Elinor."

"Your Grace."

Her voice was cool, but the fluttering of the little vein in her neck betrayed her. She was not as collected as she appeared.

"Would you grant me the honor of the next dance?" He kept his gaze firmly on her face, lest it dip lower, where it didn't belong. Red tinged her cheeks. Was it a reaction to him or to the fact that they were currently the subjects of curious glances?

She bit her lip as if considering, and it took everything in him not to groan at the seductive sight. "Yes."

The word was soft but decisive.

He held out one hand, fingers up, and she placed her own in it. Before he led her to the floor, however, he raised hers to his lips, pressing a lingering kiss to her gloved knuckles. Whispering erupted around them as she snatched it back.

"Are you mad?" she hissed, the tiny v between her brows making her displeasure clear.

He swung his arm in a grand gesture. "My apologies, my lady," he said, loudly enough for others to hear. "That is how we pay homage in Italy to those of great beauty."

People tittered, but he ignored them as the strains of a waltz began. He took her hand once more, careful to adopt the appropriate, respectable form. As respectable as a waltz could be, that was; many, especially of the older generations, did not approve of partners holding each other at the shoulder and waist and remaining coupled for the duration of the intimate dance.

He'd never been so in favor of the waltz as he was right now.

"You are a goddess," he murmured as they turned.

"Come now, Your Grace. The masked ball is long over. We've seen each other for who we really are, and it's clear what you think of me." Her forehead creased as if she lamented her revealing words.

"What I think of you? How do you know what I think of you?"

Her emerald ear bobs dangled enticingly. How he longed to press his lips below them, to the place where her neck met her jaw.

She snorted, the unexpected sound catching him off guard. "You've gone out of your way to avoid me since the very night of the masquerade. You obviously regretted our —our *exchange* that evening. You've made no secret of your feelings."

"You think I regret that kiss?" He clutched at her waist, drawing her closer, then leaned in, his lips closer to her ear than they ought to have been. "Do you?"

She stumbled but quickly found her footing again. They sailed through another two turns before she spoke. "I do not understand you, sir."

Her forehead wrinkled again, and her tongue darted out to wet her lips. How he wished to join his own with them, or to kiss her brow, to smooth her cares away. Instead, he muttered, "That makes two of us."

Unexpectedly, she laughed.

He raised a brow.

She shrugged. "What else can I do? This is doubtless one of the most absurd situations in which I've ever found myself."

"Absurd?"

"Of course! We do not know each other, and yet we've exchanged intimacies. You've eschewed me since, only to attempt now to work your wiles on me, as on many other women."

"Work my wiles?" He made a misstep, nearly trodding on her slippered foot. "A man does not have wiles."

"You do. And you wield them with careless ease. Your reputation precedes you, Your Grace."

His lips pulled into a line. "Don't believe everything you hear about me, Goddess."

"Likewise. And don't call me that."

"Goddess? Why not? I would think you'd see it as a compliment."

"That proves you know me not at all."

"So, tell me."

Her eyebrow winged up. "Tell you what?"

"Tell me about you. And why you are no goddess."

"Whatever for?"

"Because," he whispered, his eyes never leaving hers, "I find I want to know."

❧

NELLE SHIVERED, though she was far from cold. What a dashing figure Gavin cut in his ebony kerseymere coat, pantaloons, and gray silk waistcoat. His starched white cravat bore a lion's head pin with ruby eyes. Above the cravat lay a hint of bare throat and then that masculine jaw, shades darker than her own skin. His hair brushed his coat collar, and the impulse to smooth it back nearly over-whelmed her.

Someone must have added spirits to the lemonade. That was the only explanation. One moment she'd been doing her best to encourage Lord Grennet, and the next, she was in Gavin's arms, gliding through a waltz. Why had she said yes? Then again, had she refused, wouldn't that have caused a stir, as at the house party?

More of a stir than a duke kissing your hand in the middle of a crowded ball? Though the Malford ball was a private affair, upwards of one hundred people were in attendance. And this was no Twelfth Night masquerade. No excuse for such untoward behavior could be found here. He'd shrugged it off as a difference in culture, but would others accept that? Did she?

What was he about? This sudden attention should vex her, and yet surely, she could enjoy this one dance. When the music ended, they'd part. The evening would resume its tiresome regularity, this interlude all but forgotten—by others, at least. Likely by him, as well. She'd never forget. Not with what he did to her.

Her pulse pounded. She longed with a fervor she'd never known to taste him once more, right here. She wouldn't, of course. The scandal would devastate her family, and it would mean nothing to a man like him. She'd heard whisperings of whom he'd bedded. A Don Juan, just as Mother had said. It made her heart ache. But for this moment, what harm could it do to pretend she was once again that goddess and he her knight—hers alone? What harm could it do?

Plenty. He'd distracted her from the earl. He'd distracted her since their midnight kiss, consuming far too many of her thoughts. He had her wanting what would only lead to heartbreak. For this enigmatic duke had managed to thaw her just enough that she was *feeling.* And as when a limb falls asleep and then comes awake to stabbing pins and needles, so, too, this awakening pained her. She desired when she did not wish to, especially not this man, for whom a kiss was insignificant. Better to aim for a light, teasing, meaningless exchange.

"For I'm neither Greek nor Roman, of course," she said in delayed answer to his question. She inched away, setting a more proper distance between them. "Nor immortal. A mere woman. Not one who could keep up with a legend like you."

"There's nothing *mere* about you, Lady Elinor." He dropped his hands from her person and stepped back as the music came to an end. "And you truly shouldn't believe everything you hear."

What did he mean? She'd opened her mouth to ask when Lord Grennet stepped in front of him. Nelle sucked in a breath at the slight.

"May I beg another dance, Lady Elinor?"

She peered around the earl to Gavin. A scowl marred his face.

Lord Grennet turned, as well. "Oh, Your Grace. I most humbly beg your pardon. I thought you'd finished with Lady Elinor. I didn't mean to usurp you."

His words were amicable enough, contrite, even. Yet had his voice held a hint of challenge?

The men took each other's measure for what seemed an eternity. Why couldn't they let her make her escape, rather than leave her here like a bone over which two dogs were fighting? She stifled a laugh at the image of Lord Grennet as a Scottish terrier and Gavin a wolfhound.

"Of course you didn't," Gavin answered, his expression nonchalant, though his voice held a similar edge. He broke into a devilish grin. "But whoever could say they were finished with an incomparable such as Lady Elinor? Certainly not I." He looked to her, his eyes smoldering. With anger? Desire? "I look forward to getting an honest answer to my question."

Without further acknowledgment of the earl, he gave her a courtly bow before walking off in the opposite direction, the crowd parting as he sailed through the room. She couldn't help but watch his retreating form. As he exited, several women made noises of disappointment. It was all she could do not to join them.

A finger tapped her shoulder and she spun around. Lord Grennet's mouth was a thin line, scarcely visible through his beard. He held out his hand.

She took it.

~

Rage simmered beneath his skin, but Bertie pasted on a courteous smile. "Thank you for agreeing to a second dance, Lady Elinor. I treasure time with you."

He clenched his jaw, grinding his teeth so tightly pain shot through to his cheekbones. Cortleon had looked at Lady Elinor as if he wished to devour her, the same way his loathsome father had at Albina when they'd kissed and caressed each other in that field, heedless of her marriage vows. Heedless of Bertie. How he'd wanted to kill them both in that moment. But he couldn't. Not his beloved Bee, heavy with child. And now Lady Elinor, like his wife, was succumbing to Cortleon's spell. The man, like his sire, was the seductive serpent in the garden.

Bertie rubbed at his shoulder, counting silently in an effort to calm himself. The music began, and he executed his steps, mindful not to bruise Lady Elinor's fingers, though given how she'd kept her eyes on the debauched duke, perhaps she deserved it.

"Are you all right, my lord?"

"Of course."

"You were frowning just now. I hope I've not done something to offend."

Such as ogle Cortleon?

"A woman of the highest virtue and honor could never cause offense, my lady. Though might I express a word of caution? Some gentlemen are not all that they seem."

Lady Elinor's lips narrowed, but she turned to follow the next figure of the cotillion, and when she rejoined him her expression was nothing but congenial. *Good.* A woman who could control her emotions. Albina could not deny her passions. Her exuberance in all things had charmed him until he'd learned the extent to which that ardor ran. And until she'd lost that vitality, Loughton Knight even in death taking every bit of Bee from him.

This Cortleon would not do the same.

As the dance ended, he made a knee. "You are the crown jewel of English society, Lady Elinor Greene." Taking her fingers as Cortleon had done, he brought them to his lips, setting a firm, protracted kiss on the top of her gloved hand. *There.* Let that replace the actions of that miscreant. And let Bertie make clear his claim on the lady, for she was the prize. *His* prize.

He'd do whatever it took to capture her.

CHAPTER 18

$\mathcal{N}$elle lay abed the next morning, her head swimming. Why had Gavin sought her out and spoken to her in such an impassioned manner? Why had he kissed her hand but then abruptly left her to Lord Grennet? Not entirely abruptly, perhaps; there'd been those uncomfortable few moments while each man had assessed the other. If they'd puffed out their chests and beat on them like apes, she'd not have been surprised.

Why had they engaged with each other at all? Gavin had no interest in her. No lasting one, at least. If he had, he'd not have been so quick to make light of his actions at both the masquerade and the Malford ball. Lord Grennet, on the other hand, had made his intentions clear, especially with that kiss to her knuckles—and with no pretense of denying what it might signify. If he'd meant to erase her memory of Gavin's mouth on the thin fabric covering her skin, he'd failed. Why did the duke's touch elicit such a heated response whereas Lord Grennet's lips had done nothing but mildly shock her?

Both men had complimented her beauty. How tiresome. More than once she'd wished she were ugly. Then people would value her for her character, not her countenance. Had she not this face and figure, perhaps she'd be left well enough alone. As it was, however, her parents' ultimatum rang in her ears.

"We'd hoped for a connection at the house party, of course," her mother had repeated last night, "though apparently your charms, while enough to provoke the Duke of Cortleon into that disgraceful kiss, were not enough to win his lasting affections or those of anyone else. But now it's the middle of the Season, Elinor." Lady Rutley set her hands on her hips. "Lucy-Anne has caught the attention of Lord Ashvere and even Tabitha has several beaus pressing suit. What do you have?"

Nelle could only sputter in response.

Her mother stared at her, chin up, eyebrows raised.

"Mother." She took a breath, clenching her fists at her sides. "You needn't wait for me to wed in order for my sisters to do so!"

"Of course, we do."

"Many families have daughters who remain spinsters."

Lady Rutley sucked in her cheeks. "*This* family shall not. It's a matter of pride."

"Of *pride*? Whose? Yours? Mine?" Nelle's shoulders shook with anger. If her visible distress moved her mother, the woman didn't show it.

"Pride in the family name. Each daughter must make the best match and obtain the best marriage settlement possible."

"It's not pride. It's *money*, isn't it?"

"Money means nothing until you don't have it." Her mother inched closer, so near that the odor of fish on her breath was unmistakable. "And you'll not have it if you don't marry. We'll provide you no further funds if you're not betrothed before your next birthday, Elinor. December is long enough. We've granted you a full year after our initial request. Most parents would not be so generous, especially with a daughter already twenty-five."

"Mother!" Nelle sank onto a nearby chair. "You can't mean it!"

"I am sorry, my dear, but sometimes we must do things we wished we did not. I did not want to marry your father."

"Is that why you're doing this? So that I, so that *someone*, will suffer as much as you have? You, an earl's wife, in your fine gowns and your grand country home?"

"I was to marry a marquess!" her mother shrieked, all hint of composure gone. "But he'd run himself in on the tables, so my father forbade it. I married Rutley instead. And look where we are. In the same financial ruin! That 'grand' country home is gone! I will not bear it. I will see my daughters well married and our fortunes restored."

Nelle gazed dully at the worn carpet. "Do you care nothing for us, Mother? So little that you'd barter us for gold?"

"Don't be absurd. Of course, I wish my girls happy." Her mother's lips twitched. "And you could have been happy. You've had London society at your beck and call from the moment of your debut, and yet you've turned every suitor down, one by one, even Lord Bonstaff, who, though only a baron, possesses wealth to match that of Croesus. You'd have been well set, Elinor. Your family, too. But no, you've been selfish. Only ever selfish, wanting to help those less fortunate without once ever considering helping us!" Angry splotches of red rose on her cheeks as she spoke, her voice cutting like a knife.

Nelle didn't move, even after her mother stalked out with one final grunt. How long she sat there, she didn't know, but the same thought reverberated through her head: *was she so very selfish?*

She'd always believed herself a generous soul. She'd regularly given the Home her own funds to aid with expenses. She'd even considered selling a necklace or two if she could have been sure her family wouldn't find out.

Why hadn't her mother sold the family's jewels? No doubt to keep up appearances. And if things were as dire as her mother alleged, a necklace or two wouldn't bring in enough to make a difference.

Shaking off memories of that painful conversation, Nelle rolled over in her bed. It'd come to this: choose herself or her family. If she opted for the selfish choice, she'd lose. She'd be cast off completely, like a foundling.

Nonsense! Shame enveloped her like a smothering shawl. Her current situation in no way compared to that of abandoned babies. She'd had twenty-five years of familial love and material comfort.

She'd agreed to find a husband, but had pushed it off, hoping her parents would reconsider. How naïve. How selfish. Her mother was right. It was time for her to live up to her obligations to her family, not just to the Home.

A scratch came at the door. "Nelle?"

Lucy-Anne. Nelle flung an arm over her eyes. She didn't wish to converse with her sister, sure that Lucy-Anne wanted nothing but to gush over the dashing Ashvere, for he'd kissed her again and she couldn't be happier.

Nelle could. If before she'd felt the prize goose, today she felt the poor rabbit caught up in a trap, with nowhere to go and no way to make a sound. But she'd been selfish long enough; she could at least allow her sister to share her bliss, even if she couldn't join in the emotion herself. "Come!"

Lucy-Anne peeked around the door. "Are you ill? You've been abed clear through breakfast."

Nelle swallowed. She didn't wish to lie to her sister, but she couldn't confess the truth, either. "Fatigued from recent events, is all. You know you're more suited to the social whirl than I."

"Good." Lucy-Anne raced to the bed, launching herself next to Nelle. "He wants to marry me. Hugh wants to *marry* me!"

Nelle's mouth dropped, but no sounds emerged.

Lucy-Anne bobbed her head. "I know, is it not too fantastical to believe?"

Joy for her sister battled with a weariness that had nothing to do with physical fatigue. Her parents would never allow it unless Nelle married first. And unlike Lucy-Anne, no one had proposed to her as of late. Not yet, anyway.

Lord Grennet had been increasingly attentive. If she made more effort to entice him, surely she could persuade him to make an offer. How horrid that made her sound, as if she were a snake charmer. The earl was no snake!

On the other hand, his recent interactions with Gavin troubled her. Why? Suitors had fought over her before. But sometimes there seemed an edge to the earl, visible only in the briefest of moments, in the shadows of his words. If one blinked, one missed them.

What nonsense. She was finding excuses again. Lord Grennet had been nothing but kind to her. He remained the ideal candidate. "Has Ashvere talked to Father?"

Lucy-Anne rubbed her hands over the wrinkled coverlet as if to smooth out any challenges to her happiness. "Not yet. But Father will approve, won't he? Hu—I mean, Ashvere is titled. And someday he'll be Earl."

"Yes, but not for years. His father is in good health and Ashvere young—as are you."

Lucy-Anne laughed. "I'm already twenty! Many of my friends married at eighteen or nineteen. And he's not so young; he's turned twenty-four!"

And I, twenty-five. "You're right. But why not enjoy more time with this secret? That way you and Hugh can become more thoroughly acquainted."

Lucy-Anne scoffed. "I know him well enough."

"I meant no offense, but it's been mere weeks."

"*Months*." The stubborn set of Lucy-Anne's jaw was unmistakable. "Two weeks at the house party and now six weeks here in London. That makes two months."

"And you believe that sufficient time to make such an important decision? Marriage is permanent. Forever."

"You think I don't know that?" Lucy-Anne clasped one of Nelle's hands. "I know Mother and Father aren't happy. But some marriages are. You saw the Duke and Duchess of Claremont at the Redbury ball. I believe Hugh and I will have such a marriage. I believe it with all my heart."

"I don't doubt you do, but just last autumn you wanted to wed Lord Stoneleigh."

Her sister waved a hand. "That lasted less than a week once I experienced his taciturn nature for myself. I need someone with spirit. I need *Hugh*."

"Then I truly hope you shall get him. But..." Nelle bit her lip.

"But what?"

"Surely you remember Mother and Father's ultimatum?"

"That I—that none of us—may marry until you do?"

"Yes."

"Horsefeathers. Hugh has funds. He'll help us. He's promised as much."

"Ah, but will his father let him? As Earl, he controls the purse strings."

Lucy-Anne looked down, puckering her lips. Her eyes raised slowly as a smile spread across her face. "You simply must marry him. That would solve our problems!"

Yes. Yes, it would. So why was she still fighting against it?

"That assumes too much, dear sister. But ..." Nelle bit her lip again, the words not wanting to come out. Once said, she couldn't take them back. Yet she must salvage not only her family's fortunes but also Lucy-Anne's hope at happiness. "I shall encourage the earl. I agree he's the best choice for me, especially given the ... situation."

Lucy-Anne shrieked and threw her arms around her sister. "Oh, this will be perfect. We'll all be so happy!"

If that were the case, why did Nelle feel like crying?

CHAPTER 19

"*M*y mother received a letter from her friend, the Dowager Duchess of Engelsfell." Arthington waved a paper in the air. "She says the duchess has been ill, which kept her from responding more promptly to my mother's request."

He handed the letter to Gavin before sitting down in his usual chair. They were waiting in Arthington's drawing room for Emerlin to join them for an outing to Tattersall's, as Arth had his eye on a new bay.

Gavin furrowed his brow. Why should he care about this elder duchess?

"You may read it." Arth waved an imperial hand.

Suppressing a snicker, Gavin scanned the message's contents.

My dearest Irene,

How I miss you. I was most disappointed to miss the house party, as well, but my stomach pains have not relented. Most days I remain abed.

You asked if I remember particulars from that ill-fated party. How awful it was! I still think of the horrors that poor boy witnessed. It is no wonder Anna took him from the country.

Anna? This duchess had known his mother well enough to call her by her Christian name? Mama had listed Engelsfell among the English dukes and duchesses, of course, but hadn't mentioned a personal connection.

I consulted my notes of that year—for you know I keep records on everything. I'm certain that is why you asked me. I transcribe exactly, in case any detail be of interest:

A grand fete, as always. Lord M openly smitten with Lady C ... a betrothal likely. Arthington's cook Mrs. Fay outdid herself; such a Yorkshire pudding, and the fowl! But, oh, the terror of New Yrs Eve. The Duke of Cortleon MURDERED. Discovered by his son. Wynhawke could not say who'd done the monstrous deed. Arthington took things well in hand but found nothing. Many of us thought to leave, fear weighing heavy, but a sudden snow bound us two days. Grennet chafed to remove Albina, who felt poorly on account of the babe. A surprise she came, being near her time. Such a vivacious wit! This likely ends Irene's Christmas parties.

Reading again of the tragedy rouses so many emotions, does it not? And then Albina's death so soon thereafter! Poor Ashvere, to lose his mother when he was only months old, and to laudanum. I'd warned her against its dangers. She insisted she'd stopped. How sad. Is it any wonder Grennet nearly went mad with grief? How many lives that foul formulation has ruined; that is one reason I refuse it, though my pain increases.

And now the younger Cortleon has returned. You must tell me of him, though Percy will meet him soon, as I've convinced him to return to Town. He does not wish to leave me, but Deandra should not miss out on the joys of London—and the chance of a good match—on my account.

Give my love to James. Has he any intention yet of taking a wife? I suppose not, or you'd have told me. I live for such news, for at this age, what else is there?

Yr ever-affectionate friend,

Minerva

He looked to Arth. "I see nothing here that sheds any light."

"I thought not, either, but wanted you to read it in case anything would be meaningful to you. I'm sorry it yields no new information."

Something tickled at the back of Gavin's mind. He studied the paper once more. "You said Grennet's wife died from complications relating to Ashvere's birth."

Arth nodded. "That's what Mother told me."

"She said nothing of laudanum?"

"Not that I recall. But remember, I was a child."

Gavin gnawed at his thumb. Grennet's wife died within months of the party at which his own father had lost his life. A party at which the earl had been present and from which he'd wanted to hurry away. Gavin's thoughts spun. Lady Grennet had been heavy with child. Even his rake of a father wouldn't have ... Unless the child ... No. Ashvere was the spitting image of his father.

This line of thought was ridiculous. He was springing at shadows, looking for connections that weren't there.

Emerlin swept into the room. "How do I look?" he said, spreading his arms wide. "Handsome?"

"If by handsome you mean like a strutting peacock, then yes," Arth retorted.

Emerlin ran his hands over his blue superfine coat then adjusted his red cravat. "I can't have Cort draw *all* the ladies' attention, can I? I do have a reputation to uphold."

Arth snorted. "A reputation I thought you didn't want."

Em shrugged. "Old habits die hard. Shall we to Tattersall's?"

They looked to Gavin.

"Yes, let's. I do enjoy a fine horse."

Arthington's eyes rounded in mock horror. "You're not thinking of replacing Gringolet, are you?" He paused as if considering. "Then again, if you return him to me, we might avoid Tattersall's and retire immediately to White's."

"Not on your life." Gavin rose from his chair and returned the letter.

"It was worth a try," Arth said, tucking it into his coat before clapping Emerlin on the shoulder. "Good news! Engelsfell is coming up to Town."

"Meaning there'll be even fewer ladies for me?" Em quipped.

"Now you know how I feel."

Gavin chuckled as he followed them out. What diversions they provided. *But not too many diversions.*

His quest came first.

∾

"FATHER, I wish to ask for Lady Lucy-Anne Greene's hand, with your blessing."

Bertie looked up from his desk in the study. Hugh stood before him, pulling at the bottoms of his coat sleeves. The boy was nervous.

Boy. He studied his son. Though not as tall as he was, Hugh still topped most other gentlemen, and his chest was nearly as brawny as Bertie's own. No, Hugh was a boy no longer. He was a man. When had that happened? "You're too young to marry."

Hugh's brow rose. "Too young? I'm twenty-four! You met my mother at the same age."

"Met, yes. Married, no. Though I pleaded, my parents

insisted I give it at least a year or two more to determine if my passion was lasting or momentary." He tapped his fingertips together. He'd dutifully waited. His hunger for Albina had never wavered, however. How he'd looked forward to their few stolen moments, the kisses and occasional caresses. He'd never pushed her, for she was an innocent. So he'd thought. If only he'd seen her for the two-faced whore she was before they'd tied the knot. His love had blinded him. He'd not allow his son to make the same mistake.

"Then we shall form a betrothal but wait to marry. Surely that would satisfy you?"

"I think it better for you to gain more ... experience ... before you make such a promise."

"I do not want *experience*, Father. I want Lucy-Anne." His son's voice rang with disgust.

Bertie nearly slammed his hand on the desk. *Victory*. He'd raised a man of honor. Not like Loughton Knight—or his son. But now was not the time for levity. "Hugh," he said, softening his tone. "Rutley would likely refuse, anyway."

"Why? I am everything respectable in a gentleman and a future earl, to boot."

He winced. His son's reference to his eventual demise was as painful as it was true. "Of course. But Rutley is deep in debt and needs his daughters to marry into money."

"I *have* wealth!"

"No," Bertie shot back, his voice rising. "*I* have wealth; you live at *my* pleasure."

Hugh approached the desk. "I don't understand. I thought you approved of my attentions to Lady Lucy-Anne."

His words were calm, but his face was not. Red mottled his cheeks and neck, and his jaw twitched.

Did Hugh have his same temper? Bertie had thought

not, as he'd never seen Hugh act this way. Then again, never before had he given his son cause. He'd tended toward overindulgence in atonement for Hugh's lack of a mother, even as he'd insisted on a strict regimen of studies to train his heir in both academic subjects and in the gentleman's code. "I didn't curb your attentions because I didn't think you'd take it this far this fast."

Hugh threw up his hands. "What else were you to think? What else was *she* to think?"

Bertie drummed his fingers on the desk but said nothing. His patience was wearing thin.

"I am a man grown," Hugh bit out. "A man of station. Viscount Ashvere. I believe I ought to control a share of our fortune. And I believe I should be able to wed whom I please."

"If you marry without my blessing, you also marry without my fortune. And unless you intend to commit patricide, you will remain under my control for years to come."

Hugh spat and sputtered, a vein throbbing in his temple. With one final glare, he stormed from the room.

Bertie exhaled forcefully as he leaned back in his chair, waiting for his ire to cool. He did hate to disappoint his only son, but far more was at play here than an infatuation. He could allow Hugh and Lady Lucy-Anne to marry, of course, and bestow on them enough largesse to rescue Rutley from any level of debt. But if he did so, he'd lose Lady Elinor's interest. He was not so naïve as to think her naturally attracted to a man nearly thirty years her senior, especially given her disinterest in any suitor so far. Lady Rutley had undoubtedly nudged her eldest daughter in his direction.

It had amused him at first. He'd had no wish to remarry, though he admired Lady Elinor for her wit, her comportment, and her sincere devotion to her charity work. She was everything Bee was not, despite their physical resemblance. But anything beyond pleasantly diverting dinner conversation hadn't crossed his mind until the miscreant duke had stolen her attention, just like his father had Albina's love. Until Cortleon had kissed Nelle in front of a crowd then dismissed her as meaningless, just like his father had dismissed Bertie.

He ought to have left well enough alone. He'd avoided discovery. No one suspected the truth. And yet, he couldn't. Not when this vile young rakehell had swept back into English society, taking up a status and reputation he hadn't earned. He'd become society's darling, the toast of the Town. The Legendary Duke. Just like his libertine father.

Bertie had defended his own honor in ridding the world of the previous duke and Albina. He'd not let history repeat. *This* Cortleon would not corrupt another innocent woman. No, Cortleon would not win *this* prize.

The duke desired Lady Elinor. He had at Camlon; he did still. That made marriage attractive to Bertie in a way it hadn't been since he'd spotted his wife in the woods copulating with Loughton Knight. Yes, by marrying Lady Elinor, he'd not only acquire a wife of impeccable reputation, noticeable intellect, and noble heart, but he'd deny Cortleon the woman he wanted.

That thrilled him most of all.

~

"GOOD HEAVENS, Lucy-Anne, whatever is the matter?" Nelle raced to her sister, who lay sobbing against the wall in the far corner of her chamber. Sitting down, she pulled Lucy-Anne into her arms.

"He won't let us marry!"

Nelle frowned. "Who?"

"L—Lord Grennet! He's forbidden it!"

"What?" She pulled back to see Lucy-Anne's face. Her sister's red eyes and puffy, tear-stained cheeks tore at her heart.

"Hugh asked permission to request my hand, and his father forbade it."

Lord Grennet had refused a union between his son and Lucy-Anne? That made no sense. He himself had commented on their affection for one another. And he and his son had made several morning calls in which Ashvere was obviously paying suit. Had something happened to change the earl's good opinion of Lucy-Anne? Or of her? She *had* rudely turned her back to him as she'd stared after Gavin. Had that damaged *Lucy-Anne's* standing with Lord Grennet?

She closed her eyes. *Oh, please not.* What her mother would say if she'd ruined two matches with one blow. "Did he give an explanation?"

"H-He said Hugh is too young. That we must wait two years!" Her sister's sobs increased. "*Two years,* Nelle. Mother will never allow me to wait that long."

"So, he didn't ban it entirely."

"He might as well have. He swore to cut Hugh off entirely should he marry without permission!" Lucy-Anne sniffed. "He doesn't approve of me. Why else would he do this?" She dashed a hand across her cheeks. "Why does he not approve? Damn him! Damn him to hell!"

Nelle sucked in a breath. Her sister had never spoken thusly. "Lucy-Anne!"

"Why would he get in the way of a marriage that will make his son so happy? We are in *love.* Am I such a poor match for an earl's son? My own father is an earl!"

Lucy-Anne extracted herself from Nelle's embrace and leaned against the wall, her head lolling to the side. "If I cannot marry him, I shall *die.*"

"Oh, come," Nelle countered, annoyance lacing her

words. "Do be sensible. I understand that your affections for Ashvere run deep, as do his for you. If that's the case, two years of being in love doesn't sound so awful to me."

"It wouldn't to *you*. *You've* never been in love!"

She gasped. Lucy-Anne's words stung more than they ought to. But they held truth; Nelle had never felt anything near approaching what had Lucy-Anne in its clutches. Except on that Twelfth Night, underneath blazing candles and mistletoe, when she'd kissed a knight at midnight. When she'd kissed Gavin. But that wasn't love. That was desire. The two differed.

What would it be like to combine physical passion with deep admiration? With the giving of one's whole heart? Not that it mattered. She'd never know. She'd set her cap for Lord Grennet and while she held a friendly respect for him, that was all. At the moment, though, she simmered with anger toward the earl. Why would he refuse Hugh's request? Did he think Lucy-Anne a fortune hunter?

Nelle sagged against the wall herself. Wasn't that the truth? Neither she nor her sisters had any sizable dowry to offer, and each must make good matches for the sake of their parents' situation as well as their own. And soon. A two-year delay was impossible. They hadn't the time to wait.

At least she didn't. She chewed on a finger. She'd pinned her hopes on Lord Grennet. She'd thought him enamored of her. They'd spent a few evenings in conversation and shared several dances. In total, however, their interactions amounted to less than two full days, if that. How vain to believe she could catch the widowed earl at will because other gentlemen had always schooled around her.

Except Gavin. With Gavin, she was the fish desperate for any bait he offered.

Her sister snapped around, spearing her with an

accusatory stare. "Oh, why couldn't you have *married* already, Nelle?"

Nelle flinched. "From whence comes this attack?"

Lucy-Anne huffed. "If you'd married and saved us from the brink of ruin, Lord Grennet wouldn't worry for his own fortune. He must think me after money, especially as Father's struggles have become known." She crossed her arms, jutting out her chin. "I'm *not*. Hugh and I wouldn't need much on which to live. We could wait it out until ... until Hugh was Earl, if we had guaranteed financial security from *our* side."

Nelle leapt to her feet. "Why must *I* be the sacrificial lamb?" she bellowed, throwing her arms in the air. "Why must *I* be the one to save this family?"

At length, Lucy-Anne whispered, "I'm sorry. I shouldn't have spoken so. It's wretchedly unfair. Every bit of it."

Nelle didn't respond, long-suppressed emotion propelling her back and forth across the chamber. It *was* unfair. Why must she atone for her father's sins? Why must she accede to her mother's demand she marry before any of her younger sisters? Anger ate at her, her very flesh tingling with fury. Was *this* why she wanted to rescue everyone else? Because she'd somehow always known she couldn't save herself?

Mayhap she should just walk into White's and offer herself to any man willing to pay her father's price. That'd save her family and set her free, as it'd ruin any chances of her making a decent match. She cackled, a high sound she'd never made before. The idea of prostituting herself had never occurred to her, and yet wasn't it what her parents' demands amounted to?

"Nelle?"

She turned.

Lucy-Anne had risen from the floor and was shaking

out her skirts. "What if ... what if you spoke to Lord Grennet?"

Nelle snorted. "I doubt I hold any influence with him."

"I disagree. I believe he feels something for you."

"If that were the case, why would he deny my sister her happiness?"

Lucy-Anne shoved at a lock of loose hair. "I don't know. But would you consider it, at least?"

Nelle's shoulders dropped. "I will. For you. *If* I should see him again."

"Thank you."

"At present, however, may we leave this sad matter and see what our other sisters are up to?"

Lucy-Anne nodded then followed her through the door. "I do so wish you could be in love, Nelle," she said as they descended the stairs. "It's the grandest of feelings. Like ... floating. Like you and he are the only two people in the world, your only wish to be with him. To kiss him!" She giggled. "I want to kiss him again and again until the end of time. Kissing is so grand!"

Memories of a night not so long ago and yet so far away, of a dance, of a look, of a kiss at midnight, attacked Nelle. Curse the man. He hounded her day and night.

Lucy-Anne turned at the bottom step. "You kissed the Duke of Cortleon. Was it anything like that? Or must it be someone you love?"

Yes, it was everything like that. Grand didn't even begin to describe it. But she shook her head in response; some things were too private to share, even with her sister.

They entered the drawing room, where Tabby was tying on her bonnet. "Ah, there you are! Pru and I are off to Gunther's for an ice. Would you like to join us?" As they neared, she ran to Lucy-Anne, touching her fingers to her sister's still-red cheeks. "Whatever is the matter?"

Lucy-Anne looked to Nelle as always, waiting for her sister to rescue her.

"We're allowed to have some secrets from each other, are we not?" Nelle quipped.

"I suppose," Tabby sulked.

Pru hurried into the room, tugging on a glove. "Why do you want to go *now,* Tabby?" she grumbled without looking up. "It's because Lord Farnham mentioned he might take his sister for ices today, isn't it?" She stumbled to a stop at realizing she and Tabby weren't the only ones in the room.

"Aha!" cried Nelle. "I see you have a secret of your own."

"Not anymore." Tabby's voice was petulant.

"Come, come, dear sisters." Nelle looped her arms through Tabby and Lucy-Anne's. "Let's away to drown our troubles in lemon ice."

"I was hoping for mint," said Lucy-Anne.

"And Tabby is hoping for a serving of green eyes." Pru tittered.

It wasn't Lord Farnham who leapt to Nelle's mind at her sister's words, of course. It was Gavin and his amaretto irises.

Even more unnerving was the thought that she might enjoy licking him more than an ice.

CHAPTER 20

*G*avin wiped his face with a towel, clearing away the sweat sparring with Percy Valfort, Duke of Engelsfell, had drawn forth. The two had only met the previous week, but they'd taken an instant liking to each other, not in the least because both relished fierce training. Engelsfell actually held the advantage in pugilism, but with time, Gavin was convinced he could take the man on, though Engelsfell had a good four inches on him in height. Their fencing skills, however, were equitable—and far superior to most, which is why they'd drawn such a crowd at Angelo's.

"Shall we have another go?" Gavin's chest heaved, the exertion of the past hour—or had it been two?—making itself felt in his shoulder.

A chorus of cheers went up from the men around them, who immediately exchanged bets, but Engelsfell held up his hands. "I do not concede defeat, Cortleon," he said. "I merely concede that I'm to meet my sister at the modiste."

"Are you seeking a new gown, Your Grace?" chirped a gentleman.

The tall duke swung around, grinning wickedly as he

pressed the tip of his rapier to the man's coat then trailed the blade down, hovering it just above the man's privates. "Say that again, Wingate, and you shall forever be in need of one yourself."

Wingate blanched.

Arthington clapped the man on the back. "Never fear, Wingate. Engelsfell talks big, but he's one of the most soft-hearted men I know."

Engelsfell threw up his free hand even as he lowered his weapon. "How is that helping to defend my manly reputation?"

Chuckles surrounded them.

"Shall we see you in the park this afternoon, Engelsfell?" Arth asked while the other two dukes divested themselves of their fencing gear.

"What is it with you and parading about Hyde Park? If I didn't know better, I'd swear you fancied yourself a king."

"Don't let Prinny hear you say such," Emerlin interjected.

Engelsfell chortled as he batted away the fencing mask Arth chucked at him. "In any case, yes, I shall be there. In a carriage. With my sister. Because my task this Season appears to be chaperone—and matchmaker."

"For yourself or for Lady Deandra?"

Engelsfell poked Emerlin in the arm at his comment.

Contentment spread through Gavin as they exited Angelo's School of Arms. Was there anything better in the world than true friendship?

Nelle's Sevres blue eyes and honey-sweet lips whispered *possibly* the entire way down Bond Street.

～

WHEN LORD GRENNET called that morning to invite Lucy-Anne for a carriage ride with his son, with Nelle chaperoning, she'd wanted nothing more than to dismiss him. She hadn't got the opportunity, however; their mother immediately accepted on both her daughters' behalf, unmistakable excitement in her voice.

But how could Nelle explain her reticence when her mother didn't know of Ashvere's wish to propose—or Lord Grennet's refusal? Of course, she didn't know; Ashvere hadn't approached Lord or Lady Rutley, nor would he without his father's permission, and Lucy-Anne had sworn Nelle to secrecy.

"If she knows, she'll interfere in some way—a way that will ruin my chances with Hugh *forever*."

Lucy-Anne had been so histrionic over the whole affair, it was hard to believe she hadn't sunk into a faint for good measure. But she was likely right, especially with their parents growing increasingly frantic.

How Nelle would like to give Lord Grennet a piece of her mind, denying Ashvere and her sister their happiness! But she couldn't say anything in the presence of the two people in question.

While Lucy-Anne exclaimed in glee at the invitation —"Do you think he's changed his mind?" she'd whispered in Nelle's ear before running off to select her apparel for the outing—Nelle had taken a seat in the drawing room, mulling the best course of action. Letting her anger toward Lord Grennet show would only hurt, not help, Lucy-Anne's chances of getting the earl to change his mind.

Besides, it made sense for Lucy-Anne and Ashvere to wait longer. Given how rapidly her sister gave her heart and then withdrew it again, perhaps seeing if her infatuation lasted was best. Its intensity and the fact it had outlived most of Lucy-Anne's other interests inclined Nelle to think her sister's affections real. In which case, more time wouldn't hurt anyone.

Lucy-Anne's upset was understandable, however; Lord

Grennet did seem to have passed judgment on her. But if that were the case, why had he called in person this morning, much less requested to ride out with both of them?

Nelle wrinkled her brow. Was it possible he wished to ride out with *her* but needed chaperones himself to avoid impropriety? Ashvere and her younger sister would provide the perfect opportunity, as they'd so engross themselves in each other that they'd let Lord Grennet and her well enough alone.

She snorted. Despite her reputation for rationality, sometimes she had the most harebrained notions.

As the appointment time neared, however, she dressed carefully, at war with herself. Should she choose her finest attire, setting herself off as well as possible to encourage his attentions? Or should she, out of loyalty to Lucy-Anne, be cool, even make a pointed comment or two? Should she pursue the earl via her original plan or set her sights elsewhere because he'd refused his son and her sister?

"Ugh!" She threw her hairbrush onto the dressing table.

"Milady?" Polly was busy readying Nelle's articles of clothing. The outburst must have startled her, given her squeaky voice.

"Nothing, Polly." She glanced at the gown the maid had pulled from the armoire. "Not that one. The blue walking dress, I think."

Polly smiled. "I like that one, milady. It brings out your eyes."

Yes, it did. Nelle would let Lord Grennet's behavior guide her own interactions, but either way, no harm came in garbing herself accordingly. For whether courting or confronting, she was going into battle.

∾

GAVIN, Arth, and Emerlin had just begun their slow amble

down Rotten Row, Gringolet shaking his head in impatience to go faster, when Engelsfell appeared astride one of the largest stallions Gavin had ever seen. The horse was so strong and wide, it could easily have served as a medieval knight's destrier.

At his awed look, Engelsfell laughed. "Never seen a horse as big as Hopper, eh? I fear I'd strain any other steed to the maximum of his capabilities. You might have noticed I'm not exactly a small man."

"So say all the ladies," Arth cracked.

Engelsfell smirked in response.

"I thought you were riding with Lady Deandra?" Emerlin said.

"Sad to have me to yourself, Em? But to my luck, her friend, Miss DeSeese, asked my sister to ride with her—and her parents. According to Dea, poor Miss DeSeese didn't wish to be stuck with them alone, as her mother can be quite overbearing."

"Aren't all mothers?"

Emerlin hooted at Arthington's quip. "Seems to me your mother has always been quite biddable where you're concerned, Arth. Why else would she have agreed to a Twelfth Night masquerade? I'd have thought it too risqué for her tastes."

"It was." A cheeky grin spread across Arthington's face, revealing his crooked tooth. "But it was my condition for agreeing to invite so many unmarried ladies ... and their mothers ... to Camlon. *I* needed something to look forward to. Mother, of course, hoped I'd make a match from the lot."

"No such luck, eh?" Engelsfell swung in line with the other men, and they continued on.

"Not for my mother. And the rest of us enjoyed two weeks surrounded by the prime jewels of England, did we not?"

Prime beauties indeed, Nelle chief among them. *Goddess among them, really.*

Gavin hadn't seen her for nearly a fortnight. Then again, he and Engelsfell had spent much time the past week at White's, dined at Offley's, and won a respectable sum playing hazard at a Pall Mall hell—and in doing so had managed to avoid most social invitations per Engelsfell's request.

"I've had enough of women during the day," he'd explained upon inviting Gavin out a second night in a row. "Our townhouse is full of them ... morning calls, afternoon tea ..."

"This is a problem?" Gavin teased. "A bevy of beauties in one place, without competition from other gentlemen?"

"A swarm of ladies, beautiful or not, seeking the best match they can make? Namely, me? I'm not interested. But do feel free to come calling if you are eager to take up the matrimonial yoke, Cortleon."

"Not I."

How he'd wanted to ask if Nelle was among their number. He longed to see her pert, pretty face and hear her sweet voice. A frustrated groan escaped. Why did she dominate his thoughts so?

A barouche-landau rumbled toward them along the other side of the path. The park pulsed with people at this fashionable hour, but something about the figures in this particular vehicle caught his attention. He narrowed his eyes as the identities of the barouche's occupants became clear. Nelle. And Grennet.

He swallowed. Why was she riding out with the earl? What did this signify? He pulled Gringolet to a stop. The reddish hair of the gentleman in the reverse position set him at ease. Ashvere. The young lady next to him was no doubt Lady Lucy-Anne. Perhaps Nelle was simply chaperoning. It'd make sense; Ashvere and Lady Lucy-Anne had made no attempt to hide their affection for one another, but unless betrothed, riding alone was forbidden, and Lady Lucy-Anne might feel uncomfortable with only Ashvere's father as additional company.

A strange relief rushed through him. The idea of Nelle and Grennet formally courting roused unexpected, intense emotions—jealousy the primary one. Pure and simple. He was jealous of Grennet's position next to the woman he'd kissed on Twelfth Night, the woman with whom he'd shared several far too brief but titillating conversations at Camlon and here in London, and the woman with whom he'd danced twice—and whom he'd not wanted to let go.

It was time to admit this attraction was no passing fancy. Not when he longed to know her more intimately and not only in the physical sense, though that certainly played a part. Never had he wanted to kiss a woman more, to lick at the mole on her cheek, the expanse of bare skin above her bodice, or the ankles her gowns occasionally revealed. And to taste every inch in between. Never had such desire coursed through him for any other woman. It'd nearly driven him mad over the course of the past week, and he hadn't even seen her.

And yet, his oath bound him. He'd not dishonor her by indulging in his base passions. He nearly sniggered out loud. As if she'd allow him! No doubt such a suggestion would earn him a rightly deserved strike across the cheek. Yet she'd responded ardently when they'd kissed. More than once he'd caught her looking at him. And the air vibrated with invisible electricity whenever they neared one another.

It didn't matter. He couldn't pursue her, regardless of whether his intentions were noble or not. Marrying Nelle with his past unresolved was no more an option than bedding her.

The carriage was feet away. Grennet's brow lowered

upon spying him. Almost immediately, the earl pasted on a false grin and turned to Nelle—but she was staring directly at Gavin.

He soaked in those blue eyes, eyes as blue as the paint Michelangelo had used on the Sistine Chapel. He'd thought nothing could render them more beautiful, yet the luxurious, deep hue of her dress magnified their brilliance. A delectable blush infused her cheeks, and a jaunty bonnet covered her hair. If only he could untie its ribbon and pull it off to let those tresses fall free. How long was her unbound hair? How would it feel caressing his shoulders?

Her tongue darted out to lick at her lower lip, and desire punched him in the gut harder than Engelsfell's fists.

Grennet whipped forward again as the carriage passed, but Gavin only had eyes for Nelle—and she him, as she turned her head, their gazes locked until the barouche-landau had passed by a good number of feet.

"I say, Cort! What are you doing back there?"

He twisted in his saddle at Arth's voice. His three companions watched him from their mounts with amused expressions. The whole exchange with Nelle couldn't have taken more than a minute, probably less, and yet it was as if time had stood still.

"If you want the lady, I suggest you pursue her now," Engelsfell said, his bluntness startling. "Otherwise it looks as if you may lose her to Lord Grennet. And that'd be a shame."

"A shame? How so?" He nudged Gringolet forward. He certainly had his own opinions about the earl, but he was eager to hear what Engelsfell had to say.

"Because it's clear as day you're half in love with her."

Gavin pulled his mount to a stop. The horse shook its head in irritated response. "You've known me half a month, none of that in Lady Elinor's presence, and you make such a bold claim?" He thrust out his jaw.

Engelsfell laughed, long and loud. "I merely said so to gauge your response, and yet your righteous indignation and lack of denial prove me right."

Emerlin grinned, his cheeks dimpling. "I dare say he's right, Cort. I've thought as much myself but hadn't the nerve to say so aloud." His eyes dropped to Gavin's hands. "I feared being on the receiving end of your fists again."

Arth raised his own hands, palms forward as if swearing innocence. "I can only say whomever you kiss at midnight, and seek out at dinners, and study at the opera, and mention more than once, and dance with too closely at a ball is your business. I'm sure it means nothing."

Had Gavin something, anything, even an apple, he'd have thrown it at them. He shifted on the saddle, torn between wanting to look back once more—and wanting to kick Engelsfell. Though Engelsfell was right; he could no longer deny it.

The question was, what to do about it?

~

ALTHOUGH THE FIRST moments in the barouche-landau had been somewhat strained, Lucy-Anne and Ashvere swiftly fell into private conversation, whispering to each other while occasionally glancing at the couple seated across from them. *Lord Grennet and me.* That was the couple and could forever be. Nelle peeked at the earl.

A smile parted his beard. "How lovely to have you accompany us, Lady Elinor. You look exceptionally well this afternoon."

Her hackles rose. A compliment on her appearance, of course. *You dressed for it, you goose. Why complain now?* Besides, what else could he say? For a gentleman to compliment her intelligence or her giving nature would be highly unusual, though the earl had previously praised her

197

foundling house service. She was peevish on account of Lucy-Anne, but indignation wouldn't save her sister's prospects. She must put aside personal feelings and pursue this man with every weapon at her disposal.

She fluttered her lashes. Besotted women did so, didn't they? "How kind of you to invite us out today, my lord. The weather is superb, isn't it?"

He'd nodded as the coachman steered the carriage into Hyde Park, which teemed with polite company out to enjoy the sunny afternoon. Several gentlemen tipped their hats in greeting, and Lord Grennet touched his own in return.

Nelle sought a suitably bland topic for conversation. "Do you enjoy London, sir?"

"I far prefer Swythdon. The noise and odor of the city are unpleasant."

"I agree."

He turned to her. "So, you'd be satisfied to remain in the country? You'd give up City life?"

"I would—except for the children. I love Inglewood, especially my animals. I miss them when I'm here. But while away from London, I fret over what I could be doing for the Home."

"I see. I admire your good works. Helping the less fortunate is laudable. Lady Grennet on occasion provided meals to the families around Swythdon." His eyes flashed when he said his deceased wife's name.

This was the first he'd shared of her. Should Nelle ask more? Given his dark expression, no. Of the estate, then. "Could you tell me about Swythdon?"

"With pleasure." He launched into a description of the hall and its history. At length, he paused, clearing his throat. "It is a pleasure to have a female companion, Lady Elinor. It's been quite some time."

The poor man. He'd lost his wife so long ago. He must be lonely. Why hadn't he remarried?

"You remind me of Lady Grennet."

Her eyes widened, but he went on before she could respond.

"Much of your look is similar to hers, though your beauty exceeds her own." He shifted in his seat. "But good looks are not everything in a person. You have a steadiness, a sense of purpose she lacked. Her passions drove her. You, if I may be so bold, exhibit admirable restraint, as one expects of a lady of gentle breeding."

Was that what had set him against Lucy-Anne? Her sister's open emotionality? Nelle's brow knitted. She had deep feelings, too. She didn't reveal them often to the world, but she certainly had them.

"A restraint that earned me the title of Ice Princess." Her tone was light, teasing, even as it betrayed vulnerability. How she hated that moniker.

"I don't see that. I see a woman of honor."

She ducked her head at the unexpected commendation. When she looked up again, her gaze caught on a man riding toward them on a great gray horse. The dusting of hair at his collar left no doubt as to his identity, but she'd recognize Gavin's physique anywhere. Those broad but not overly broad shoulders, his narrow waist, long, muscular legs, and that way he had of moving—carefree, yet intentional at the same time.

Yes, she'd know him anywhere. *For shame!* She derided others for appreciating a person's appearance over his or her character but had done just that regarding the duke—had done so from the start—and she couldn't stop absorbing every inch of him.

As they neared each other, he halted his horse, his companions riding on ahead of him. Her lips rounded into an o. Why had he stopped?

The closer Lord Grennet's carriage neared, the more Gavin's every feature sharpened: those chiseled lips, marked jaw, striking brows—and those eyes. Eyes wholly on her.

She drew in a sharp breath. He made no secret of his regard, though she was in the company of another gentleman. His smoldering sherry-colored eyes ravaged her, never once glancing at anyone or anything else. His behavior was unthinkable, beyond forward, but she couldn't look away. It was as if he were a hawk and she the mouse caught in his trap—except she didn't in the least wish to escape. She wanted him to devour her, to swoop down and haul her from the barouche, to kiss her and surround her with his entire form.

She squirmed in her seat, disconcerted to the extreme. For heaven's sake, he'd paid her no attention in weeks. The abounding gossip about his amorous conquests confirmed he held no special affection for her. Yet, his stare was more intense than any she'd ever experienced—and she'd not lacked male attention. The carriage rumbled on, but she turned to watch his retreating figure. Ire rushed in, drowning her desire—for she must admit that's what it was. Desire. What was she to make of the infuriating man? She jerked around. How dare he single her out in such a way and behave so outrageously, when he by his own admission had no lasting interest in her?

Someone cleared his throat.

Lord Grennet. Nausea enveloped her. She'd blatantly ogled Gavin while seated next to him. How could she have behaved so inappropriately, especially when he'd just praised her supposed honor? She set a hand against her stomach. The carriage's movements had already unsteadied it; now it threatened to cast up its contents.

Oh, if only she could erase the past few minutes! Whatever must the earl think? She didn't wish to look at him, but she owed him an apology. She turned to him, even as her insides spun and her fingers trembled in her lap. "My Lord.

I beg your thousand pardons. The duke's unexpected attention caught me unaware, but I shouldn't have—"

"You've nothing for which to apologize. The fault lies entirely with that rogue." His eyes were cold.

Nelle swallowed, fear slithering up her spine. He looked a different man entirely, less a gentle giant and more like an adder readying itself to strike. *You goose.* She'd compared Gavin to a hawk and Lord Grennet once more to a snake. And her the mouse in both instances. Yet neither man was an animal—and she was no mouse.

"That *scoundrel!*" The earl's words burst forth as if he couldn't contain them.

Lucy-Anne and Ashvere quieted, both looking to the older man.

"That vile, libertine seducer of women. No better than his *father.*" He spat the words, his enmity startling, then barked to his driver to turn around. "The hour grows late. It's best to return."

Nelle could only nod. Lucy-Anne stared at her, ashen-faced. Ashvere glanced between his father and Nelle as the carriage lapsed into silence once more.

The earl did not look at her again.

CHAPTER 21

*B*ertie affected an air of indifference as best he could. Inwardly, he fumed. Damn Cortleon. *Damn him.*

Bertie had planned on declaring his intentions toward Lady Elinor at the end of their ride. She'd listened with interest as he'd spoken of Swythdon. She'd asked numerous questions and seemed to understand his love for his ancestral home. Her attentive, intelligent conversation assured him she was not only a woman of exceptional character but would make a competent countess. Encountering Cortleon had been an unexpected gift, an opportunity to taunt him with Bertie's possession of the eldest Greene sister.

Until Cortleon's shameless leer—and Lady Elinor's response. Lust. Naked lust. Not only had she leered in return, but she'd also twisted to watch him long after they'd passed, her shameful behavior visible to everyone. *Ice Princess? Hah.* Had she lain with the cur? Was she as deceptive and unfaithful as Bee? Had he once again completely misjudged a woman?

He gripped his thighs to the point of pain. He would not

look at her, couldn't bear to have her near with his temper raging so. Half of him wished to take her by the throat and squeeze, pressing out his anger and hurt.

No. He had to control the monster within, the monster he'd thought locked away. Cortleon's reappearance had unleashed it. Lady Elinor's behavior enraged it. For the sake of his son and his own honor, however, he must contain it.

Four horsemen sat astride steeds just before the park's exit. Arthington, Emerlin, Engelsfell, and Cortleon. Bertie gritted his teeth to keep from snarling. Would he never be free of this devil's spawn? He looked to Lady Elinor, but this time she bent her head toward her lap, giving the riders no notice. *Good.*

He shifted his attention to the horsemen. The other three men joked and laughed, but Cortleon met his glare with an unflinching one of his own. The duke's eyes narrowed as the barouche-landau neared, his motionless posture like that of a bird of prey readying to strike. When their paths crossed, Cortleon raised his fingers to his hat, tipping it and his head with such exaggeration that the action was clearly a slight.

White-hot rage burned through Bertie. *I'll kill him. I will* kill *that man.*

Hugh, however, touched his own hat in return. "A pleasure to see you, Your Grace," he called out, before returning his attention to Lucy-Anne.

Bertie froze as a new thought struck. Cortleon had treated him with disdain before, but never so openly or with such malice. Did he know? Was that stare the duke's way of acknowledgment? If so, Bertie's life was in danger. Was Hugh's? What if the bastard struck at his son as the ultimate revenge?

Black spots stabbed at his eyes as his heart seized in his chest. He fought to breathe. Losing his only child, his heir, would be worse than dying himself. *No.* He'd not fear the mongrel. He'd triumphed before; he'd win again. No cursed Cortleon would steal his loves a second time.

Bertie looked to Lady Elinor, who sat preternaturally calm, her hands in her lap. Oh, but he could take something from this duke.

And he would.

~

NELLE CRINGED when the carriage arrived at their townhouse. Guilt and remorse tugged at her like the hungry hands of beggar children. She shouldn't have reacted to Gavin whilst in the company of another man. She shouldn't have reacted to him at all.

Mother would be livid. Before the outing, she'd pressed yet again. "You must get the earl to offer for you, Nelle."

Lucy-Anne had bobbed her head in avid agreement, her earnest eyes wet with unshed tears. Those same eyes now gushed rivers down her sister's cheeks as they ascended the front stairs. "How could you, Nelle?"

She swallowed. What could she say?

"You've ruined my chances with Hugh. *Ruined*!"

Nelle bristled. She'd done wrong, but this was too much. *She* wasn't obstructing Lucy-Anne's happiness; Lord Grennet was.

Their mother flew into the hall. "My dears! What's happened?"

At Lucy-Anne's continued sobs, she rushed to her second eldest, enfolding her in a stiff embrace. "Well, Elinor?"

If only she could escape to her chamber. If only she could determine how to remedy this disastrous situation— if it were, indeed, possible—without her mother critiquing and censuring her every action.

"Nelle was ... was ..." Lucy-Anne said, sucking in air

between each sob, "*rude* to Lord Grennet. She angered him. Now he'll no doubt forbid Ashvere from ... from seeing me!"

"Elinor Elizabeth Greene! *What* have you done?"

"Mother!" Nelle exclaimed in protest of her mother's outraged tone. And yet what could she say? She *had* been rude. "I—" She faltered.

"She *ogled* the Duke of Cortleon. And for some time!"

Nelle's shoulders wilted. Of course, her sister could force out the crime, even in the midst of her tantrum.

Their mother gasped. "Elinor! While in the company of your suitor?"

"Who says he's courting me? He's never declared his intentions. I was merely there to chaperone."

"Lord Grennet was chaperone enough. He intentionally sought your company." Her mother's voice grew shriller with each word. "Oh, what if you've destroyed things beyond recovery? Did you not apologize?"

"I did. Perhaps he'll come to forgive me with time." Nelle set a hand to her aching forehead, as much to shield her from this onslaught as anything.

"Time is not something you have. You will write the earl a letter expressing your deepest regrets."

"A letter!" Unmarried ladies did not exchange letters with single gentlemen.

"Yes, a letter. Make it clear you not only welcome his attentions, you desire them. Make it clear that if he offers for you, you'll accept."

"Mother! I will not!" A woman essentially proposing to a man? It wasn't done.

Lucy-Anne sniffled. "Please, Nelle. It's my only chance with Ashvere. I will simply *die* if I cannot have him!"

Had she not been near hysterics herself, she'd have rolled her eyes at her sister's dramatic proclamation. There was no escape now. Unless Lord Grennet refused her completely. Given her behavior this afternoon, he almost certainly would.

She wanted to scream, to flail her arms into the portrait of the third Earl of Rutley on the wall, to kick over the large, empty urn underneath it. Gavin had undermined everything. Yes, she'd gawked at him—but only because *he'd* leered first. Perhaps she should write to *him* and demand he rectify the mayhem he'd caused. Perhaps she should demand *his* hand in marriage.

She stilled. Propose to the duke? Giddiness overtook her, maniacal giggles threatening to escape. No, she couldn't do that. It made even less sense than the cursed letter she must now draft to Lord Grennet. She'd have nothing further to do with Gavin. She didn't like how he made her feel. She didn't like that he made her feel at all.

"Excuse me, please, Mother. Lucy-Anne," she beseeched. "I need time alone."

Lady Rutley nodded once, her mouth a circle of disapproval.

Nelle trudged to her chamber, her resolve firmed. She'd write the letter. Not tonight. She'd beg a day or two. But then she'd prostrate herself before Lord Grennet, the sacrificial lamb on her family's altar.

She judged others for fancying her solely for the sake of her appearance, and yet, did she not desire the Duke of Cortleon because of the same? They'd shared conversation a few times, but she knew relatively little about him. No, his face and form stirred these feelings, longings which had likely lost her any chance with the earl. Lost her this chance to save her family.

Shame consumed her like a starving man did bread. Gavin must be dead to her. Never again would she give him one whit of attention. She must never think of how his thick hair curled around his cravat, or of those brandy-colored eyes, or the heavy brows framing them. Never again should she admire the strength of his jaw and the curve of those masculine lips. Never again would she acknowledge how her stomach quivered at the broadness of his shoulders, the narrowness of his hips.

No. Never would she feel anything again.

❧

HOW BADLY BERTIE had misjudged Elinor Greene. He'd not grant her the title of Lady. The alleged Ice Princess lusted like a common whore. Did no woman exist who did not hunger after one man while with another? He slammed his fist into his knee.

"Father." Hugh swallowed. "I've never seen you like this. What's set you off so?"

Bertie glowered at his son, his jaw working. "Did you not see *them*?"

"Whom?"

"Cortleon and Lady Elinor!" He barked the names.

"I saw him look at her, yes."

"And her at him!"

"What of it, Father? Wouldn't such open regard divert any lady's attention?"

Bertie snorted.

"I certainly think his behavior forward," Hugh added, "but perhaps gentlemen behave differently in Rome. He's not so long returned to England, after all."

"Why do you defend Cortleon? Do you also lust for him?"

His son recoiled as if struck, then arched forward, jutting out his chin. "What's got into you? If I didn't know better, I'd say you were drunk."

The carriage hit a rut and swayed, but the men remained as they were, two bucks locking horns.

"I don't excuse him, Father," Hugh said at length. "But I

do think you rush too quickly to judgment. I like the man. We've conversed at gatherings and shared drinks at White's. He is honorable. Several ladies at the theater made their interest in him—and me—known while we spoke after the show—yet he declined them all. I, too."

Bertie's snort was louder this time. "Come, my son. That does not prove his honor. I've heard far too many *ladies*"— he put snide emphasis on the word— "claim intimacies with the cur."

"Not Lady Elinor. This is the first I've seen her pay him notice."

"You are blind, your own attentions centered on her younger sister! They kissed at the masquerade." The memory sent fresh waves of resentment crashing over him.

"It was Twelfth Night, Father; many people did. Besides, she rode out today with *you*, not him. Doesn't that suggest where her affections lie?"

"It suggests she chaperoned her sister, as requested. Nothing more."

Hugh leaned back against the squabs. "I'm not sure what else to say."

"Then say nothing. But you might think twice about Lady Lucy-Anne, given her sister's behavior."

"What utter nonsense! Now you slander my love?" Hugh shouted at the coachman to stop the carriage. Bertie could have contradicted his son's command but didn't.

"I will walk from here," Hugh said, leaping down from the barouche. "We'll not speak again until you apologize for the way you've insulted the two Greene sisters."

Bertie stood, looming over his son. "You dare threaten me? Your *father*?"

"It's no threat. It's common decency. I think you will agree once you have calmed down. Good day, sir."

And with that, he stalked off.

Bertie sat and signaled to the driver. As the carriage

jolted into motion, he turned to watch Hugh's retreating form. His son refused to meet his gaze.

After a few more minutes, the fight went out of him and he slumped against the side of the carriage. So it often happened; a grand and terrible temper gripped him in its talons ... but then left again nearly as quickly.

If only he'd waited all those years ago. If only he'd called Cortleon out properly, honorably, instead of shooting the man on sight. How differently things might have turned out. Perhaps he could have won Bee back.

No. The fault lay not with him but with Bee. Just as it lay with Lady Elinor. He closed his eyes. History was repeating, a woman betraying him with the Duke of Cortleon. First Albina, now Lady Elinor, but the result was the same.

When the carriage arrived at his townhouse, Bertie flung himself from it, marching directly to his study, where he downed first one and then a second tumbler of brandy.

Pouring himself a third, he settled into the chair behind his desk. As the alcohol spread through him, his muscles relaxed. His mind did not. He didn't love Lady Elinor, not like he'd loved Bee. That was irrelevant; he'd not let Cortleon have her. No, he'd offer for her the next morning and make it clear that only with her acceptance would he allow Hugh and Lady Lucy-Anne to marry. Should Lady Elinor refuse, he'd never permit the match. She wouldn't let that happen to her sister. He was sure of it. Once wed, he'd take her north to Swythdon, out of reach of Cortleon's clutches. She'd be his. And she'd not betray him again, even if it meant he had to lock her up.

He drained the liquor from his cup before slamming it on the table. By all that was holy, he'd win against Cortleon. Lady Elinor would agree, especially after he promised a preposterously large marriage settlement, enough to relieve her family's dire straits and more.

A door opened and closed below. Hugh. Remorse crept

over Bertie and he dropped his head into his hands. His rage had consumed him once again, leading to this row with his son. But Cortleon and Lady Elinor were at fault for this fury—and Hugh would forgive him when he announced his blessing for his son's match with Lady Lucy-Anne. Hugh would have his love, he would have Lady Elinor, and because of his generosity, she'd both grant her sister's dearest wish and save her family. Yes, everyone would have what they wanted. Except for that loathsome whoremonger.

Bertie would make sure of it.

CHAPTER 22

Gavin lounged in a high-backed chair in White's, Arth, Em, Stoneleigh, and Engelsfell seated around him. His attention was not on his friends but on the fireplace. The fire's rhythmic dance of orange and red soothed him. Many a night in their villa, he'd sat up long after his mother had gone to sleep, letting the flames lull him into a carefree, peaceful state.

"I received a note from my mother, Cortleon. I learned of it after I returned from the park."

Engelsfell's direct address pulled him from his fantasies of devouring Nelle the way the fire did its wooden fuel. The fellow duke must have moved his chair, as he now sat with their knees nearly touching, his back to the other men, blocking them from view. And perhaps earshot.

"Oh?" Gavin had no interest at the moment, but he didn't wish to be rude, either.

"She enclosed an old letter from Grennet's first wife." Engelsfell handed over the letter without further comment.

Dearest Minerva, it began,

I do hope this letter finds you in good health. How I've missed your darling face this Season! London was utterly divine, as usual! I'd happily live there year-round, but of course, Grennet insists we remove to Swythdon at the earliest opportunity. I believe he'd give up his seat in the House of Lords and live out the rest of his days in this mausoleum if he could.

Oh, forgive me my unkind words. I try to love him, I do. We've had a terrible row this very day, however, so I write seeking comfort from a friend who might provide the secret to a happier marital life. His affections threaten to smother me. I needn't know of his every activity; why should he need to know mine? If he were to take a mistress, for example, I'd turn a blind eye, as wives do. Are you shocked to hear me say such? I'm sure you'd never allow it of your husband.

But mine believes I've taken a lover, *simply because he saw me speaking with a certain peer at the Malford ball and then again at Lady Brockhurst's salon. How am I to answer that, Minerva? Would you love me less if I had, dear friend? No, no, do not put any seriousness to that silly question.*

Perhaps it will placate him to know I'm with child. Is this not the best news? I do hope the babe looks like the man I love. Grennet, of course. Whom else could I mean? You see I'm in a playful, teasing mood, despite this evening's discord. How can I not be, when we've the Camlon house party to look forward to? Isn't being in the presence of dukes divine? Didn't you once fancy the Duke of Cortleon yourself?

May the weeks fly until we are together again!
Yr most loving,
Albina

Gavin raised his head. "You think this concerns me?"

"It might. It mentions your father. And Grennet."

The fire crackled with a loud pop as its logs settled. He studied it a moment before saying, "You think the affair to which Lady Grennet alludes was with my father?"

"Possibly. He was known for his numerous liaisons."

Gavin winced at the reminder of his father's dishonor. He'd considered the same in regard to Loughton and Lady Grennet, but to hear it from someone else's lips? "What did your mother say regarding this?"

Engelsfell leaned forward. "She discovered it among her trove of papers, and because of my recent inquiry, sent it in case it should yield useful information." He shifted in his seat. "She said at the time she didn't think anything of the innuendos; Lady Grennet often spoke in a bold and what others might deem scandalous way. But she's been thinking about how sudden and unexpected her friend's death was. Lady Grennet never wrote again after the house party. Mother attributed it to the babe, knowing herself the irregularities such a condition can bring."

Engelsfell fell silent as Gavin stared at the flames. If his father and Grennet's wife had been having an affair, it certainly gave the earl motive. And Grennet was a large man. He would have seemed enormous to a child. A giant.

But Lady Grennet had named no lover, neither in writing nor in person, or wouldn't someone have said so? She hinted at a possible affair but stated nothing overtly. And although she mentioned Gavin's father, there was no proof he was the peer to which she'd earlier referred.

"An affair also occurred to me," he admitted, angling his face toward Engelsfell. "But this letter isn't enough to prove a connection or to implicate the earl."

Engelsfell shook his head. "It's no confession, I admit. But it could be something."

"But not enough. And without proof, I can't do anything." If Grennet was the perpetrator and he confronted him, who was to say the earl would tell the truth? And if innocent, Gavin would have falsely accused another person. His sense of honor could not bear that.

Sulpicio's fourth rule sprang to mind. *Be willing to wait.*

Damn it all. He'd like to think Grennet was guilty. But

did that stem from their animosity over Nelle? Or because he was desperate to catch the murderer? No other inquiries had yielded fruit, but that didn't mean he could accuse an innocent man. If only he could remember! Each night, he prayed the dreams would come again, in hopes he could make out the blurry visage that had haunted his childhood nightmares. Green. Green was the only detail still crystal clear. The man had been all in green. More, he didn't know.

Gavin knocked back the rest of the claret. Maybe he never would.

❧

BERTIE ADJUSTED his coat before exiting the carriage. He'd come unannounced to the Greene home, impatient to make Lady Elinor his betrothed. On previous days, she'd received visitors at this hour, so he assumed today would be no different.

He assumed wrong. Lady Elinor was not at home, the reedy footman announced, but he'd be more than happy to pass on the earl's card. Just as the servant made to close the door, Lady Rutley hustled into the hall. "Lord Grennet! How lovely to see you. Pellnore, do welcome the earl in."

Bertie gave the countess his widest smile as he crossed the threshold. "A pleasure, Lady Rutley. Though I'm saddened to hear Lady Elinor is not at home."

"She's gone to the foundling home once again."

"Her service is admirable."

She waved a hand. "Indeed. But one she ought to give up; it's long since time she found a husband."

The woman was nothing if not obvious.

"I do not mean to be indiscreet," she continued, "but it is our understanding that my daughter gave offense yesterday. I assure you she was most distraught and hopes to make amends."

He gave a rather imperious nod. He needn't let her think him easy to assuage. "I've put it behind me; my affection for Lady Elinor is too great to do otherwise."

She beamed. "Come, sir. May I offer you a cup of tea?"

"Please." He followed her into the drawing room, the walls of which were the exact shade of Lady Elinor's eyes.

Lady Lucy-Anne poked her head into the room, followed by Lady Tabitha.

"Oh, I beg pardon, Lord Grennet." Lady Lucy-Anne's cheeks flushed as she curtsied. "I did not mean to interrupt."

"Good afternoon, sir," said Lady Tabitha, before addressing her mother. "We should like to go to the milliners, Mama, to see if our bonnets are ready."

"Take Prudence and a footman."

"Thank you," both said, then made their exit.

"You are blessed with beautiful and gracious daughters, my lady," Bertie said, as he took a seat on the settee.

Lady Rutley's eyes brightened. "Why, thank you."

"I know my son has become quite fond of Lady Lucy-Anne."

The countess shifted, folding her hands in her lap. Her face beamed. "And she of him."

"I myself have developed feelings for Lady Elinor."

"Oh, this is good news, indeed!"

"I'd hoped to speak with her personally of those feelings, but perhaps it is better if I make my addresses to you and Lord Rutley."

She hesitated. "Pardon me for being so bold, Lord Grennet, but may I ask as to the exact nature of your intentions?"

Bird-witted simpleton. What did she think he was suggesting? Thank goodness once he and Lady Elinor were wed and back at Swythdon, he'd likely have little interaction with her mother, whose ingratiating manner annoyed him. "I should like to make a formal offer for her hand. The marriage settlement will be generous, of course. Such a beauty is well worth it."

Worth getting the final revenge on Cortleon, at least.

The woman nearly leapt out of her chair. "Oh, our Elinor. To be married at last! But yes, yes, let me ring for Lord Rutley."

A maid entered, bearing a tray of tea and scones. Lady Rutley shooed her away. "I shall pour, Polly. Please ask Lord Rutley to join us at his earliest convenience. His very earliest convenience."

She'd barely served his tea and begun her own when the portly Lord Rutley entered the room, his cheeks ruddy. Had the man run? The earl and his wife must be desperate, indeed.

Bertie rose as Rutley crossed to him and extended a hand. "A pleasure, a pleasure," he said, shaking Bertie's hand before taking a seat next to his wife.

Satisfaction swept through Bertie as he sat down again. He was so close ... "I've spoken briefly with your wife, Rutley, but I am here to ask permission to marry your daughter."

"Which one?"

Lady Rutley elbowed her husband. She'd likely intended to do so without notice, but the earl let out a small cry. No doubt the woman's elbows were sharp as a blade.

"Lady Elinor, of course."

"Oh, very good. Very good."

"But I do have one condition."

The earl and countess stiffened, nervousness creeping into Lady Rutley's visage.

"I'd not intended to let my son marry at such a young age. However, his feelings for Lady Lucy-Anne cannot be denied and from what I understand, she's led him to believe the same. I would most heartily give my blessing if Lady Elinor accepts my proposal. But if she were to refuse

... well, I'd have to reconsider Hugh's request, as seeing Lady Lucy-Anne would prove too painful if I cannot have her sister. I do love her so."

And hate Cortleon.

Lord Rutley's brow furrowed. Before he could speak, his wife rushed ahead. "Of course, of course! Elinor admitted yesterday evening that if you had asked, she'd have accepted, so we are thrilled to accept on her behalf!"

The earl looked less sure, but his wife set a restraining hand on his knee.

Victory is mine. Bertie's lips tipped into a grin. "Splendid. Will you attend the Effingham ball?"

"Indeed. We've been looking forward to it."

"I'd like to make the announcement there—unless, of course, you wish to do so at a ball of your own?"

Unlikely. The Effingham ball was this Season's last big event; the majority of the *ton* would retire to their country houses in the next week or two. Plus, even if Rutley and his wife wanted to host such an event, the immense cost was not something they could bear. Not until he and Lady Elinor were wed.

Rutley's brow wrinkled once more, but he gave a short nod. "That sounds excellent, Lord Grennet. I'm sure my daughters would like to share their joy as soon as possible."

Or you *would, to show you've secured husbands at last for two of your girls.*

"Wonderful. Lord and Lady Effingham are of long acquaintance. Lady Effingham will be most pleased. She's expressed concern many times that I'd never marry again and would instead remain a lonely bachelor." Bertie rose. "We shall meet soon to negotiate the marriage settlement. Settlements, rather."

The earl and his wife stood, as well. Rutley gave him a nod, while the countess executed a deep curtsy.

Bertie turned to leave. "Oh, and if you please? Could

you not speak of this to your daughters until I've had the chance to propose to Lady Elinor myself?"

"Of course, Lord Grennet. We are utterly delighted that our families shall be joining together."

"As am I," he responded with genuine warmth before exiting the room.

His joy stemmed not from his upcoming nuptials, however, but from denying the duke the prize.

SLEEP WOULDN'T COME for Gavin. Nelle lingered in his every thought. He waffled between desire and fear—desire for the lady in all its inappropriate forms and fear for her safety if Grennet turned out to be the murderer. Was it possible the earl pursued Nelle in an effort to strike at *him*, rather than out of real interest? Or was that wishful thinking? That idea certainly only made sense if Grennet was the monster of his nightmares.

He tossed again, pulling at the pillow. If only he could know beyond doubt. Lady Grennet's letter tormented him, but any proof of conflict between his father and the earl was tenuous at best, non-existent at worst.

Gavin understood his worry for Nelle's safety. He prided himself a champion of women; he'd offer his assistance to any lady in peril, any damsel in distress. If Grennet were courting someone else and Gavin found indisputable evidence the earl was, indeed, his father's killer, he'd rush to the lady's rescue without hesitation. Of course, he would. This fear didn't limit itself to Nelle alone.

He pounded his fist into the mattress. He was fooling no one, least of all himself. Yes, undoubtedly, he'd aid any woman in need, but for Nelle, he'd lay down his life without a second thought. Why? He hardly knew her.

And why this unholy desire?

How her exquisite eyes, that porcelain skin, and those irresistible lips tempted him. How he'd like to lay her down naked on the silken spreads atop his great bed at Wainsbury and feast on her, tracing every inch of her skin with his fingers, tasting her with his tongue.

He rolled over, pressing his pelvis into the mattress. It did nothing to assuage the ache, however—an ache he'd denied for so long. This was madness. He must wrestle these feelings under control. But how?

He flipped to his back, staring up into the darkness. Perhaps if he spent time with her in an ordinary setting, doing ordinary things, he could break this spell. He needed to take her down off the pedestal on which he'd placed her, to learn who she was as a person, as a human being, rather than the goddess into which he'd crafted her.

And he needed to know what lay between her and Grennet. Had the two ridden out with Ashvere and Lady Lucy-Anne as chaperones or was there something more to it? Could Nelle have feelings for the earl? Gavin shuddered. Whether or not Grennet was whom he sought, the earl was more than twice her age. She deserved better.

Yes, he needed to spend time with her to ferret out her status with the older man—and to defuse this lust. But how to manage it? To call on her directly would indicate stronger intentions than he had, plus a chaperoned social call guaranteed no privacy for conversation.

He could invite her to ride in Hyde Park, as she'd done with Grennet. Doing so would still require a chaperone, however. Engelsfell could come along with ... with ... With whom? Lady Deandra? Or Nelle's sisters?

If Engelsfell asked one of Greene ladies, his intentions could be misconstrued. Gavin's, too, in asking Nelle to ride out. Any time an unwed duke made notice of a particular lady, rumors instantly abounded, as he himself had discovered. That was one reason he'd done his best to keep his distance from women as of late; he didn't want to engender false hopes or more rumors. A second, of course, was his obligation to his quest. A third was quite simply that he didn't trust himself around Nelle. And that distressed him.

If only he could meet with her alone ... No, no, that was exactly the wrong approach. Not only would immense scandal arise were they discovered, but it might also prove too tempting not to beg a kiss, or more, from the seductive Aphrodite.

Sounds in the hallway alerted him that the servants were up and about. Only the barest of light peeked around the edges of the bed curtains, however, indicating it was still very early. Arthington and Emerlin probably wouldn't rise for some time. Like he, they hadn't fallen into bed until the wee hours of the morning.

He rolled over once more, the heat in the room from the warm July nights encasing him like bandages around a mummy. Sitting up, he yanked off his nightshirt. His skin was slick with sweat, but once exposed soon cooled to a more manageable level. If only he could do the same for the heat in his smalls. He could satiate himself, of course. It wasn't as if he hadn't over the course of this long, celibate existence. It'd take little time, given his increasingly detailed fantasies about Nelle. Which was precisely why he wouldn't. Not when he was thinking of a specific woman— a woman who wasn't his.

He rose, stalking back and forth across the chamber.

Wait. Hadn't Nelle spoken of visiting the foundling home most every Thursday? Today was Thursday. The Home was public, but few if any members of society would be there. He could pay a call on the pretense of making a sizable donation—which he'd be more than happy to do. In fact, he ought to have done so before now.

Yes, he'd go to the Home. Even if Nelle weren't there, he'd offer his aid. But he hoped he'd see her. He must put a stop to this perpetual preoccupation, must douse the passions she'd ignited. Seeing her with children, in a plain dress rather than an ethereal ball gown or that dashing walking habit, perhaps with spit-up pap or worse on her skirts, would render her less the mystical maiden and more a simple woman.

And then he could move on.

He paced, bouncing on his heels or toes at points, wanting to slake the energy bounding through him. It was too early to see her, of course; she likely wouldn't commence her visit until after ten, perhaps noon. It couldn't be much past five now, given the dim glow permeating the room. It was too early even to ride in the park. *Damn.*

He lay back down. Further sleep might aid the wretched state of his head. Even if not, it'd while away the hours until he could execute his plan. For he'd go, today. And that would end this bizarre state of affairs between them.

CHAPTER 23

*N*elle rocked the screaming baby in her arms, smoothing his wispy hair with her hand. The poor thing burned with fever, his face red as he wailed out his discomfort. "Has Doctor Turner come today, Nan?"

"Not yet, milady. In due course."

Though Mrs. Piper, the Home's matron, preferred Nelle call her Nan, she refused to address Nelle as anything other than Lady Elinor or milady. "You are a lady and a lady deserves respect."

If anyone deserved respect, it was Nan. She came from the lower gentry herself but had lost her family to a bout of typhus that wiped out most of the residents in her village. "I suppose I was lucky to be spared," she'd confessed, "but being left an orphan had me doubting that. Now I see God's purpose for me was to aid other orphans like myself, especially the wee ones."

"I'm concerned about William," Nelle said.

Nan dipped her head, the movement brisk and austere. She'd seen too much loss within these walls to show any outward reaction. Nelle had caught her crying more than once, however. Nan's no-nonsense demeanor stemmed not from lack of feeling but rather the excess of it. Still, she bustled about from dawn until dusk and often into the night tending to the children.

Three other nurses also helped at the Home, one at night and two during the day. They had a cook, plus two maids for the cleaning and washing. With so many nappies, the washing never ended, the lye soap rendering the maids' fingers perpetually raw. Nelle had offered more than once to help, but they'd shooed her away. "This is no work for an earl's daughter."

How it frustrated her, but they'd not be dissuaded. Caring for the babies, however—that was something she could do. She pressed her lips to William's soft head, breathing in his sweet smell.

Nan looked at her. "Do you ever want ones of your own, milady?"

Nelle started. Though they often spoke intimately, Nan had never asked that question.

But why bring more children into the world when these poor darlings were in desperate need of homes? *Because highborn ladies must bear their husbands highborn children,* her mother would no doubt respond.

She stared at the tyke in her arms. If a husband, especially a peer, *were* to take orphaned children such as these into his home, even if he developed a sincere affection for them, he'd still want offspring of his own to whom he could pass on his family name and heritage.

One of Lord Grennet's advantages had been that he already had an heir. She needn't necessarily bear him children, though perhaps he'd have wanted them. As she rocked William back and forth, his cries gradually lowering until he slipped into a fretful sleep, she could envision the love she'd pour into her own children, the same love she showered onto these fragile babies. Especially if she bore them out of love for her husband, rather than out of duty.

Love and husbands. Neither often went together. If she'd married Lord Grennet, they wouldn't have. He might have earned her respect, even admiration. But he'd never have occasioned any greater feeling. It hardly mattered now. She must write to him tonight, but she had no faith she could redeem herself.

Nan gasped, and Nelle whirled, clutching William carefully in her arms. The older woman pointed toward the window. A coach had halted outside the Home. It bore no mark to indicate its passenger, but a well-dressed gentleman exited the cab, his long legs easily descending its two high steps. Once in the street, he paused, looking up at the house.

Gavin. The Duke of Cortleon was standing in front of the Home. Despite the nondescript coach, people recognized him at once. Men on the street pointed and whispered. He ignored them, though he did stop to hand a boy several coins before he made his way forward.

A knock sounded at the door. She and Nan looked at each other.

"You should greet him, milady. We've never had a duke here."

"Me?" Nelle squeaked.

Meanwhile, someone opened the door and welcomed him inside. Gavin's voice echoed in the hall, but she couldn't quite make out what he was saying. Without warning, he rushed into the rather shabby drawing room in which Nan and she stood.

"The Duke of Cortleon, Mrs. Piper," a maid called from behind him, her voice wavering.

He turned. "I beg your pardon, miss. I was so eager to meet the owner of this admirable establishment that I rushed in ahead. I was unforgivably rude."

"T—Tis quite all right, Yer Grace," the young woman stammered.

He turned again to the room's occupants, and Nelle held her breath. Why was he here? And why must he always look so ... so ... *edible*? He wore the same attire as any gentleman—though made of the finest materials—and yet somehow he seemed *more*. More masculine, more majestic, more everything. No wonder others called him "the Legendary Duke."

"Lady Elinor. It is a delight to see you again." He gave her a smile that made her insides buzz like bees around honey.

Nan's mouth rounded into an o of astonishment. Nelle hadn't revealed they were acquainted.

"Your Grace." She rocked the sleeping babe in her arms, offering a polite nod. She'd not let him see how he affected her.

He addressed Nan. "And you must be Mrs. Piper. Lady Elinor has spoken of you with the highest praise."

Nan's cheeks took on the hue of cherries, but she curtsied politely. "We welcome you to Home for the Salvation and Advancement of Abandoned and Illegitimate Foundlings and Small Children, Your Grace, and are most deeply honored by your presence."

A little girl of about two toddled into the room and right up to Gavin, wrapping her arms around his leg.

"Oh, heavens! Morna!" Nan exclaimed, but before she could retrieve the child, he leaned down and scooped the girl up in his arms.

"Hello there," he said.

The girl stared at him with wide eyes.

I know how you feel.

"I—I beg your pardon, Your Grace," Nan said. "I'll call for Sally to get her."

"Nonsense," he said, his eyes still on the child. She

reached up and patted his chin. He responded by pursing his lips and making cooing noises at her.

Nelle's breath caught. The Duke of Cortleon, one of the most powerful men in the land, was playing with an orphaned child. Morna touched his lips then stuck her fingers into his mouth. His eyes rounded, and Nelle fought to suppress a laugh. He hadn't been expecting that. But against all expectations, he made a show of pretending to eat her fingers. The girl giggled.

He charms us all, from the oldest of the old to the youngest of the young.

"You have a way with children, Your Grace." Admiration laced Nan's voice. How often had she spoken with open disdain about the nobility's disregard for those less fortunate? Yet in less than a minute, this peer had earned her respect.

He looked up, the girl's fingers still in his mouth, and this time Nelle couldn't hold back. She laughed so hard she shook William awake, who immediately began screeching.

"Oh!" She crooned softly into the baby's ear, hoping to soothe him back to sleep, but he was having none of it.

Meanwhile, Morna wiggled, pressing against Gavin's chest, and he set her down. She toddled off, indifferent to the fact she'd just interacted with a duke.

"Here, may I?" He held his arms out.

Nelle hesitated. Did he truly wish to hold a squalling baby? But she complied.

William quieted for a moment as he studied the new person holding him but then returned to full-lunged crying. She pressed her knuckles to her mouth to stifle her mirth. At least this proved Gavin wasn't some sort of magical god. Not for the male side of the species, at least.

"Sally," Nan called, as she removed the unhappy baby from the duke's arms. When a plump young woman appeared, Nan handed William over. "A new nappy, I think."

The maid nodded and hurried from the room.

He gave a rueful shrug. "I tried."

The winsome grin that followed nearly made Nelle cry herself. Or want to stick her own fingers into his mouth. Good heavens. She ought to commit herself to Bedlam for her reaction to this man was madness.

"Might I ask the reason for your attendance here today, Your Grace?" Nan's fidgeting hands revealed her nervousness.

Gavin nodded toward Nelle. "Lady Elinor has told me of her work here." He paused. "You may know of my own upbringing. I've always had a heart for children without parents, as one of mine was stolen from me years ago. I saw many struggling in the streets of Rome. I see them now in London. As I'm in a position to help, I decided to seek out a charitable home I could support."

His face had gone from charming to serious over the course of his speech, the corners of his lips pulling down when he'd mentioned his father. That brief moment of vulnerability made her heart pound as much as his sherry eyes.

At the mention of support, Nan touched a shaky hand to her lace cap. They'd had patrons in the past but never someone of his rank. With a duke's commendation and financial support, the foundling home could see vast improvements in its ability to care for children. "We are deeply honored by your attentions, Your Grace. Would you like a tour? I would be most happy to show you about."

"Thank you," he said, his speech rapid, "but I hoped Lady Elinor might be the one to provide such a service."

Nan sent her a curious glance. Nelle, for her part, wasn't sure how to respond. He'd stated why he was here, but why this particular attention to her? Had he more of a sincere interest than she'd thought? Heated looks were one thing, but coming to a foundling home? That seemed in a different category entirely. *Unless he was such a knave he'd use a house serving those in greatest desperation as a setting for seduction?*

She pressed a hand against her midsection. Despite Gavin's rakish reputation, she didn't believe him a man of such low character, nor should she assume he'd stoop to such measures, especially when he could have nearly any woman he wanted with a mere crook of his finger.

"She is at your disposal, Your Grace." Nan's cheeks rounded in a smile. To Nelle, she added, "Take all the time you need. We want to ensure His Grace has as detailed a tour as he would like."

Why did it sound like a second meaning undergirded her words? She had little time to consider before Nan departed, leaving Gavin and Nelle to themselves.

Tingles traced across her skin at being alone with a man not her relation. This was entirely improper. Or was it? They weren't in a private home, after all, but a perfectly respectable house for orphaned and abandoned babies.

"Hello, Lady Elinor."

"Your Grace. Shall we start in the main nursery?"

"Anywhere you'd like. As Mrs. Piper said, I should like to see every inch."

She gave him a look, even as tiny shivers tickled her skin. Had he intended that double entendre? No guile shadowed his face, however, his expression merely that of polite curiosity.

Dipping her chin, she set off, leading him up a narrow set of stairs to a large chamber lined on either side with cribs. Infants lay in many of them, some crying, others sleeping. Older babes sat, staring silently around the room. Two nurses scurried from one child to the next, offering what comfort they could. One small boy, maybe a year in age, bounced exuberantly upon spying Nelle, his arms reaching up.

Little Georgie. One of her favorites. He'd been left at the house only hours after his birth, a tiny, screaming, purple-faced creature. His survival had been far from sure —several illnesses sickened him in his first few months, and once he'd nearly died of a violent stomach ailment. And yet, he always had a happy smile for her. He liked her hair. She often loosened a lock for him to latch onto. She did so now, picking him up with a coo and settling him on her left hip before pulling out a hairpin so that a tendril fell.

"He likes you. The children here like you. You're obviously kind to them and treat them well."

Respect undergirded Gavin's tone. Respect for her. Not for her appearance, but for *her*, in her service to these children. Her eyes moistened as an unusual, joyous satisfaction overtook her. So this was how it felt to be admired for what she *did*, not for how she looked.

He walked to a crib and plucked up the crying infant within.

One of the nursemaids scurried over. "I'm so sorry, milady," she said, looking toward the duke with nervous eyes. "We haven't the arms to tend to them all at once."

Nelle smiled as George traced his fingers over her jaw. "We know, Patsy. You're doing as best you can. You always do. Your loving heart would never willingly leave any child to suffer."

Patsy dropped a curtsy, flashing one last look at the duke before rushing over to catch a child near to falling from his bed.

"Nor would yours," Gavin murmured, his voice low. "No one could ever call you the Ice Princess if they but saw you here."

She bristled at the detested epithet but then nuzzled

her nose against Georgie's as he tugged her hair, making him laugh with delight.

"Yes, this paints you in an entirely different light." A hint of something further undergirded his voice, something she couldn't decipher. Something beyond even admiration. *Wonder?*

"One could say the same of you, Your Grace," she answered pertly, nodding toward the baby girl in his arms, who'd quieted and now lay contentedly still, her little eyes never leaving the duke's face.

"It seems we all participate in a form of perpetual masquerade."

"Would we truly want to see others without those masks?"

People hid truths and lies most would never know. These parentless children bore evidence of that. As did her own life. Others might think they knew much about her based on her parentage, her status in society, or her alleged frigid demeanor. But they did not know *her*. To the *ton,* she was Lady Elinor Greene, the aloof beauty. The Ice Princess. Few outside her sisters and one or two close friends understood how she burned to help those in need: babies, orphans, animals. And her family.

What drove Gavin? His reputation for courtliness, charm, and physical prowess preceded him. He was gallant with the ladies, the envy of gentlemen. Despite his different, foreign upbringing and occasional faux pas, he'd brought London society under his spell. But was that all there was to him?

He gazed at the child he cradled as if she were the most beautiful thing he'd ever seen, his eyes soft, his lips moving with silly, nonsensical sounds meant to soothe.

No. That devil-may-care attitude hid something deeper. Richer. How many dukes would come to a place such as this, much less be enraptured by poor, cast-off children?

Peers might wrangle in parliament over reforms to help the common people and ladies adopt causes to aid those less fortunate, but few members of the upper ten thousand challenged their 'natural right' to power and privilege. Many, like her mother, looked down on the lower orders while professing a devotion to improving their lot. And how rapidly the *ton* closed ranks if someone attempted to rise above his or her station.

Gavin, however, was as attentive and polite to servants as to those they served. On more than one occasion, she'd seen him thank footmen and maids for their service—much to their surprise and the amusement of those they served. Look at how he'd reassured the Home's nervous nursemaids. He treated everyone according to their behavior, not their societal position. And to witness him now ...

She didn't know his real reason for coming here today. She rather doubted he'd done so solely for the children's sake. No, he'd deliberately sought her out. Why? Regardless, his heart was certainly open to children. Even these children—the unwanted, the abandoned.

What would Lord Grennet think of this Home? He'd expressed admiration for her charitable endeavors, thus she'd assumed he'd not mind if she continued to work here after marrying. But had she erred in thinking such? She'd thought him gentle-natured, but his hostile reaction in the park suggested otherwise. Though little chance of marrying him remained, he might not have been the easy, malleable spouse she'd envisioned. He'd played a ruthless hand in regard to Ashvere and Lucy-Anne, denying his only son his dearest wish. Would he have applied the same ruthlessness as a husband?

Yes, the facades people fostered could hide so many different realities. How terrifying.

"I'd like to see you without yours," Gavin said after several moments had ticked by.

"*What?*"

What was he suggesting?

"Your mask."

"Why?" she cried, at an end with this dance. This charade. Had she not had Georgie in her arms, she'd have thrown them up in exasperation. She lowered her voice to an angry whisper. "Why are you even here? Why do you pursue me then dash away? You profess to have no interest in me, yet here you stand. Yet there you were yesterday, eyeing me in the most . . . indiscreet fashion."

He set the now-sleeping baby girl back in her crib. Nearing Nelle, he leaned in close. Too close. His breath fluttered against her cheek. Georgie clasped onto his cravat, tethering him inches from her face. "You're right. I've behaved dishonorably. I beg your forgiveness."

Every movement of his lips drew her closer. The finest of lines were visible around his eyes, and she could make out each individual eyelash framing those hazelnut circles.

"The truth is, I don't know. Oh, I know why I came. I wanted to spend time with you, to get to know you." Georgie yanked on his neckcloth, and Gavin bent lower, his lips now hardly two fingers' width from her own. "I thought in doing so, I'd break this spell. Set you free from goddess to a mere woman. A woman who could rival Helen of Troy, but a woman, nonetheless."

His tongue wetted his lower lip and her own lips parted. How she wanted to arch forward that last bit of space and touch her mouth to his. And that with a baby in her arms!

"And yet I am more entranced than ever."

The confession robbed her of breath.

"You are no goddess. You are a sorceress. Like Morgan le Fay against the knights of old."

Nelle stiffened. "That's hardly a kind thing to say. No woman wants to be considered a witch." She pulled at the boy's fingers until he released Gavin's cravat, then stepped back. "I'm neither goddess nor sorceress nor Helen of Troy, sir. I'm simply a woman trying to do my best in a world that doesn't want to let me."

He grimaced as he also stepped away, establishing a more proper distance between them. "My apologies, again; I meant no insult. The opposite."

She glanced around. Had Patsy seen them? Or anyone else? The only eyes watching them belonged to children too young to speak. No other adult was in the room.

"You are a woman," he said, "but anything but simple. Do you see me as just a man? Here in England, I am Cortleon. A duke. Society defers to me because of my title —a title I did nothing to earn and knew nothing about until I was seventeen. People no more see me for who I am behind this ducal mask than they see you."

She stilled, halting the unconscious rhythmic swaying women adopted when holding infants. Gone was the usual, insouciant charm he threw out as if it were second nature. No, a hint of anger stood in its place—anger and ... and what? Frustration. Sorrow.

The exact same as she.

She met his eyes directly. Openly. "Who are you, then?"

Patsy entered at that moment, followed by another nursemaid. Nelle tucked Georgie back in his crib then ushered the duke into an adjacent corridor, shutting the door behind her.

"Gavin Knight," he said, as she turned to him. "No more, no less. A boy who lost his father to a murderer. I lost my entire life, actually, as my mother took me from everything and everyone I'd ever known to a foreign city and hid our existence." He ran a hand through the top of his hair, holding it from his face. "I am that young man who, as promised, stayed at his mother's side as she suffered through her long illness, even as I yearned for more: more adventure, more knowledge, more understanding of the world—and if I had a place in it."

The pain on his face made her long to reach out, to touch him, but she held back, sensing he didn't wish it.

"I yearned not only for the truth about my father's death but for vengeance. The sole reason I came to England, this land I no longer knew, and took up this title and its obligations was to seek justice for everything taken from me and my family." He crossed his arms, leaning back against the wall behind him. "I am a duke. But I did not wish to be, Lady Elinor. Just as I did not wish for a woman with the finest face I'd ever seen to deter me." He held up a hand at her bristled brow. "There's more to you than that. Much more. But just as I formed an opinion of you without knowing much about you, so did you of me."

She winced. He was right, of course. She *had* made assumptions about his character based on his looks, his mannerisms, and the talk about him. The man before her now was a far cry from the self-assured rogue he'd always appeared.

"I've lived months in frustration," he went on. "For not only can I—*will* I—not allow this unwelcome attraction to divert me from my quest, but the feelings you arouse threaten my very honor."

Wait. She threatened *his* honor?

He arched a brow. "No doubt you've heard of my reputation with the ladies? According to the gossipmongers, I've seduced half of the *ton*."

Her cheeks flamed. Why was he speaking of such things to *her*?

"The rumors hold no truth." His eyes pierced hers. "The only woman I've done so much as kiss in England is you."

She gasped. How could that be? She'd witnessed his flirtations—Lady Tutledge at the opera, for one—and had herself heard several ladies claim to be direct objects of his ardor.

"Do you know much about my father?"

She shook her head. "Not much beyond that he was killed ... and that he had a reputation."

"A reputation." He gave a sardonic snort. "Yes. He was not an honorable man. He was a womanizer. A rogue. A rake. A rapscallion. Whatever word one wishes to use. His exploits were legendary, to use everyone's term. He seduced what women he could, young, old, married or not."

Gavin's mouth twisted in a painful grimace. "My mother loved him anyway. But Loughton Knight was a lecher and an adulterer. There are no two ways about it. His lust got him killed. I may not know much else, but of that, I'm sure." He pressed his palms into his forehead. "If only I could remember! I was there, Nelle. I *saw* the man who killed my father. But I cannot remember his face!" His voice shook.

She moved closer and laid a hand on his arm. He looked at it, then to her, his fingers falling from his forehead to trace a tender path along her cheek. "You see, dearest Nelle, this is why I *must* curb these feelings for you. I cannot sink to such dishonor as attempting to seduce you. I swore to my mother and to myself I would *never* be like him." He dropped his fingers. "But I also cannot marry you. I cannot offer for anyone with this uncertainty, this danger over my head. I may not remember my father's murderer, but I've no doubt he remembers me."

She stilled. How was she to react? He'd called her by her Christian name. No, even more intimate: her nickname. He'd spoken of seduction and marriage. And why neither was possible.

She'd thought if she wanted a man at all, she preferred one who roused little feeling. She'd thought wrong. She wanted *this* man in whatever way she could have him. She'd never once considered an illicit liaison. Never once considered lying with a man outside of marriage. Yet now, if they were truly alone instead of in this Home surrounded by children and caregivers, she'd haul him into a chamber without stopping to think and kiss him senseless, sliding her hands inside his coat, under his waistcoat, closer, under whatever fabric she found, until she could touch his bare skin. Until she could not tell where he stopped and she began.

"Your Gr—"

He set a finger against her lips, halting her words. "No. Gavin. Not Your Grace, not Duke, not Cortleon. Just … Gavin." He brushed her loosened hair from her face. "Tell me, Goddess. Have I frightened you? Your expression reveals nothing of what you may be thinking."

"No," she whispered. "Not at all, Gavin. But you have broken me."

He reeled back.

"I did not want to feel. Not like this. Nothing like this. I've never felt anything for any man. But I *feel* for you. I'm no freer to pursue this passion than you are, however. My family is facing financial ruin. It is on me to marry well in order to save them."

He shook his head. "Why you? It's not escaped my notice that your sister and Ashvere are enamored of each other."

"Quite." Her lips pulled into a pained smile. "But my mother insists it's unseemly for the younger daughters to marry before the eldest."

"That's nonsense!"

"I am in complete agreement, Your Grace."

"Gavin," he corrected.

"Gavin."

"You don't wish to marry." It was a statement on his part, not a question.

"No, I do not."

"Yet you are acceding to your parents' demands."

She set her hands on her hips, lifting her chin. "What choice do I have? I'm not a woman of independent means. Should I defy my family? Insist I shall live as a spinster? I could, but Mother has threatened to disown me. Oh, I could become a governess, I suppose, or move in to become a permanent nurse here." Her shoulders drooped. "Perhaps I should. But I've just enough pride and have lived in just enough luxury that I don't want my own fortunes to drop thusly. I suppose that reveals much about my selfish nature." Tears filled her eyes.

He reached for her hand. "If you are willing to marry in order to rescue your family from a financial mess you didn't create, I must argue you're one of the least selfish creatures alive."

She shook her head, even as she let him wrap his fingers around hers. "If that were true, I'd have married several Seasons ago, when I had my pick of men. Instead, I rejected all comers. Marriage never appealed. Not when so many husbands and wives share lives of mutual apathy at best, misery at worst. Like my parents."

His thumb traced over hers, a rhythmic caress that both calmed her and sent her pulse racing.

"Naively I thought I could go on as I was," she added, a complex cavalcade of emotions cutting through her. Misery. Desire. Confusion. "I thought I could escape time."

"I, too, have thought the same." He laughed, but it was a bitter laugh. Pulling her to him, he nestled her in a loose embrace. She could have moved if she'd wanted to. She didn't. She lay her head against his chest.

"My mother took ill years ago," he whispered. "I feared I'd lose her, but as days, then months, then years went by with her never fully recovering but never succumbing, either, time ceased to seem real. I couldn't imagine her not with me. I kept believing it simply couldn't happen, that she'd never die." His breath tickled the top of her head as he spoke. "Then one day, she was gone. The only parent I could remember, the only parent I'd ever known, was gone. I was alone in the world. And to follow through on my vow for retribution, I had to travel to a foreign land and move within a society whose ways were alien. I had to confront the past, though I remembered nothing of it." A pained chuckle shook his chest. "Now here I am, no closer to finding my father's murderer than I was months ago, unsure of my next course or if I'm even capable of fulfilling my quest, holding in my arms a woman I desperately want but cannot have."

She looked up. "Why can't you have me?"

He stilled. "I've told you. I'll never dishonor any woman, especially you, in such a way."

That wasn't what she'd meant, but how could she clarify? He'd insisted less than ten minutes ago he'd not *marry* before he'd succeeded in his goal, but what if they promised now to marry at some point in the future?

She worried the inside of her cheek. What if he never completed his quest? Or worse, what if the person who'd killed his father killed him, as well? The notion of Gavin dead was too much to bear. Besides, there were too many practicalities to consider, too many insurmountable realities. What would happen to her sisters should she become engaged but remain unwed? Would Gavin settle her father's substantial debts without a legal bond? Would her parents agree a betrothal, rather than a wedding, satisfied their requirements? And what about Lucy-Anne? Nelle's behavior may have upset Lord Grennet, but he certainly bore the duke no good will, either. Because of her. If she promised herself to Gavin, would the earl forever refuse Lucy-Anne as a wife for Ashvere?

Cries from the next room pulled her from her thoughts.

Rushing feet sounded from down the hallway, and she sprang back, freeing herself from the duke's arms.

"Come, Your—Gavin," she said, false brightness in her voice. "I believe our conversation has drifted further afield than either of us expected. Shall we go below to the yard to see where the children play and take a little air?" Without waiting for his response, she strode off, arms swinging with determination. Her silly idea was a momentary fantasy. An interlude. She didn't know exactly what had passed between them, but once they each left this house, it'd be gone.

And the masks they'd both discarded would be firmly back in place.

Gavin trailed after Nelle, feeling naked after such an intimate exchange.

Her skirts swished in front of him. The loose-fitting dress with its high waist and bodice full up to the neck revealed nothing of her form below. Just as her brisk, no-nonsense pace revealed nothing of what she was thinking, the openness and vulnerability of the past fifteen minutes clearly tucked away.

He wanted it back. He'd learned to play the rules of high society and played them well, but he treasured the connections he'd made that broke through the social veneer of expectations and allowed behaviors. Such as with Arthington, Emerlin, Stoneleigh, and especially Engelsfell. They'd trained together, ridden together, drunk together, talked into the mornings together. Those men knew him. And yet much of what he'd revealed to her he hadn't shared with them. He'd certainly never admitted the full extent of his doubts about his own abilities. He'd needed to live up to his legendary reputation, been grateful for it, even, in hopes it'd send a message to his father's murderer. Gavin Knight, Duke of Cortleon, had returned, and this time he wasn't backing down.

But he'd shared those hidden secrets with Nelle. Why? He'd come today in an effort to lessen his attraction to her, to make her real and thus less desirable. He'd failed miserably. He only wanted her more. Because he *liked* her. He not only admired how she interacted with children but also the respect she showed Mrs. Piper and the nursemaids, women below her on the social scale. He also appreciated how she'd spoken directly and honestly about her wants and needs—and her frustrations with how the world saw her.

They wove their way through a long corridor and out a door at the rear of the edifice. Several babies sat or crawled about on a rather sorry patch of dirt and grass that served as the lawn. Mrs. Piper conversed with a stout woman of indeterminable age, and another young woman sang songs to the small group of babies kicking their legs on the ground in front of her. Despite the paucity of provisions and the sparseness of the area, it exuded an unexpected aura of happiness. A light breeze blew, ruffling the hair of some of the older babies. A boy crawled along rapidly on all fours. He stopped suddenly, picking up something between his fingers and making to pop it into his mouth.

"Oh, Richard, no!" Nelle darted forward and grabbed the offending object, whatever it was, from his hand. The child whimpered but crawled on. Wrinkling her nose, she carried the retrieved treasure at arm's length to a nearby bucket and dropped it in, then wiped her hands several times on a piece of cloth draped on a nearby chair. "Beetle," she said, as she returned to him, her nose still twitching with disdain.

He erupted in a gale of laughter. How prissy she'd looked just then, denying a baby boy his prize and making the most amusing expressions in her rush to dispose of it. If only he could drop a kiss right on that adorable little tip above those luscious lips. But they weren't in private anymore, a point driven home when every eye turned to him. "I beg pardon," he said, executing a low bow. "I was feeling sympathy for the poor child, denied the thing he wants most."

The woman next to Mrs. Piper tittered.

"I want to thank you, Mrs. Piper, and dear Lady Elinor, for accommodating my unexpected visit. I've been most impressed by what I've seen. You can be sure I shall communicate my pleasure to the Regent and the House of Lords."

Mrs. Piper gasped.

"I should like to return in the near future to discuss ways in which I might be of service," he added. "Generous service."

Now the matron looked as if she might faint.

He turned to Nelle. "Thank you for allowing me in today."

He wished to say more, but they were in company. The pinking of her cheeks, however, suggested she'd understood the multiple meanings of his words.

"We are indebted to you for honoring us with a visit, Your Grace." Her words were crisp, clear. Everything that was proper.

Ah. There it is. The mask was back in place.

Nelle's gaze slid from him to Mrs. Piper and back again when he made no move to leave.

"Perhaps you might show His Grace out?" Mrs. Piper's voice squeaked.

"Oh, of course!"

He followed her once more, her rigid shoulders proof she'd resurrected her walls. She paused with him at the front door while Patsy retrieved his hat and gloves. For just a moment, after the maid had come and gone, her lip trembled. It was all he needed. He ignored his gloves, reaching for her bare hand with his and pressing a kiss against its back. He didn't release her fingers. "Thank you, Nelle, for an illuminative afternoon."

Her eyes rounded, those eyes reminiscent of the blue flowers of the rosemary Mama had grown in their Italian garden, eyes which reflected the same turbulent emotions ricocheting through him. He didn't want to leave. He didn't want to let go of this woman—the woman he'd come to see with the idiotic notion that spending more time with her would make him want her less.

He was the Fool Grennet had played at the masquerade.

Grennet. He hadn't thought of the man all afternoon, but the suspicions Lady Engelsfell's latest communiqué had fostered flooded back. Though the connection was tenuous at best, the earl was the most promising lead in his hunt for his father's executioner. And Grennet was the man with whom Nelle had ridden out the day before.

Gavin frowned. He'd considered speaking of his concerns before they'd got ... distracted. But he had no real evidence, only a suspicion—a suspicion that flew in the face of society's opinion of the earl. If he impugned an innocent peer, not only would he irreparably damage his own reputation, but he might ruin a beneficial match for her—though the idea of her marrying the earl wrenched his gut in ways he didn't wish to examine. Grennet's attentions to her and her presence yesterday in his carriage indicated his intentions, as had his challenging stare. The earl was guarding what he already saw as his.

Was there a chance Grennet posed any danger to her? Surely not. Even if he *were* the monster, the earl's enmity was for Gavin, not her. Though given the events at the masked ball, the Malford ball, and yesterday in Hyde Park ...

Nelle pulled her hand free and opened the door. His

footman descended from the waiting coach and readied it for his entry.

"Thank you, Your Grace, for visiting today. Mrs. Piper looks forward to your return." She folded her hands primly against her abdomen.

The Ice Princess had returned to her tower.

Gavin tipped his hat before climbing into the cab. No other words were necessary. As the carriage pulled away, his thoughts continued to spin. It was highly unlikely the well-respected Grennet posed any danger to her.

His heart lurched. But what if he was wrong?

CHAPTER 24

*B*ertie adjusted the folds of his cravat, pleased with the intricate design his valet had crafted. He wished to look his best when he announced his engagement to Lady Elinor this evening—and Hugh's to Lady Lucy-Anne.

Neither Lady Elinor nor his son knew of his plans. No, surprising them would be much more satisfying. Though Hugh had remained cool since their altercation in the park, this would win him back.

As for the Greene sisters, Lord and Lady Rutley had assured him both daughters would accept with delight, but Bertie hadn't risked asking Lady Elinor privately, lest she decline him. He needed to remain in control of this chessboard. Once their betrothal was announced, she'd not beg off, not when her sister's happiness and her family's fortunes were at stake.

And Cortleon had not come for him after their encounter in the park. Had the duke known anything, he'd certainly have shown his cards and confronted him by now. No, Bertie and Hugh were safe.

The fool.

This Cortleon, the spitting image of his father, would not be victorious. *This* time Bertie would save his wife from the lecherous duke—and from her own concupiscence. This time, he'd triumph. And redeem himself at last.

~

NELLE CLIMBED into the coach after Lucy-Anne, swallowing a sigh. She did *not* want to attend the Effingham ball, but her parents had insisted.

"A certain someone expects you there, I am sure," Mother had said, her tone unexpectedly cheerful. "You don't want to miss your chance to shine."

Surely, she didn't mean Lord Grennet? When Nelle had returned after her afternoon with Gavin at the Home, her mother had informed her she needn't write the earl after all. "Your father thought it inappropriate," was her only explanation.

When had Mother ever so readily acquiesced to her husband? Nelle hadn't challenged the reversal, however, grateful for the reprieve. Her parents had been strangely silent thereafter about the whole debacle. They must have accepted she'd ruined any chance with the earl, but she'd not asked, not wanting to open Pandora's box.

She'd neither seen nor heard from Lord Grennet since that ill-fated carriage ride more than two weeks ago. He'd been absent from the few soirees and dinners she'd attended, and though Ashvere was present for Tabby's most recent musicale, his father had declined the invitation.

Nor had she seen the Duke of Cortleon, though Lucy-Anne mentioned his appearance at the theater the previous evening. Nelle would not think of him by his Christian name. The intimacy they'd shared at the foundling home had been an extraordinary but fleeting experience.

She had skipped the theater herself, pleading fatigue.

Indeed, she was tired of London. Tired of the constant social obligations, the artifice of conspicuous display, and the unabating pressure to hook a husband. Even Tabby, her normally confident sister, had lamented the cutthroat nature of the marriage market.

"I expect you to be on your best behavior, girls," Lady Rutley said presently as the carriage crawled along the crowded streets. "Do not linger long away from the ballroom." A self-satisfied purse of the lips followed that strange statement.

"Of course, Mama," said Lucy-Anne, ever eager to please. "Lord Ashvere has promised me two dances. Oh, if only we could also dance a third!"

"Mayhap."

Their mother's response stupefied Nelle. Had she no shame? Dancing three dances with the same man was tantamount to declaring an engagement. Then again, Mother had no idea of the machinations behind the scenes, of the earl's threat against his own son, or of Lucy-Anne's dependence on Nelle to right the situation.

Her sister had been remarkably close-lipped about Nelle's faux pas in Hyde Park, Lord Grennet's heated reaction, and his noted absence. Why? Did she believe if she didn't speak of it, it hadn't happened? Nelle hadn't asked; if she did, the dam might burst, and she'd drown in Lucy-Anne's tears and recriminations.

Numerous coaches waited outside Effingham House, as families and couples streamed from their vehicles into the columned abode.

"We might as well get out and walk from here," Tabby groused. "Getting to the front shall take hours."

"Nonsense," said their mother, even as she fanned herself against the summer heat, which had rendered the inside of the carriage nearly unbearable, despite the late evening hour.

Nelle pulled at her gown's bodice. Her chemise clung to her damp skin. By the time they entered the ballroom, the Greene ladies would look like wilted flowers, hair and cheeks drooping under the weight of the humid air. The visual amused her. Given the hues of their gowns, Lucy-Anne would be the palest of pink hydrangeas, Tabitha a lavender delphinium, and Lady Rutley a sunflower, her bright yellow gown nearly blinding. Nelle's own dress might be a snow star, the type of green-tinted white astrantia that grew in abundance at Inglewood. All were new. Why had Mother insisted on such a luxury at the tail end of the Season? Did she believe the fashionable dresses would somehow compel eligible gentlemen to declare themselves on the spot? A nervous giggle escaped, earning Nelle a sharp look.

When their turn arrived, they alighted from the stifling carriage as elegantly as possible—but how polished could one appear when rivulets of sweat ran down one's spine? Luckily, the outside air was considerably cooler, and the gentle breeze eased her discomfort.

The height of London society milled about in the grand hall and receiving rooms. She'd thought much of the *ton* already removed from Town, but whoever remained must be here, as the crush was immense—and the warmth so many candles and bodies generated oppressive.

When the butler called everyone to dinner, Nelle shuffled along behind her parents and siblings. Each place at the table bore a name card, but the seating order had no rhyme or reason, completely disregarding traditional precedence. How *very* odd. Doing so in a private home such as Camlon was one thing, but she'd never heard of such at a Town ball. A general muttering indicated others were perplexed, as well.

Lord Effingham's voice rose above the chatter. "We hope not to cause offense but rather to stir excitement by partnering ladies and gentlemen with companions other than their usual fare."

"As the lord and lady often do themselves," whispered a lord behind her. "No doubt they each seek a new bed partner tonight."

May she not be seated next to Lord Effingham, then.

Her parents and Tabby discovered their placards at the first table, but Lucy-Anne had to search farther, finding hers at the third of the long tables crowded into the dining room. Nelle, however, was near the head of the center table. She glanced at the name cards for the empty seats next to hers and nearly stumbled over the chair the footman had pulled out. Gavin had been placed to her left, Engelsfell to her right. She'd been seated between two dukes. It must be a mistake.

Arthington entered the room, followed by Emerlin. Behind them came Engelsfell, then Stoneleigh, and, at their rear, Gavin. A slight hush fell over the room as this handful of the most prominent men in the realm strode through. Stoneleigh sat next to Tabby. Arthington and Emerlin took seats opposite each other at the other end of Nelle's table. Engelsfell and Gavin continued in her direction, of course.

She gulped.

A broad grin swept across Gavin's face when he saw her. He said something to Engelsfell, who nodded in return, mirth playing at his lips, then slid into his chair. "Good evening, Nelle. This is indeed a great pleasure," he murmured.

Her pulse leapt at his use of her Christian name. Or was it that wolfish grin, the slightly disheveled hair, or the lion pin gracing his cravat that did her in?

Drat and blast. She'd never make it through the evening. Maybe the heat, rather than his presence, was making her feel faint. *Ha! Don't lie to yourself.* If only she could plead a headache and return home. It was too late for that, however. She must make do.

"Good evening, Your Grace." There. That should indicate where things stood.

Her formality didn't deter him from winking at her. Winking! "You look particularly ravishing this evening, Goddess."

Could she stab him with her fork? Anything to stop this flirtatious behavior. Had he not declared the impossibility of any future at the foundling home?

"Your delicious blush sets off the hint of green in your gown to perfection."

"*Gavin!*" she hissed, to his answering bark of laughter.

"There it is. Thank you, *Lady* Elinor."

Her lips curled up. She couldn't help it. The man was deucedly appealing. No wonder his reputation as the most charming of lovers had spread far and wide, even if it weren't true.

"You know, I've never cared for the color green," he went on as a footman filled his glass.

"Not care for green? Who doesn't like green? It's my favorite color." The words streamed out before she could stop them.

He took a sip of his wine. "You've made me reconsider. I find I'm rather fond of the shades you wear, at least."

Oh, good heavens. The man was incorrigible. The evening was looking up if such repartee was to be had. How entertaining it was to playfully spar with a man. How electrifying to spar with this one.

She took a sip of her own wine then touched her napkin carefully to the corner of her mouth. She was about to greet Engelsfell when a man at the next table caught her eye. Lord Grennet. His eyebrows pulled together and his lips thinned into a white line as he stared at her. He looked for all the world like Zeus angrily readying his next thunderbolt.

The napkin fell to her plate. *What on earth?* She glanced at Gavin. Had he noticed the earl? The rigid set of his jaw and the fierceness in his eyes said yes.

He leaned in, his breath tickling her neck. "I hope you'll favor me with a dance. A waltz, if possible; it does seem to be our dance."

Goosebumps spread across her skin at the way he said *our*, and yet a tinge of irritation followed in their wake. For whose sake was he charming her—hers or Lord Grennet's? "Perhaps you'd prefer to dance with the earl? You do seem to have eyes for each other," she said tartly.

"Ah, the Ice Princess launches her offensive." His voice lowered to an intimate whisper. "No, Nelle. I promise you are the only reason I came tonight."

"Me?" What a thing to say! Was she supposed to believe him? And if so, *why*? She deserved an answer. "Why?" she demanded, edging away to put more space between them. She didn't want to draw further attention.

"Because I need to hear more stories of Georgie and Richard, of course," he said easily. Annoyingly easily. "Has Richard moved on to worms yet?"

Another smile threatened her cheeks. The dashed rogue—every time she sought to establish distance, he pulled her in again.

A familiar laugh caught her ear, even in the midst of the many conversations. Lucy-Anne. She was seated a few places down from Lord Grennet directly next to Ashvere, joy lighting her face at her beau's attentions. Someone who knew both the Rutley family and the Effinghams must have had a hand in these seating arrangements.

"Happy to oblige," commented Engelsfell from her other side.

Nelle's gaze flew to him, but the tall duke was talking to

the gentleman across from him. How silly to assume he'd been addressing her, that he'd somehow heard her thoughts and confessed to playing matchmaker.

When she turned her attention back to Lord Grennet, this time he smiled. Or was it a grimace? The beard made it hard to tell. She smiled in return, not wanting to rouse further ire. She must still try somehow to salvage Lucy-Anne's chances with his son.

Deliberately, she set to the roast goose in front of her, taking slow bites to limit any conversation. A fetching ebony-haired woman to Gavin's other side was doing her best to command his full attention. Gratitude for the respite warred with jealousy. It seemed an eternity until Lady Effingham called for the ladies to retire briefly before the dancing commenced.

As Nelle rose, Gavin grazed his fingers along her arm, startling her. "I trust you'll not forget our dance," he said.

She did not look at him, giving the barest of nods in response.

Engelsfell cleared his throat. "Will you save a dance for me, as well, Lady Elinor?"

"Of course, Your Grace."

The duke threw Gavin a teasing grin.

She bristled. She was no piece of meat for snarling dogs to fight over. Though Lord Grennet was the only snarling fellow nearby—or had been. He'd moved to sit with her father and a passel of other older gentlemen. With a loud guffaw, he slapped his hand on Lord Rutley's shoulder. Her father beamed in response.

What was that about?

BERTIE COUNTED to one hundred and then again as the ladies departed the dining room. He'd put on a good face for Rutley and Lady Elinor herself, but inside he fumed. Most of the gentlemen availed themselves of a glass of port. He did not. He needed his wits about him, especially after having to bear Cortleon being seated next to his soon-to-be wife.

To her credit, though she'd initially responded to several of the duke's comments, after a few glances toward Bertie, she then ignored the bastard. *Good*. She knew her place. Cortleon, on the other hand, had leered first at her and then at that raven-haired wench to his other side.

Had the toad no shame? So like his father. Women had laughed and simpered at whatever Loughton Knight said. Bee had, too. Bertie had excused it as part of her naturally effusive manner. Plus, those in the top echelon of society had always awed her. In hindsight, however, he'd seen it for what it was: evidence. Proof of his wife's perfidy with that loathsome lecher.

He steered clear of the younger Cortleon. He didn't trust himself to keep his temper. At best, he'd blurt out his coup at securing Lady Elinor; at worst, he'd challenge the damned duke. And he'd not risk his life on that wretched cur, not when he was about to hand the man an ignominious defeat.

He pulled at his beard, anxious to escape and rejoin the ladies, grateful at last when Effingham excused them to the ballroom. His cheer dimmed, however, at the sight of Cortleon bowing before Lady Elinor. She gave him her hand. *Maggot*.

Bertie turned to a rather homely young woman and extended his own hand. "Miss Dowding, would you grant me the honor of this dance?"

She nodded an enthusiastic yes, her protruding front teeth pressing into her lower lip. "Yeth, thank you, Lord Grennet."

Poor thing. Unless possessed of a sizable fortune, she'd be hard-pressed to make a match.

They moved into their positions for the quadrille, but his partner might as well have been a broomstick for all the attention he paid her. He kept his eyes on Cortleon and Lady Elinor, though they exchanged but few words. When the dance ended, Lady Elinor hurried away toward the retiring room. The duke, meanwhile, headed in the opposite direction, meeting up with Emerlin at a far corner of the room.

Bertie relaxed, pleased his future wife had resisted the knave's seductive ways. And soon, very soon, he'd announce Lady Elinor was his. He merely waited on Hugh to be in the room, so that his son could hear his good fortune. The lad was nowhere to be seen at the moment, but given Lady Lucy-Anne's presence with her mother and sister, he rested easy that she wasn't seeking indecent liberties with his son, as so many did at events such as this.

He scowled. Those of rank and prestige ought to behave with honor and respectability. He'd certainly ensure his new wife would. He'd protect her at all costs. And she'd not dishonor him. No woman would again.

NELLE SAGGED against a wall in the corridor, her heart racing. How could the touch of Gavin's gloved hand send her into such palpitations? It wasn't just his hand, though. At each turn of the dance, he'd whispered something short and simple, quietly enough that no one else could hear.

"You are radiant."

"I cannot tear my eyes away."

"I should like to meet you in the gardens."

"I shall wait there the next quarter hour."

"If you do not come, I'll understand."

And then, on the final turn, "I cannot stay away from you, my goddess."

She ought to refuse his outrageous offer, of course. What good could a clandestine meeting do? And yet, after visiting the retiring room to recover her senses, she found herself at the courtyard doors. She glanced around. Her mother was in close conversation with Lady Effingham. Lucy-Anne and Tabby nursed lemonades. Lord Grennet spoke with someone she didn't know. None of them faced her. Before she could reconsider, she slipped out. If anyone were to ask, she'd say she needed some air. The oppressive evening heat would lend credence to her claim.

A voice called softly to her and she whirled. Gavin stood bathed in the light from the windows behind him, which cast his face in shadow, hiding his expression. Without a further word, he walked into a darkened alcove shielded by ivy-laced trellises.

She shivered, despite the sultry weather. She'd been alone with him before, of course—they'd spent more than an hour in each other's company at the Home. But this was different. This was in private, under the cover of darkness, at a ball in which she wore her newest gown and he a raven-black coat over an ivory waistcoat, with the black silk breeches common for formal dress. His stockings and shoes did not differ from other gentlemen's, but he cut a finer figure than any she'd ever seen, the breeches hugging his muscular thighs, the stockings emphasizing his well-formed calves. Not that she should notice. He was not for her. And yet here she was, hidden outside with the altogether too enticing Duke of Cortleon.

"I need to caution you," he whispered.

Caution? She wanted to cast caution to the wind. Perhaps it was the three glasses of wine she'd imbibed in an effort to calm her nerves. Perhaps it was her growing sense of desperation over the whole wretched state of things.

Whatever it was, she threw herself at him, her arms encircling his neck, her fingers lacing through the hair dusting his coat collar.

He hesitated but a second before his own arms slid around her, his wide hands caressing her back. He bent his head but paused as their mouths were about to meet as if reconsidering.

No! She desperately wanted his lips on hers, wanted to rekindle the fire that had been burning ever since the masquerade ball.

"Please," she whispered and barely before she'd got the word out he acquiesced, nibbling at her lower lip before moving his mouth over hers.

She sank into him, a satisfied purr emerging from her throat, and at the sound, he increased the pressure, teasing at her lips until she opened them. He explored her inner recesses and she returned the caress in kind, their tongues thrusting and parrying as if in some sort of duel, a duel in which there were no losers. His own low growl met her ears as he pressed her to him, their bodies melding. *Oh, how delicious!*

Despite the hot, humid air, she wanted nothing more than to get closer, to remove his cravat, to slide her fingers over his bare skin, to ... His hand moved up her side, near her breast, and she gasped at the ache it produced. She wanted him to move higher, to take the mound in his hand. She wanted him to—

With a sudden jerk, he pulled his mouth away and disentangled her arms from his neck. He stepped back, chest heaving. "I'm sorry." He held up a hand as if to ward her off. "I never should have—To dishonor you in—"

She swallowed. "No, 'twas— 'twas me, Gavin. I—"

"*No*," he said forcefully. "The fault lies with me for asking you to meet here." He edged closer, the faint glow from the ballroom illuminating his face. His eyes swam with something—desire? Frustration?

"You have my highest admiration, Nelle. If things were otherwise ..."

The music from the ballroom ceased. Voices hummed nearby.

"Oh!" she exclaimed, the danger of this situation washing over her. She shouldn't be here. If they were caught ... Without further thought, she ran from the alcove, pausing only to check that the terrace was clear of people before slipping back into the ballroom. She'd made it three steps in when Lord Effingham called out over the room.

"Lord and Lady Rutley and Lord Grennet have an announcement they would like to make."

What? She pushed through the crush, spying her parents on the empty dancing area, the earl to their side. Her mother impatiently gestured her over, but her face beamed with joy. Unease sparked in Nelle's stomach as she crossed to her mother, who motioned her next to Lord Grennet. The earl gave her an eerie smile before stepping forward.

"It is my great pride and honor to announce," he said, his voice ringing through the room, "that I have asked for Lady Elinor's hand in marriage and she has accepted."

Applause burst forth from around her as she stood, stunned. He'd never done any such thing!

Her father pressed a kiss to her cheek. "I am so happy for you, my dear."

Surely, she was in a dream. She pressed a hand to her stomach, her head spinning. As Lucy-Anne rushed to her side, giggling with glee, she looked to the terrace door. Gavin stood just inside, still as a statue, his face betraying nothing. When their eyes met, he crossed his arms over his chest, his jaw tightening as his mouth twisted in ... in what? Betrayal? Disgust?

No doubt hers would do the same, if she weren't the object of so many appraising faces, though her fury aimed at Lord Grennet and her parents. How dare they? *How dare they?*

"One thing further," the earl said, as the clapping died down. He gestured Ashvere over. "Ours is not the only celebratory news. My son and my betrothed's sister, Lady Lucy-Anne, are also to be married."

Lucy-Anne shrieked, rushing to Ashvere, who took her hands in his, their elation evident. The ballroom once again erupted into applause, guests nodding to each other in approval, the sound of a hundred voices nearly deafening. Her parents and Lord Grennet accepted congratulations as Ashvere swung Lucy-Anne in an ecstatic circle.

Nobody seemed to notice Nelle, standing completely rigid as the chaos swirled around her.

When she looked again to Gavin, he was gone.

CHAPTER 25

*E*uphoria surged through Bertie. He wanted to shout, wanted to punch the air in victory, wanted to strut about the ballroom. He'd won. Given Cortleon's reaction from the back of the room, the duke knew it, too.

Lady Elinor was safe from the rake. Or would be, as soon as they'd wed. There was no guarantee this Cortleon would respect an engagement or marriage any more than his father had, but Lady Elinor would. She was different from Albina.

His newly betrothed's cheeks had burned red and her breathing been rapid, however, as she'd come through the crowd before his announcement. Where had she been? He'd thought her in the retiring room, not having seen her reenter the ballroom. Then again, Lord Bickville had occupied him in conversation. Had she been in the gardens? *With Cortleon?*

A knot formed in his chest. The damned duke *had* stood near the place from which she'd come. Bertie had scanned the room to find the rogue before he'd spoken, wanting to see Cortleon's face the minute victory was his. *Had they … ?*

Surely not. It'd not been above five minutes, ten at most,

since their dance and despite her flushed face, her hair and attire weren't mussed. The warmth in the room likely explained her deepened color, then; many ladies fanned themselves, their own cheeks rosy and foreheads pearled with sweat. Nor had Cortleon the look of a man satisfied. The man's cravat remained starchily creased and his clothing showed no sign of disarray.

"An honorary waltz is in order!" called Lady Effingham.

Bertie turned to his betrothed, who stood behind him, her skin rather ashen. Irritation curled his lip. Was she not pleased? He'd forgiven her rudeness in the park and granted her greatest wish: financial security and her sister's happiness. He reached for her hand and pulled her into position. She complied, but her body was stiff, her arms rigid. As the music began, she strained against him as if seeking as much separation as possible.

"I did *not* accept any offer of marriage from you, Lord Grennet. You never made one." Her eyes snapped, but her voice was low so as not to draw attention.

"Ah, but your mother did. She said you'd indicated your eagerness to wed after our ride in the park."

She jutted out her chin, looking away. Why wasn't she giving him the gratitude she owed?

He tightened his grasp on her hand. "Let us show good cheer, my dear. It would not do for my bride-to-be to appear unhappy. My pardons for not having asked you personally. I suppose young ladies expect that. But surely, you're overjoyed that I've rescued you from a life of spinsterhood, that your sister now basks in unadulterated happiness, and that your family no longer faces complete financial ruination?"

At length, she gave a stiff nod. He heaved an irritated sigh. Once his wife, she'd cease these fruitless snits.

"Now smile. People expect excitement in a lady newly betrothed."

～

NELLE WINCED at Lord Grennet's grip. He was immense, far larger than she. Despite his size, he'd always seemed gentle. Not now. Now, for the first time, he truly frightened her.

She'd never actually agreed to her mother's demand she accept any proffered proposal, never voiced out loud willingness to write the letter her mother had demanded. No doubt Mother's desperation for the match had conveniently erased that detail from her mind—or did she simply not care whether or not Nelle had given consent?

She swallowed. Was there a chance he'd seen her in the gardens with Gavin? That'd explain this change in demeanor. But if so, he'd not have gone through with the announcement. He seemed agitated, but not as much as she'd expect if he knew of her tête-à-tête with the duke.

Her head pounded. She wanted to pull free and run from the room. Doing so would accomplish nothing, however, beyond making her the subject of gossip. As she and the earl made the next turn, Lucy-Anne floated by in Ashvere's arms, her expression that of pure bliss. Nelle's eyes caught on her mother, who'd clasped her hands at her chest as she watched her daughters dance, satisfaction permeating her upright posture. Even her father beamed, accepting congratulations from fellow guests as he proudly held his lapels.

Her stomach heaved as the walls closed in around her. This was the outcome she'd wanted: Lucy Anne's happiness recovered and the family's fortune solidified so that her other sisters need not also sacrifice themselves. Yes, this was exactly what she'd wanted ... before Gavin. Before he'd charmed her with his tenderness with children—and moved her with his own vulnerability. Before she'd kissed him in a shaded alcove, setting her aflame with desire. She wanted *him*, not Lord Grennet.

"If things were different," he'd said.

But they weren't. And he didn't love her. If he did, he'd have declared it in the garden or challenged Lord Grennet's claim in the ballroom. She almost laughed at the fantastical image of the Duke of Cortleon charging across the floor to rescue her like a chivalrous knight of old. This was no medieval tale. Gavin Knight could not save the Ice Princess. A betrothal was binding.

The disgust in his face told her he thought she'd thrown herself at him while already promised to the earl. If only she could find him and explain. To what end, though? If she begged off from Lord Grennet, she'd ruin her family.

The inevitability of her fate dragged on her like a sodden cloak, its ties choking. But this was the mantle she must don. She had no choice. She pasted on her brightest smile for her future husband. "I hope you can forgive my ungracious reaction, sir. This turn of events caught me by surprise. I thought, given recent events, that I'd lost your good favor."

There. If he knew of the alcove encounter, surely he'd reveal so now.

His brow rose, but then his beard cracked, his teeth gleaming in a self-satisfied smile. "Any fault lies entirely with that bastard Cortleon."

She inhaled sharply at his coarse language.

"I beg pardon," he said, "but if you knew the duke as I do ..."

Nelle wrinkled her nose. *As he did?* What did he mean? The two men hardly sought each other's company, and given Gavin's long absence from England, what history could lie between them?

"You're nothing like him. Nor my first wife, thank heavens. You possess the sense and rational demeanor she lacked. It pains me to say this, but she let her desires drive her into—" He broke off, frowning deeply. "I don't demand much in a wife, Lady Elinor, but fidelity is a must. I trust you will never deceive me in such a way."

Relief washed over her. He didn't know of her garden dalliance. That didn't change the fact she'd thrown herself wantonly at Gavin and still wished for more. She shook her head, chastising herself for the continued yearning. The die was cast.

"That's what I thought." Lord Grennet puffed out his chest. "I've won in all ways." He released her hand, giving her a formal bow. "Yes, I've won."

Goosebumps pricked her skin, the words nagging at her. *Won what?*

∾

GAVIN THREW DOWN HIS PLAY, his concentration solely on the cards in front of him. Or it should have been. Anything to avoid thinking of Nelle's treachery. He'd considered leaving entirely, but he'd not let that temptress have more power over him. Instead, he'd made for the card room and hurled himself down at the table at which Engelsfell and Emerlin were playing. His mood communicated itself well enough, as neither man attempted to engage him in conversation, though Em's eyes revealed his concern. Two other gentlemen were at the table, however, and Gavin was not going to speak aloud of Lady Elinor Greene's duplicity.

How could she have deceived him so? To be engaged to Grennet—*Grennet!*—but yet kiss him so passionately in that alcove. She'd initiated such intimacy, knowing full well she was promised to another, knowing full well his vow of honor.

He grabbed his cup, gulping down the liquor. He was as much at fault for their actions in the alcove as she. More so, in that he'd asked her there, intending to ... intending to what? He'd fooled himself into believing it a noble request, a chance to talk to her of Grennet. He'd not asked her about the earl at the Home, as he'd determined to do. No, he'd assumed given their ... connection ... that his concerns of an attachment were unfounded.

At seeing the earl's intemperate reaction to them talking at dinner, however, he'd decided he must warn her. What he would have said, he knew not. He still lacked proof.

He ought to have rejected her advances. He ought to have refused her. Why hadn't he?

Because ... because it was Nelle. The woman who'd drawn his regard from the very start then captured it completely at the foundling home. Her character was even lovelier than her appearance. Now, when he looked at her, he saw not only her fine features but also how tenderly she'd gazed at William, how she'd let Georgie tug on that magnificent golden hair, and how she'd pressed those berry lips to several infants' brows, her love for them evident in every movement. He saw her generosity and her warm, caring nature—the one she hid from society. Why she hid it, he didn't know. Perhaps she only wished to share herself with those special few she trusted.

She'd shared herself with him. She could have kept their interactions at the Home strictly impersonal, but she hadn't. Neither had he. The most intimate exchange of his life had taken place not in a bedroom, not in the midst of lovemaking, but in the hallways of a public home.

Somehow that rendered it all the more special.

Nelle's quiet devotion to helping the ones she loved reminded him of his own mother and the sacrifices she'd made on his behalf. She'd given up her entire life, the only world she'd known, to protect her son. She'd moved them to a foreign land and chosen to live in secrecy, in a situation that, while comfortable, was far below what a duchess would expect.

And she'd done it for him. Just as Nelle had promised herself to Grennet to save her family.

If only ... If only what? If only he'd offered for her himself? He'd never declared formal intentions because he didn't have any. He *couldn't* have any, not if his father's killer still lived. The father for whom he sought justice—but to what end? He hadn't known him. He certainly didn't admire him. Loughton Knight had been unfaithful to Gavin's mother countless times, infidelities that cost him his life. Why avenge the man who'd wronged them so? Yet surely the murderer must pay. He'd taken his father from him. And now he'd taken the woman he loved.

It was as if Gringolet had kicked him in the gut.

He loved Nelle. Loved her as he'd never loved anyone. Beyond his mother, but that had been different, the affections of a child for a parent. This was the passion of a man for a woman. And he'd lost her because he'd prized this quest above love. Lost her to Grennet, the very man who might have stolen his father's life. If only he had proof! *If only* ...

He growled.

"Do you want to sit this one out, lest I win even more off of you?" Engelsfell teased as he dealt.

A massive figure appeared in the doorway, one that had to bend down to enter so as not to bash into the doorjamb. *Grennet.* Other men congratulated the earl as he sauntered into the room. Unbelievably, the oaf crossed to their table and took a free chair across from him.

Though Gavin fought to retain a nonchalant manner, every muscle in his body tensed. He wanted to pummel Grennet with his fists, wanted to pound the snake into the ground. How he hungered to call him out.

The man to Grennet's side nudged the earl. "Well done, sir, landing the woman most of us coveted at one time or another over these many years."

Gavin clenched his fists against the table. Was that a poke at Nelle's age? If so, the lord was an idiot. Any man of sense could see she outshone every young debutante, not only in beauty but also in depth of character.

Emerlin and Engelsfell's gazes slid to him. He steeled himself, winging that winsome grin his mother had always said could make any woman fall at his feet. But he didn't feel it.

"Congratulations, Lord Grennet." He infused his words with false insouciance as he bit back an oath.

The earl curled his lips in a smug grin. "Thank you, Your Grace."

Was it his imagination, or had Grennet shaded his words with derision?

"But why be here when you could be with your new fiancée?" Emerlin said.

He'd asked what Gavin likewise wondered. Why sit with men when he could be with the most magnificent woman in the world?

"Lady Elinor wished some time with her sister and mother to celebrate the dual engagement and to begin planning the weddings."

"Will it be before the Season lets out? That's only a matter of days." Engelsfell's question sounded innocuous enough, but he shot a glance at Gavin.

"No, no. Now that she's mine, we have time. I'm thinking a Christmas wedding at Swythdon." His steely gaze met Gavin's. "A long engagement helps ensure there are no … unexpected surprises, does it not?"

It took every ounce of restraint not to rise up with a roar from the table. Was the man implying concern about a possible pregnancy? On whose behalf: Nelle or Lady Lucy-Anne?

Emerlin placed a calming hand on Gavin's leg under the table. "No worries she might change her mind?"

The Irishman's words were light, teasing.

"No." Grennet took up the cards he'd been dealt, again looking at Gavin. "She's well and truly mine."

He tensed but said nothing. He'd not give the vile dog the satisfaction of knowing his needling had any effect. Conversation lapsed into small talk between the two less familiar lords and Grennet. Gavin played without care, consumed with fantasies of challenging the damned earl, but he took a number of hands anyway, the pile of guineas in front of him increasing as the hour went on.

Grennet leaned back in his chair after Gavin beat him in yet another round. "Perhaps, Your Grace," he said, his tone wry, "given my poor luck here, I should seek to win what you've already gained from my betrothed this evening."

Gavin froze. What did he mean? Did he know about his stolen passion with Nelle earlier? Drumming his fingers on the table, he casually slung his other arm over his own chair back, his eyes meeting Grennet's directly. "I can't say I know what you mean, sir. Though a lesser man might think you impugn my honor or that of Lady Elinor. Again."

The man next to Grennet sucked in a breath.

"No, no," the earl said. He gave an awkward chuckle, holding up his hands. "We all know you are a man of ... impeccable honor. I merely meant another dance." Rising from the table, he touched his hand to his forehead. "Good luck, gentleman, against Cortleon. He does seem to be on a winning streak. Then again," he added, his face cracking into an odious smile, "gambling is like courting, don't you think? Sometimes the person least expected ends up with the prize."

With that parting shot, the earl left the room.

CHAPTER 26

*N*elle packed for Inglewood in a daze, still flabbergasted by the events of the Saturday prior. She'd kissed the Duke of Cortleon again. She was betrothed to the Earl of Grennet.

How she wished she could explain to Gavin she'd known nothing of the engagement. She had no respectable way to seek him out, however, and what good would it do? Her course was set.

Lucy-Anne talked endlessly of wedding plans. "Hugh says his father wishes a double wedding at Swythdon," she'd said at breakfast. "They'll hold a large house party at Christmas, and we'll marry on New Year's Day. An auspicious way to begin this new chapter in our lives, don't you think, Nelle? Oh, 1814 shall be a grand year, indeed!"

"Why the long delay?" Not that she was complaining; the longer the better. But it seemed odd.

Lucy-Anne had waved a hand. "Oh, to allow us to assemble our trousseaus, no doubt. And to ready ourselves for our move to Swythdon. Isn't it wonderful? You and I shall live under the same roof!"

Now they sat in the drawing room, Lord Grennet and

his son across from them. When Lucy-Anne suggested she and Ashvere take a turn about the room, the earl moved next to Nelle. How she wished to scoot away.

"My dear, I hope you understand the reason for waiting to celebrate our nuptials. Such a delay will ensure everything and everyone is in … order."

She gritted her teeth. Was he implying a possible *pregnancy*? And did he suspect her, or Lucy-Anne? The earl's eyes *had* trailed to her sister as he'd spoken. The insinuation made her sick. *She* may merit his doubts—she *had*, after all, behaved inappropriately with Gavin—but Lucy-Anne did not! Her sister had been besotted with Ashvere from the minute she'd laid eyes on him.

He took one of her hands in his. "I will treat you well, Lady Elinor, provided you remain faithful and let no hint of scandal touch you."

She yanked her hand away. "If you think so lowly of me, sir—"

"No, no. That was a bad way to broach this topic," he interrupted, tugging at his beard. "My first wife was not loyal. She carried on an affair with—" He paused. "With whom isn't important. But her deception is the reason I've not remarried. I couldn't bear having my heart broken in such a way again."

How awful. A spark of pity formed for him. And yet, something gave her pause. His manner seemed unnatural, his voice lacking emotion. Or had he walled away his pain, as she'd done?

The earl's eyes turned flinty. "I will never allow a woman to dishonor me in such a way again."

The spark petered out, replaced by fear. He'd just threatened her, had he not? Why had she ever assumed him likely to acquiesce to her every need, grateful to have her as his wife? How arrogant she'd been. How naïve. She gave him a nod, even as her stomach reeled.

"I've no doubt, however, my dearest," he added, his serpentine smile back in place, "that you'll be the perfect wife. You're Albina's opposite in nearly every way. We'll make our home at Swythdon. I'm sure you will come to love it as much as I do."

She swallowed. Swythdon. In Staffordshire—nearly Cheshire, he'd said. She'd never been so far north. Most of her travels had been between Rutley Manor, Inglewood, and London. She'd been as far east as Margate and as far west as Glastonbury, but the Cotswolds were the northern-most she'd visited. How often would she and Lucy-Anne be able to see their family? Or come to London?

He rose. "Hugh, though you'd undoubtedly prefer to spend the rest of the day in Lady Lucy-Anne's lovely company, it's time to make our good-byes. We've much to do before our journey tomorrow."

"Tomorrow?" Lucy-Anne's face fell. "Oh, must you leave so soon?"

The earl gave her a patronizing smile. "I'm sure the months will fly by until we are in company again, dear lady."

Lucy-Anne nodded, but her eyes moistened. "I shall miss you most ardently," she said to Ashvere. "Write to me every day!"

"I promise," he responded, moving to stroke her cheek with the back of his hand.

"Oh, Nelle, isn't it sad that the Season has come to a close?" her sister exclaimed. "Lady Deandra wrote that she and her brother were off this morning, Cortleon and his friends, too. Tabitha will be most disappointed. I believe she holds a tendre for Emerlin."

"Does she now?" Ashvere's eyes twinkled. "And here I thought all the ladies mad for the Legendary Duke."

Nelle's heart pounded. He was gone. Gavin was gone. *Would she ever see him again?* She choked back the lump in her throat. It mattered not; if and when she did, she'd be a married woman.

This time last year, she'd thrilled in the Season ending, having made it through once more unscathed. Then her parents had issued their ultimatum. Because of that and Lucy-Anne's love for Ashvere, Nelle had set her cap for the moneyed Earl of Grennet. And she'd done it. She'd secured an engagement. She'd rescued her family from penury, had given her sister her heart's desire, had done everything she was supposed to.

The one thing she hadn't planned on was falling in love with the Duke of Cortleon.

∿

GAVIN PUSHED GRINGOLET HARD, the horse eating up the miles between London and St. Graele. When Engelsfell said he was returning to his ancestral home, he'd invited himself along. He'd needed to leave London. He couldn't bear the idea of seeing Nelle again, especially if she were in Grennet's company.

After the Effingham ball, he'd drunk himself silly in Arthington's townhouse, refusing Arth and Em's company. Hoisting the bottle of brandy, he'd given them a caustic grin. "Merely drowning my frustrations at having made no further progress in my quest."

"I shall leave you to it, then," Arth responded, "but I am off to bed; one too many late nights of carousing for me. I'm getting too old for this." He pointed a finger at Emerlin. "If you repeat that to anyone, I shall beat you."

Em wrinkled his nose. "Is that anything to say to a friend?"

Arth sauntered off with a laugh, but Emerlin remained in the doorway. "Are you sure you don't need company, Cort?"

"No." Gavin tossed his hair back, winging a pained smile. "Some defeats a man must face alone."

His mind swirled with suspicions. Had his father slept with Grennet's wife? Had the earl killed him in a mad rage? Or as calculated retribution? If so, if Grennet *was* the green monster, then Gavin had shot him all those years ago. But then why on earth would the earl antagonize him? Wouldn't it make the most sense for Grennet to keep his distance, lest Gavin learn his secret?

The questions circled, with no clear answers. He'd swirled the brandy in the bottle, his mind spinning as well as his head. Engelsfell's mother had known Grennet's wife —and Grennet. If he spoke with her personally, might she remember something further, some additional information that could help?

His request to accompany Engelsfell had elated his tall friend. "Of course. You'll relieve the tedium that arises when I have no one with whom to train. No one whom I can beat." He'd punched Gavin in the shoulder with that statement. Gavin retaliated with a strike to the abdomen, both erupting into good-natured laughter. "Just be sure," Engelsfell had said, slinging an arm around his shoulders, "that you do not go after my sister, or I'll have to pummel you for real."

No chance of that. Though Lady Deandra was a sweet girl, his heart beat for only one woman.

"Not much farther now," Engelsfell called presently. The man's massive steed pulled near to Gringolet, the horses' hooves flying. "Two miles at most."

With that, he kicked his heels into his mount's side, encouraging the equine to gallop even faster. Gavin did likewise, the exhilaration of flying over the ground, wind whipping through his hair, overtaking him.

It'd been Engelsfell's idea to leave the carriage behind and ride these last few miles themselves. "Deandra is safe with the coachman and two footmen. And no doubt she needs a respite from our talk of weapons and combat."

As they flew around a hill, a large sandstone manor came into view. "St. Graele," Engelsfell called over his shoulder.

The immense estate home's castellated roof reminded Gavin strongly of Camlon. Wainsbury was by no means small, but it couldn't compare. When they pulled up the horses just short of the stables, the beasts' chests heaving, he shook his head. "Do all you dukes live in bloody castles?"

"All we dukes? *You* are a duke."

A gray-haired woman raced out a door, her chubby cheeks belying the slim form below. "Percy!" she cried out. "Oh, your mother shall rejoice to see you again. How we've missed you!"

Engelsfell enfolded her in an embrace, his giant form dwarfing the lady's petite build. "Aunt Ellen, I would like for you to meet my friend, the Duke of Cortleon. Cortleon, this is my aunt, Lady Kingsfisher."

"Oh, my pardons, Your Grace," she said, not releasing her nephew. "It is a pleasure to make your acquaintance."

Gavin smiled. How could he not? This tiny, unexpectedly spry woman was charming. "Likewise, Lady Kingsfisher."

"But where is Deandra?" The lady sent her nephew a sharp glare as if she suspected Engelsfell of harming his sister.

"She'll be along shortly, Auntie. Cortleon and I needed to give the horses their head."

The woman snickered. "More likely you than the horses. But come, come, your mother will want to see you."

Engelsfell nodded, falling into step behind his aunt. "My valet, Chretien, will show you to a chamber," he said to Gavin as they walked. "He can also serve as your valet for your visit. I'm certain my mother will be eager to meet you, however. May we ask you to join us in an hour?"

"Gladly." The sooner he could meet the dowager duchess, the sooner he might gain new information.

A scant thirty minutes later, a servant came to indicate Her Grace was most desirous of meeting him. Thank goodness Chretien, a rather somber fellow of few words, had rapidly set him to rights after the long journey. He followed the valet down a wide corridor. Entering a side chamber, the servant announced, "Your Grace, may I present His Grace, the Duke of Cortleon?" then quietly made his exit after Gavin stepped into the room.

A frail, aged woman lay in the large bed at the center, Engelsfell standing to her side. Their resemblance was unmistakable—the same curve to the cheek, the same nose, and same smile. How this slight woman had ever given birth to a man as huge as her son, however, was a mystery.

"Oh!" She raised her hands to her mouth as several tears spilled onto her cheeks. "You are the very image of your father."

He rocked on his heels. He'd seen a portrait of his father at Wainsbury, of course. He couldn't deny the similarities, but that didn't mean he welcomed them.

"I'm an old woman, one stranded in this bed." She patted a space next to her. "Come, let us not stand on formalities."

With a smile, Gavin took a seat, happy to drop polite society's rigid rules.

"How proud he would have been of you, dear boy." She settled a thin, wrinkled hand over his. "And your dear Mama. My friend. How I longed to see her again. All these years with no communication. We'd thought the both of you ..." She trailed off, but her meaning was clear.

Gavin choked back the grief that had arisen at her reference to his mother. "Duchess, if we are dispensing with formalities, might I ask you immediately of that day?"

She nodded, her eyes watering once more. "Such a sad day. Though everything I recorded I sent to Irene ..."

"You wrote of Lord Grennet and his wife?"

"Ah, yes. Albina was quite charming. So full of life and energy. Vivacious. Winsome. She was never the same after that frightful event." She broke off, giving his hand a weak squeeze. "None of us were. You, most of all, no doubt." Engelsfell says you remember nothing?"

He swallowed. "No."

"Perhaps that's fortunate. We couldn't imagine the horror of seeing your father like that."

He fingered the signet ring on his free hand. "Though if I had, we could have brought the murderer to justice. If only I could remember, I could do so now."

"Sometimes it's best to let the past remain the past." The words were Engelsfell's, his voice strangely soft. When Gavin glanced at him, the large man straightened. "Though I'll aid you however I can, of course."

"I was never quite sure why Albina married him, truth be told," the dowager said, drawing the men's attention back to her. "I suppose her parents pressured her. He was a nice enough fellow, but not at all like her. Overly proper, especially for a mere earl." She sniffed.

Engelsfell laughed. "Come, now, Mama. Not everyone can be a duke."

"I suppose not. But what airs he put on, always attired as if to present himself at court. Such a fop in those green clothes. Not that it's a bad color; I have several green gowns myself and it was quite popular in that era. Many gentlemen wore suits of vert. But to dress head-to-toe in such! Green hose, green shoes. Green hat!" She made a dismissive noise. "Albina thought so, too. She never cared for his fancy waistcoats embroidered with ladybugs and butterflies and such. 'Golden thread for insects! How garish,' she'd say with that giddy laugh. Though I suppose there were worse offenders ... Lady Gadsworth with her bug-infested wig, or Lord Dumplesworth, whose puce satin breeches drooped so around his skinny legs."

Gavin stilled at her mention of embroidered waistcoats, his head filling with images. A man in the woods, his long white hair secured with a green ribbon. A periwig. Gold thread shining on a green waistcoat. Butterflies at Gavin's nose. A threat ringing in his ear: *I will chop off your head.* And then a memory of reaching ... reaching ... lifting Papa's heavy pistol as the monster lunged for him, hands outstretched. A deafening noise, the giant falling, red everywhere.

The waistcoat was sickeningly clear. The man's face was not. But given the duchess's description of his clothing, it could easily have been Grennet. A giant man in green. The green monster of his nightmares?

He homed in like a hawk. "Was Lady Grennet true to her husband?"

The dowager sighed. "I suspect not. She never said anything openly, but there were hints—as you saw from the letter."

"Do you know who her lover might have been?"

She frowned, turning her eyes to her son.

"Could it have been my father?" Gavin asked directly. Perhaps she hesitated to incriminate the previous duke.

"I do not feel well speaking ill of the dead," she said, slowly. "And I don't know for sure if Albina was unfaithful. She was such a flirt, always making suggestive comments and innuendos, that separating fact from fiction was sometimes difficult. However ..." Her fingers plucked at the bedclothes. "Your father's reputation was well-known. I suppose it possible. She *was* quite distraught at his murder —though we all were, of course."

"Of course."

The dowager sucked in a breath. "Are you suggesting Lord Grennet might be the one who killed your father? Oh, I can't imagine it; honor was always paramount to the earl. Despite his large stature, he was unfailingly polite and well mannered. I don't believe a man of such esteem could stoop to so dishonorable an act."

"Such esteem?" Engelsfell snorted. "Moments ago, you were decrying his low birth."

"This is no time for jokes, my child." Her voice was steel. How amusing to see Engelsfell draw himself up straight, like a little boy shaking off a scolding. Only this little boy was well over six feet.

"I'd never publicly accuse any man of such a heinous act without definite proof, which I do not yet have," Gavin said. "I'm simply gathering as much information as possible. It's equally likely it was a brigand." He didn't think anything of the sort, but he didn't want to distress her by saying so. He rose, pulling down the edges of his coat. "Thank you for your willingness to speak openly and frankly with a man you've just met. I ought to leave you to rest now, Duchess."

"Do tell me you'll stay at St. Graele awhile. My son would certainly enjoy the company. He spends far too long as it is cooped up here with only his female family members for companionship."

"Mother," Engelsfell said, irritation in his voice, "I do actually have estate duties to which I must attend, you know."

"Yes." Her eyes drifted shut. "But I know your secret, Percy."

At that, both men's eyebrows rose.

"What secret?" Engelsfell said after a moment.

His only answer was a soft snore.

CHAPTER 27

*B*ertie paced Swythdon's long halls. It'd been weeks since his return, and yet his usual peace from being at home had not come.

Lady Elinor and her family had returned to Inglewood, as Lucy-Anne's voluminous correspondence confirmed. Nearly daily a new letter arrived for Hugh, but Lady Elinor had not written. Neither had he; he'd never been much for letter writing. But his betrothed ought to have put pen to paper, especially given her sister's frequent missives.

He scowled then quaffed from the goblet in his hand. It was only three in the afternoon, but a man was allowed an early drink now and again, wasn't he? No matter that he'd had such drinks with increasing frequency since his return.

Was Lady Elinor being unfaithful? Had Cortleon perhaps gone to Inglewood? Though the duke had left Town a number of days before he and Hugh, he'd not been in residence at Wainsbury. A local inn master confirmed as much when they'd passed near the Cortleon seat, which was not far from the main road used to reach Staffordshire and Swythdon.

Had Albina stopped there? Had she trysted with the

blackguard in his own home? She'd traveled often from Swythdon to visit her mother in Coventry. Wainsbury was fewer than nine miles away. The thought brought the glass to his lips again. Had Cortleon entertained Bee under his own roof? Perhaps even with his wife in residence?

The notion was abhorrent, but then again, who knew what the wretched cur had been capable of? He'd swived Albina when she'd been heavily pregnant—a repulsive notion on many levels. How often had Cortleon and Bee made love—no, not made love, fucked—yes, how many times had Cortleon and his wife fucked while at Camlon that Christmas? How many times had they made him a fool? How many times?

He raised his glass once more, irritated to find it empty. "Brandy!" he bellowed.

After a moment, a footman entered the hall, decanter in hand. This wasn't the first time Bertie had called for more liquor of late. He held his glass for the servant to pour.

"No, no, more than that!" he chided when the man pulled the decanter away when the glass was barely half full.

As the servant retreated, Bertie studied an enormous portrait on the wall of a rather stout woman in an ornate gown, an embroidered stomacher sprouting from voluminous green skirts and leading up to a wide ruff. A former Countess of Grennet, a century and some removed. Had she been loyal to her husband? Or had she also been willing to spread her legs for any man who came along?

Albina's portrait hung farther down the hall. He hadn't been able to bring himself to get rid of it, despite its constant reminder of the unfaithful bitch. He'd loved her. Oh, how he'd loved her. And she'd made a mockery of him.

He stumbled toward the painting, halting before it. There she was. That same blonde hair, those same blue eyes. Lady Elinor's were a shade or two darker, but the similarities were undeniable.

His face crumpled. Perhaps he should cry off. If she proved as perfidious as his first wife, he'd surely go mad. It was why he'd never taken a second—not when the first had led him to such dishonor. To *murder*. That's what it was, he'd since admitted to himself. He'd not given the duke a fair chance to defend himself. *Because Cortleon was indefensible!* Still, Bertie had always lived by the rigid code of honor his father and grandfather had instilled in him.

Until that day.

He took another swig of brandy. Why *had* he offered for her? Why had he made their betrothal the condition upon which his blessing for Hugh and Lady Lucy-Anne depended? Hugh was too young to marry, especially to the silly Lucy-Anne Greene. So different from her levelheaded sister. And yet, he'd given permission. He'd even promised Rutley an absurd sum for Lady Elinor's hand. Why?

To thwart Cortleon. Plain and simple.

But *why*? The duke had shown no signs of recognition. If Cortleon suspected him in any way, he'd have confronted him, particularly after losing Lady Elinor to him. The rash temper which had led the duke as a small child to shoot the man who'd just threatened his life must still be there.

Bertie groaned. Why had he poked the tiger? He should have left him well enough alone. Cortleon had shown remarkable—and unexpected—restraint, given his own provocative behavior. Why did a Cortleon always drive him to behave in dishonorable ways?

If anything, Bertie should have slain the lion when he was but a cub. He *should* have cut off the head of the only witness to his crime and ended the Cortleon line. That would have been the greatest revenge.

Revenge. Yes, he still wanted revenge for the ruin Loughton Knight had wreaked upon his life. Revenge for how the knave had stolen his love. He'd deprived Hugh his mother, as well. Bertie may have been the one to end her life, but Albina had wanted it. And Cortleon had made it necessary. Bee's melancholy over their son being a legitimate Grennet instead of a bastard Cortleon had been too much to bear.

His head spun, his stomach threatening to empty its contents. He ought to have eaten before he started on the brandy. He should go downstairs and request a meal, but his feet wouldn't move. He stared at Albina's portrait, Lady Elinor's face blurring onto Bee's and then off again.

With an angry growl, he whipped his glass toward the painting. It hit Albina's forehead, scuffing the paint. Brandy streamed down her face, looking much like tears. The same tears she'd wept for months after Cortleon's death and then Hugh's birth.

Clutching his head, he sank to the floor. No. The monster would not win. He would marry Lady Elinor. She'd be an honorable, dutiful, and faithful wife. And he'd have back everything he'd lost at Cortleon's hands.

∿

NELLE SAT in Inglewood's garden, petting the rabbit on her lap. Isolde, the rotund gray cat who'd simply appeared at the cottage one day, nosed her way under her skirts as Tristan, the white-pawed black tom who'd joined them only weeks after Isolde, chased a butterfly through the flowers. Normally stroking Caera's soft, white fur was enough to diffuse her worries. Not today. It'd turned October and thus a month closer to her nuptials.

She did not want to marry Lord Grennet. Their last few exchanges had made her uncomfortable, even afraid. It was as if another person lurked behind the gentleman he portrayed to the world. Like he was wearing a mask.

At the thought, her mind skittered to Gavin, though it often did. Memories of their masquerade kiss and then that second, more impassioned encounter at the Effingham ball preoccupied her dreams—and her waking hours, too.

She missed him. She missed the man she'd met at the foundling home, the one who'd showered those babies with genuine affection and revealed intimate parts of himself. They'd shared a true connection, not the surface facades adopted in most exchanges.

She missed the excitement of wondering if he'd be at the same social events, disappointment overtaking her when he wasn't, delight secretly surging when he was. She missed their teasing dinner conversations and the dances they'd shared. She missed the intensity of his eyes, the way he looked at her as if stripping her bare. Not of her clothes, though that notion titillated her. No, of her defenses. Of her very being, so that he saw the raw, sensitive center of her— the one she didn't show anyone else.

Lucy-Anne might have no compunction about her open sensibility, but Nelle never felt she could be free with her feelings. Mother had chided her since she was young for any such display.

Nelle had wept for days over a robin with the broken wing she'd attempted to nurse back to health, only to watch it die in her hands.

"'Tis but a *bird*, Elinor. A wild thing. Stop this absurd crying at once."

Her mother's harsh words had echoed in her ears long after, including a few years later, when Nelle had discovered Galahad, their old English bulldog, with his hindquarters caught in a trap, whining in great distress.

"There's nothing we can do, Nellie. We must put him out of his misery," Father had consoled her, but oh, how the bullet that had pierced the dog pierced her heart, too. She'd cried long hours, but always away from where she might be discovered.

She preferred to be among animals or children; they, at least, were honest in who they were, whether reveling in their joys, as Isolde did now, her belly up and feet stretched out under the warm sun, or lamenting their sorrows, as abandoned babies did with their cries, constant reminders there wasn't enough love in the world to counteract suffering or to save everyone.

But she tried. How she tried. If she could rescue one animal from pain, keep one child from loneliness, then her life had purpose. What purpose would she have as a wife?

If she bore children of her own, she supposed she'd have something, someone, into which she could pour her love. Did the earl wish for more? He did once, he'd said, but he was a younger man then. At his age, with an heir of good health and sound mind, was he satisfied? She certainly hoped so.

The image of a brown-eyed boy scampering about the garden, laughing with joy, slammed into her, taking her breath away. For the little boy, blond but with cognac eyes, ran to his father, who scooped him up and tossed him in the air, to ecstatic giggles. His father. Gavin. Gavin was the man in her imaginings. The father of her children. The man she loved.

A bitter cry burst forth, sending the rabbit scampering from her lap. When she'd finally found a man she could love, a man she *did* love, he was out of her reach. She was betrothed to another, one she didn't love or esteem. But what options did she have? No tenable ones.

Lucy-Anne bounded into the garden, a paper clutched in her hand, no doubt another letter from Ashvere. "Oh, Nelle, why can't time fly faster, so that I may see my Hugh again? And then be in his arms, as his wife." She tittered as she plopped down next to her sister. "How do you think it will be? The wedding night, I mean?"

Nelle gulped. Her wedding night was not something she wished to consider.

"Do you think it will hurt? Some of the girls say it hurts. I hope not. I can't imagine anything being horrible with Hugh!" At her continued silence, Lucy-Anne frowned, setting a hand on Nelle's knee. "I know you don't feel the same way for the earl as I do for Hugh, but he'll be a good husband. He must be."

Was Lucy-Anne trying to convince her, or herself? Did her sister feel any guilt over her situation?

"I'm worried for you," Lucy-Anne said, unusually serious. "You've grown thinner, your complexion paler. Are you truly so set against marrying? Do you ... do you wish to break with Lord Grennet?"

The catch in her voice revealed her apprehension over Nelle's answer. For if she said yes, she'd ruined her sister's happiness. "Not at all," she lied, forcing a smile. "Only nervous at the changes to come."

That was the truth, at least.

Lucy-Anne grinned with relief, leaping to her feet. "I must go tell Mother my new idea for my trousseau! Oh, let the days rush by!"

With that, she scurried off, leaving Nelle to her thoughts once more.

Time was passing too quickly and yet also too slowly. Too quickly, in that she wasn't ready. Christmas loomed on the horizon. By Twelfth Night, she'd be a married woman. And too slowly, in that starting her new life would aid in forgetting Gavin. If she were to wed *him*, she'd not have such dread. No, she'd very much look forward to spending their days together—and sharing his bed. If only she could have spoken to him after Lord Grennet's announcement. If only she could explain she hadn't known. If only she could tell him she loved him, come what may.

If only ...

～

GAVIN LEANED ON HIS SWORD, his chest heaving. "I must say, you're by far the best I've ever encountered outside of Sulpicio. Few men will battle with actual swords anymore, preferring the lighter—and safer—rapier."

Percy spun the large weapon in his hand. "Yes, but this is much more fun, don't you agree?"

"I agree it's a good idea the blades are blunted, or I fear I'd be bleeding from multiple holes. You might be my better, though I hate to concede such."

"Worried you could lose your reputation? The *Legendary* Duke, so they say?"

Gavin blew his lips in disgust. "*I've* never said so. Though," he added, flashing a cheeky grin, "I've never denied it, either." He straightened and pulled the sword from the soft ground into which its tip had sunk. "How better to ensure my father's killer knows what he's up against?"

The words were tossed off in a carefree manner, but Percy frowned. "You truly think it's Grennet?"

He paused. "I do."

"Then why are you still here?"

"So eager to get rid of me, are you?"

It'd been a good six weeks since they'd arrived, but he must admit he was loath to leave. Not only did he enjoy Percy's company immensely—he was the brother Gavin never had, who'd insisted after the first day here that they call each other by their Christian names, a sign of their close friendship—but leaving meant he had to face the realities of his current situation. He was increasingly convinced Grennet had killed his father, but his strict code of honor insisted he couldn't challenge the man unless he had incontrovertible proof. Without it, Grennet could deny any and all accusations. Without it, Gavin might never truly know.

The dowager's discussion of the earl's wardrobe, of his waistcoats, seemed damning enough, but still, his memories would not clear. Was his recollection of such an embroidered waistcoat true? Or was it possible he *wished* it to be true and had therefore imposed that image onto the shadowy figure in his head?

"To be honest," he said to Percy, kicking at the ground, "I still have doubts. My mother, your mother, Arth's mother, hell, even Arthington himself, have insisted Grennet could never have done such a thing. Then there's the issue of the gunshot. I fired the pistol, I struck the man at close range. But Arthington's father examined every guest and none were injured."

"Examined them without clothing?"

He frowned, looking at his friend. "Doubtful. You think someone could have hidden such a wound?"

Percy shrugged. "Perhaps. Especially if it wasn't as serious as presumed."

"How am I ever to know?" He swung his sword in frustration.

"Well, you could always get Grennet naked." Percy's eyes danced with mirth, and he erupted in full laughter when Gavin struck out at him, easily countering the blow with his own blade. "Just a suggestion."

They sparred another quarter hour before Gavin raised his arms, then fell down into the soft grass, panting. "I yield!"

"As well you should, brave knight. Thou art valiant, but I am ... I am ..." Percy broke off, his forehead wrinkling.

"Legendary?" Gavin supplied, to a hoot from his friend.

After a moment to catch his breath, he rose. "But you're right. I must return to Wainsbury, must see if there's anything more there to discover. I cannot stay here when there is a dragon to slay."

And a goddess in need of rescuing.

CHAPTER 28

*G*avin had been at Wainsbury for a week but had found nothing further, despite searching the estate high and low. Not that he knew what to look for. Was he expecting a written confession from his father?

He'd also queried the few remaining servants who'd been here when Loughton Knight was alive. He hadn't wished to discuss such personal matters, but then again, it wasn't as if they were unaware of what had transpired, nor were they ignorant of the previous duke's reputation.

When asked about his father's extramarital activities, Mrs. Stewart had given a disdainful sniff. "Your poor mother. She did love him so. But once a rake, always a rake."

The housekeeper had immediately apologized for speaking ill of his father, but he'd have none of it.

"I asked for your honesty, and it's what I wanted. Thank you, Mrs. Stewart."

She'd curtsied to leave but then exclaimed, "Oh," one hand flying to her cheek. "Perhaps Malmesbury ..."

"Malmesbury?"

"His Grace's old valet."

He wrinkled his brow. No one had ever mentioned any former valet.

"He took up another position at Badon Hill after His Grace died but lives now in the village with his daughter. He's lost most of his sight. If anyone were to know more of His Grace's intimate dealings, it would be Malmesbury."

"Thank you, Mrs. Stewart."

He'd wanted to rush to this Malmesbury immediately, but it'd been late in the day. Better to wait until the morning. Now he sat astride Gringolet, the horse's hooves lapping up the short distance between Wainsbury and the local village. It didn't take long to find the cottage Mrs. Stewart had described, and a rather harried-looking woman of some years instantly welcomed him in.

"I must beg your pardon, Your Grace; I have the grandchildren under my care while their mother—my daughter—visits her sister in Warwick proper and have not had time to set things to rights. They are an energetic lot." Her voice squeaked, and she pulled at her frayed apron.

Nervous. She was nervous. No doubt dukes didn't often visit.

A bundle of skirted legs and unkempt hair shot through the room, the girl screeching as a boy chased after her. Two more boys followed in their wake, younger than the first two. One clutched a toad as he ran, the poor animal's eyes bulging out in sheer terror. Likely it was more frightened of the girl than she of it.

"Oh, gracious," the woman squawked.

"It's quite all right, Mrs.—?"

"Mrs. Hobbles."

Hobbles? What an unfortunate name. He stifled a chuckle as the woman ushered him toward a side room.

"Father is in there. I must warn you; he mostly sits. Tires easily." She poked her head in through the doorway.

"Papa?" she called in a loud voice. "You have a visitor. His Grace, the Duke of Cortleon."

"His Grace," came a raspy response, "is dead."

"No, Papa." Mrs. Hobbles cast apologetic eyes at Gavin. "His son."

"His son?" The energy in the man's voice picked up. "Lord Wynhawke has returned?"

Mrs. Hobbles moved aside to allow him entry. An aged, frail man sat in front of a fireplace, a heavy blanket covering his lap. Rheumy eyes looked in his direction.

"I am Cortleon now," Gavin said, taking a seat in a rickety-looking chair to the man's side.

"Oh!" Malmesbury's face lit up. "If only I could see you! My eyesight is not what it once was."

"I'm told I look like my father." He couldn't hide the edge of distaste in his voice.

"Then you must be quite popular with the ladies," Malmesbury answered, a rather cheeky smile crossing his face for a man of his years.

"My father is why I am here."

Malmesbury sobered.

"What can you tell me about his indiscretions?"

The air hung with a pregnant pause. "He did have many," the old man said at length, his words cautious.

"Have no fear, sir. You do not dishonor my father or my family by speaking the truth. I seek answers about his death and the identity of his murderer."

Malmesbury's shoulders relaxed. "You witnessed the act."

"I did. But I cannot recall the details of that day with any clarity."

"Yes, you were so young. Poor boy."

"Did my father ever speak of any paramour in particular?"

The man's lips tipped down. "He was quite careful. Had

to be, to protect your mother. He did care for her in his own way."

Gavin nearly growled. How could one care for a woman and then be unfaithful to her? That would never be him. Never.

"But several times, when in his cups, he'd mention his beloved B."

"Bea?"

"I never knew if it was her name or perhaps her initial."

His heart sank. Grennet's wife was Albina. Not Bea or any name that began with a B. This Bea might be but one of his father's many lovers, however. Lady Grennet could still number among the rest.

"His Grace had a secret compartment in his desk." Malmesbury's cloudy eyes looked up as if he were trying to remember. "I saw him tuck papers in there a time or two. Never looked, of course; a valet wouldn't ever do so. Couldn't help but notice a distinct air of perfume often pervaded the room, though."

The man's memory was certainly not failing with his eyesight.

"Thank you, sir." Gavin rose. He pressed several guineas into the man's hand and then took his leave, nodding to the frazzled Mrs. Hobbles, now carrying the toad in her hand, as he left.

Once at Wainsbury, he searched every inch of his father's desk. At the back of one drawer was a slat with a strange indentation. He pushed at it, but nothing happened. Mayhap it wasn't anything, but he grabbed a short candle off the desk and bent down, using the flame's light to peer at the mark. A lion's head was carved into the wood. The barest bit of space around it hinted it might turn if one had the key. He looked to the signet ring on his left hand. Tugging it off his finger, he pressed the golden lion's head against the indentation.

A perfect fit.

Giving some pressure, he turned the ring against the wood and the slat popped open, revealing a compartment. From it, he extracted a handful of letters. He sat back on his haunches, not bothering to move to the chair in his hurry to examine this find. All of the letters were addressed to Loughton in a flowing, feminine hand. All were explicit in content, erasing any doubt this woman and his father had been on most intimate terms. Each was signed, "Your ever-loving Honey Bee."

Honey Bee. So, B was not an initial. Not a Christian name. A pet name. He ran a hand through his hair, pulling on it in frustration. He was no closer to discovering the woman's identity than before.

Except the scrawl looked familiar.

He studied it again. Did the hand not resemble that of the letter Percy had shown him, the one from Grennet's wife?

He scanned the contents of each letter again, looking for any missed clue. One referenced a house party at which she hoped to see her lover again. "I hold an unexpected treasure," it said, "one I hope might be yours. How green with envy my husband would be if he only knew of my love for you, dearest Lought."

The word green stood straighter than the rest of the words. For emphasis, perhaps? And the treasure—surely that referred to a pregnancy? This Honey Bee had to be Lady Grennet. Had to be. His hand shook, the paper rustling. Was this not proof? Unfortunately, the letters were undated, signed only with an alias, and he had no other script to which he could compare them.

But Percy did: Lady Grennet's letter, which Gavin had returned upon their arrival at St. Graele. As much as he hungered to race off to Swythdon and confront the nefarious earl, it'd be best to wait and have Percy send the letter.

If the handwriting proved a match, then he'd form a plan of action. Charging madly into Grennet's domain was not a wise course.

With a curse, he scrawled a missive to Percy, asking his friend to send the letter with all haste. He gave the note to a footman, commanding him to deliver it personally.

Then he waited.

～

FOUR EXCRUCIATINGLY LONG DAYS LATER, a carriage rumbled down Wainsbury's front lane. *At last!* But why a coach rather than a single rider?

Gavin had paced the grounds with impatience then ridden Gringolet out far and wide when no letter had arrived by the end of the second day. St. Graele lay less than thirty miles from Wainsbury; why hadn't he gone to retrieve the letter himself? He could have ridden there and back several times over and by day three was considering it—but then a note had finally arrived from Percy stating he'd be here on the morrow. That he was coming in person elated Gavin, but the terseness of the note was concerning. Had his mother taken a turn for the worse? Surely not, or Percy wouldn't leave her.

As the carriage pulled up, Percy leapt out before the wheels had come to a full stop. Gavin eagerly embraced his friend then started in surprise when Arth and Emerlin emerged, as well. "What?"

Percy grinned. "I thought the boys might be going mad at Camlon on their own, with no clubs to visit, whist to play, or women to charm."

Arth shoved at the larger man as Emerlin crossed to Gavin. "Good to see you, Cort. How quickly you've become one of us."

One of us. A sharp stab of emotion hit. He belonged.

He'd found his home. It wasn't at Wainsbury, an estate that still didn't feel like his, but amongst these men. He gave a grateful nod, not trusting himself to say more. Emerlin returned it. No other words were needed.

"I say, it's not a problem that we'll be housing with you for the winter, is it, Cortleon?" Arth curled his lip up over that famed snaggletooth. "You do have enough brandy and port put by, correct? And chicken. I like a good chicken."

"For you? Doubtful."

The men ascended the stairs into the main hall. Arthington let out a low whistle as he surveyed the space. "A fine house you have here."

"It is, though it can't compare with Camlon. That house ought better to be called a palace, as it's fit for a king."

"Need I fear our Prince Regent should wish to acquire it for himself?"

"And venture this far from London?" Em raised a dubious brow.

Arth pursed his mouth, nodding in agreement. "A worthy point."

"I'm delighted you're here," Gavin interjected, "but the letter?"

"Of course, of course." Percy pulled a folded paper from his waistcoat pocket. "I did not trust it to my trunk."

Gavin took it and opened it. Chills ran through him. The writing looked the same. This was it. This was final proof, was it not?

"Come." He beckoned to the men as he sprinted to the stairs, taking them two at a time in his haste to reach his father's study. He spread Lady Grennet's letter on the desk then pulled out the others. Opening the top one, he placed it side-by-side with the one freshly delivered.

Percy let out a low whistle. "Identical."

Arth nodded in concordance.

"I knew it. I *knew* it." Exhilaration flooded through him,

his entire body tingling as if set on fire. Moments later, his euphoria drowned under a tidal wave of rage. He pounded his fist on the desk with such force the inkstand jumped a good inch. It'd been Grennet the whole time, taunting him at Camlon, testing him in London. Taking Nelle from him.

Nelle. She was to marry that monster, the monster who'd murdered his father.

"I'll kill him," he shouted as he stalked the room. "Kill him!"

Percy and Arth made noises of understanding, but Em cleared his throat, waiting until Gavin looked at him to speak. "I admit, this evidence appears damning. It certainly proves Lady Grennet was having an affair with your father. But ... does it prove the earl is the one who murdered him?"

Gavin made a noise of complete exasperation. "How could it *not*?"

"I, too, want it to be true, if only so that you finally have your answers." Emerlin's blue eyes were earnest. "But as you noted, the letters are undated. It's still possible they're not connected."

It was Arth's turn to snort. "Surely you don't believe that?"

"What I believe doesn't matter. The truth is what matters, and Cort insists on definitive proof before he challenges any man. I think we'd all agree that's the utmost sign of a gentleman's honor. We do not accuse lightly; it does not befit our status."

Arth raised incredulous eyes to his friend. "Since when have *you* cared about status?"

Emerlin returned the stare, unblinking. "Since I committed to aiding Cortleon in whatever way I could. Sometimes that way is to be a voice of reason, sometimes of dissension, even if I do not wish to be."

Gavin stilled. "Em's correct."

Arth threw his hands in the air. "For all that is holy,

what more do you need? The words directly from the man's mouth?"

"Yes."

"Well, all right, then." Arth set his hands on his hips. "How do you plan on achieving that?"

He didn't know. The earl had proved quite slippery, but he was circling closer—and even a snake could be caught in a trap.

~

THE UNEXPECTED ANSWER came the next day when an invitation to the weddings at Swythdon arrived.

"Why on Earth?" Gavin mused aloud as he held the perplexing invite.

"Who cares?" Percy responded. "This is your chance. *Our* chance."

"What if you were not invited?" With a chuckle, Gavin leapt out of the way of his friend's fist-swinging response.

"I've no doubt I am, at least," Arth put in, "given how many times we've hosted him at Camlon. Our invitations must be there."

"Of course. Omitting the grandest duke in the land would not do."

Now it was Emerlin's turn to duck as Arth reached out to box his ear.

Percy looked to Gavin. "The party lies some four weeks hence. Should we return to our own estates, then?"

"By no means. I need you here to keep me from storming the castle myself." His tone was light, but inwardly he felt anything but. Why *had* Grennet invited him? Had it been Ashvere's request? Most likely Grennet relished one last opportunity to torment him by marrying the woman Gavin loved. The maggot must think he'd not be able to stay away. He was right.

He missed Nelle. Oh, how he missed her. He longed to see her face, those eyes alit with tenderness as she coddled a child. He ached to see her graceful figure as she glided across the ballroom, her pleasure in dancing evident in her every move. He yearned for more time with her, to learn everything about her. His desire for her on all fronts had only grown, not lessened, in these months apart. Yet, she'd deceived him. She'd kissed him and encouraged his advances, knowing full well she was promised to another. *How could she?*

The shock on her face at spying him in the ballroom, her duplicity revealed, had etched itself into his memory. Though of late, another thought had wriggled its way in. Was it possible she'd looked so stunned because she hadn't known? Had Grennet sprung such a thing on her publicly so she couldn't immediately refuse, lest it cause a scandal?

Lord and Lady Rutley had rejoiced at the news, no surprise evident in their countenances. They'd known. Could they have arranged her betrothal without her consent? It was beyond the pale, and yet Nelle herself had confessed her family's desperate straits. Landing a wealthy earl like Grennet would remedy that.

He castigated himself over the possibility she'd had no clue. He doubted it was the truth, but he hadn't given her a chance to explain. He'd spent the remainder of that night stewing in the cards room, then left London as soon as possible thereafter to avoid having to encounter her again.

"Do you think she's already there?" Gavin said as the men walked to Wainsbury's stables, each eager for a bracing ride. The November weather had turned cold, but he craved the brisk wind against his face.

Arth arched a brow. "She?"

"Unlikely," Percy answered without addressing Arth's question. "Deandra went to visit Lady Tabitha just last week."

He blew air from his cheeks, relief surging through him. At least Nelle was not in immediate danger. The thought that the earl might have also killed his wife was one he couldn't shake. He'd even less evidence to support that suspicion than of Grennet's involvement in his father's death, but the idea of Nelle within the earl's lair terrified him.

He swung himself into the saddle, immediately urging Gringolet to charge forth.

"Whoa," Emerlin called in a teasing voice, but he ignored the receding sound, intent on riding out his fury—and his fear.

Would Nelle be in mortal danger when she became Grennet's wife? Gavin bared his teeth to the wind. *If* she became his wife. He had to hear it from her own lips that this was what she truly wanted.

No need to rescue a goddess from a tower if she was exactly where she wanted to be.

CHAPTER 29

*N*elle pulled the thick woolen blanket across her lap, grateful for the warming stone at her feet. The air had turned miserably cold, the sky gray and threatening. She'd prayed several times for the heavens to open up and inundate the land with snow so as to render travel impossible.

No such luck.

The coach labored on, the horses straining under the weight of the six of them inside and the massive trunks stowed on the vehicle's roof. At this rate, reaching Swythdon might take a full week. Not that she was complaining. Dread consumed her as each mile eked by. Bars might as well have lined the carriage windows, for she felt a prisoner in a prison of her own making. Or perhaps like a princess in a high tower, waiting for her knight. Only instead of her knight, her Gavin, the dragon had arrived—in the form of Lord Grennet. He'd devour her alive.

Lucy-Anne prattled on about the passing scenery—scenery they'd seen a thousand times before, as they'd traveled only fifteen miles or so, but her sister narrated as if every detail were new. Tabby occasionally disputed Lucy-

Anne's descriptions, while Pru dozed in a corner, as did their father on the opposite bench. Lady Rutley sat with her hands tucked primly in her lap, a self-congratulatory smile on her face. Would her mother hold that for the entire journey?

Nelle blew the air from her cheeks, her shoulders slumping. Was this how the virgins of old felt when others sacrificed them to the gods in hopes of better fortunes? Had those ancient women ever wished to save themselves, everyone else be damned? What would her family do if she insisted right now that they turn the carriage around, that she would not, *could not* marry the earl?

The words hovered on the tip of her tongue, her indignation rising. She looked to Lucy-Anne, dreamily rubbing her fingers over her betrothed's most recent letter. To Tabby, who'd rejoiced at hearing they were to have a new pianoforte, their other having been by necessity sold some time ago, and who'd been copying music from friends for weeks. To Pru, who'd chattered excitedly of the new gowns she'd have for next Season—her debut at last.

"I'd feared I should have to make do with cast-offs," Prudence had admitted one evening. "The youngest rarely gets something new."

And she looked to her parents. Her father walked taller with the weight of his crushing debt off his shoulders. Even her mother had become more amiable, especially when Lord Rutley raised the possibility of returning to Rutley Manor.

Nelle slumped, her protest dying within her. How could she deprive her family of such joy when they'd lived under this cloud of darkness? She couldn't. She'd seen what hope ripped away looked like far too often at the foundling home. She'd not allow her selfish desires to sabotage those she loved. She wrapped her hands deeper in the blanket, chills overtaking her.

Every mile north felt a step closer to hell.

~

BERTIE'S final revenge on Loughton Knight and the cur's damnable son was close. So close. They'd tried to take everything from him: his wife, his honor, his very life. But he'd persevered. And won. The younger duke did not suspect him. The fool.

He took another swig from the decanter. He'd ceased for some time bothering with a glass. They didn't hold enough. His free arm crossed to rub at the perennial ache in his shoulder. The pain always worsened in the winter as if an intentional reminder of the injustice young Wynhawke had done him that cold New Year's Eve.

Cortleon had paid. Now his son would. The man deserved to watch him win.

Hugh entered the drawing room then bared his teeth at the drink in Bertie's hand. *Ungrateful wretch.* Look at all he'd done for his son. He'd hired the best tutors, sent him to the best schools, trained him up to be the best, most proper of gentlemen. He'd given Hugh the *world*. And now he'd even given him permission to marry that flighty Greene sister.

He raised the bottle in silent toast. *May she prove less duplicitous than your own bitch of a mother.*

"Father," Hugh said, sharply. "It's two o'clock in the afternoon. Too early for drinking."

Bertie waved the decanter, nearly knocking it into his teeth as he brought it back for another swig. "Nonsense. Perfect thing to warm one on cold days like these. You should join me."

The boy thrust his hands on his hips, his chin taking on a dangerously defiant air. "I am concerned. Since we've returned, you've not been yourself." He pointed at the bottle. "And that is to blame. The amount of alcohol you imbibe is cause for worry."

Bertie made to stand in outrage at his son's verbal abuse but flopped down as the room spun around him. "You dare challenge your *father*?"

Hugh sighed. "I'm not challenging you, sir. I'm expressing concern."

"No need! I'm simply celebrating our upcoming nuptials. They're cause for rejoicing, are they not? We are each marrying the woman we love." Though he didn't love Lady Elinor. Did he? Her face swam before him, conflating and combining with Albina's. He'd loved one of them. Which one?

"It is certainly to be a happy time—if you cease consuming that poison long enough to be present for it."

Bertie growled. Snippety upstart. *He* was the boy's father. He was the boy's *savior*, having protected him since he was but a babe. Now he'd given his son his greatest desire. He deserved respect. He deserved recognition! He deserved ...

Hugh's retreating footsteps shook him from his stupor. He set the decanter down, then pressed his fingers to his temples, where the familiar aching had already begun. Perhaps the boy was right. He couldn't properly inflict the revenge about to be his unless he was sober enough to keep his wits about him.

Picking up the bottle, he hurled it at the wall, the shattering of glass a most pleasing sound. He'd destroyed it.

Now to destroy the duke.

As THE COACH labored up the steep path to Swythdon, Arth let out a low whistle, his brows rising. "Not bad for an earl."

"Afraid it outshines Camlon?" Emerlin flashed his infamous dimpled grin.

"Nothing outshines Camlon."

"Except maybe St. Graele," Percy said.

Gavin held up his hands. "I cannot compete."

Arth was right. The gray stone castle rising from the woods was a sight to behold. And the edifice was definitely a castle; its origins must go back centuries. If archers appeared on the roof and guards in armor at the entryway, it'd not have surprised him in the least.

He couldn't care less about the home, however; his only pursuit was Grennet. This was it. He'd find undeniable proof or wrangle a confession from the earl one way or another. There was no doubt in his mind now that Grennet was the green monster, but as Emerlin had cautioned more than once, he needed irrefutable evidence. He couldn't call the earl out without absolute certainty. He'd never forgive himself if he killed a guiltless man. Grennet wasn't guiltless, though. Far from it.

And in a mere two weeks, he was set to marry Nelle. The woman Gavin loved.

What a tangled mess. If he declared his feelings for her, would she break off the engagement? It needn't ruin her family; he could certainly provide the same or greater monetary benefit to her parents as the earl. On the other hand, if she reneged on the betrothal here in Grennet's very seat of power, would he retaliate in some fashion? Could he risk him hurting her—or anyone else?

Gavin looked to his companions, an unwelcome thought intruding. What if she didn't love *him*? What if she truly *wanted* to marry the earl? If he were to then find the proof or obtain the confession he sought, he'd be left with a terrible choice. If he told her the truth about Grennet and she cried off, the danger of the earl's unpredictable reaction remained. Grennet knew of his interest in Nelle; Gavin was increasingly convinced the earl had pursued her to strike at him. To what lengths would the man go to deny him his love? But if he revealed Grennet for the villain he was, and she held real feelings for him—Gavin wanted to retch at the thought—what then? Would she ever forgive him, especially if he ended the earl's life?

Or ... He could let Grennet live. He could sacrifice his quest, the purpose that had driven him for more than a decade, out of his love for Nelle. He could let her go. Grennet would win. The monster would have taken everything.

The agony that idea evoked made Gavin want to yell, to kick the coach doors, to wreak havoc on everything within reach. *No.* Best not to wrestle with that now. Best to search out the needed evidence and then decide how to proceed.

In the meantime, he must act as if he held Grennet under no suspicion, lest he tip his hand to the real reason he'd accepted the befuddling invitation. He must flirt with the ladies, as he'd gained a reputation for doing. He must not pay too much attention to Nelle, must not single her out, though that'd be the highest test of his restraint yet; he wanted nothing more than to rush to her and confess his idiocy for not realizing his feelings earlier. He could not. Not while his father's murderer—while *Grennet*—was still alive. Not while he might cause her harm. For now, she was still promised to the earl. For now, she was lost to him.

He roared, slamming his fist against the side wall.

"Down, Cort. Or should I say, Sir Lion?" Percy cracked a smile at his own witticism. "Slaying our host upon arrival would not be the chivalrous way to present ourselves for a wedding."

As they reached the tall tower at one corner of the castle, several footmen greeted them then collected the men's trunks and attended to the horses and coach. A second man, outfitted in fine livery, bowed. "Welcome to

Swythdon, Your Graces. I am Hightower. I will show you to your chambers."

Hightower? In a castle with a high tower?

Emerlin cast a mischievous look over his shoulder, indicating he'd also noticed the amusing oddity.

"I beg your pardons that Lord Grennet and Lord Ashvere are not here to greet you personally; they've gone hunting with several other members of the party but look forward to meeting everyone at this evening's dinner."

That was probably for the best; Gavin's nerves were strung taut at the thought of seeing both his worst enemy and greatest love in short order. A respite was exactly what he needed to calm the pounding in his veins and the insistent voice demanding satisfaction. He needed to bury that voice, needed to concentrate only on the current moment, on determining how best to go about things.

They followed Hightower up a set of stairs through an inner courtyard. Everything about Swythdon suggested age. Ivy covered many of the walls, and the tops of several turrets had begun to crumble. When they entered the great hall, the medieval origins of the castle couldn't be denied. Tapestries and antlers hung on rustic wood-paneled walls, the open timbers of the roof on full display. Had this space changed in hundreds of years? It wasn't difficult to imagine rushes covering the floors, men in armor banging on long tables and hoisting tankards of ale while their host feasted on mutton drumsticks and mead, his lady to his side.

Hightower led them up narrow stairs just outside the hall that led to an equally narrow corridor running the entire length of the castle wing. "The rooms were originally interconnected," he explained as if apologizing. "A previous earl added these corridors to create private chambers and allow for outside entry, but space was limited, given the courtyards below."

A glance out one of the windows revealed a second

courtyard with a stone fountain. Hightower led them to the far end of the corridor. The dukes each had their own chamber, one next to the other. "Many guests must share, as we expect a large number and there are fewer rooms than one might expect in a house such as this, but of course we would never dishonor Your Graces in such a way."

"Of course," answered Arthington as if it were his due. As much as Gavin loved the man, he certainly accepted his privilege with ease.

A door closed at the opposite end of the corridor, and he glanced over his shoulder, then froze. *Nelle*. Her three sisters flitted around her, though she, like he, stood as still as a statue. He couldn't discern her expression from this distance, but her hand flew to her throat.

He turned his head back around. He wanted to charge the expanse of the narrow passageway and take her in his arms, begging a thousand pardons for his behavior at the Effingham ball. He wanted to kiss her cheeks and plead for her to forgive him, to ask if she could accept him into her heart and love him as a wife should love a husband. As he loved her.

Instead, he walked into the chamber without a further word to his friends and shut the door.

CHAPTER 30

"*O*h, the dukes have arrived," Tabby said.

Pru clucked. "So blithe about men of such stature. I doubt Mother would approve of your tone."

"I doubt Mother approves of anything," Tabby tossed back.

Nelle might have chuckled if she'd had the ability to do so. He was here. Gavin was here, looking every bit as appetizing as that evening at the Effingham ball. And every bit as lost to her as when they'd locked eyes at that same ball, his brimming with betrayal and disgust—feelings he clearly still held, for while he'd glanced their direction, he'd not acknowledged her before entering his chamber.

Oh, how long this fortnight would be! Two weeks in his presence. Two weeks of wanting, wishing, remembering. Two weeks of torment and temptation. And yet also how short, for at the fortnight's end, she'd be the Countess of Grennet—and Gavin Knight would be gone from her life forever. *Foolish goose!* She drew herself up straight, setting her hands over her restless stomach. He was already gone, as his behavior just now confirmed.

Lucy-Anne looped an arm through hers, unaware of the

turmoil churning in Nelle's insides. "Come, let's take a stroll through the courtyard."

"In this weather?" Pru clutched her shoulders and shuddered as if to prove her point.

"I dare say in a drafty old mausoleum like this, the temperature is likely to be the same inside or out."

"Tabby!" exclaimed Lucy-Anne, even as she pulled her own pelisse tighter. "That's no way to talk about Nelle's and my new home."

"At least you'll have your husbands to keep you warm," Tabby retorted.

Lucy-Anne giggled.

Nelle, on the other hand, nearly cast up her stomach's contents.

~

BERTIE STRODE INTO THE HALL, head pounding but holding three grouse at his side. A good day's kill. He handed the birds to a footman and unbuckled the mantle at his throat.

"His Graces the Dukes of Arthington, Engelsfell, and Cortleon have arrived, along with the Marquess of Emerlin," Hightower imparted as he took Bertie's cloak.

Cortleon. He was here. At last. Aching head forgotten, Bertie bounded up the stairs and into his chamber, reaching automatically for the ever-present decanter on the side table, but it was gone. Being without a drink for several days had left him surly and ill-tempered, but he'd done his best to hide it when Lady Elinor and her family had arrived yestereve, releasing his irritability only later on the servants.

Calling now for his valet, he dressed with care. How he looked forward to the events of the next few weeks, especially to seeing Cortleon's face when he took Lady Elinor to wife. He'd feared the duke might decline the invitation;

what reason had he to come to Swythdon when Bertie had already captured the lady? Whatever the impetus, he only cared that Cortleon was here.

Dinner that evening was a festive affair. Giant fires burned in the massive stone fireplaces to either side of the tables, warming the cold room. Wine and spirits flowed freely, and guests chatted with anticipation, happy to see each other after months of separation and looking forward to the planned entertainments. Tomorrow was another hunt, this time for foxes.

"Your Graces, my lords," Bertie called from his position at the head of the table. "I hope you'll join us tomorrow for the hunt. Swythdon's forests are ripe with prey. It should provide for an adventurous day."

Cortleon, of all people, raised his glass. "I shouldn't miss it. Hunting is one reason I'm here."

Bertie pressed his lips together. Did something lie below the surface of the duke's words? He flicked a glance toward Lady Elinor. She sat to his left, Hugh to his right, with Lucy-Anne next to Hugh. His betrothed's posture and her every gesture were precise and proper. She'd made no acknowledgment of Cortleon. He'd given her no spare glance this evening, either.

He furrowed his brow. Had Cortleon's interest in Lady Elinor waned over these past months? Had the rake moved on to someone else? Or was his pointed disinterest an artifice? Perhaps he should thrust them together as a final test of Lady Elinor's fidelity—and Cortleon's continued desire. "Let us retire to the long gallery. It's a comfortable place to stroll, hold conversation, and indulge in a round or two of cards."

The guests clapped politely then made their way to the gallery, one of the most magnificent spaces in Swythdon. It doubled as the ballroom, but for tonight, the servants had laid out a side table with a selection of fine wines and spirits, with lemonade for the ladies. Several card tables lined the inner wall, and the three dukes and Emerlin promptly took seats at one. A few of the ladies sighed, no doubt having hoped one or more of the peers might take them for a turn around the room.

Bertie remained at the far end, observing. Hugh strolled with Lady Lucy-Anne, their eyes only for each other—so much so that his son nearly walked into a marble statue along the outer perimeter. Other ladies and gentlemen ambled about, while many of the older folk took seats near the fireplaces on either end.

Lady Elinor made the rounds with her sisters Lady Tabitha and Lady Prudence, the youngest one quiet, but Lady Tabitha engaging in animated conversation. Each time the three sisters neared the card tables, he held his breath, but after a brief nod of acknowledgment from the dukes to the women and back, neither Cortleon nor Lady Elinor exchanged glances or words of any kind.

Relief and irritation warred within him. Relief that he was not being played for a fool; the heat between the pair seemed to have cooled and crumbled to ash. Irritation, because he wanted a reason to call the damned duke out. To end what he should have ended that day in Camlon's field, this time in an honorable fashion.

His hands shook, itching to clasp a decanter off the table and drink it down. The dryness of his mouth and constant hammering at his temples had done nothing for his mood this evening, but he played the part of the gracious host to the hilt. He was long accustomed to masking his true feelings, after all.

After several more circles of the room, Lady Elinor paused before him, offering a curtsy. Two red splotches marred her cheeks. "I beg pardon, my lord. I wish to retire to my chamber. I find myself still fatigued from the journey."

"Of course, my dear," he responded, his suspicions rising again at the undisguised agitation in her person.

Cortleon looked in their direction for the barest of moments before jerking his head back to his table companions.

Bertie smiled. The chase was on. And the duke was Bertie's prey.

~

THE NEXT MORNING dawned sunny but bitterly cold. The men amassed near the stables seemed not to mind the frigid temperatures as they mounted their steeds with excitement and boasting.

How hunting charged Bertie's blood. Nothing exhilarated him like the rush of sighting one's prey, of cornering them, of prevailing in the fight for survival. Yesterday it'd been birds—a mere shooting exercise. Today, however, they'd hunt foxes and tomorrow a boar. The varied challenges each target presented excited him like almost nothing else. Almost.

For he had to admit, the dance of shadows he'd been playing with Cortleon for nearly a year had provided him with no small outlet for the darker urges he disliked acknowledging. Ferreting out what the duke might or might not know and baiting him with his own attentions to Lady Elinor had been a different kind of hunt. A game. A game in which Bertie was in control, in which he held the cards and had the upper hand.

Not like with the bastard's father. Albina and the duke's deviousness had shredded Bertie to the bone. He'd known nothing of their lengthy duplicity, of their disloyalty, until he'd caught them in that forest clearing, Cortleon's hands up her skirts, her own in her lover's breeches. He'd watched them couple, rutting like animals. He'd watched Albina depart.

"We mustn't arouse suspicion," Cortleon had said, stroking her cheek when she'd begged him to walk with her.

She'd left.

And he'd killed the bastard.

Now the game had come full circle, to Swythdon—with Bertie holding trump.

The horn blasted, signaling the start of the hunt. A score or more horses raced after the hunting dogs, following their mad barking. He charged into the fray, leaping over logs, sprinting across clearings, the euphoria the chase engendered nearly matching that of brandy. Over field and dale they sped, men calling when they'd sighted one of the three foxes. It seemed as if the hunt had barely begun when the huntsman again blew the horn, indicating the sport was finished.

What? Bertie rode into a clearing where a handful of lords gathered around Cortleon, who held all three foxes in his hand. *How?*

Men cheered and clapped. "A miraculous feat," one shouted. "No wonder we call you the Legendary Duke."

Cortleon held up his free hand. "Pure luck, I assure you," he said, though his cocky grin belied his professed humility. "In the right place at the right time." He looked to Bertie. "I offer these to our host. In gratitude for inviting me to hunt him." He chuckled, shaking his head. "Hunt *with* him, I meant, of course. A slip of the tongue."

Bertie's nostrils flared. *A slip of the tongue, my ass.* He sidled his mount closer to the duke, straightening in his saddle, his shoulders rigid.

"Lord Grennet!" called Engelsfell, pulling his horse up next to Cortleon. "Cortleon here should be banned from tomorrow's hunt. To give the rest of us a fair shot."

The men chortled, noises of agreement rising in the winter air.

Cortleon tossed his absurdly longish hair away from his face. "'Twould be a most welcome respite, I must confess," he said, pulling at the neck of his mantle. "I'm not used to these English winters. Should tomorrow prove as cold as today, I'd likely be frozen through before sighting the boar once."

Bertie scowled. *The duke alone at Swythdon the entire day, while the rest of the men were away?* Lord Cobshire and Mr. Eschel would stay in residence, likely Lord Rutley, as well, but they were aged, the earl rotund. That Bertie so avidly took part in the hunt despite his ever-increasing years remained a point of pride.

"Then ye are banned, Sir Knight!" Arthington joked, riding close to slap the back of Cortleon's head.

The detested duke merely chuckled. Bertie grit his teeth. The title reminded him of that night nearly a year ago on which Cortleon as a medieval knight had stolen a kiss from a goddess—and he'd been a Fool. No more. Never again. He'd instruct Hightower to keep a close eye on Cortleon—and his betrothed.

"You'll be stuck with the old and infirm," another man teased.

Cortleon winked. "Aye. And the ladies." He took a knee, bowing low. "On the pelts of these vixens, I do pledge my troth to guard and protect all women in Lord Grennet's castle, like a valiant knight of old."

"One set of vixens for another, eh?" called Hugh, as the duke rose and handed the foxes to a groomsman.

Cortleon's only response was a wink, but his eye caught and held Bertie's before he turned and remounted his horse.

Bertie seethed, blowing frosty breaths into the air. Oh, yes. The hunt continued.

CHAPTER 31

*G*avin rose the next morning no more rested than when he'd gone to bed. His thoughts constantly churned over ways to find the evidence he needed. And ways to keep his mind, and eyes, off of Nelle.

How had medieval knights kept to the chivalric code? How had they maintained purely platonic relationships with the ladies to whom they'd sworn eternal devotion and service— often ladies who were the wives of the lords to whom the knight had pledged fealty? Not that the earl was in any way his lord. But Nelle was certainly his lady. His goddess. As unreachable now as those ladies were to the courtly knights who'd served them.

Unless, of course, they hadn't *kept the code.*

He batted at the air as if to rid himself of the heretical thought. Were Percy to see him striking at nothing, he'd call him mad. It'd not be so far from the truth. It was a form of madness to be here, his enemy to one side, his love to the other, and to have no obvious recourse with either.

A knock came at his chamber door. "Enter," he called, before remembering he was clad only in his breeches.

Emerlin poked his head in, his brows rising at Gavin's bare chest. "Expecting someone else?"

He threw a pillow at him.

"Merely wished to check that you are not joining the hunt," the marquess added.

"No." Gavin pulled a shirt from the wardrobe and yanked it over his head. "This might be my only chance to survey Swythdon more closely to see if I can find anything." What, he didn't know. Did he think Grennet had waistcoats from two decades ago lying about? Or a letter in which he'd made a complete and full confession? He snorted. *Not bloody likely.* Though what if his wife had written something down? Was there any chance she'd kept a journal of some sort?

"Do you want me to stay with you to help?"

Gavin shook his head. "No. One man sneaking about is less apt to garner notice than two."

"Yes, but one of us the earl has in his sights and one he does not."

"Thank you, my friend. But I'll not risk you incriminating yourself in any way. This is a matter I must pursue on my own." He shrugged on a waistcoat.

Emerlin's blue eyes crinkled. "Then it's up to just me to keep Arth and Engelsfell in line."

"Good luck with that!"

"It'd take more than luck," Em called as he ambled down the hallway. "I'd need pure magic."

Gavin chuckled as he donned his coat. How probable was it that any chambers would be empty? Voices echoed in the hall below, along with the clinking of plates and utensils. Hopefully, most guests would be breakfasting. He scouted the area around him, following the corridor until it rounded a corner. These rooms were more remote from the other chambers, and larger in size, given the space between doors.

A man carrying a fine coat of dark green exited one of the chambers. Grennet's valet, perhaps? Gavin waited until the servant had disappeared then put his ear to the door of the room from which the man had exited and listened. When no sounds came, he carefully pressed the handle, opening the door a few inches. From the dark paneled walls and heavy furniture, this must be Grennet's chamber, not his deceased wife's. Unless they'd slept in the same bed —though, given the apparent nature of their marriage, he doubted it.

He moved to the next room, making sure no one witnessed his actions. Once again, he pressed an ear to the door. Silence. This time when he cracked open the door, sunny yellow walls and white wainscoting greeting him, along with a French turned-leg table on which a porcelain basin and pitcher stood. The room had a far more modern feel than the rest of the castle, which looked like it hadn't changed in centuries.

He pushed his way in. Sunlight streamed through diaphanous curtains on the two windows lining each side of the poster bed. A small writing table sat to one side, paper and quill at the ready. A chest of drawers hugged the wall across from the bed, ornately decorated with inlays of marble and featuring a painted pastoral scene. Definitely a woman's chamber. The quality of its furnishings and proximity to the earl's affirmed it must have been Lady Grennet's.

Gavin shook his head. What was he doing? How feasible was it that a room empty of its mistress for twenty years contained any hints as to her lover's demise? He hadn't anything else to go on, however, so he carefully closed the door and looked about. Though the room was currently empty, someone was obviously staying there. Not surprising, given how many people had gathered for the double wedding. A green ribbon lay across the dressing table, a shawl draped over the chair back. He paused. That shawl looked like one Nelle had worn the previous evening. Was this her chamber?

His eyes drifted to the bed. Oh, how easy it was to imagine her there, her blonde hair spread out in waves around her, her arms reaching up for him.

"No," he muttered, annoyed at his body and mind, both of which threatened to get him into trouble.

Moving quietly, he ran his fingers over and around the writing desk and the dressing table, opening and shutting drawers, but found nothing of interest. No obvious letters lying about or any secret compartments. He blew the hair out of his eyes in exasperation. Stealing about into chambers expecting to find evidence of a crime committed decades ago was a fool's errand.

A click sounded, and he whirled.

Nelle walked in.

~

"GAVIN!"

Nelle cringed. She shouldn't have called him by his Christian name. It implied an intimacy that wasn't there, especially given his pointed avoidance of her. Oh, he'd greeted her civilly, inquired cordially after her health, made the requisite small talk. But nothing in his words or eyes hinted at any deeper level of feeling. The man she'd met in the foundling home was gone.

How having him close and yet so very far unnerved her. Her eyes hungered to soak in the familiar curve of his jaw, his glorious mane of hair, and those sherry eyes. She'd been careful not to do so. Not only did she not want to give Gavin—the *duke*, rather—the satisfaction, but she didn't want to provoke Lord Grennet in any way.

While she couldn't point to any one thing, the earl

seemed ... different. Not as frightening as in their last encounter, thank heavens. He was a perfectly respectable host, even jovial at times. He sang her praises to her parents and professed how glad he was that she and Lady Lucy-Anne would soon be joining his family. Yet it often seemed an act—as if he were strutting his hour upon the stage. As if he were Shakespeare's Macbeth himself.

When she'd hesitantly asked Lucy-Anne if the earl seemed changed, her sister had laughed it off. "He seems the same proper older gentleman he's always been." She clapped a hand over her mouth. "Er ... he's not so *very* old."

"I'm well aware of the earl's age, thank you," Nelle responded but without bite.

"Think of how you will comfort him, Nelle! He's been alone these many years. What a poor existence for a man."

"He had his son."

Lucy-Anne tutted. "Yes, but that's not the same as a loving wife caring for you and looking after you."

That sounded a more motherly than wifely role, but she hadn't bothered to respond. Nothing would dissuade Lucy-Anne from her idea of matrimony as a state of complete bliss and harmony. For her sister's sake, Nelle prayed it was. She didn't hold such hopes for herself.

Swythdon was a cavernous mass of loud, dark, echoing rooms, with little comfort to be had. This chamber was one of the few areas that brightened her spirits. Thank goodness Lord Grennet had assigned it to Lucy-Anne and her.

Her father hadn't liked the idea of his two daughters in a separate hallway so near to their future bridegrooms, but the earl had set him at ease. "Never would my son or I dishonor your daughters in any way, Lord Rutley. You have my word on that. Their chamber is the best at Swythdon."

Father had begrudgingly agreed. What else could he do? He knew where his fortunes now lay.

Nelle had abandoned breakfast in favor of time here

alone. She loved Lucy-Anne beyond measure but being in the presence of her sister's overriding joy made her own misery that much harder to bear. She'd needed to escape. The wedding was now only a week away. Her stomach had given her fits all morning, especially since her mother had taken last night as the opportunity to talk about marital duties—"In case it gets lost in the rush, dearest,"—a conversation awkward on both sides. What her mother had described sounded far less pleasant than she'd even anticipated. Messy. Uncomfortable. Embarrassing. Envisioning those acts with Lord Grennet made her want to vomit.

She'd imagined herself with Gavin, instead. Through the night, she'd dreamed of them blending together, their naked bodies moving against each other. Those vague, blurry visions had combined with vivid memories of their first kiss and their torrid exchange at the Effingham ball. Yes, intimacies with him appealed far more. In fact, she'd been lost in a fantasy of his hands caressing her everywhere when she'd entered her chamber to discover him standing there.

How much time had passed since she'd said his name? Seconds? Minutes? She had no idea. She took a step forward at the same time as he, then another, and then he ran, sweeping her into his fierce embrace. *What in heaven?* She must still be dreaming. He couldn't actually be in her private chamber, holding onto her as if she were the only thing binding him to this earth. His hands came up to cradle her neck, his eyes searching hers in silent question.

She nodded, and his mouth came down, taking hers in frenetic possession, his lips nibbling, his tongue touching, tasting. She moaned as he moved, trailing little kisses along her jaw, then down her neck. He lifted his head, and her eyes, which had drifted shut, flew open. But he only smiled as he leaned in again, this time kissing her in much more leisurely fashion, his fingers tangling in her hair.

He tasted of everything male. Or at least everything male about the Duke of Cortleon—a hint of something exotic, a dash of spice, a heavenly mix she never wanted to give up. She broke off the kiss to pepper his nose with light pecks as she traced her fingers across his cheek before kissing her way to one ear, breathing into it softly.

The most enticing noise rumbled low in his throat, almost like a purr. Without words, he reached for her again, drawing her face back to his, their mouths meeting once more in a third kiss of desperate passion. She wound her fingers through his hair, luxuriating in the silky strands. How she loved his longer tresses, though they were far from the current fashion. She hoped he never cut them. Just as she hoped she'd never wake from this dream, her fantasy of fantasies come true.

One of his hands reached behind his head to cover one of hers, his fingers tracing over her knuckles, though their mouths remained melded. He jerked unexpectedly, ripping his lips from hers as he took a step back. But he retained his grip on her hand, turning it now to examine the large emerald on her fourth finger. His lips tipped down.

"This isn't a dream, is it?" Her words came out a whisper.

He didn't respond. His eyes were on the cursed ring with its ridiculously large stone. The ring Lord Grennet had presented to her the first night at Swythdon and insisted she wear. How could she refuse, with her family looking on in wonder and encouragement?

"Not a signet," he murmured, his brows low.

She yanked her hand away. "Why are you here?" Her words could have been shrill, perhaps ought to have been, but they weren't. They were simply questioning, her tone soft.

"I don't know."

He shouldn't be here. In her bedchamber. With her, alone. "Why did you kiss me?"

"I don't know." His eyes simmered with unnamed emotion, but when nothing further followed, she tore the ring off her finger and thrust it at him.

"Here," she cried. "Take it. I don't want it. He gave it to me. I have nothing else I can give you. Nothing."

"I didn't ask you for—"

"Oh, but I'd like to," she said, breaking him off. "I'd like to give you myself."

His jaw dropped.

She might have laughed at his comical expression, but it would have come out a maniacal cackle. For this was madness. All of it. She poked a finger into his breastbone, then again. "I know you won't accept. I know it renders me the worst sort of woman in your eyes, the kind willing to give herself to someone who isn't her husband."

The anger building had her poke him a third time, hard, for good measure, before she turned her back to him. "I can't break off the engagement. It'd devastate Lucy-Anne. Ashvere. My family. I have no choice; I *must* marry him."

She whirled around again, tears cascading down her cheeks. "But I beg one night with you, Gavin. One night to put *me* first, to be with a man I ..." She pressed her fists to her mouth to prevent the words from spilling. She couldn't confess her love. It'd change nothing and revealing such a thing without reciprocation would irrevocably wound her. She carried no illusions that he loved her; his casual disregard this past week proved that. But he still desired her. His ardent kisses proved as much—as did his hard length that had pressed into her as he'd held her. "One night to be with a man to whom I am at least attracted."

The lame completion of the sentence grossly understated her true feelings. But there it was; her open confession. She wanted one night with the man she loved before being shackled for the rest of her life to a man she didn't. She held her breath as he exhaled.

He studied her for a long, uncomfortable moment then handed back the ring. "No."

CHAPTER 32

*N*elle crumpled at his feet, her low cry tearing his heart. But how could she offer such a thing, knowing he couldn't accept?

He leaned down and tucked his hands under her arms, lifting her up. Instead of withdrawing, as he might have expected, she clung to him, her shoulders shaking in great sobs.

"Oh, Nelle," he whispered, wrapping his arms around her and stroking her back. He'd said no for himself as much as for her. For even beyond the question of honor, the truth was, he didn't know how he could make love to her and then never have her again. The thought tore at him like a thousand arrows piercing his heart. "I couldn't dishonor you in such a way," he said, pressing his lips to her hair. "I couldn't dishonor myself."

His words only made her cries more ragged. To hold her in his arms and yet be the cause of such sorrow nearly killed him. She was caught between duty and desire, the same as he. Did she not deserve happiness? Shouldn't she know one night of true love? For if he took her to bed, that is what it would be—making *love*. Never had he felt so torn.

Never had he questioned his commitment to his vow as much as he did at this moment. Would it be so unforgivable to be with the woman he loved?

Through his torment and temptation, his mother's tear-streaked face forced its way into his head. No doubt his father had said similar things to justify his infidelities. Loughton Knight's promises had not mattered to him; he'd followed lust and passion wherever he wished. Had he thought it love? Had the women he'd seduced and then abandoned?

Even knowing he was right to refuse her, Gavin couldn't seem to let her go. He cradled her, breathing in her light, feminine scent, knowing this was the last time he would hold her in his arms, would feel the softness of her cheek, or would know the taste of her lips.

A noise sounded in the hallway, jolting him out of the cocoon in which they'd wrapped themselves. He shouldn't be here. He must take his leave, lest they be discovered together. "I must go."

She raised her tear-swollen eyes, their rawness electrifying their magical blue. He stroked the wetness from her cheeks with his thumbs, his own heart pounding. He didn't want to leave her. He never wanted to leave her. But honor forced him out of the door.

Desire drove him to ram his fist into it. He welcomed the pain. Anything to keep from going back in.

BERTIE URGED his horse over the upturned log, excitement surging as the boar veered, charging out of sight. He yelled to the men behind him as he shifted course, dogs baying as they tried to corner the animal. A flash of tusk and the crisp crackle of twigs indicated the beast had switched paths yet again. It crashed through the nearby underbrush as he jerked his mount around. Where had the damn animal gone? He'd lost track of it several times today, much to his irritation. The creature was wily.

As was Cortleon. *Were he and Lady Elinor—*

A loud gunshot and huzzah broke off the thought, and he twisted in the saddle. The boar's crazed eyes locked on Bertie, blood spurting from its neck as it charged at his horse. He raised his rifle and pulled the trigger. The wild pig squealed once then shuddered and fell to the ground.

Victory! He leapt down and approached the beast, setting his hands on the animal's bloody side to ensure it was dead.

"We've earned our dinner tonight, haven't we, Father?" Hugh said as he pulled up on his own mount, the other lords following behind him calling congratulations to the earl.

"Indeed."

After instructing the footmen on the conveyance of the boar, Bertie remounted his horse then spurred it toward Swythdon. Normally he enjoyed a full day of hunting, but this time he was eager to return home to learn if Hightower had noted anything unusual. Eager to ensure his second bride was not the two-faced bitch his first had been.

He gave the horse its head, relishing the power between his legs. He'd instruct the stable hands to give the horse a good rub down; it certainly deserved it. As did he. The dust and dirt the hunt had kicked up plus the blood on his hands from examining the boar's wound had him in no condition to serve as host.

A long soak in the giant oak bath, a shave, and fresh clothing had him in quite the convivial mood as he entered the hall. Hightower had witnessed nothing between Lady Elinor and Cortleon. According to the manservant, she'd spent the day in the company of her sisters and hadn't so much as glanced the duke's way when they'd crossed paths in the inner courtyard.

This wife might turn out to be a blessing after all.

His guests slowly drifted into the dining hall. Bertie had decreed this dinner an informal affair, asking only that everyone be present by nine. Lady Elinor took her seat at his side just before the clock struck, offering him a wan smile. As the meal progressed, she said little, sipping from her wine cup but only picking at her food.

"Are you unwell, my dear?"

She looked up from her continued study of her plate, her face paler than usual. "I am fine. Merely tired."

"Do make sure you rest up. I don't want an exhausted bride for our wedding night."

She swallowed.

"Shall we have dancing tonight, Father?" asked Hugh from his other side. "Lucy-Anne says the ladies are longing to dance."

"Why not?" His mood was buoyant given the outcome of the hunt, both in the field and at home. He turned back to his plate. Lady Elinor was staring down the table. She immediately shifted, casting a question at her sister across from her, but something had obviously caught her attention. Or someone. For Cortleon sat several seats away, flashing that nauseating smile at the young woman next to him.

Bertie ate carefully, observing his betrothed's every movement from the corner of his eye. Sure enough, she peeked at the duke again then hastily glanced elsewhere as if to pretend she hadn't sought the man out. As the second course was laid, he ground his teeth. The small, furtive glances continued. And Cortleon returned them. Not directly; when she looked away, he looked to her. If she glanced his way, he turned his attention to the women on either side of him.

Bertie wanted to stab them both with his knife. Had Hightower missed something? Had he himself? With a curt motion, he beckoned the wine steward. Hugh shot him a frown, but he didn't care. He'd abstained for nearly two weeks; that proved he was well in control.

Two goblets later, he rose, lifting his refilled cup in the air. "A toast!" he called, all eyes turning to him. "To the hunt!" He raised his glass higher. "To the ladies!"

The men cheered as the women smiled.

"To the *victor*!"

At this last, he fixed his gaze on his nemesis. Cortleon lifted his own glass, twisting his mouth as he nodded. Elation surged. The duke had just conceded defeat, had he not?

He drained the cup, signaling once more to the steward. "Let us retire to the gallery for dancing," he called, then addressed Lady Tabitha. "My lady, would you grace us with your excellent playing?"

Lady Elinor's sister dipped her head in acquiescence, and the company rose, chattering echoing through the corridors as they made their way to the gallery. After Lady Tabitha settled herself at the old pianoforte, he spoke again, his voice booming.

"Yesterday's champion ought to have a prize, think you not?" He spread his arms wide. "The Duke of Cortleon presented me his winnings of the three vixens. I, therefore, need to offer something in exchange."

The crowd murmured as Cortleon's mouth pulled into a tight line, his brows dipping deeply over his eyes.

"I give you my fiancée, Lady Elinor."

An uncertain hush fell over the room. Lady Elinor, who stood some distance from Cortleon, said nothing, but two bright spots burned on her cheeks as the color drained from the rest of her face.

He reveled in their discomposure. Let them be as out of

kilter as he. Let him lay the trap and catch them in the act. Oh, not in anything so flagrant as a tryst or even a mere kiss, not here in the gallery-turned-ballroom. But Bertie was a hunter, born and bred, trained to watch for the littlest indication of his prey's next movements. If there was anything between the damnable duke and the lady, they'd not be able to completely disguise it.

"For the first dance, of course," he added with a wink.

Cortleon bowed deeply. "It'd be my deepest honor." He brandished that notorious grin then walked to Lady Elinor, extending his hand. "Only if you wish," he said to her. "A lady should always be able to refuse an offer."

Bertie snarled. This was supposed to ruffle both of them and show that *he* was in control.

After a second, Lady Elinor took the duke's hand, giving a curt nod. She did not meet his eyes.

Bertie moved to the side of the room, goblet firmly in hand, as Lady Tabitha struck up the opening strains of a waltz. *Good*. Such an intimate dance would betray anything dishonorable in their reactions to each other. To his surprise, however, though they danced with grace, they maintained an even greater distance between them than decorum decreed and did not seem to share a single word. Lady Elinor, in fact, hardly looked at Cortleon.

"You won today."

The deep voice startled him. Engelsfell. Bertie raised a brow, the fourth glass of wine starting to muddle his head.

"In the hunt," the tall duke clarified.

They were near equals in height and stature. How unsettling. He was long used to being the dominant man. Should they spar, whether by rapier or fist, Engelsfell, with the advantage of youth, would undoubtedly best him. Bertie scowled. With guns, however, size didn't matter. Only speed. And accuracy of aim.

Cortleon's friend studied him so intently he shifted on his feet. What was he about?

"Well done." Engelsfell nodded toward Cortleon. "It'd be most interesting to see which of you prevailed in a one-on-one contest, don't you think?"

Something undergirded Engelsfell's words, something Bertie was missing. Was the duke goading him? To what end?

Engelsfell whacked his shoulder, giving him a good-natured grin. "To being sportsmen. Men of honor!"

Men of honor. He'd drink to that.

His eyes skirted back to his betrothed, stiff in her movements, then to Cortleon, moving with impossible finesse, his body relaxed but distant, a bland, nearly bored expression on his face. The duke did not look at Lady Elinor.

Bertie took another drink. A man of honor, indeed.

NELLE WANTED to sink into the floor or better yet, take that axe down off the wall and strike her blasted betrothed with it. Never had she been so humiliated. She was no commodity to be given in an exchange of goods, traded as if in a game. The indignity of it all!

Fury filled her, although she kept her face neutral, suppressing her emotions a long-honed skill. Fury at the earl, but also at Gavin. And herself. She'd begged him for one night together then spent the entire day mortified by her own shamelessness and his refusal. And now to be thrust into his arms, forced to parade about on display for the rest of the company, her future husband included? She kept every part of herself as far from Gavin as she could, her arms rigid, her back unyielding beneath his grasp.

"Goddess," he whispered, then fell silent. "No shame."

Could the infernal man read her mind in spite of her effort to don a mask of indifference?

"The fault lies with him." Again, a pause. "And with me."

Each time, he spoke rapidly. When he stopped, his face returned to the nonchalant, easy expression he might have worn while dancing with anybody.

What was he about?

They swung again, Lord Grennet now behind her. On the next turn, Gavin said, "I am so sorry." And on the next, "for all of it."

He addressed her only when his own back was to the earl, so her betrothed couldn't see. He was protecting her. Against her future husband. Against the challenge and suspicion in Lord Grennet's voice. Tears pricked her eyes.

His fingers caressed her waist, the lightest of touches. "Goddess. Proud, fierce warrior. My queen."

"Stop." *Stop.* He couldn't say more, or she'd burst, her rage and frustration and desperation and desire pouring out in an uncontrollable torrent of tears.

"Of course." His fingers ceased their movement and his arms locked into place, his eyes drifting to somewhere over her shoulder.

He'd misunderstood. She wasn't rejecting him, only trying to halt his unbearably tender attempts to buoy her up.

The waltz came to its end and he stepped back, bowing politely. In the next moment, he'd asked someone else to dance.

She was forgotten.

She slunk off to the corner. If she were an animal, she'd be licking her wounds right now. As it was, her injuries weren't visible, but she certainly wished for something to soothe them. Footmen had wheeled in a bowl of punch and she walked to it now, mostly for something to do. She needed to show she was fine, that she was in complete control, that the earl's outrageous behavior meant naught to her.

One sip revealed the punch was as much liquor as anything else. She downed the first glass faster than any lady ought and ladled herself another. If her mother discovered the true nature of this libation, she'd forbid it. Well, Mother would soon hold no power over her. Not when she was Lord Grennet's wife.

Gavin whirled by, another besotted young lady on his arm. Engelsfell and Emerlin each asked her to dance, but she claimed an aching head. Their faces softened with greater sympathy than a simple headache ought to have produced.

As the evening wore on, she refused all offers, though few came, sipping instead at her punch. Lord Grennet, thank goodness, never came her way. Gavin, however, danced with nearly every woman in the room, showing partiality to none.

Not once did he look at or approach her again.

CHAPTER 33

*I*f Gavin had had his way, he'd have skewered the jackass then and there—this time *not* because Grennet murdered his father but because he'd shamed Nelle so openly with his cruel antics. The asinine fool.

For her sake, however, he'd kept himself in check, making light of it as if dancing with her were the highest honor. Because it was. It was his opportunity to hold her once more.

All day, desire had wrestled with honor. She'd offered herself to him. Openly. Without further demand. He ached with longing, his shaft hard in his breeches, its opinion making itself well known. It very much wanted to bed her. But he'd spent years taming those urges and tempering his body to the demands of the oath he'd made to his mother —and himself.

Never had he been so tested.

And then to see the pain and shame in her eyes as she acquiesced to Grennet's command. He couldn't bear it. He'd done what he could, whispering encouragement when the mongrel couldn't see, pouring his love and respect for her into his voice, his eyes, his hands.

She'd told him to stop.

Though it'd cut deeply, he'd respected her wish and had resumed his mask of the carefree, debonair duke, flirting and dancing through the evening. Until she left.

He'd overheard Lady Lucy-Anne tell Ashvere that she'd pleaded a headache and retreated to her room. That she hadn't done so immediately after their forced waltz testified to her strength of spirit, though it hadn't escaped his notice that she'd not danced again.

As Lady Tabitha took a break from performing, he sought out Percy. "Billiards?"

The single word sufficed. Percy immediately beckoned to Arth and Em.

"Gladly," said Arth when asked. "If I have to watch one more woman make calf's eyes at Em and Cort, I'll go mad."

"Don't worry, Arth." Emerlin's brow arched wickedly. "I'm sure *someday* a woman will come along who'll only have eyes for you."

Arth shot him a glare. "It's not as if I'm unattractive," he muttered as they exited the room. "And I'm a duke, for heaven's sake!"

"A duke who thinks he's a king," Em teased, skirting out of the way when Arth made to shove him. "Come down off your throne and you might find someone whom you can then treat like your queen."

"Or don't." Percy grinned broadly. "And leave me the rest."

Gavin availed himself of the brandy in the billiards room cabinet, refilling his cup thrice as they played through several rounds. Though the alcohol fogged his head as he'd hoped, it wasn't enough to halt his constant questioning of his every action since returning to England. It was, however, enough to erase any interest in the game. "Sorry, friends," he said, after swigging the last of the liquor. "I must retire for the night."

He ambled into the corridor, intending to return to his chamber. Instead, he angled toward the ballroom, peeking in through an open door. Though the hour grew late, many guests still danced, Lady Tabitha once again drawing forth exquisite music from the ancient pianoforte. How could she play for such lengths of time and with such variety?

Grennet and a widow partnered for a country dance. The earl hadn't danced once with Nelle, another snub of the woman he was to marry. Ashvere passed by, Lucy-Anne in his arms. That was one benefit to being betrothed; they could partner as often as desired.

He desired. Oh, yes, he desired.

Before he could reconsider, his feet moved, leading him with a mildly unsteady gait to his chamber. Wait, no. This was not his chamber. This was Nelle's. And if Lady Lucy-Anne was in the ballroom, it meant she was within. Alone.

His hand raised as if of its own volition and knocked softly. A rustling within followed, and a moment later, the door opened. She stood there, still in her gown, a lovely confection of green. Funny how he hated the color less and less, especially when it was on her body. Her hair, however, was askew, great locks having fallen loose from her chignon, and her face was tear-streaked. At seeing him there, she sucked in a breath, her eyes widening.

"Gavin?"

At the whispered sound of his name on her lips, he leaned in, cupping her cheek with his hand. "Oh, no. No, no, no. You mustn't cry, dearest Nelle. You mustn't."

She leaned into him. "Why are you here?"

"Because …" He paused. Why *was* he here? This wasn't proper. *Proper be damned,* screamed the brandy in his brain. Maybe he ought to listen. "You are my goddess and I am your knight."

A wan smile greeted his words. "I'm not. This is no masquerade." She closed her eyes for the briefest of moments. "And Lord Grennet is no Fool." She swayed slightly in the doorway, a surprising giggle bursting forth. "Did you know I've sometimes thought him a dragon, one set to devour me?"

"Then I must slay him." The words were said in jest, a response to her imagery, and yet she held her fingers to his lips to silence him.

"Never say that," she whispered. "I'm not a princess who needs rescuing." She paused, biting her lower lip. The seductive sight sent shivers through him, though he was far from cold. A haunting sadness filled her eyes. "I'm not your quest, Gavin."

You should be.

He didn't want to think of his quest or of Grennet or dragons or fools. Or even of princesses and knights. He wanted nothing other than Nelle. No masks between them. Right now. He reached his other hand up, cradling her face between them, that dearest face. "Come with me."

"With you? Where?"

Away. Far away from here. Wainsbury. Rome. "My chamber."

Her own hands came up and pulled his away. She stepped back, unsteady on her feet. "Are you foxed?"

He frowned. Was he? Did he care? He knew what he wanted. And she was right there. "Not quite. More ... half-sprung. You?"

She set a hand to her head. "I did have punch."

The air went out of his lungs. He couldn't take advantage of her, not when she was in such a state. His heart pounded, his body pulsing with longing. A lone, sober thought floated through the fantasies playing in his mind: he should not take advantage of her, drunk or not.

He was about to step away when she touched his chest, looking up at him. "Yes."

"Yes?" He could drown in those eyes.

"Yes, I will come to your chamber."

The blood rushing to his groin made it difficult to think rationally. He wanted to swing her into his arms and carry her to his room. But ... "It would not be honorable in the least to ... to make love to you when you are not of clear mind and therefore cannot in good faith grant permission."

"Of course it would!" she protested, her lips forming the most adorable pout. "I gave you permission this morning. I *begged* you. You refused me."

"I was a fool." He enfolded her in his arms, her heavenly breasts pressing against his chest as his lips took hers in a torrent of emotion, his tongue ravaging the insides of her mouth. But she gave as good as she got, her arm tracing its way down his back to settle on his rear, pulling him closer as the most enchanting sounds emerged from her throat. He groaned as long-slaked passion roared to life, then abruptly broke from her, his breath ragged. "We cannot stay here."

"Then lead on, Sir Knight." She giggled again, an unexpected sound from this normally sensical woman, but he reveled in it. Her eyes sparkled, her nose wrinkling in adorable fashion. Gone was any hint of the meek, restrained Nelle from earlier in the evening. She'd shed the burdens bearing down upon her like a milkmaid's yoke. If only he could keep that joy on her face forever.

Without further thought, he did exactly as he'd wished to do a moment before; he lifted her into his arms, mindful to shut her door behind her, and carried her down the corridor. Her arms wrapped around his neck and she bit her lips together, mirth showing in her eyes.

"Your arms are quite strong, Sir Knight," she whispered as he maneuvered his chamber door open and steered them over its threshold.

He gave her a wolfish grin. "The better to hold you with."

As he set her down and shut the door, she said, "And what great lips you have."

Warming to the game, he pressed kisses to her pert little nose then to that delicious mole on her cheek. "The better to kiss you with."

She laced her fingers through his hair. "And wolf, what a fine mane you have."

"The better to—" He broke off, and she laughed.

"I haven't a good one for that," he admitted. "Though I'm more hawk than wolf."

"No," she whispered, suddenly serious. "Not a hawk. A lion. Cortleon. *My* lion."

He growled and caught her up in his arms again, his lips drinking in all of her—her mouth, her brow, her earlobes, the shapely expanse of her neck. Together, they weaved a slow dance toward the bed. She fell back on it and he followed, moving to her side so as not to frighten her, though every inch of him wanted to crawl on top, to possess her, to consume her, to feel her underneath him.

They both wore far too much clothing for that, however, so he settled for dropping kisses onto whatever bare flesh he could find, his lips dipping lower until they lapped at the pale skin above her bodice. She gasped, her fingers trailing through his hair as she clasped him closer.

"May I loosen this gown?" he murmured against her skin.

She did not hesitate. "Oh, yes. Yes, please. But only if I can remove your coat and waistcoat."

"By all means." He stood, pulling her up with him.

She ran her hands over his clothed chest, a wondrous innocence to her touch, though her eyes expressed anything but. Those endless wells of blue mirrored his intense desire, and her tongue darted out as she pushed his coat from his shoulders. He shrugged free of it, aided by her impatient hands, and let the garment drop. Her fingers returned to his chest, tracing his rigid muscles through his shirt, pausing to squeeze his upper arms.

"So solid. Nothing like me. Nothing like anything I've ever touched."

"Both of those statements make me stupidly happy."

She laughed, a light tinkling of sound, as she pulled at the folds of his cravat.

"Here, now, you only said coat and waistcoat," he challenged, chuckling as her hands stilled.

"So I did." Her lips turned up in a suggestive smile. "But I'm done playing by the rules. By the strictures I've set for myself. For tonight, I want to break them all."

"All? Are you sure you know what you're asking?"

"Teach me."

She tugged the neckcloth free and moved to his waistcoat buttons as the discarded cravat joined the coat. The waistcoat followed its companions in short order, as did his shirt, which he happily removed at her command. Chest now bare to her gaze, he held still as she took in the naked expanse of his skin. Her hand moved to touch his mother's ring and crescent necklace, which he'd worn every day since receiving it. "What's this?"

"From my mother. I wear it as a sign of my love for her."

Her eyes softened. "You cared for her very much."

"Very much. But I don't wish to speak of her now."

"No, indeed." With a soft, sultry laugh, she pressed a kiss to the ring then traced her fingers through the hair dusting his upper torso and down over the veins and muscles in his arms before returning to his chest, her fingertips lightly grazing his nipples.

"Goddess," he uttered hoarsely. "What power you hold over me."

She gave him a saucy smile. "Indeed?"

"More than you'll ever know." Truth rang behind his words. "But now you are quite overdressed."

"Am I?" The coy tilt of her head contrasted with the bewitching moué of her lips, her eyes alit with awareness of her own allure.

"Let us remedy that." He reached for her, holding her against him as his hands loosened the lacings at her back. His attempts to remove the dress foundered, however, as the material wouldn't give.

With a sweet little laugh, she pushed away. "I must say, it pleases me that you're no better at removing my garments than I yours."

Reaching up, she took out several pins anchoring the gown's bodice, then looked for a place to put them.

"Here." He took them and set them on the table beside the bed. When he turned back, the gown lay on the floor. He drank her in, his Nelle, standing there in her petticoat and stays, a hint of uncertainty in her eyes.

"Goddess. Nelle." His fingers traced the smooth skin of her cheek. "Do you want to stop? We can at any time."

Every inch of him screamed in protest, but he meant it. He never wished to do anything to scare or harm her. Not ever.

"No." Her voice was firm. "Most definitely not."

She loosened the petticoat's ties and it fell, leaving her only in stays and her chemise. Though nearly as long as the petticoat, no doubt to provide additional warmth in this cold winter season, the chemise did not conceal the sensuous shape of her legs underneath.

His fingers itched to follow her limbs to the spot at which her stockings ended and her naked flesh began, but he held himself still, scarcely daring to breathe. "You are beautiful. Everything about you is beautiful. Inside and out, dearest Nelle."

He stepped forward, leaving less than a hand's width between them. "May I do something?"

She looked up, those intoxicating blue eyes locking with his. "Yes."

No questions. No indecision. She didn't know what he was going to do, and yet she trusted him completely. His heart swelled. Carefully, he pulled the green ribbon encircling her mass of hair free and dropped it to the floor before loosening the remaining hairpins, which allowed it to fall over her shoulders, its ends reaching to her bosom.

"What a glorious mane," he whispered, his fingers tangling through the luxurious locks. "You are my lioness."

"Lionesses don't have manes," she whispered back, and he nearly howled with laughter. So Nelle, to insert logical facts at a moment like this.

"Mine does," he insisted, moving his hands from her hair to the laces underneath securing her stays. "May I?"

"Please." She turned, pulling her hair over her shoulder to expose the laces, and he bent to press a kiss to the nape of her neck as he worked the ribbons loose. She shivered as they released from around her midsection.

"Are you cold?"

"No." She turned to face him. "I'm on fire."

Her hands came out to grasp his waist at the place where his breeches met bare skin. She traced over the flesh there, her fingertips dipping below the edge of the fabric. He inhaled sharply, his cock pulsing. She had to remove her hands to allow her loosened garment off and the minute her skin left his he missed it, ached for it.

The stays fell. Only her chemise remained, her nipples budding against the garment. He exhaled, his blood pumping so intensely he could feel it in his neck. He slid his hands over the thin fabric at her waist, marveling at its narrow span, then moved them up her ribs to just under her breasts. Her breath caught, but she nodded. It was the permission he needed. He took the mounds into his hands, caressing, marveling at their soft fullness even through the chemise. "Good God, Nelle. You are perfection."

Gently, he lowered his mouth to hers, pouring all the emotion, all the need raging through him into this kiss. She responded with abandon as his fingers teased at her nipples, a shudder ripping through her at the touch.

"I want more of you," she breathed against his mouth, "All of you." Her hands skittered to the front of his breeches, but she fumbled in trying to release their buttons. She broke free from the kiss. "Drat it! I'm hopeless at this."

"Oh no," he said, even as his fingers undid the fall front. "You're exactly as I've dreamt you would be."

He'd just revealed how he'd fantasized about her, about this, but he didn't care. Nothing mattered in this moment except Nelle and the exquisite sensations she aroused. The breeches dropped, and he kicked off his shoes, letting them fly toward the pile of clothing.

She looked down and promptly burst into giggles.

"Nelle?" Her reaction was not what he'd hoped for—or expected.

"I'm sorry." She pressed her hands to her mouth as her shoulders shook with laughter. "It's only—a man in stockings with bare legs above is a comical sight!"

He looked down, too. At least she hadn't been laughing at the sight of his cock straining against his smalls. "I suppose you're right. Let me see you in yours only, so I can decide if the same is true of women."

Her cheeks flushed, but she complied, pulling the chemise over her head and letting it drop. She folded her arms across her abdomen, as if embarrassed.

"No," he whispered. "No. Please never hide from me. You are ... you are ..."

But no words would come. Her rose-hued areolas surrounding those pert nipples, the smooth expanse of her abdomen, and the triangle of dark blonde hair covering her mons had captivated him. He wanted to taste her there. Wanted to taste her everywhere.

She moved to roll down a stocking, and he made a sound.

"Please," he said when she looked to him. "If it'd be all right with you, I should very much like for you to leave them on."

"Might I at least remove my slippers?"

He laughed again at the beautiful combination she was: sensible and yet unbelievably seductive at the same time. "Of course."

"And now, those." She pointed at his smalls after she'd rid herself of the offending footwear.

"These?" he teased, pulling at the waistband.

"Yes." She swallowed, betraying her nervousness.

"Perhaps in a bit. When you decide to take them off yourself. For now, let us try the bed."

The wide smile she gave him as she pulled him to the bed confirmed he'd made the right suggestion. She'd said she wanted it all, but that didn't mean they needed to sprint to the finish. If this was to be his only night with her, he'd be damned if he'd rush it, no matter how many years it'd been since he'd lain with a woman. He was with Nelle now, and he'd not allow things to be less than perfect.

They lay as they had before, on their sides, facing each other. He ran a finger over her brow, down the ridge of her nose, across those lips. She surprised him by drawing the tip into her mouth and sucking it. The erotic fantasies her actions unleashed nearly had him undone before they'd begun. She released the digit, her hand sliding over his ribs to his back, pulling him closer. He happily complied, especially as it brought her glorious breasts in contact with his heated skin. He was aflame, on fire for her. He took her mouth in a fierce kiss again, his hands caressing her hip before clasping her derriere and pushing her into him.

With a groan, he left her lips, moving down to lick at her neck, then her collarbone, and then down, down, bending so that he could take a nipple in his mouth, suckling at her like a starving man. And he was starving. For Nelle and Nelle alone.

"Ooh ... I never ..." The words came out a sultry croon, and so he intensified his ministrations, growling with glee when she wove her hands into his hair, tugging him closer.

Slowly, slowly, he pushed her shoulder, turning her onto her back so he could lavish the other breast with equal attention. As he did, he trailed his fingers down her soft, warm abdomen, dipping a tip into her navel and then south, farther south, until they slipped into the curls at the junction between her thighs.

He paused, gauging her reaction, not wanting to push her further than she truly wanted to go, but she merely raised a leg, allowing him easier access. The trust she placed in him moved him like nothing else. She was inexperienced in the ways of lovemaking, and yet she innately allowed him closer, allowed him access, giving herself over to him.

He dipped his fingers between her folds, absurdly pleased at her wetness—evidence of her desire. For him. He eased a finger inside, slowly, carefully. She bucked up against him, mewling noises emerging as she grasped the back of his head, clasping him to her breast. As if he ever wanted to leave. He slid his finger out and then in again, slowly, carefully, and she moaned, the moan increasing as he pressed further, then slipped in a second finger. His cock pulsed, desperate to replace his fingers.

"Oh ... Oh, God." The words eased out of her like honey off a spoon.

"Why, thank you, Goddess," he whispered against her

breast, but she didn't respond, lost in her own haze of pleasure.

She whimpered as he withdrew, but he made up for it by moving his finger higher, finding her nub and rubbing against it lightly, rhythmically.

"Gavin!" she cried as her hips jerked. "It's ... it's ..."

"Yes," he murmured, his own breath labored. He watched as she danced in response to his ministrations, his own loins tightening almost painfully as her pleasure built.

"Oh!" she cried again, and he moved his mouth back to her breast, drawing in a nipple and sucking it as her panting increased, her body growing more rigid. "Oh!"

Yes. Let go, Goddess. Let go.

With a guttural cry, she arched off the bed, pulsing against his hand as she held onto his shoulder, her fingers digging in. As her spasms eased, her hips fell, her legs trembling.

"I ..." Her eyes drifted open, pleasure writ across her face. "I had no idea."

He pushed himself up and moved to all fours, dipping his head to kiss her thoroughly, one hand cradling the side of her face, touching her gingerly, in awe of the precious treasure he held.

"And now?" she said as he pressed a gentle kiss to her brow.

"That is up to you."

The most darling v appeared between her brows. "I want ..." She looked down toward his bulging smalls. "I want those off."

He lifted up into a kneel, spreading his arms wide. "I'm all yours."

Her eyes narrowed, her lip darting out. "So you are."

She pushed herself into a sitting position, wiggling back so that she could sit cross-legged before him. The childish position in the midst of very adult behavior amused him, but then thoughts of anything else fled as Nelle pulled at his smalls. When they caught on his upright cock, her mouth ticked sideways as her face took on a very serious expression. Without compunction, she lifted the edge of the fabric up and over it, pushing the piece of cloth down to his knees. Then she sat back, considering. "It's rather strange-looking, isn't it?"

Her words came after several hushed moments of careful observation, and at the wholly unexpected question, he collapsed face down on the bed, roaring with laughter. "Oh, Nelle," he said, his shoulders shaking. "You are never what one expects you to be. And that's—"

He broke off. He'd almost said, *that's what I love most about you*. But he didn't. He couldn't. Not when she wasn't his to love.

The thought nearly extinguished his erection, but then she reached out, pushing him over and rising above him so that she could take his length in her hand, her fingers slipping over his skin, and his attention riveted to the feeling of her holding him, her explorations tentative at first but then growing bolder.

"I can't imagine always having this between my legs."

He nearly exploded. Good God, he could. What heaven lay between those thighs, lay in her entire person. He'd like nothing better than to do this, to be with her, loving her, every day for the rest of his life. He sucked in a ragged breath as her hand tightened.

"Does that hurt?"

"No."

"Should I do more?"

"Yes."

"How do I—how do we get you inside me?"

His cock pulsed in her hand. "Are you su—"

She set her other hand against his mouth, stopping the

question. "Do not ask me again. I am sure. I've never been surer about anything in my life."

With a groan of pure desire, he rolled, pushing her gently onto her back as he moved over her. He nudged her legs apart, so he could settle against her. She readily complied, bending her knees as he rose enough to trace through her folds again and thrust in a finger and then a second when she asked for it.

"More, Gavin," she moaned, and he knew what she meant. He withdrew his fingers, his shoulders taut with anticipation as he rubbed his tip against her. "More."

He eased inside, using every ounce of his reserve not to sink into her immediately. He would not spill his seed, not now, not before she—before he—experienced all this could be. Inch by inch, he entered, mindful for any sign of restraint or pain on her part. There was none.

"This is odd, too." She lifted up on her elbows to witness where their bodies joined. "But the very best kind of odd."

Yes, the very best kind of odd, his Nelle.

He moved back, then in once more, and she gasped. "Do that again."

"With the greatest pleasure, my lady," he said, driving into her again, this time to the hilt.

She cried out, and he stilled. "Did I hurt you?"

"No. I don't think so. Do it again."

He did, and this time she exclaimed in pure wonder. "Why do people not do this all the time?"

"Oh, dearest Nelle, they do. They do."

And then he lost himself to pleasure, to the feel of her around him, of her breasts against his chest as he thrust, again and again, his tempo increasing, driving himself on and on toward that cliff.

Her hands grasped at his arms, taut with effort and

exertion, then at his shoulders as she urged him on. "More. More. More."

He panted and roared as the tension built to a nearly painful precipice. When her hands sank to clasp his hips, her legs rising and curling around him until her heels touched his buttocks, he exploded, leaping into the exquisite release, holding Nelle, his precious Nelle, to him, wanting her with him, needing her with him as he tumbled deep into something he'd never known.

After the spasms diminished, he reluctantly withdrew, not wishing to crush her with his weight. He rolled to her side but pulled her to him so that her back nestled into his chest, her bottom against his hips. Settling his arm around her waist, he wrapped a hand loosely around one breast as he peppered the nape of her neck with kisses.

"Nelle," he whispered. But in truth, there were no words. Nothing to encompass the intense emotions battering him from every side.

She turned her head, her blue eyes, relaxed now, meeting his. "Thank you."

Thank him. Thank *him*? It was he who should be worshipping at her altar. His goddess.

"Gavin?" she murmured, hugging his hand to her breast with her own.

"Yes?"

"Can we do that again?"

CHAPTER 34

*T*hrice more they made love before Gavin fell into a deep sleep, his chest rising and falling against her hand as she lay in the crook of his arm, her head on his shoulder. Even in slumber, he held her hip, those large fingers claiming her.

She longed to sink into the shelter of his body and stay forever in this bed, but she should return to her own room. She blinked sleepily. What time was it? She looked to the fireplace. The fire that'd burned brightly when they'd first entered had reduced to smoldering coals. Panic seized her. Had Lucy-Anne returned to an empty chamber? What if her sister alerted their parents? Oh, what had she *done*?

She eased free of Gavin's embrace, praying he'd not rouse. Thankfully, he hardly stirred. She donned her clothing as best she could, leaving her hair loose to hide the disheveled bodice. With great luck, she wouldn't encounter anyone in the hallway, Lucy-Anne would already be abed, and she could slip in with nobody the wiser to her clandestine activities.

Now that hours had passed since her overindulgence in punch, her head pounded. While she felt no remorse over her own actions, guilt hit her like a hard fall from a horse. Gavin had sworn never to dishonor a woman—not that she felt the least dishonored. The opposite, in fact. He had, however, refused her earlier out of fealty to his strict code of conduct and out of respect for her. Nothing had changed between then and now—except the amount of alcohol they'd each imbibed.

Would he rue this night come dawn?

She studied his jawline, illuminated by the moon rays streaming in through the window. Everything about the man exuded strength and vitality. His body was exquisite, muscled but not overwhelmingly so, his shoulders broad, his waist narrow. And his sex ... her own throbbed just thinking about it. How could they fit together so perfectly? Was it the same for all men and women?

How could she—how could he—regret what they'd shared? How beautiful that mingling of physical and emotional passion had been. How overwhelming. For her, at least. She'd infused every movement, every touch, every caress with love, wanting to envelop him in it even if she dared not confess it. If only she could freeze time and remain here for the rest of eternity, nestling with him. But she couldn't.

He shifted onto his side, and she stilled as he reached for the coverlet and pulled it over himself. Was he awake? Had he noticed her absence? A moment later, soft snores signaled she was safe.

Gingerly, she opened the door. The corridors were empty. *Thank heavens!* Closing the door as silently as possible, she hastened to her own chamber.

Her good fortune held as Lucy-Anne was abed, snoring loudly. *Whatever will Ashvere think of such racket?* Shoving away the errant thought, she shed her clothing once more, keeping on only her chemise, and climbed into the bed. Would her sister notice her lack of nightgown in the morning? Hopefully not, but if so, she'd come up with some sort of excuse.

For now, though, she huddled under the quilt, the cold from the room seeping in despite the thick bedcovers. If only she were still curled into Gavin, the heat of his body radiating through her. She scrunched up into a ball, fighting for every ounce of warmth as memories of his mouth on hers lulled her into a restless slumber.

Her last thoughts before drifting off were of lions and dragons—and her a Fool.

~

GAVIN WOKE WITH A START. Where was he? And why was he naked?

Memories of the previous evening, Nelle in his bed, under him, on top of him, stormed through like a charging bull. No. *No, no, no, no, no.* Why had he ... *Why?*

His temples pounded like a hammer on an anvil. He'd been three sheets in the wind, at least in the earlier part of the evening. By their last round of lovemaking, however, sobriety had returned, though clearly not his reason with it, as he couldn't tear himself away. Not that it'd have made a difference at that point. The damage had been done. He'd taken a woman to bed, and not just any woman, but a woman betrothed, the woman promised to his enemy.

He sat up, gripping his aching head. What had he been thinking? He'd been drunk many times over the years and never once broken his vow. Never once. *But this was Nelle.*

The woman he loved.

"That might be an explanation, but it's not an excuse," he growled, rising in order to don a damned nightshirt and then stoke the fire. The room was freezing cold. Not the time to be lounging about in the buff.

He stared at the rumpled bedclothes. When had she

gone? The why he could imagine; she wouldn't want to be caught in his chambers—especially not when set to marry another man the day after tomorrow. No, wait. The sliver of light in the sky indicated it was dawn. Just tomorrow, then.

She couldn't marry Grennet now. Not when she'd lain with him. Honor—what little he had left—demanded he offer for her. Why hadn't he done so before? For Nelle to break off the engagement while in Grennet's home and with the wedding so imminent would be awkward, to say the least. But she must. What reason would she give? Would she share the truth of this night?

And what would Grennet do? He didn't fear for himself, but the idea that the earl might lash out at Nelle sent nightmarish chills through him. What if he was not there to protect her and Grennet harmed her—or killed her? No. Surely, he wouldn't stoop to hurting a woman. Unless he'd harmed his own wife.

Gavin kicked at the pile of clothing on the floor. He should challenge Grennet *now*, despite lacking definitive evidence of his guilt. Weren't the letters damning enough? He pressed his hands to his forehead. He wanted counsel from his friends, but he couldn't betray Nelle by revealing their intimacies, nor did he wish to confess his own moral failing. No, before he could decide on a course of action, he must speak with her, must make her see honor demanded he make this right. Honor demanded they marry.

The thought shot joy through him. Yes, he would marry her. His love.

But what about Grennet?

～

NELLE WOKE after only an hour or two of fitful sleep. The sun was creeping over the horizon, bathing the room in faint light. Lucy-Anne slept on.

She'd always appreciated the day's early hours. Prudence was the only other family member who left bed before mid-morning, but she usually busied herself with drawing or tinkering with mechanisms and such, leaving Nelle alone to enjoy the respite before Lucy-Anne and Tabby enveloped her with their ceaseless energy and chatter. This morning, however, she longed to lose herself again in the Land of Nod. Her body twinged in unfamiliar places. Her head throbbed. She was to marry someone she didn't like, much less love, on the morrow. In sleep, she could forget.

As it was, she tossed and turned. Was Gavin awake? Had her absence surprised him? She slipped out from under the covers, not sure what to do. She needed to talk to him. She must convince him he'd lost no honor and bore no blame for the previous evening. And she must assure him she'd make no claims on him. She wanted no false declarations, no insistence they wed out of some misguided notion that honor required it. He'd made his priorities clear—and she'd never ask him to give up his quest.

Nor did she want to marry a man she loved. Lucy-Anne would pronounce her mad. But she didn't want to lose herself in that way. Better to marry without expectation of affection than to have one's heart shattered.

She pulled a plain morning dress from the chest of drawers, one that buttoned up the front so she could manage it herself. She didn't bother with stays or petticoat; she'd simply check if Gavin were in his chamber and then return straightaway. If anyone noticed her, she'd say she'd wished to visit Swythdon's chapel, which lay at the far end of the corridor.

She scurried along swiftly, alert for any faces, though no one was about. She paused outside Gavin's door. Should she knock? Enter silently?

Before she could choose, the door flung open, and he pulled her inside.

~

SHE'D COME BACK. She'd made her choice. She was his.

Gavin pushed the door closed and pressed her against it, burying his hands in her hair as he kissed her, his hips melding into hers through her gown. At first, she returned the kiss as eagerly as he gave it, but then, unexpectedly, she pushed against him. Immediately, he retreated, his brow furrowing.

"That's not what I came here for!" Her voice was sharp, irritation evident in the way she thrust up her chin, her hands settling on her hips.

He swung his hair from his face, confusion puckering his brow. He waited, unsure what to say. When the silence stretched, he tugged a hand through that same hair. "Nelle. Though it isn't what I wanted, there is no shame in last night."

Her eyes widened, her lips tightening.

Damn. That wasn't what he'd meant. Wanted *at first*, he should have said.

But before he could amend his statement, she held up a hand, as if warding him off. "No, there is not. I got exactly what I wanted. Thank you."

Last night, when she'd thanked him, he'd wanted to crow from the rooftops. Now, the words made him feel tawdry. Used. She'd wanted a service and he'd provided it. His abdomen tightened, indignation filling him. How dare she reduce what they'd shared to such an emotionless transaction?

"I want you to know I meant what I said. You are free. I have no expectations of you."

The words cut through him like a sword through flesh.

She could have been talking to anyone, so indifferent did she sound. *Who was this woman?* She was not the woman who'd been in his bed last night. This was not the Nelle he knew.

"You must know we—I—am honor-bound to marry you."

She exhaled. "I feared you'd say such."

Had her lip trembled or had he imagined it?

"No, you're not, Gavin. I made that clear from the start." Her tone was matter-of-fact as if they were discussing the weather or something equally as innocuous.

"But, Nelle."

She crossed her arms, her spine rigid. "No. This changes nothing. I will marry Lord Grennet on the morrow."

"This changes everything!" He threw his arms up, his voice rising. "You *know*. You know how important my honor is to me. You know I swore to my mother, to *myself*, that I would never disrespect a woman, especially one promised to another. You know I vowed never to be like my father."

"You haven't disrespected me, Gavin."

"I slept with you! I took your virginity!"

"No, I willingly gave it."

He stared at her, unable to comprehend, unwilling to believe that last night meant so little to her when it had shaken him to his very core. Was she really so heartless? So cold? The Ice Princess, claiming her next victim?

His chest heaved, his teeth grinding as rage surged through him. "You seduced me. Stole my honor. Forced me to break my vow."

"I did not!" Her eyes snapped. "*You* are the one who came to *my* chamber!"

"I was in my cups!"

Her eyes narrowed. "All four times?"

"Damn it, Nelle!" It took everything he had not to slam

his fist into the wall. "You should have turned me away. You should have rejected me if you were still going to wed another man!"

"Nonsense. I'd told you exactly what I wanted that morning. *You* are the one who sought me out."

Bloody hell. She was right. Still, he wanted to lash out. Didn't she know the pain she was inflicting?

"I thought you the highest of women. Never did I think you'd dishonor me in this way. Never did I think you would dishonor yourself. You're no better than the women my father slept with." The minute the words were out, he wanted to take them back. Damn his temper! He hadn't meant any of them, had only wanted to hurt as he was hurting.

Her face turned a deep red, her whole person shaking. "I did no such thing. I gave myself to the man I love!"

He went rigid. Loved him? *Nelle loved him*? He didn't understand. Didn't ... The fight went out of him, leaving him trembling. "You say you love me but insist on marrying another man? No. If you loved me, you'd call off the wedding."

"It's too late! Don't you see? The die is cast. I must marry the earl, for my family's sake as much as my own."

"Your own? What do *you* gain by marrying him?"

"I—I—," she stammered. "I must honor my pledge."

His fury mounted. "*Your* pledge? What of *mine*? I'd vowed to give my body to my wife only. My wife! Now I've thrown it away for momentary pleasure. Because of *you*."

She sucked in a breath. "I refuse to be disparaged by a man who was as willing as I. Had you any true feeling for me, you'd not seek to shame me for that."

"Had I—" he began, but before he could get any further, she jerked open the door and backed out, slamming it shut.

He stared at it. What had just happened? How had everything gone so wrong?

And how had he not told her he loved her?

He sank to his knees as her angry footsteps echoed down the corridor. He'd failed. He had failed her. He had failed himself. Should he chase after her? Swear his love? Would she believe him after he'd unforgivably compared her to his father's flights of fancy?

A flash of green peeping out from under the bed caught his eye. He crawled to it, lacking the power to stand, and pulled it free. Her hair ribbon. He stroked it, the satin slipping through his fingers. A token from his lady, though not one she'd intentionally given. Nor was she his lady, as she'd just made clear.

But he would keep it close to his heart, a memento of the woman he loved. A reminder of the woman he'd lost because he'd valued honor and vengeance above love.

CHAPTER 35

*B*ertie pulled at his beard in anticipation. He'd set up a day of sport for the gentlemen. A day for him to show off his prowess. He looked forward to battling Cortleon, to prove he could hold his own against the so-called Legendary Duke. He might not have youth on his side, but he had strength.

And he had anger.

It mattered not that the duke had treated Lady Elinor with nothing but courteous respect yesterday, despite Bertie's trap. Every day the knave was here, his resentment and rage had grown. If Lady Elinor was his Albina in new form, Cortleon was his father's in old. The bastard was nearly the spitting image of his sire, in looks and in his attitude toward women. He'd flattered and flirted with every woman present. Only an hour ago, a company of ladies in the courtyard, including a matron near his own age whom he'd thought respectable, had made wagers as to whom the detestable duke would bed next, several admitting they hoped to be the one.

Bertie had set eyes and ears on his guests from the house party's beginning, demanding his servants relay any untoward behavior. He didn't care about any report unless it concerned Cortleon, however. None had come. The rake-hell was wily, indeed.

He strolled now among the gathered gentleman, the thirst for revenge running rampant through his veins.

Engelsfell and Arthington swung their swords, testing the blades' balance and strength. Arthington ran a finger along the dulled edge. "Impressive," he called to Bertie. "Training with actual swords is quite the treat, Lord Grennet."

"I thought it fitting in a medieval castle such as this."

Emerlin stood off to the side, observing.

"Are you not joining us, my lord?" Bertie called.

"This is more Arthington's strength than mine, I'm afraid. I'm content to play the observer, as I prefer to be able to lift my arms tomorrow."

Coward. He turned to the circle of men. "Gentlemen! I've drawn partners for each of us. We shall battle as if in a medieval tournament."

"Luckily the blades are dulled," called one young lord, eyeing his sword with uncertainty.

Or unluckily. Bertie gave a smug smile. "If anyone feels the need to bow out like Emerlin, now is the time to do so."

The marquess merely shrugged, but Arthington took a step forward, hand gripping his sword as if he wished to issue a challenge over the implied insult.

"Duke," Bertie called, "You shall spar with Engelsfell."

Arthington stopped and turned to his tall friend. "Well, this will be interesting."

Bertie called out further matches until only one remained. "And I shall battle Cortleon."

His nemesis stepped forward, dexterously swinging his

chosen sword, his face impassive. The other gentlemen, however, whispered amongst themselves. The murmurings irritated him. Were they questioning his ability to take on the younger man?

As the sparring began, the men crowded around, yelling encouragement and studying moves. Some gentlemen speedily conceded; others took longer. Arthington and Engelsfell put on the best display, each striking and parrying with vigor until at long last Arthington stabbed his sword into the ground and raised his arms, his breath labored, his hair coated with sweat.

"I concede. Damn it all." He gave Engelsfell a grin. "Though you must admit, I did pretty well for fighting a massive tree trunk."

Several men chuckled, bobbing their heads in agreement.

Bertie intentionally saved his match with Cortleon for last, wanting his defeat of the duke to resonate longest in the other men's minds. And in Cortleon's. As the two circled each other, their eyes locked, the intensity palpable in the air. Cortleon took the first swing, but Bertie countered easily, a smile on his face. He'd trained Hugh himself, spending long hours in practice with a claymore. Sword-fighting was one of his strengths.

Cortleon, however, was no easy mark. As the fight labored on, Bertie's breathing grew heavier. Cortleon acted as if this were mere child's play, his brow barely dotting with sweat. *Curse the man!* White-hot fury spread. The duke was clearly superior. Why must a Cortleon best him at *everything*?

The bastard grinned, a grin of confidence, of arrogance. With a surge of revived energy, Bertie lunged, swinging and slashing with all of his might, but with lightning-fast reflexes, Cortleon twisted out of the way, landing on the his sword, his face a mass of pulsing veins and clenched muscles, white with exertion. Gavin took one last look at him, then thrust his own sword into the ground, as Arth had done. As courtesy demanded, he held out a hand to help the older man up. Grennet ignored it, climbing to his feet, though with much effort.

Gavin forced an easy grin. "A well-fought match, Lord Grennet."

The earl made no response.

Gavin shrugged then pulled the padded coat over his head, tossing it to the ground. He, like the other men, had removed his coat and waistcoat before donning the defensive garb. When he picked up his waistcoat, Nelle's green ribbon slipped from the waistcoat's pocket and floated to the ground. As he reached for it, Grennet's sword slammed into his side.

Gavin fell to the ground, agony ricocheting through his ribs.

"You whoreson! That's Lady Elinor's ribbon! You've no respectable reason to have it." Grennet's face purpled, spittle flying from his lips. "You seduced her, didn't you? You seduced my wife!"

Percy halted the earl's arm when he raised his sword again. Gasps emerged from the gathered gentlemen as Gavin fought to catch his breath. With determined effort, he rose.

Grennet rammed his blade into the ground between them. "I demand satisfaction. I challenge you to a duel!"

Gavin grinned. A true, wide, heartfelt grin. *At last.* He tossed his hair over his shoulder. "I accept."

"Cort," Percy said, raising his hand, caution in his voice.

"The earl has publicly dishonored Lady Elinor with his vile allegations. Had he not challenged me, I would have him."

Regardless of the truth in Grennet's assertion, the

pads of his feet. "Shall we call it, Lord Grennet?" he taunted, readying for the next strike.

Bertie snarled. He'd be damned if he'd concede to this man, even as his heart hammered in his chest, perspiration dripping from his face. "Never."

～

THAT MORNING'S horrible argument with Nelle fueled Gavin to drive relentlessly at the earl. Though evident early on he was the superior fighter, he toyed with Grennet, doing his best to exhaust the man. If only this duel were real, and he could win his Nelle merely by besting this beast.

At the earl's challenge of "*Never!*" every fiber of Gavin's being fixed on his opponent, just as Sulpicio had taught. He knew Grennet's every move before he made it, knew the man's strengths and weaknesses, knew where to attack and how to defend.

Irritated by Grennet's unwillingness to concede, he lunged, dealing blows to the earl's thigh, ribs, and shoulder. A full strike smarted, despite their blunted blades and thick-padded sparring coats. Grennet had landed more than one such hit; Gavin would no doubt sport a bruise or two.

He slashed at the earl as if possessed, wanting to swing at his neck, though that'd be disgraceful sportsmanship. He roared out his anger at the man's claim on Nelle, at her for seducing him, and at himself for breaking his vow.

"Cortleon!" called a voice then again louder when he didn't respond. Percy faced him just outside the battle circle. "Our excellent host is twenty-some years your senior. Grant him mercy and call enough."

Grennet had fallen to one knee though he still swung

reptile should not have publicly disparaged Nelle. He'd asked for no explanation, merely leapt to the conclusion Gavin had bedded her then voiced his accusation for all to hear.

He clutched his side. Grennet had hit him when he was down, a testament to the fool's complete lack of honor. His fury rekindled, his elation at the long-awaited excuse to duel the abominable earl fleeing. That he was still angry with Nelle himself didn't matter. He'd not allow slurs against her to stand. He must protect her honor. He was the one at fault for the previous night. She was right; he'd come to her. And because of the punch, she'd not been in full command of her senses.

"Emerlin. Will you serve as my second?"

The Irish lord raised his brow. "Yes, my friend. But may I have a word?"

He nodded tersely.

Em beckoned to Arth and Percy. Together they descended on him, as Grennet demanded his son serve as his own second.

"I beg you to reconsider." Percy's voice was low. "Refute his charges, but to duel a man your social inferior, a man so much your elder? Where is the honor in that?"

"You ask *me* to stand down when he himself issued the challenge? After having made such grievous charges against Nelle? No. I must defend her."

Em shook his head. "Are you sure you're not letting your enmity outside of Lady Elinor color your decisions?"

"Of course I am!" Though he whispered, his vehemence could not be missed. "He killed my father. Destroyed my mother's and my life. Slandered the woman I ..." He faltered.

"Pistols," Grennet bellowed, each syllable an assault. "At dawn."

"Father," Ashvere pleaded. "Stop this madness. We're to wed in the morning."

Grennet ignored his son, fixing Gavin with a murderous glare, like a boar preparing to charge.

Gavin pushed forward through his friends, his chest lifted high. "Agreed."

CHAPTER 36

*P*rudence, of all people, was the one who burst in
with the news. Most of the women had gathered
in the green drawing room for an afternoon of cards, letter
writing, and reading. Pru, however, had begged permission
to examine the castle's walls, wanting to calculate their
thickness and investigate how the stones had been joined
together.

"Fine, fine," their mother had said at breakfast. "But do
not wander far."

Now Nelle's youngest sister stood before her, chest
rapidly rising and falling, her face so white it seemed she
might faint. "A duel! Lord Grennet has challenged the Duke
of Cortleon to a duel!" she cried.

Exclamations and exhalations filled the room. Lucy-
Anne tossed her cards on the table and hurried over.
"Whatever for?"

The panic in her voice matched that building in Nelle's
stomach. He must have learned of her liaison with Gavin.
But how?

Pru swallowed. "He accused the duke of ... of ...
improper behavior with Nelle."

"*What?*" Lady Rutley spun to Nelle, visibly shaking. "Daughter?"

Nelle closed her eyes. *Why* could Pru not have come to her privately or at least held this to the family? What to say or do? The accusation was true, though she refused to think it improper. She'd dreamt all morning of their heavenly night. That wasn't something she wished to confess to her mother, however—or to anyone else. She rose from her seat. "I must talk with him."

"With whom?" Her mother's words came out more a shriek than a question.

How like Mother to presume guilt, despite Nelle's years of impeccable behavior. "The earl, of course."

And Gavin. For this was madness. She ran from the room. She must convince Lord Grennet ... but of what, exactly? She refused to let herself think as she scurried through the labyrinthine castle, avoiding others as best she could in her frantic search.

At length, she spied Ashvere. "Excuse me, Lord Ashvere. Where is your father? I need to speak with him."

"I don't know. He left his chamber a few minutes ago."

She'd missed him. *Confound it all!*

"He may have gone riding or for a walk. Sometimes he does that when he is—is ... upset."

He hadn't looked at her while speaking and he'd stumbled over his last words.

She let out a sigh. *Might as well confront it directly.* "Do you believe your father's accusation?"

Ashvere raised wary eyes. "It doesn't matter what I believe, only what my father does. Now please excuse me. I must attend Lucy-Anne, as she's quite distraught."

He left her without another word.

At least he hadn't openly shunned her or leveled his own charges. But *Lucy-Anne* was distraught? What about *her*? The man she loved but couldn't marry was to duel the man she didn't even like but whose wife she was to be on the morrow. She made for her own chamber, needing to escape prying eyes and gossiping guests. Closing and bolting the door, she fell against it.

What if Gavin lost? The idea of him lifeless, blood seeping from his magnificent body, brought up such bile that she scrambled to find something into which to throw up. Luckily, the chamber pot had been cleaned and was within easy reach. She sank to the floor, the smell sickening her further.

Where was he? How could he have agreed to this duel? They were guilty of the crime for which they'd been accused. If Lord Grennet died because of their actions— because of *her*—she'd never forgive herself. Nor Gavin. She may not want to marry the earl, but she certainly didn't wish him dead.

Several knocks came at the door, but she ignored them, her head spinning. Lord Grennet was gone, though what would speaking with him accomplish, anyway? And at this point, even if she found Gavin, any attempt to talk would not go unnoticed. She couldn't risk adding fuel to the fire. Panic clawed at her. She had to escape, even if only temporarily. After exchanging her slippers for kidskin boots, she pulled on a red woolen cloak over her day dress. The cloak's large hood hid her face, allowing her to sneak down the stairs and out a side entrance. If any of the people she passed knew it was she, they let her be.

Once in the cold, she inhaled deeply, the harsh winter air a welcome penance for the guilt shrouding her. She'd done this. By giving in to her selfish desires, she'd brought this on. Shame wrapped its suffocating arms around her. If either man were to die because of her own foolish choices, she wouldn't be able to bear it.

What could she do?

How could she save them both?

~

THE HORSE'S hooves clattered on the rocks embedded in the forest path. Gavin didn't know where the path led, nor did he particularly care. He'd needed refuge from Swythdon, a chance to clear his head following Grennet's challenge, and so he'd saddled a steed from the stables and ridden off.

Percy and Arth had argued with him for a good half hour about why he must cry off, but he'd remained silent in their onslaught, his own conscience at war with itself. He'd been grateful, even joyous when Grennet had issued his challenge. At last, he'd meet the enemy on the battlefield! After the initial jubilation ebbed, however, his struggle had begun. He still hadn't the final proof he'd needed. Killing Grennet without it meant he might never know the truth. Could he live with that?

If I got to live with Nelle. If Grennet were dead, the obstacle she'd set between them would be gone. If Grennet were dead, he could marry her. But wanting him dead to mete out final justice was one thing; how could Gavin claim any sort of honor if he killed the earl over a woman? Was that not exactly what Grennet had done to begin this whole madness?

The path twisted through a chasm lined with tall towers of rock. Late-afternoon sunshine dappled the moss-covered walls. The horse whinnied in protest of the ever-narrowing space, so he dismounted and patted its withers before walking on. Hopefully, the steed would wait for him.

After a short distance, the chasm widened. A raised, roughly rectangular slab of stone sat in the center of a circular area. Beyond it, the walls narrowed once more, perhaps into solid rock, as it was far darker than the preceding space. He took a seat on the stone, its icy coldness seeping through his breeches. What should he do? If he cried off, he'd destroy not only his honor but Nelle's, too, by essentially admitting the validity of Grennet's claims. But those claims *were* true. He *had* bedded her. And therein lay the problem. His dishonor might now cost him his life.

Perhaps he should delope, for if he killed the earl, where would that leave him? Could Nelle forgive him? Could he forgive himself? And would he never know the truth about his father's death?

A clattering sounded, and he lifted his head. Horse hooves. *A second rider.*

He'd brought no weapon. If it were Grennet, he'd be at his mercy. His chest tightened, his body stilling as footsteps neared. But it wasn't a bearded head that peeked around the corner. It was Emerlin.

How had he found him?

His friend approached the stone, saying not a word as he took a seat. For a time, neither spoke. Finally, Em turned, his earnest blue eyes full of compassion. "Will you tell me?"

Gavin needed no clarification. He knew what his friend meant and somehow knew he'd receive no judgment, no matter what he was about to say. He told Em everything. Of meeting Nelle, of his attempts to subdue his growing attraction, of their afternoon at the Foundling House. And of last night. Not in any great detail, but enough to admit Grennet's accusations were not without merit.

"I love her."

Em nodded. "You do."

"You see why I have to protect her. I cannot let him dishonor her. Not any more than I already have." He shifted on the rock. "I want to kill him. He murdered my father. Honor demands he pay for that crime." He went silent for a moment. "But if I kill him, she'd think I'd done so to cover my own sin."

"You could tell her."

"Of my father? Of my surety of Grennet's hand in it? Yes. But what if she doesn't believe me?"

Emerlin gave a mysterious smile. "Is that what you truly fear?"

The question brought Gavin up short. "I don't know," he said at length.

"I think you do."

What did Em mean?

The Irish lord hopped up. "I'll leave you now. Should you want further counsel, you know where to find me," he said, before vanishing behind the rock.

Gavin remained frozen in place, the stunning answer to Emerlin's question striking him like one of Grennet's blows. What he feared was not Nelle's incredulity, or even dying at Grennet's hand. No, his true fear was that he was a man driven only by passion, first for vengeance, now for desire. A man without honor.

Exactly like his father.

BERTIE STORMED across the wooded expanse on the northeast end of Swythdon, the area that melded into the forest beyond the castle. He'd seen Cortleon ride this way, following the trail that wended towards Lud's Church, the chasm not more than a mile away. He needn't go that far, as the path was the single entry and exit. The duke would have to return the way he'd gone.

Bertie would be waiting.

He fingered the two pistols, one tucked into each pocket of his greatcoat. Yes, he'd finish this now. No sense waiting until tomorrow; he'd not ruin his son's wedding day.

After he'd left the sporting ground, he'd gone to his chamber, screaming for Hightower. When the knock came, he'd bellowed "Enter," expecting his manservant.

Instead, his son threw open the door.

Bertie had hissed at him, insisting this was no time for discussion, but Hugh refused to budge. "If you're considering killing an innocent man, it's exactly the time."

"Innocent? *Innocent?* How can you claim that whoreson is innocent?"

Hugh winced at the raw language. "How can you prove he's not?"

"Lady Elinor's ribbon!"

"Yes. He had her ribbon. But a hair ribbon is not something genuinely intimate, like a garter."

Bertie glowered, his chest heaving with rapid, angry breaths. "He bedded her. I know it."

Hugh crossed his arms. "How? And don't say the ribbon again; there could be other explanations for that."

"Because!" His temples throbbed, and he itched to hit something, throw something, even as his battle-sore ribs protested. "There's much you don't know, Hugh. This is the only way to right the wrongs done to me."

"What wrongs?"

"Your mother!"

At that, his son's eyes went wide. Bertie never spoke of Albina to Hugh. He'd not wanted to reveal her duplicitous nature, had wanted to protect his son from the painful past.

"What can Cortleon have to do with my mother?"

"Not him. His father! *Loughton Knight killed your mother.*"

Hugh stilled, his face whitening. "You said she died from fever."

"As I said, there is much you do not know. And *this* Cortleon is no better than his sire."

A knock sounded at the door, and Hightower entered without waiting for permission. At seeing Hugh, he stumbled. "I beg pardon, my lord."

"No," Hugh said. His rigid shoulders and tight jaw

bespoke his turmoil at his father's revelation. "I was just leaving."

Half of Bertie wanted to call after his son. The other half, however ... The other half commanded Hightower to retrieve his set of dueling pistols and to ensure they were loaded.

He needn't wait until morning. No, he'd start the New Year fresh, with Cortleon dead.

Then he'd turn his thoughts to what to do with Elinor Greene.

CHAPTER 37

*G*avin urged the horse on, yearning to go faster but knowing the animal must navigate the rocky path. He wanted—no, he *needed*—to talk with Nelle, to beg her forgiveness for his inexcusable behavior that morning. Even if she couldn't forgive him, she needed to know he loved her. God, how he loved her. She needed to know he wanted to spend the rest of his days with her and that he'd never forgive himself for not realizing the truth earlier: she was the only future he wanted. She mattered more than his honor, more than this fruitless quest. He wanted nothing more than to marry her.

The horse broke into the clearing between the forest and the shallow woods bordering Swythdon. A man stood at the far end, clad in a green greatcoat.

Grennet.

As Gavin neared, the earl pulled out a pistol and aimed it at him. "Dismount!"

Gavin narrowed his eyes, homing in on the earl like a hawk. He could charge the fool as he was on horseback and Grennet was not. But he was no coward. He'd not run, despite being unarmed. He swung down from the horse, whacking its hindquarters to send it from the field, and crossed to Grennet, his stride confident and cocksure. The earl needn't know he had no weapon.

Sulpicio's first rule: *Show no fear.*

"Stop!" Grennet commanded when he was some ten yards away.

Gavin complied. What else could he do? His mind spun, searching for the best course of action. Was Emerlin still in the vicinity? Would the horse alert others? Not that he liked the idea of needing others to rescue him—but he didn't care for being shot, either.

Grennet's red hair and beard encircled his head like a halo of fire. Like a dragon about to roast him alive. The earl retrieved a flask with his left hand from his greatcoat pocket, undoing the seal one-handed. He took a long swig, all the while keeping his pistol trained on Gavin.

"I thought we were to meet tomorrow," Gavin said, shrugging a shoulder.

Command the stage. Sulpicio's second rule.

"Ah, but does this not bring back memories?" Grennet ambled unsteadily toward him as he took another swig. He stopped close enough to reveal the smell of the alcohol. Close enough to show his eyes, the whites so shot through with blood they appeared red.

Third rule: *Observe your opponent.*

Red eyes. Red eyes on a giant man in green. Gavin sucked in a harsh breath.

"That's right," Grennet said. "I was there. *You* were there." A crazed smile cracked his beard. "You weren't supposed to be, you know. I didn't want to have to kill a mere boy."

Every muscle in Gavin tensed. Proof at last—from the murderer's own mouth.

"Then you shot me! You vile little brat." Incredulity laced the earl's words. "But I hid the wound," he said, triumph in his voice. "Such pain you caused me. Though nothing like the pain your father inflicted when he *fucked my wife.*"

He tilted the flask to his lips again, then tossed it away with a noise of disgust. "Empty." He took a step back, wobbling on his feet. "I meant to properly challenge him, you know. An honorable duel. I was a *gentleman*. A man of principle. Of *honor*. Nothing like your whorish father."

How Gavin itched to lunge at him and beat the sorry snake to a pulp. He heeded Sulpicio's fourth rule, however: *Be willing to wait.* Despite Grennet's unsteadiness, the pistol held firm, and from this distance, the man could hardly miss.

"I didn't mean to shoot him in the face. Yet I can't say I'm sorry. That handsome countenance beguiled so many women. Innocents. And I destroyed it." He stepped closer, his eyes tightening to slits. "Maybe I'll take yours."

"Grennet—"

"Silence! Your father stole *everything* from me. Everything. He took Albina. My love. My life. He took my honor. And he *kept taking*, even after I killed him. Even after he was gone."

Gavin's brow furrowed. *What did he mean?*

"She never came back to me. I thought after, and with the babe … But she was inconsolable from the day he died, and when *our son* had my red hair and my same green eyes? She did nothing but weep for weeks, lamenting that Hugh wasn't *his.*"

Grennet circled around him as he spoke, increasing the distance between them as he went. What was the damnable man about now? Gavin turned, not willing to put his back to the earl. He was *il falco*. The hawk. And a hawk never loses sight of its quarry—though for once, he was the hunted, rather than the huntsman.

"I sent her to seduce you, you know," Grennet said, stopping, their original positions now reversed.

Gavin fought to keep his expression implacable. No. It couldn't be true.

"I needed to see. Needed to know if she'd be unfaithful again."

Again?

"The whore. Albina. Elinor. All of them! Whores."

"How dare you?" Gavin roared, lunging a step forward. "How dare you speak so of her?"

"I knew it!" Grennet crowed. "I knew you'd fucked her. You're just like your father."

"I. Am. Nothing. Like. My. Father."

It took everything he had not to charge the odious ass, consequences be damned. But he didn't. For something in the woods behind the earl caught his eye. A figure in a cloak. The figure tilted its head and even from this distance, he recognized Nelle instantly. *Oh, no.* He had to keep Grennet from turning again, had to keep him from noticing her. Why didn't she leave? Didn't she know how much danger she was in?

Sulpicio's voice echoed in his head: *Disarm them with charm.* The fifth rule.

But what could he say to—

"Take this!" Grennet exclaimed, pulling a second pistol from the same pocket in which the flask had been hidden. He held it out, keeping his own trained on Gavin, his arm surprisingly steady.

Would the earl shoot him at close range? Gavin approached, taking the weapon. It was loaded.

"Now return to where you were, then we'll count our paces. On ten, we fire! I'm a man of honor. A peer. This time, I do it properly."

Honor? Ambushing a man in the woods, demanding this farce of a duel?

Gavin flashed the briefest of glances to Nelle. Her hands cupped her mouth, her eyes wide. He prayed with all he had she'd remain silent, that she'd not call the earl's attention to her. He retreated but did not turn. He'd be damned if he'd let the man shoot him in the back, though Grennet had lowered his arm, his pistol now at his side. As he reached his origin position, Gavin could not help calling out, "Honor is defined by behavior, not birth. A man who shoots another in the face and then flees can *never* be honorable."

A bellow of rage left the deranged earl. "You are *exactly* like your father. A cocky libertine whoremonger. And *she's* just like Bee. I thought I'd found better in Elinor Greene. Thought I'd found a woman of virtue and honor. I was wrong. I'll have to find a way to rid myself of her without suspicion, too, after I kill you. Just like Albina."

Gavin's instincts had been correct; Grennet had not only murdered his father but also his own wife. The man was fully mad. Insane.

"Ten!" the giant monster screamed, stepping forward.

He followed suit, moving each time the earl did. At the count of four, however, Grennet whipped up his gun. Dishonorable to the end. Everything moved in slow motion, Gavin's attention narrowing until all he could sense, all he could see, was the end of the pistol pointing at him and the broad chest rushing forward behind it.

Sulpicio's final rule: *Don't miss the killing shot.*

He raised his own arm.

A desperate cry echoed across the clearing as Nelle sprang from the forest, racing toward him.

A shot rang out.

The monster froze, astonishment rippling across his

face. Grennet fell to his knees, grasping at his chest, where a red circle widened across his green waistcoat.

Confusion reigned. All sound faded. *Why had the earl fallen?* Had he shot him? He looked at his pistol, but it remained cocked.

"Hugh."

The word was Grennet's, although the ringing in Gavin's ears was so strong he could scarcely hear it.

Ashvere stepped in front of him, giving a raw scream. "*You* killed her. You killed my mother!"

"To protect you, my son." Grennet's voice was raspy, weak. He collapsed to the ground.

Nelle ran past the felled earl, legs pumping. "Gavin!" She launched herself against him. "My love!"

"Nelle, no!" he cried, shoving her to his side. For behind her, Grennet had twisted. Mustering what little strength he must have left, the earl gave a malevolent smirk and raised his pistol.

The gun exploded.

∿

NELLE SCREAMED as Gavin and Ashvere both dropped. Had he killed them both? She fell to her knees, shrieking at the blood oozing from Gavin's neck. His eyes closed. He lay motionless.

Oh, please, God. No! What should she do? He couldn't die. Not her love. How could she save him? She had to save him! Tearing off her cloak, she pressed it against his neck, desperate to quell the flow of blood. Next to him, Ashvere held his hand against his side, red wetness seeping between his fingers. Her heart hammered frantically. She needed to find help. But if she left them, would they die?

A rhythmic drumming sounded in the distance. Horses' hooves?

A great stallion broke through into the clearing.

Arthington! Oh, thank God. Great sobs of relief overtook her as he thundered toward them, Engelsfell and Emerlin at his rear. The blond duke leapt from his horse, flying toward the two fallen men.

"Is he ... Are they?" His face was white, his voice full of fear.

She shook her head. "Not yet. But I don't know the extent of ..."

Emerlin rushed to Ashvere. "He's been shot in the side. We must get them both to the castle at once."

"But how? We haven't got ..." Her whole body shook, though from terror, not the cold. "They can't die! Gavin can't die!"

Engelsfell knelt near Ashvere, who was moaning but alert. "Can you sit a horse if we tie something about your waist?"

The young lord lifted his head, his cheeks ghostly pale as he nodded.

The tall duke pulled off his coat then carefully raised the injured man off the ground enough to wrap the makeshift bandage around him. Ashvere groaned but retained consciousness.

"Em, mount your horse!"

Emerlin's long limbs made the leap into the stirrups and the swing over the saddle look effortless.

Engelsfell lifted Ashvere, his biceps bulging with effort as he carried him to the horse. "Place your leg over the horse," he urged.

Ashvere complied as best he could. Engelsfell pushed him onto the saddle as Emerlin's arm came around the young lord's waist to hold him firm.

"I'm sorry for the pain this pressure must cause you," Emerlin said when Ashvere groaned, "but it will help hold in the blood." With a nod to Engelsfell, he turned the horse and made for Swythdon.

Meanwhile, Arthington came to Gavin and bent down. "Let me see."

Reluctantly, she removed the cloak, wanting to avert her eyes from the bloodstained shirt and cravat. But she couldn't. Not when this was the man she loved.

Arthington pulled at the neckcloth, discarding it before moving the shirt to the side to gain a better view of the wound.

She gasped. Around Gavin's neck, along with his mother's necklace, was a green ribbon nearly ripped in two. *Her* ribbon. He'd worn her ribbon like a token given by a lady to her knight. Had the bullet torn it?

Arthington blew the air from his cheeks in a huge sigh of relief. "Thank God. It missed his jugular. Despite all the blood, I believe the wound largely superficial."

Tears of relief spilled over as the duke tugged off his own cravat, folding it into a square. Setting the clean linen against the neck wound, he then bound it with Gavin's sullied cravat, tying the cloth underneath his armpit.

"But then why is he unconscious?" Nelle asked, her fear returning.

"He must have hit his head when he fell. But if anyone's hard-headed, it's Cort. He'll no doubt rouse soon."

The reassuring smile he gave her rang false, but she nodded. What else could she do?

Beckoning Engelsfell, who stood at the ready, Arthington mounted his own horse. He grabbed Gavin's leg as Engelsfell lifted the wounded duke sideways then wrapped his arms under Gavin's to hold him as Engelsfell pushed him fully onto the saddle.

"Got him?"

Arthington gave an affirmative nod, then followed after Emerlin.

Engelsfell turned to her. She rose from the ground, her legs trembling. He tipped his head toward his horse. "My lady?"

With unsure steps, she followed him to the animal. He lifted her so that she could place a foot in the stirrup then stepped back while she swung her leg over the saddle. Her skirts bunched awkwardly as she straddled the horse. How strange to ride like a man.

The duke mounted behind her, one arm coming around her waist while his other hand took the reins. If only it were Gavin. If it were *her* duke, she'd lean into his chest, inhaling his beloved scent and reveling in the intimate feeling. Still, she wasn't about to complain; Engelsfell and his friends had come to the rescue when she'd thought all hope was gone.

As the duke turned the horse, she cast a glance at the earl's body lying face down in the grass. *Let him rot.* Her stomach heaved, and she vomited over her skirts. How close she'd come to marrying him. She'd thought in doing so, she'd rescue her family. Instead, she'd almost cost the man she loved his very life.

"I'm sorry," she whispered weakly, embarrassed at the sick now covering her.

"Absolutely no need," Engelsfell said as the horse picked up its pace through the woods. "I was close to doing the same."

She doubted that but was grateful for his attempt to soothe her, regardless. Closing her eyes, she prayed fervently that Arthington was right and that Gavin would be fine. And that Ashvere would survive. He'd saved her love, shooting the earl as he had. His own father.

Would he regret his actions? Would he be able to forgive himself? She hoped so. This was *her* fault. Had she not been so selfish, had she not been intimate with Gavin, none of this would have happened. After hearing the earl's ghastly confession of having murdered both Gavin's father and his own wife, she held no remorse for him. But if God forbid, Ashvere should die, if she should have cost him his life and her sister her greatest love, how could she ever live with herself?

CHAPTER 38

SWYTHDON – JANUARY 1814

*T*he green monster charged at him from the darkness. Only this time, the monster morphed into a man. Grennet.

A cacophony of sights and sounds crashed through Gavin, memories of his father falling, the echoing of the gun, of the earl's threat, the man's gigantic hands reaching. Of the retort of his father's pistol, the giant clutching at his neck. And of running for all he was worth.

His eyes blinked open. The room was blurred. Unfamiliar. Where was he?

"Gavin!" exclaimed a soft voice, a loving voice, as warm fingers gripped his hand and a face leaned over his.

As his vision cleared, he took in the heavenly blue of her eyes. Nelle. "Goddess." He gave a wry smile, even as pain lanced through his shoulder. "I knew you were a goddess. An angel. You've come for me from on high."

A tear splashed onto his cheek. She squeezed his hand. "And you my valiant knight, my warrior. My champion."

"I remember. All of it. It *was* Grennet." Closing his eyes, he licked his dry lips. "Water?"

"Of course!" She rushed to the pitcher on its stand, returning with a ladle, which she carefully maneuvered to his mouth.

After several sips, he pushed it away, frowning. "I didn't kill him."

"No. Ashvere did."

"It should have been me. To avenge my father. My mother. It should have been me."

She brushed the hair from his forehead. "He's dead. What does it matter?"

It mattered. *How could she not see it mattered?* He stilled. Grennet had wronged him. But in killing his own wife, in stealing Ashvere's mother, he'd grievously wronged his son, too. Nelle was right. Ashvere had deserved justice, as well.

"Where is Ashvere?"

She frowned. "Recovering."

"Recovering?"

"The bullet that hit you hit him, too."

"What?" He pushed up on his arms then sank back as pain spasmed through him.

"Don't worry; he's doing fine. Lucy-Anne is tending him well." She hesitated, more tears slipping down her cheeks. "I'm actually more afraid for his spirit. He killed his own father."

"He had good reason. The man murdered his mother. No one will challenge his honor on that accord."

She let out an exasperated sigh, even as her hand sought his. "What is it with men and honor? Do you think it matters to Ashvere at this moment whether others find his actions honorable or not?"

Gavin wrinkled his brow. "Honor is the mark of a gentleman. It guides a peer's every action."

"That's stupid. Clearly, it does *not*."

He laughed. He couldn't help it, though the movement hurt. Her indignant tone was adorable. He pulled her hand toward him, pressing a kiss to her knuckles. "As stupid as sacrificing yourself to appease everyone else?"

"*What?*"

"Why were you so insistent about marrying Grennet? It can't be that you had feelings for him." He wrinkled his nose. "Did you?"

She harrumphed, pulling her hand away. "No. But I needed to marry *someone.*"

"Why?"

"My family insisted. Gave me an ultimatum. Said it was —" She broke off.

"—A matter of honor?"

Her eyes wouldn't meet his. "No ... it was for my sisters. And to save my family."

"Save their honor, you mean."

"Why are you being so ... so ... obnoxious?"

He grinned. "Partly because I want you to see that what you were doing and what I was doing, both fighting on behalf of our families, wasn't so different after all. And partly just because you're charming when you're cross."

She opened her mouth, her eyes flashing, then closed it. After a moment, she said, "You're right." She cupped his stubbled cheek, her fingers caressing his face. "And it almost cost me you." Uncertainty shadowed her features. "*Did* it cost me you? You insisted your search superseded everything else, but now—"

Ignoring the twinge in his neck, he pulled her to him. "You're right," he whispered against her lips before leaning back and adjusting his shoulder in an attempt to mitigate the pain. "I am stupid."

"What?"

"I nearly lost you, Nelle. Because of my misguided notions of honor. Because of those horrible things I said, blaming you because I—" He swallowed. "I did not mean them. On my honor, I—" He broke off again with a derisive chuckle. "The wrong phrase. But you're right. I couldn't let go of the past. I couldn't let myself imagine any sort of future until I'd righted the wrongs of years ago. Wrongs I couldn't even *remember*. Honor demanded it, I thought. It was my life's purpose, that which I trained for, the entire reason I returned to England. But I was so busy fighting for ghosts that I didn't fight for you." He grimaced. "I should have. By all that is holy, I should have. For if there's anything worth fighting for, it's love. And I love you, Nelle. My God, how I love you." Swallowing, he added, "Can you forgive me?"

"Forgive you?" Her voice was soft, her eyes brimming with emotion. "There's nothing to forgive. You *were* fighting for love, Gavin. Love for your mother."

"Yes. But she is gone. You are here."

"Yes. That doesn't make your love for her or your desire to honor her any less strong, however."

His own eyes welled up. "No. It doesn't. She was all I had. Because of *him*."

"Yes." She traced his nose with her finger. "But now Grennet is gone."

"Not him. My father."

She raised a questioning brow.

"Had my father been faithful to her, had he truly loved her, none of this would have come to pass. None of it."

He sucked in a breath as shame settled over him. Shame for who his father was but also for what he'd been willing to sacrifice to avenge such an unprincipled man. He'd been willing to walk away from the love of his life. The love who'd almost married his mortal enemy. He closed his eyes, turning away, unable to bear the compassion in her loving gaze.

"Perhaps," she said, her fingers feathering through his hair. "But Grennet chose his own actions. Then, and now. He chose the dishonorable course every time."

He turned his head back. "Yes, he did. He shot my father in the face. Tried to kill me then threatened my mother's life. Murdered his own wife. And then, upon my return, seeing my feelings for you sought to—"

"—To marry me," she broke in. "As vengeance against you." She nodded. "Yes. It makes sense now, why he reacted so whenever you were about. As does his sudden reversal regarding Ashvere and my sister—and why he was willing to settle such a ridiculous amount of money on my parents for my hand." She shrugged. "So much for being the most beautiful woman in England. In the end, I had absolutely nothing to do with his interest in me."

He stroked her hand. "He was a Fool. Capital F. He even wore the costume, remember?"

"I remember."

"Nelle?"

"Yes?"

"I was a fool, too."

"If you insist on donning that jester hat, you must let me share it."

He furrowed his brow, but she set a finger to his lips when he made to speak.

"I nearly lost you, Gavin. Because of my misguided notions of love. What other woman would insist to herself she didn't want to marry the man she actually loved?" She moved her hand to his chest. "I couldn't see love as compatible with marriage. I couldn't see a husband as congruous with independence. I longed to be valued for my character over my appearance, and yet ... yet I built a tower and locked myself in. I became that Ice Princess everyone called me, wearing my coolness as my armor, my work as my shield. I told myself long ago that I would only marry for love, and yet when I found it, I rejected it, fearing I would lose myself." She smiled, the tenderest smile he'd ever seen. "And then ... you. You melted me, Gavin. My walls tumbled down. And I, the Fool, tried to build them up again. I ... I became my own dragon."

"Nelle ..."

"I didn't understand I could *find* myself in love, as well. But I have with you, Gavin Knight. My legendary duke in shining armor. I've found myself. Because you saw me. You saw past my mask. You rescued this princess."

"Oh, Goddess." He raised her hand, pressing a lingering kiss to her knuckles, his eyes wet with tears. "It was you who saved me. You've given me a new quest."

This time, her brow puckered.

He chuckled, moving her hand back to his heart and covering it with his own. "I pledge my fealty to you, Lady Elinor Greene, and I pledge my troth. I am your Knight, now and forever. And from this day forward, my single quest is this: to love you and only you. Always."

CHAPTER 39

Gavin stood in Swythdon's chapel, Nelle at his side. Next to him was Lucy-Anne and to her other side, Ashvere, though he sat in a chair.

Lucy-Anne had suggested postponing the wedding in order to allow him more time to heal, but Ashvere had been adamant. "I will not wait one more minute to have you as my wife."

Gavin had to admire the young man not only for his physical fortitude but for his strength of mind, as well. As the tale had come out, everyone agreed the new Earl of Grennet had acted with honor, especially since his father had been about to shoot the Duke of Cortleon.

Still, two days ago he'd confessed to Gavin he didn't feel the least bit honorable. "I killed my *father*. The man I looked up to as the most proper, the most respectable, indeed the most honorable of men. I thought he'd led a faultless life. Though we occasionally sparred, I was *proud* to be his son." His face contorted. "But he killed your father. *My mother*. How am I to live with that?"

For a long moment, Gavin was silent. "I don't claim to

know how this must feel. But I've lived my entire life in my father's shadow. It took nearly losing Nelle to see I need to live for me." He pressed his hand into the younger man's. "Neither of us can change our pasts. But we *can* decide how we live in the future."

With that, he'd left Ashvere to Lucy-Anne's loving care and sought out Nelle, finding her in the library, a large orange cat on her lap. He'd halted, nonplussed at the animal's presence. He'd noted no felines at Swythdon.

She raised a shoulder, an amused smile lighting her face. "I don't know where it came from, either. But I won't deny I'm grateful for its company. I miss my animals. Just like I miss the children."

The cat purred so ridiculously loud as she stroked its fur, he burst out laughing. "I know how you feel, cat." He leaned toward the feline's face. "I want to purr when she strokes me, too."

Her cheeks colored at his more-than-suggestive comment.

The cat gave him a baleful stare before jumping down with a meow. It padded near to the window then sprawled in the sunshine-covered floor.

Gavin dropped to a knee. "In fact, I'd like nothing more than for you to stroke me forever." He lay his head on her lap. "I am already your knight. I would like to be your lion. Your ever-loyal, ever-faithful husband." He swallowed. "I'll even attend the opera with you. Every night, if you wish."

She smoothed a hand over his hair, just as she'd done to the feline.

"But," he said before she could speak. "It's up to you." He looked up into her sweet face. "You must choose for yourself, Nelle. You have a say. I'll still aid your family. I will provide for the Home. But you need never marry if that's your true desire. I never wish to clip your wings, Goddess. You may fly free."

~

NELLE SEARCHED Gavin's warm sherry eyes, giving him a tremulous smile, her heart overflowing. A week ago, her only future was one of staidness at best, misery at worst—a life empty of everything she now knew it could hold.

Gavin had saved her. He'd thawed her, opening up a rainbow of emotion she'd never before experienced. How silly she'd thought Lucy-Anne and other young ladies for making calf-eyes at lords, yet here she was as lovesick as any of them over the Duke of Cortleon.

Trying to land a spouse through artifice and coquetry rather than sharing one's genuine self *was* silly. Only by taking off the masks and being willing to see the other person for who they truly were could real, lasting love exist.

Lucy-Anne had found such. What Nelle had initially dismissed as passing infatuation clearly was not. Her sister refused to leave Ashvere's side, insisting on ministering to him herself, despite her family's pleas for her to rest. "If I need rest," she'd said to her parents the third morning after the horror, "I'll sleep here. With Hugh."

"That'd be indecent," Lady Rutley responded. "You're not yet married."

"Nonsense," Lucy-Anne snapped, much to Nelle's amusement. "He's my life. I will not leave his side."

Their mother swished out of the room, Lord Rutley trailing behind.

"I know I often seem melodramatic to you, Nelle," her sister said, shaking her head when Nelle tried to protest. "We are different, you and I. Emotion drives me in the way practical thinking does you. But the love I feel for Hugh? It's as if I found the part of me I didn't know was missing." She flashed a saucy smile. "I do hope you've found the same outside of the duke's bed now as well as in it."

Nelle's mouth fell open.

Lucy-Anne winked. "I pull off a convincing snore, do I not?"

"But how did you ...?"

"Know it was Cortleon?"

She nodded.

"I'm a lover of love. Think you I can't see it when my dearest sister has fallen into it?"

Hugh stirred on the bed, and Lucy-Anne immediately turned. "My heart," she said when he opened his eyes.

"My treasure," he responded.

"I am happy and blessed to be yours."

"And I yours."

Nelle had slipped from the room unnoticed and gone to the library, seeking her favorite chair for a few moments of solitude. When she'd arrived, however, a long-haired orange cat, its ruff so large it resembled a miniature lion, had been stretched across its seat.

"You've stolen my place," she teased the cat, surprised when it meowed and then leapt down. "I didn't mean you had to move." But she took the spot, warm from the feline's presence. A minute later, the cat jumped onto her lap, circling around as it kneaded her thigh before sitting down as if this were a ritual they'd done for a thousand years. It purred contentedly as she scratched its head.

Gavin had found her there. He'd given her freedom.

And she'd given him her whole self.

"I want nothing more than to be yours." She ran her fingers through his silky tresses, amazed such a man loved her for *her*. He knew her strengths, her fears, and her weaknesses. He knew who she was behind her mask. And yet, he still wanted her. Still loved her.

He took one of her hands, enclosing it between his own as his face grew solemn. "I will never be like my father. This I vow to you."

"Neither shall I," she responded. "I haven't got the balls for it."

With a roar of laughter, he pulled her from the chair until they fell backward, her body resting full length against his. He winced when his shoulder hit the floor. "I fear I'll always bear a mark there."

"A badge of honor," she insisted, before pressing her mouth to his.

In no time at all, they'd both been purring.

The memory brought forth a smile as she stood in Swythdon's medieval chapel, Gavin to her side, as the priest united them in holy matrimony. Beside her, Lucy-Anne squealed and jumped before throwing her arms around her husband. When he groaned, his new countess contritely apologized.

"The only thing that hurts is your absence, my wife."

At that, Lucy-Anne kissed him, a kiss so openly passionate the remaining party guests tittered.

Gavin nudged her. "Well, now. The Legendary Duke has a reputation to protect. We can't let them outshine us, can we, my Legendary Duchess?"

She catapulted herself at him, laughing out loud as he raised her in the air before thoroughly worshipping her mouth. "My legendary love," she whispered against his lips.

Despite his neck wound, he lifted her and carried her from the room, ignoring the exclamations and cheers surrounding them.

"Promise me one thing?" he said, kicking the door shut as they entered his chamber.

"Anything."

He lay her on the bed then stretched alongside her, nibbling her neck. "Let's never attend a Christmas party again."

Laughing, she rolled on top of him. "Agreed, my dearest husband. Agreed."

EPILOGUE

WAINSBURY - TWELFTH NIGHT, 1815

"Georgie, give the doll back to your sister." Nelle mustered a stern expression, though she never could hold it for long.

The darling boy gave her an impish grin then continued to chew on the doll's head.

"He learned that grin from you, I fear," she said to her husband.

Gavin looked up from the floor, flashing her the exact same smile before Morna, bouncing on his chest, covered his mouth with her chubby hands. "Me, Dada, me! No Mama. Me! Me!"

Nelle pressed her lips together to suppress her mirth. "From day one, she's tried to steal you away."

He pried his daughter's fingers away, dropping kisses on them as she giggled. When the little girl hopped off of him, running over to pet the orange cat sleeping near the fireplace, he sat up, resting his arms loosely on his bent knees. "What can I say? I have that effect on ladies."

"You are incorrigible!"

"Always."

Mrs. Stewart entered the room, dropping a curtsy. If she thought it odd the Duke of Cortleon was on the floor, coat off, she said nothing of it. "William has settled for the night but Cook has warm bread from the oven. I thought I might take the other children?"

"By all means. I'll never turn down a chance to be alone with my wife." He gave a wry chuckle as he stood up. "It's getting harder and harder to have her to myself."

Mrs. Stewart settled Georgie on her hip then reached for Morna's hand.

The girl eyed her. "We have chockit?"

"Yes, dear, we may have some hot chocolate."

She grinned, granting the housekeeper her hand as they exited the room.

"She learned that from you," Gavin said.

"What?"

"Oh, yes. She knows to make her conditions clear before agreeing to anything. Clever woman."

Nelle laughed, rubbing a hand over her rounded belly.

He crossed to her chair, setting his hand near hers. "Is she kicking?"

"Not right now. And it could be a boy, you know."

"Yes, I do suppose there's a fifty percent chance of that."

She laughed. Again. She spent much of her days laughing, her hours filled with joy, every minute a treasure with her husband. Her knight.

"I have a present for you." He removed his hand to reach into his waistcoat pocket and withdraw a small box.

"For me?"

"It *is* the twelfth night of Christmas, after all. I take it you forgot to get me anything?"

"Oh, you oaf."

He tucked the box behind his back. "Tsk, tsk. What kind of wife hurls insults at her husband when he is showing her his love?"

"This one."

Chuckling, he set the box on her stomach then stepped back.

Picking it up, she lifted the lid then gasped, a hand flying to her cheek. Nestled inside was a signet ring, an exact copy of Gavin's, though in a much smaller size. Instead of the ruby of her husband's, however, this one held a dazzling emerald, the majestic Cortleon lion peering at her from its top.

She looked up, speechless.

"You are my duchess. My partner. My lioness. My equal. You deserve a ring commensurate with your status."

"But it's green ..."

He chuckled. "Yes. Your favorite color. You've even got me wearing green waistcoats now." He helped her from the chair, his eyes smoldering. "But more importantly, you are Elinor *Greene* Knight. A person in your own right. Separate from me and yet joined. By these rings. By our vows. By our love."

"Gavin, I—" She swallowed. "I do not know what I did to deserve you."

"Nor I, you," he said, taking the ring from the box and slipping it on her finger.

"But ... but you've given so much. To my family. To the foundling home." A knot formed in her throat. "You've taken these children into your home—"

"—*Our* home," he interrupted.

"—our home and made them your own. You've helped me establish a home for children in Warwick. You've let me move my menagerie into Wainsbury. And now this." She sniffed as she ran a finger over the ring. "What have I to give that could ever be comparable?"

"You've already given it." He pulled her into his arms, nestling his chin on the top of her head.

She leaned in, breathing his familiar scent, though the

growing babe between them made it difficult to achieve the closeness she craved. *Patience, Nelle. A mere month more ...*

"What do you mean?" she murmured against his chest.

"You gave me you. And—" His breath hitched. "You gave me a family. I never had that. I had a mother, one as loving to me as you are to our children. I miss her fiercely. I always will. But I did not have a *family*. I grew up a lonely child. Now I'm surrounded by babies and rabbits, by boys and girls and cats and even chickens. I'm an orphan no more. You saved me."

"No," she corrected, her own eyes moist. "We saved each other. Remember?"

"Yes, dearest wife." He pressed a tender kiss to her hair, his hand cradling her face. "We fought our dragons and defeated them. Together."

AUTHOR'S NOTE

ON GAWAIN AND THE GREEN KNIGHT

The Legendary Duke is loosely based on the Arthurian legend of *Gawain and the Green Knight*. For those not familiar with the story, I include a brief summary here to show how I incorporated as many elements of the story as possible into Gavin and Elinor's tale and also to explain why some had to be left on the plotting room floor. (If you've skipped to this note before reading the story, you may want to reconsider, as I've included many spoilers here.)

Gawain and the Green Knight opens at Camelot, where King Arthur and his knights have gathered for a New Year's feast. In the midst of their celebration, a mysterious giant knight bearing a massive green axe thunders in on a horse. The knight, entirely green from head to toe, challenges Arthur's court to a game: "Chop off my head now, and I'll chop yours off a year hence."

When King Arthur rises to accept the challenge, Gawain leaps ahead of him. The green knight offers him the axe, and Gawain dutifully chops off the knight's head. The knight, however, merely picks up his severed head and remounts his horse, the head telling Gawain to find him at the Green Chapel in a year so that he may chop off Gawain's head, as agreed.

Nearly a year lapses and Gawain sets off north to fulfill his end of the promise, a testament to his bravery and honor. His travels bring him to a castle on Christmas Day. The castle's lord and lady welcome Gawain in and feed him lavishly at their celebratory feast. The lord, Bertilak de Hausdesert, strikes a bargain with Gawain: for each day Gawain stays with them, whatever Bertilak gains in the day's hunt he will share with Gawain, provided Gawain share with the lord whatever he likewise gains that day in the castle.

The first day, while Bertilak hunts deer, his wife attempts to seduce Gawain, from whom, despite his resistance, she manages to steal one kiss. That evening, Gawain grants one kiss to the lord. The second day, Bertilak hunts a boar while his wife again hunts Gawain. This time, she secures two kisses. Gawain thus likewise gives Bertilak two kisses that evening. On the third day, Bertilak goes hunting for foxes. His wife tries once more to seduce Gawain, begging him for a love token such as a ring. He refuses. But when she mentions her green girdle can protect its wearer from death, he accepts it, fearing the beheading he faces once he finds the Green Knight. This time, however, although Gawain gives Bertilak three kisses that evening in exchange for Bertilak's offering of three fox pelts, he mentions nothing of the girdle.

The next day, Gawain sets off again on his quest. Though a servant tells Gawain everyone will understand if he bows out of the agreement, Gawain refuses, saying his honor prevents it. When he finds the Green Chapel on New Year's Day, the Green Knight, who turns out to be Bertilak in magical disguise, spares his life but knicks him on the neck with the axe for failing to disclose the gift of the girdle. Gawain is hailed as the greatest knight in the land, though he wears the girdle from that time forward as a sign of his sin in failing to tell the whole truth.

~

The impetus for this book came from friend and fellow Regency author Cora Lee, who dreamt up the idea of a Regency series whose heroes and/or heroines were based on legendary figures. I volunteered to write about the Arthurian knight Gawain and specifically the legend of *Gawain and the Green Knight* but pulled myself from the series after my mother died, as I felt I could not commit to a publishing schedule when in the midst of grief.

The idea never left, though. I loved the idea of adding Gawain alongside my already established Arthur and Merlin characters, namely the Duke of Arthington and the Marquess of Emerlin, who've appeared in *A Matter of Time* and *The Demon Duke*. The inspirations for those two, as many of my readers know, are Bradley James and Colin Morgan, who played Arthur and Merlin in the BBC series Merlin. Eoin Macken played Gwaine, another character I adored, and provided the physical inspiration for Gavin Knight, Duke of Cortleon.

I'd also studied this particular Arthurian legend in grad school, making it an ideal story to tackle—or so I thought. You see, my memory is terrible, and I'd forgotten the legend's key elements, including the beheadings and the theme of adultery, neither of which lend themselves well to a romance novel! Thus began my own quest to transform the medieval plot into a story for lovers of Regency romance.

But how to make the beheadings that bookend the story work? The Hamilton musical soundtrack provided the answer. I was making dinner one day while singing quite loudly to "The Ten Duel Commandments" when the idea hit me: a Regency duel! I'd turn the beheadings into a duel.

But again, how to make that work? How do I create a giant green man and how do I reference beheadings without actually beheading anyone? Well, a man dressed in all green and getting shot in the neck seemed to work. I still wanted the green axe in there, however, so I had Bertie point to a big axe when threatening five-year-old Gavin in Camlon's ballroom (i.e., Camelot's court).

I wove other nods into the story, as well: *The Legendary Duke* opens and closes during the twelve days of Christmas, as does *Gawain and the Green Knight*. When Grennet suggests a game of cards to Gavin at the Twelfth Night masquerade, Arthington leaps in to accept, a reference to Arthur wanting to agree first to the Green Knight's challenge at Camelot. A short time later, when Grennet makes suggestive comments about the kiss Gavin and Nelle exchanged, Gavin leaps up to challenge him. Many of the character and place names reference Arthurian legends as well - see the Glossary for specifics.

Gawain and the Green Knight's other big plot sticking point was infidelity, which is not exactly a beloved theme in romance. How could I both include and not include it in *The Legendary Duke*? By having the men compete for Nelle! I also wanted her betrothed by the third exchange to get as close to that married line as I dared without going over. I'm hoping that since the betrothal lacked her overt permission, readers will accept when she seeks Gavin for one night together. Though she loves him, not Bertie, she feels honor-bound by her promise; she cannot break the betrothal, as it would destroy her family's chances for happiness, just as Gavin will not break his vow to avoid taking a wife until he's served justice to his father's killer.

To match the three kissing exchanges in *Gawain and the Green Knight*, Nelle and Gavin kiss three times before their magical night: once at the Twelfth Night ball, twice in the gardens at the Effingham ball, and three times in Nelle's chamber at Swythdon. Likewise, Bertie is obsessed with hunting and over the course of the story hunts for deer, boar, and foxes, just as in the legend. I wove in references to Bertie wanting what Gavin has acquired several times, as well, and made allusions to the sexual undertones that lie between Gawain and Bertilak in the original legend.

As for the ring and garter gifts Lady Bertilak offered Gawain? In their encounter in her chamber at Swythdon, Nelle thrusts Bertie's ring at Gavin, which he refuses. However, when he discovers her hair ribbon in his chamber, he keeps it—the very hair ribbon Nelle finds around his neck, nearly severed in two by Grennet's bullet. And Hugh even references a garter when arguing about Nelle with his father.

So, what do you think? If you knew the legend before, did you see familiar elements? Do you think I did it justice? If it's new to you, did I craft a Regency tale that adequately blended in the medieval legend? I'd also love to know what other Easter eggs you find, whether specific to the legend or to Arthurian myths in general, as I didn't list them all here. Feel free to drop me a line at AuthorMargaretLocke@gmail.com

∿

Further reading / viewing on Gawain and the medieval legend of *Gawain and the Green Knight*:

Armitage, Simon. *Sir Gawain and the Green Knight*. Faber, 2007.

Joe, Jimmy. "Arthurian Legends." *Timeless Myths: Arthurian Legends*, 1 Jan. 1999, www.timelessmyths.com/arthurian/.

Matthews, John, and Mildred Leake Day. *Gawain, Knight of the Goddess: Restoring an Archetype*. Aquarian, 1992.

Merlin. BBC One. United Kingdom. 2008-2012. Television.

"Sir Gawain and the Green Knight BBC Documentary, with Simon Armitage." *Sir Gawain and the Green Knight*, youtu.be/74glI1lg1CQ.

Tolkien, J. R. R. *Sir Gawain and the Green Knight*. Allen & Unwin, 1975.

Website, Timeless Myths. https://www.timelessmyths.com/arthurian/gawain.html

Website, Wikipedia. "Gawain." *Wikipedia*, Wikimedia Foundation, 14 Apr. 2018, https://en.wikipedia.org/wiki/Gawain

Website, Wikipedia. "The Wedding of Sir Gawain and Dame Ragnelle." https://en.wikipedia.org/wiki/The_Wedding_of_Sir_Gawain _and_Dame_Ragnelle

Website, Wikipedia. "The Marriage of Sir Gawain." https://en.wikipedia.org/wiki/The_Marriage_of_Sir_Ga wain

WHAT'S IN A NAME?

GLOSSARY & ORIGINS OF NAMES USED IN THE LEGENDARY DUKE

Not every name in *The Legendary Duke* relates to Arthurian legend, but many do. I compiled this list for anyone who might be interested in knowing the connections.

Abelard and Heloise - Not Arthurian figures but a real 12th-century theologian and nun who were passionately involved with each other and exchanged a famous series of love letters.

Albina, wife of Bertie Laxton - As far as I know, Albina is not an Arthurian reference, but I needed a name I could shorten to a nickname that wasn't obviously related to her original name and could be misconstrued as something/someone else entirely.

Anna Knight - Gavin's mother. Name of Gawain's mother in some Arthurian legends.

Arthington, Duke of - Childhood friend of Gavin Knight. Named for King Arthur. He will get his own story in *The Once and Future Duke*.

Ashvere, Viscount - Courtesy title for Bertie's son, Hugh. Green axe translates as "hache vert" in French. I created a name to sound similar and evoke the huge green axe the Green Knight carried.

Badon Hill -   Estate at which Loughton Knight's valet Malmesbury worked. Site of a famous battle involving King Arthur.

Bedeville, Viscount - Friend of Arthington and Emerlin. Named for Sir Bedivere, a Knight of the Round Table.

Bertie Laxton - The Earl of Grennet and Gavin's nemesis. In Gawain and the Green Knight, Gawain's hunt for the Green Knight leads him to a castle owned by a man named Bertilak, whom we later discover is also the Green Knight. Hence, Bertie Laxton = Bertilak.

Borswell, Viscount - Friend of Arthington and Emerlin. Named for Sir Bors, a Knight of Round Table.

Caera - Nelle's white rabbit, named for Caerbannog - the white rabbit from *Monty Python and the Holy Grail*!

Camlon - Arthington's ancestral home. The name is a combination of Camelot & Avalon, two places where King Arthur is said to live.

Cortleon, Duke of - Gavin Knight's title. Cortleon is an amalgam of "courtly love" and Caerleon, the name of a Welsh castle some believe to be the historical Camelot.

Deandra Valfort - Percy Valfort's sister. The Arthurian legend Perlesvaus names Percival's sister as Dindrane.

Elinor Greene - Gawain marries a woman named Ragnelle in the Arthurian legend The Wedding of Sir Gawain and Dame Ragnelle. I thus chose Elinor for Gavin's love, as the traditional Regency name can be shortened to Nelle. A central theme of that legend is the notion that what women really want is choice, which comes into play in this story, as well. I gave Elinor's family the surname of Greene to echo the idea of the Green Knight and to highlight the color.

Emerlin, Marquess of - Arthington's best friend. Named for Merlin, wizard counsel to King Arthur. Emerlin's story will be told in *The Irish Duke*.

Engelsfell, Duke of - Percy Valfort's title. While Engelsfell has no Arthurian connection, Engel means "angel" in German, and I liked the subtle auditory allusion to "fallen angel," an oblique reference to *The Angel Duke*, which will tell Percy's story.

Farnham, Lord - NOT Arthurian, but a reference to the singer "Colin can't name in that clip," one of my favorite videos with Colin Morgan and Bradley James and one that I think of when thinking of the friendship between Emerlin and Arthington. See the YouTube video here: https://youtu.be/LDZQGS6hoC8

Galahad - Nelle's English bulldog, named for Sir Galahad, a Knight of the Round Table.

Gavin Knight - The name Gavin is the modern equivalent of Gawain, and Knight refers to being a Knight of the Round Table.

Grennet, Earl of - Bertie Laxton's title. Grennet is my

version of Green Knight, to clue people into his role in this story.

Gringolet - Gavin's horse, named for Gawain's horse of the same name.

Hopper - Percy Valfort's horse. The actor Tom Hopper played Percival in the BBC's Merlin.

Howsden - Grennet's valet in 1788. The original, full name of the man Gawain meets while searching for the Green Knight is Bertilak de Hausdesert, so I derived his valet's name from the latter part of that.

Hugh Laxton - Bertie's son. I gave him the first name of Hugh because it was visually similar to the word huge, a hat tip to both the axe referenced in his title of Viscount Ashvere, and to his and his father's size.

Inglewood - Nelle's home. The story of Gawain & Ragnelle (see Elinor Greene, above) takes place in and near Inglewood Forest, so I adapted the name for the cottage where Nelle and her family live.

Irene - Arthington's mother. King Arthur's mother is Igraine, so I chose an English name that looked somewhat similar.

Isolde - Nelle's gray cat, named for the main female character in the Arthurian legend of Tristan and Isolde.

James Bradley - Arthington's real name, a tribute to Bradley James, who played Arthur in the BBC series Merlin.

Keswick, Viscount - Friend of Arthington and Emerlin, named for Sir Kay, a Knight of the Round Table.

Kingsfisher, Lady - Percival's aunt. In Arthurian legend, one of Percival's uncles is the Fisher King.

Loughton Knight - Gavin's father. Arthurian tradition names Lot as Gawain's father. I used Loughton, as it sounds similar and if shortened to a nickname is Lought.

Luc - Servant at Camlon. Lucan was a servant of King Arthur.

Lucy-Anne Greene - Lucy-Anne isn't Arthurian, but rather a name I picked that reminded me of Marianne from Jane Austen's Sense and Sensibility, as I think of Elinor and Lucy-Anne as being somewhat similar to Austen's sister characters of Elinor and Marianne in that story.

Lud's Church - A real site in northwestern England many believe to be the Green Chapel referenced in Gawain and the Green Knight.

Malmesbury - Loughton Knight's valet, named for William of Malmesbury, an English historian who in 1125 wrote the "Gesta Regum Anglorum," or History of the Kings of England, which references King Arthur.

Malory - Gavin's valet, named for Thomas Malory, author of L'Morte de Arthur, considered by many to be the definitive English compilation of Arthurian legends. It was written around 1470.

Minerva - Percy Valfort's mother, the Dowager Duchess of Engelsfell. In Arthurian tradition, Percival's mother's name is Yglais, which means wisdom. I could not think of any similar-sounding English name, so I went for the Roman goddess of wisdom.

Monmouth - Gavin's butler, named for Geoffrey of Monmouth, author of The History of the Kings of Britain, published in 1136. He popularized many Arthurian legends.

Morgan Collinswood - Emerlin's Christian name, a tribute to Colin Morgan, who played Merlin in the BBC series Merlin.

Mrs. Fay - Cook at Camlon; a reference to the sorceress Morgana le Fay.

Mrs. Stewart - Gavin's housekeeper, named for Mary Stewart, 20th-century author renowned for her Merlin series.

Pallemeade, Marquess of - Friend of Arthington and Emerlin. Named for Sir Palamedes, a Knight of the Round Table.

Pellnore - Nelle's family's footman, named for Sir Pellinore, a Knight of the Round Table.

Percy Valfort - Percival! Gawain's good friend and Arthurian knight. "Fort" also means strong, a reference to Percy's immense strength.

St. Graele - Name of Percy Valfort's ancestral home and a reference to the Holy Grail, the legend with which Percival is most closely associated.

Sulpicio - Gavin's fencing master, from Sulpicius, the pope who, according to Geoffrey of Monmouth, protected Gawain in Rome.

Swythdon - Bertie's home. Swythamley has been named as one potential location of Bertilak's Castle and the place where Gawain and the Green Knight fight again. The name is a combination of Swythamley and Haddon Hall, the latter of which is the estate on which I based Swythdon's appearance.

Tristan - Nelle's tuxedo cat, named for the main male character in the Arthurian legend of Tristan and Isolde.

Vero - Gavin's pistol & boxing master in Rome, named for Viamundus, the fisherman who according to Arthurian legend found infant Gawain in a river and took him to Rome. Vero also means "true" in Italian and references Gavin's hunt for the truth about his father's murder.

Wainsbury - The Cortleon ancestral home near Warrick. "Wain" is from Gawain.

Walwen - Walwein is an alternate form of Gawain. Earl Walwen is Gavin's second courtesy title.

White - Gavin's estate steward, named for T.H. White, 20th-century author of The Once and Future King.

Wynhawke, Marquess - Wyn means "white" in Welsh. Many scholars believe Gawain derives from the word "hawk." I combined the two to create Marquess Wynhawke, Gavin's courtesy title he held as a child and the name others would have called him until he became Duke.

THE DEMON DUKE

PUT UP YOUR DUKES BOOK ONE

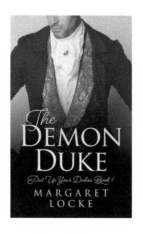

Don't miss USA Today Bestseller and RITA® Finalist *The Demon Duke*, the first in Margaret's Regency historical series.

http://margaretlocke.com/books/the-demon-duke

Behind every good man is a great secret.

Banished to Yorkshire as a boy for faults his father failed to beat out of him, Damon Blackbourne has no use for English society and had vowed never to return to his family's estate at Thorne Hill, much less London. However, when his father and brother die in a freak carriage accident, Damon must take up the mantle of the Malford dukedom and chaperone his sisters through the London Season–his worst nightmare come to life.

He never planned on Lady Grace Mattersley. She stirs him body and soul--until she stumbles across his dark secret.

Bookish Grace much prefers solitude and reading to social just-about-anything. Her family may be pressuring her to find a husband, but she has other plans, such as writing a novel of her own. She has no idea, however, how to deal with the all-too-alluring Duke of Malford.

Will she betray him to the world? Or will she be his saving Grace?

A MAN OF CHARACTER

MAGIC OF LOVE BOOK ONE

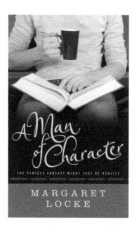

What if your book boyfriend was real?

Fall in love with the magic in *A Man of Character*.
http://margaretlocke.com/books/a-man-of-character

A MATTER OF TIME

MAGIC OF LOVE BOOK TWO

What if a magical manuscript threw you into the arms of your personal Mr. Darcy?

Eliza and Deveric's story, with several familiar faces from *The Demon Duke*!

http://margaretlocke.com/books/a-matter-of-time

A SCANDALOUS MATTER

MAGIC OF LOVE BOOK THREE

**What if your soul mate doesn't want
happily ever after?**
Revel in the magic again in *A Scandalous Matter*,
Amara and Matthew's story.

http://margaretlocke.com/books/a-scandalous-matter

ACKNOWLEDGMENTS

"Life's beauty is inseparable from its fragility." – Susan David

I lost my beloved mom, Kathleen, in August 2017. She's my inspiration and role model and was always one of my biggest cheerleaders. I'm indebted to her for so much and miss her every single day.

Thank you to my editor Tessa Shapcott for helping mold this giant of a book into a story I truly love.

Thank you to Lankshear Design for crafting such an eye-catching cover. Joy makes my books look *good*!

Thank you to Emily June Street of Luminous Creatures Press for her formatting wizardry.

Thank you to RWA's Beau Monte for answering my many questions. I quest to get it right but of course, any errors remain my own.

Thank you to beta readers Kristen Brandon, Josette Keelor, and Valeria lo Zito for their insightful comments and feedback!

Thank you to brilliant author Grace Burrowes for providing a blurb for *The Legendary Duke*. I'm truly honored!

A huge thank you to my husband and kids for their patience this summer as I buried myself in work, desperate to write again and get Gavin and Elinor's story out there. Because my mom would want me to.

Double gratitude to my non-romance-reading husband for reading every single one of my books, including this one, to help find any lingering boo-boos. A because he insists everything I write is wonderful.

And thank you to my readers. You've been a source of light, and I'm forever grateful for each and every one of you.

ABOUT THE AUTHOR

Margaret Locke, RITA® Finalist and USA Today Bestselling Author of the Magic of Love and Put Up Your Dukes series, writes binge-worthy romance that keeps you up past your bedtime. She delights in making readers laugh, cry, and think. Because love matters.

You can usually find her in front of some sort of screen (electronic or window); she's come to terms with the fact she's not an outdoors person. Newly obsessed with coffee, she also fangirls over Jane Austen, history, cats, books, and Colin Morgan.

When not writing, Margaret adores spending time with her fabulous husband, two fantastic kids, and three funny felines. And chocolate. Don't forget chocolate.

http://margaretlocke.com

facebook.com/AuthorMargaretLocke

instagram.com/margaret_locke

bookbub.com/authors/margaret-locke

goodreads.com/MargaretLocke

pinterest.com/Margaret_Locke

GET A LOCKE ON LOVE

JOIN THE KEY READERS CLUB

Interested in being the first to know about Margaret's upcoming releases or hearing other insider information?

The key is signing up for her **Key Readers Email Club**, through which once a month you'll get exclusive excerpts, giveaways, info on new releases, and more!

Sign Up Here:

http://margaretlocke.com/vipreaders

THANK YOU FOR READING

What did you think of *The Legendary Duke*?

Would you kindly consider leaving a
review on the review site of your choice?

Word-of-mouth is the best way for
authors to reach readers,
and the online version of
word-of-mouth is reviews.

Thanks so much!

- Margaret